Escape From a Canvas World

Annie's Book Stop
Freeport Outlet
475 US Route 1
Freeport, ME 04032
(207) 865-3406

Escape From a Canvas World

by

Alice Louise Hardy

Best Wishes
Alice Louise Hardy

ISBN: 1-58820-167-8

This novel is a work of fiction. Though several well known
public buildings have been used as a backdrop for the narrative
the incidents occurring within such esteemed edifices are the
product of the author's imagination as are the names of the
characters and their respective occupations.

1stBooks - rev. 10/11/00

For
my husband Bill
and
our son and daughter
Bradford and Ellyn Leslie
with love

ACKNOWLEDGEMENTS

Escape From A Canvas World was written for the most part during the chunks of time I managed to steal out of my busy life as a homemaker, which does go a long way towards explaining why it took me a decade or so to complete. Indeed many of the chapters, before being committed to paper, were scripted in my mind and committed to memory while driving countless country miles to the market, meeting the school bus, weeding the garden, getting up before dawn to watch the sunrise by candlelight, giving tours while volunteering as a docent at Bowdoin College's Museum of Art and The Peary-MacMillan Arctic Museum, and taking innumerable walks on the beach where flights of fancy often have a way of turning into reality; in my case resulting in a romantic seafaring novel.

With my literary endeavor finally in hand I found myself wondering if the opportunity would ever come my way to thank friends and acquaintances in print for their suggestions, words of encouragement and help - knowingly or unknowingly - during this lengthy time frame. Now, at long last, the occasion for me to express my gratitude has arrived.

Thinking chronologically, thanks must go to Marilyn True-Hill, Gretchen Shaw and Grace Greene as the first ones to read *Escape From a Canvas World*. Their forthcoming help in editing the manuscript and enthusiastic wishes for its success, then as well as throughout these past years, will always be appreciated. I am additionally beholden to Raymond Sipherd, author of *The Courtship of Peggy McCoy* and the *Dance of the Scarecrows*. His gift of time so generously given to read the narrative and to offer suggestions will never be forgotten.

Since those early perusals I have made many changes in the novel, some of the rewrites planned to accommodate fresh ideas and others due to unexpected personal experiences which seemed germane to the narrative. In light of the aforementioned thanks must go to Topher Browne of L. L. Bean Inc., for his erudite lecture on the art of salmon fishing and his patience with a customer who never dreamed there was more to the sport other than dropping a hook and line into the water. Thanks must also go to Emily Vogt for sharing her chart reading skills and mathmatical expertise in plotting a course. To Barbara and Roy Clark I would like to express not only my appreciation for their input on today's hip vernacular but also my sincere thanks for always "being there" in a supportive way.

I also would be remiss in not stating that a constant source of inspiration while writing the novel came from my involvement as a docent in the Bowdoin College museums. This was due in large part to the leadership and congeniality of Katharine Watson, former director of the Museum of Art, and of Susan Kaplan, director of The Peary-MacMillan Arctic Museum. Their knowledge in their respective fields was always enthusiastically shared with me for which I extend to both my appreciation and wholehearted thanks.

And last, but not in any way the least a very, very special "Thank you" to my niece Linda Hardy Heaton. Without her interest in my writing and help in undertaking the time consuming and tedious task of typing the manuscript onto a disk for future printing the novel would still be hidden in a box and tucked away on a closet shelf. I will be forever in her debt.

PROLOGUE

"The penthouse is unique!" Well, at least everyone said so, even the editor-in-chief of the architect's bible *The Pinnacle* who had written, "The rooftop apartment is truly a visual testimony to the meaning of the word unique – having no like or equal."

The owner had been pleased with the comment.

"This apartment," the article explained, "encompasses the entire top floor of Boston's most prestigious condominium, the suite having been designed in the shape of a Zodiac diagram so each room would frame a sweeping view of the city's impressive skyline."

At which point the article ended as per a gentleman's agreement between the owner and editor. Otherwise, the reader would have learned that the library, the most inner sanctum of the entire sanctum, had a different view.

The owner was touchy about this fact. To a select few invited into this special space, which offered two views of Boston's inner harbor, further explanation was always punctuated by a kingly wave of the hand. "By day, our fair city's spider-like network of bridges is in plain view as is our venerable frigate *Old Ironsides*. By night, the view is of the heavenly bodies, at times in direct competition with our earthly beacons."

The owner seated in the plush swivel chair never tired of this view, diurnal or nocturnal. He never tired of the opulent furnishings nor did he ever tire of the ambience generated by his aesthetic tastes. However, there was a practical side to his nature. He was well aware of the constant supply of money needed to indulge his rich life style. So this time, he turned around from the view of heavenly bodies to face an elegant Louis XIV writing table, picked up the telephone, and dialed direct an overseas call to Le Boucau, France.

His voice was unctuous, void of accent, pitched low. The words spoken - deliberate, brief, guarded - in total accord with the covert nature of the telephone call. "I mailed the special charts you asked for yesterday. They will come to you in care of

General Delivery, Port aux Basques, Newfoundland. Mail to such a remote area as you know takes about a week so they should be there by the time you arrive, May 31st."

The reply was equally brief and guarded, each word being chosen carefully by the man enjoying a cognac while seated in the picturesque lobby of Le Boucau's renowned Fort-de-France Hotel overlooking the Bay of Biscay. However, the response differed in tone, the baritone voice coming over the wire lightened by a slight foreign accent. "Good! I felt certain with the advent of boating season that most marinas in Boston would have on hand detailed charts of the Maine coast."

"I trust the ones that I did mail will prove helpful to our mariner friends? Especially to the two Johnny Rebs island hopping down the coast?"

It was as if the line went dead though the man in Boston could hear laughter in the background. "Are you still there?"

The man sitting in the lobby savoring his cognac was definitely still there. Though proficient in English it always took him a few seconds to convert from English into his native tongue and then translate it back again into "Americanese" so he could understand the slang expressions. Sometimes he failed. "But of course! The two Johnny Rebs, as you call them, are looking forward to exploring the many islands between Newfoundland and Boston, particularly Cape Breton and Georgetown. It will be a rewarding experience for them as well as for us, enriching their lives as well as ours. Tenfold? Yes?"

The question prompted a quick response. "I understand your train of thought. I suppose you are going to wrap-up the season as usual by having a bon voyage party for all our seafaring friends?"

Static choked the line, forcing a lull in conversation. When they finally were able to continue, a successful reading of each other's mind had occurred. Words were pointedly innocuous, to anyone listening - accidentally or on purpose - even banal.

"To answer your question about the party. Yes! Our destination for this year's celebration will be out of Portland, Maine. Halfway Rock to be precise."

"Have you chosen a date for the gathering of the fleet?"

"Yes! Weather permitting we will rendezvous August 22."

"Ah! According to my horoscope a very good day for the bestowing of the blessings."

"Plans are to hoist a few around noon. After a round or two, no more, the fleet will be blessed. We will then cast off for our respective ports."

The man got up from his swivel chair and turned to face the window-framed view of *Old Ironsides*. "A word of caution, my friend, he replied softly but emphatically. "In casting off for your respective ports I adjure you and the others to steer clear of the coast between Portland and Boston. Our President is vacationing at his seaside home and as you can well imagine the entire area is awash with Coast Guard patrols as well as the local big guns. By the way, speaking of guns I forgot to mention earlier in our conversation that the hardware you requested will be hand delivered to you in Esperance, a minute fishing village located in the Strait of Belle Isle, Newfoundland side of course. A rendezvous is planned for sometime during the first week of June."

"As usual your plans are thorough. Now, not to worry! I will heed your advice."

Having been reassured by his counterpart in Le Boucau that his warning would be taken seriously he walked across the room to a built-in bookcase, pushed a concealed switch and then stepped back while it slid open to reveal a wall safe. Still cradling the phone, he opened the safe and then removed a thick ledger before asking, "I assume as soon as you reach 'Land-ho' you will be taking off for Switzerland?"

"But of course! As usual, I will give you a call from Geneva to let you know I have arrived safely with goods in tow. Bear in mind the weather could be contrary, as much as for a day or two."

"Let us hope not! I have to make an unexpected trip down south. As soon as I hear from you I will book a flight."

They hung up, making a point of not calling each other by name, their safety depending on anonymity from all but a select few.

The man in Boston took a few seconds to tally a row of numbers in the ledger. He allowed himself the pleasure of a self-satisfied smile.

The man in Le Boucau finished his cognac. He allowed himself the pleasure of ordering another, this time sipping it slowly, relishing the aftertaste while silently making a toast, "To the land of the Midnight Sun; may thy golden rays continue to illuminate the way for a profitable run."

Chapter 1

According to my twin sister Gloria, I am long overdue for a change of pace or a change of scenery or whatever! Of course Gloria knows me well, being as how we are like two peas in a pod. That is up to a point we are like two peas in a pod, for somehow or at sometime along the way I, Serena, became a romanticist with a passion for the fine arts and Gloria became a pragmatist with a passion for order, detail and the law. Yet, despite our differences we are in tune with each other's souls and moods. For instance, when Gloria came to visit me yesterday in the hospital she sensed immediately that I was thinking about my divorce and said that I had foolishly slipped into what I called my sad and remorseful "Lips That Have Been Kissed" mood; my moods it seems often reflecting the titles of famous paintings. In this case an oil on panel by Rossetti of a titian haired woman seated alone at a table who looked uncannily like me. Then there was the day before yesterday when I ran out of something to read and ended up in a "L'Edition De Luxe" funk. Gloria clairvoyantly had saved that day too by bringing me a coffee table size book on renaissance art to peruse.

As for my mood today or for that matter what my prevailing spirit will be tomorrow only God knows. Which is why, I guess, the hastily convened jury of family members had gathered around me just to see how far they could go to brighten up my days. I smiled as I had been taught to do in the face of adversity and then mentally prepared myself for whatever mischief they had concocted as my father stepped forward masqued in his solemn court room demeanor style to deliver their verdict. He obviously was relishing the moment, his eyes and facial expression reflecting the so-called humor in the solution as he intoned, "We find the defendant guilty."

I was not the least bit surprised by his words, the practice of jurisprudence being so ingrained in our family that even as a child I always had been cross-examined about my activities while my friends were merely questioned. I was curious though about my sentence as Daddy prepared to stand down after The Judge stepped forward.

It was not long in coming. "Serena Margaret Bradford, you are hereby banned from setting foot in Boston for the next four months."

A weird sentence to be sure but then The Judge, Judge Horatio Adams Bradford that is, my grandfather, was known for his offbeat decisions. His expression was grave as he peered down at me, his hands somewhat shaky but after all that was to be expected. Judge Bradford was in his 80's. However there was nothing wrong with his voice, strong as always. Sonorous too, his words practically bouncing off the walls as he expounded upon my punishment.

"Beginning at noon, May 31st, the day of your 28th birthday in the year of our Lord one thousand nine hundred and ninety six you will leave Boston by car for Georgetown, Maine. Once there you are to be incarcerated in the house known locally as The Barnacle to serve your time for the crime of picking up pneumonia and sundry maladies. I now remand you into the custody of your parents. Case dismissed!"

His emphasizing of "Case dismissed" by whacking the foot of my hospital bed with a newspaper instead of his customary gavel broke the spell. It was like spontaneous combustion. It was like being at an Irish wake only this time I was the centerpiece. Everyone burst out laughing.

Grandfather's was the loudest. Daddy's was next in timbre. His question, "Gilbert and Sullivan were right don't you think, Serena, when they wrote 'Let the punishment fit the crime?'" prompting dear big brother Adam to interrupt. His quip-full of brotherly love, "I think a good dunking in the ocean, even keel hauling, would be more in keeping with the crime," quite in order with our cat and dog relationship.

Adam, never at a loss for words, was quick to add, "Of course, Serena, you could show a little remorse. We will be the ones stuck all summer with sister Gloria. She will be a constant reminder of you. A fate worse than death!"

Sister Gloria, my dear twin, was never one either to let grass grow under her feet. I was always the one lingering behind to inspect a wayward butterfly. She grinned impishly, speaking right up. "Best be careful, Adam, or else when the time comes for you to come in out of the cold we won't let you. Besides I'm sure Paul won't mind being stuck with me all summer."

Paul, Dr. Paul Collins that is, surgeon extraordinaire, Mass. General's young shining star, husband of two years and still obviously besotted, put his arm around her shoulders. "She is right, Adam. I can't imagine what life would be like without Gloria."

Adam just stood there, shaking his head in mock disbelief. "Let me tell you, Paul. Life without Gloria would be blissful. Life without Serena would cause great joy. Life without them both would be heaven on earth!"

As usual Mother intervened, her soft voice quieting everyone down, putting an end to all of our foolishness. "We hope you don't mind our taking charge, Serena, but you have been so very ill."

Mother bent down kissing me lightly on the forehead and then stroked my hair, pausing just long enough in between to give me an extra reassuring tuck to the sheet and to press out an imaginary wrinkle on the pillow. Her touch was soothing, erasing my aches and pains. Her ministrations comforting. For as long as I could remember this had been the path taken for my recovery. Immediately I felt better.

"No, I don't mind you taking charge. Everyone knows how much I love The Barnacle and the beach. But I do believe you have all forgotten that I am now a working girl. How can I possibly get the time off?"

My chest started to constrict from this bit of conversation. I could feel a siege of coughing coming on. That would hurt!

Mother read my mind. "Don't say another word, dear. Just lay back and listen."

I nodded, grateful for her understanding and at the same time somewhat amazed that Adam hadn't blurted, "That's not possible!"

"I spoke with Henry a few days ago, Serena," she continued. "He had called to see how you were doing and I told him the truth. Not too well!"

Daddy walked around my bed to stand beside Mother, his concerned demeanor reflecting hers. "Actually it was Henry who suggested you take a six month leave of absence. He had called the office to personally thank me for the bequest to the museum. One thing led to another. You know how it is, Serena."

I closed my eyes. "Yes, I know how it is." My parents, my family, their parents, their family and their parents before them and so forth had been and were great supporters of Boston's superb fine arts museum. In fact, one might say our family is one of Boston's tooth fairies. Still, their Henry was Mr. Smythe to me, his age and position as director dictating the respect due from a recently appointed curator.

I opened my eyes. Daddy smiled. "Henry said he expects the summer to be routine. There will be a couple of small exhibits the first part of next year. The big push will begin in the spring of the year when the museum gears up for its major exhibit on South American art."

I risked speaking. "In other words, Daddy, I won't be missed?"

"Henry didn't say that, Serena. Actually he said just the opposite. He also went out of his way to praise your work done on the recent Renoir show and that the catalog you slaved over was a huge success. In other words, bluntly speaking, he would rather you take the time now to get well than risk getting sick again in the winter when it could cause delays in scheduling shows."

This time I smiled. Not as enigmatic as Leonardo da Vinci's 'Mona Lisa' but broadly enough to show I was pleased with the compliments. "It's good to know I'm wanted back because of my work and not because the museum needs a new wing."

Gloria gasped. "Bite your tongue, Serena, for even thinking such an outlandish thought!"

Grandfather's comment was down to earth. "Damn to hell! Now that's what I call cumulative evidence. You obviously need to get away, Serena."

The prospect of having a full summer to recuperate by walking my beloved beach was overwhelming. So overwhelming I could feel a few tears oozing down my cheeks. "My four

4

legged buddy Caesar will love it too," I managed to say before succumbing to a fit of coughing.

Adam summed up the moment with a customary salvo. "Every cloud has a silver lining. In this case we will be free of that hound of yours for four months. Blind justice, I say, for having to put up with Gloria."

A round of good-natured applause confirmed his sentiments. Mother reached out, squeezing my hand. "We must all go now, Serena, and let you rest. This is the only way the bloom is going to be restored to your cheeks. By the way, you can come home tomorrow and before you know it May will have almost slipped into June. Don't forget your Grandfather has decreed that on the 31st, you must be on your way heading down east to Georgetown, Maine."

"I won't forget, Mother."

I must have dozed off because suddenly I was aware that no one was there listening to me joke about being run out-of-town. My room had changed too, from bandage white to boudoir pink. That of course explained the time of day, along with seeing the sun slip down behind the golden dome of the State House.

The hospital was strangely quiet, giving me no excuse to not think about my crime and subsequent sentence. It had been a long winter. It had been a long summer before the long winter. In fact, the past months had been traumatic. Also dramatic, especially the day I received my final divorce papers from Britton Peabody and celebrated by taking the Concorde to Paris for lunch. "Doesn't everyone?" I had blithely asked upon my return.

My return had sparked a new me. A free me, quite capable of making my own decisions - even if I fell flat on my face. I had already proven I could organize a major charitable event so I had set out to prove I was employable.

Everything Mr. Smythe had said was true. I had slaved over the catalog and it was a success, artistically as well as financially. I had worked hard on the Renoir show giving more than my share of tours when the flu bug struck down docent after docent. When the time came for my bout with the insidious germ

I wasn't properly prepared. I simply fell flat on my face. "So much for the new me," I had murmured at the time.

My room was now full of gray shadows. Soon I would be watching nature's lavish display of light and color from The Barnacle, a place so very dear to my heart, a place so far removed from the mainstream, both in locale and activity, that a breadth of attitude always seemed to spring from just being there and that a door locked against one's problems always seemed to open, showing the way.

Of course I wasn't the only one in our family who adored the old place. They all did, as had the previous Bradfords and their Adams relatives who had vacationed there for decades, ever since Grandfather Horatio's parents had built the wood and native stone house in the early 1900's when builders intended their homes to survive the ravages of the ocean for at least a century or more. Dear Grandfather Horatio, whose colorful stories of the days of his youth had always enchanted me, still did for that matter especially when he got wound up in flash-backs of a time gone by when it was fashionable to be unfashioable by vacationing in Maine instead of Newport. As a child I had particularly liked the one about how his parents had named their new summer home. He had told this story best while sitting in front of a wood snapping fire in his awesome library enjoying a "Fine Havana cigar" and a generous tumbler of port after just finishing a sumptuous meal. His eyes always glazed over and became shiny with fond memories as he began his narration, in the same way as always with, "The house was christened The Barnacle, Serena, with a bottle of fine vintage champagne from my father's private stock on the day the last nail was pounded into place. The name was chosen with great care by my mother in honor of the tiny crustacean's unmatchable glue-like habit of attaching itself to rocks. She was an Adams you know, determined not to be fitted into a mold; but on the other hand a nature lover and beachcomber at heart with an artistic rather than a practical soul. That's why you remind me so very much of her, forever straying off the beaten path."

At this point I had invariably interrupted, asking the same questions: "That's why, Grandpa, she named the house The

Barnacle, huh?; She thought it would bring good luck, huh?; Just like my lucky charm bracelet, huh?"

"Yes, yes, yes to all your endless questions, Serena," was his constant reply. At this point he had invariably sighed and I got a sip or two of his port, on the sly of course, Grandmother Martha, Grandpa's devoted wife and Daddy's mother being a stickler for observing the proprieties.

Such warm memories acted on me like a strong sedative and for the first time in several weeks I felt at peace with myself. I found that I wasn't the least bit upset with my parents for taking charge. After all I had grown up these past few months. I had grown up enough to know that a helping hand is sometimes necessary and that a wise person accepts it as such.

Chapter 2

There is nothing like being away from a dearly loved place for a few months to make you appreciate it all the more. Somehow upon returning the sky always seems bluer, the grass greener and in the case of The Barnacle, the ocean more vast, more dazzling.

Today, May 31st, the first day of honoring my penance was no exception. The minute I turned my Porsche into the private dirt road leading to our family's summer home I noticed the pines were definitely taller, at least by a foot, the shadows they cast definitely denser and by the time I got to our driveway and brought the car to a stop, which in reality is a wide outcropping of ledge, the roses were lusher and the lavender along its borders more profuse.

It had been a long four hour drive. The traffic had been heavier than usual coming out of Boston or maybe it had just seemed that way to me. I was weary, too tired to think of anything other than to let Caesar and myself out of the car. He immediately galloped off to the beach, no doubt eager to assert the territorial rights due a Great Dane, while I climbed the native stone steps to the wide front porch of The Barnacle.

Actually the wide front porch of The Barnacle is the back of the house, the part that overlooks the driveway, whereas the back porch is the front of the house, the part overlooking the ocean. As a child I had found this description most upsetting and illogical, especially since the porch encircles the entire house. I had learned not to argue about it, adults always being right, and eventually accepted the porch for what it was - a great place for roller skating and playing Monopoly on a rainy day.

As soon as my feet touched the gray painted boards my travel fatigue miraculously vanished. Eagerly I walked around to the front of the house to absorb the view that literally causes everyone to gasp when seeing it for the first time. I had been away just long enough to appreciate the experience. I gasped and then sat down on the wicker porch swing to catch my breath.

The view hadn't changed - only it was more intense - in keeping with the day. It appears to the eye like a mural you would see gracing a large inner room in need of a spiritual uplift; the center, dominated by the sky and a restless ocean kept at bay by a sandy beach fringed with tufts of dune grass, wild roses and bear berry, while the sides of the make believe mural are anchored for eternity by palisade-like cliffs studded with evergreens.

"Good to be back, Serena?"

I jumped up, surprised to hear a voice. The swing retaliated by banging me smartly on the legs as I turned around. "Mrs. Linette! You startled me. I didn't hear you drive up!"

Mrs. Linette gave me a hug. "I didn't mean to frighten you, Serena, and I didn't just drive up. Abel dropped me off. In fact I've been here since early this morning cleaning out the winter dust and cobwebs. Yesterday too, though Abel did come up to help by taking down all the storm shutters and washing the windows. Brought in a cord of wood too, not green mind you!"

I gave her a big hug in return. She was still as thin as a toothpick. "But how did you and Mr. Linette know I was coming? I had planned to call later today to see if you had some free time and could help me open the place up."

"Your family!"

"My family?"

Mrs. L. laughed and then started to count on her fingers. "First, your mother called a couple of weeks ago. Told me you had been very sick and that if at all possible it would be nice to have the house livable. Next, your father called several days ago. Told me you have been very sick and that if at all possible it would be nice if Abel could take the storm shutters down and wash the windows. He was afraid you would attempt the task yourself. Then Gloria called a couple of days ago. Told me you had been very sick and that if at all possible it would be nice to have a couple days supply of food in the house. Then Adam called yesterday morning."

"Adam!" I shrieked. "I don't believe it!"

Mrs. L. rolled her eyes. "From China, no less! Told me you had been very sick - naturally - and that if at all possible it would

10

be nice to have a supply of wood brought into the house and fires laid, ready for you to start in the study and upstairs sitting room. Mumbled something about that always having been one of his chores."

"Adam! My brother Adam called all the way from China. I don't believe it!"

"Believe me, Serena, when I tell you, you can believe it!"

I reached out, covering her fingers with mine. "So many calls. I'm sorry for all the bother."

"No bother, Serena. Your folks are nice people to work for, besides I sort of look upon you, Gloria and Adam as my family, Abel and me not having any children of our own."

"What a sweet thing to say, Mrs. Linette." I wanted to add, "We always consider you family too," but Caesar returned, his gift of a dead skate deposited proudly at our feet effectively interrupting our conversation.

Mrs. Linette retreated a few steps. "Ugh! I see Caesar hasn't changed one iota, Serena. Still dragging dead things in from the sea."

"I'm afraid not, though in Boston his loot tends to run towards brown paper lunch bags and Bon Pain wrappers."

I shuddered and pushed the fish off the porch with my feet. "I just hate skates. They are so evil looking with their slant eyes and flat bodies. I'll bury it later in the garden. At least there it will do some good."

"As long as he doesn't drag it into the clean house, Serena, which reminds me, speaking of the house that is, I made some lemonade. Why don't we go in and have a glass?"

Winking at me she added quickly, "I'll bring you up to date on all the local gossip. By the time I finish the winter's news Abel will be back and he can help unload your car."

Gossip is the staff of life in Georgetown! It is usually harmless, we "summer complaints" providing a wealth of idle talk for the locals and they a source of quaint humor for us. So I didn't wait for a second invitation and willingly followed Mrs. L. into the kitchen. A good thirty minutes and two glasses of lemonade later she was winding down. By this time I was seated on the edge of my kitchen chair, hoping I could remember all the

11

innuendoes to relate home, knowing she always saved the choicest bits for last.

"And the most shocking news I have to tell you, Serena, is that just this past month the tiny post office located in the back of Alma and Dick Graves' General Store up to Five Islands was broken into necessitating their remodeling that part of the store."

She paused long enough to make it obvious, giving me a poignant look before continuing. "The mail slot is now quite high off the floor and no longer produces a magic lollipop in return for a letter."

I felt like crying. Actually a few tears did escape to trickle down my cheeks for I had been the one, more so that Gloria and Adam when we three were tiny tots, to take the most delight in posting the mail.

Mrs. Linette was quick to see my dismay and added consolingly, "Fortunately though, Serena, nothing else has changed; their old calico cat is still sleeping on the produce counter and the penny candy case is still there by the front door, enticing the young folk into the store as always."

I managed a faint smile. "It's comforting to know that at least that part of my childhood hasn't gone by the wayside and that I can still fill a wax paper bag with my favorite penny candies just for old times sake."

Mrs. L. smiled back at me in a decidedly motherly sort of way, sighed as if she had just averted a crisis and then of all things started to laugh. "Oh yes, Serena, your parents will be interested to know that Paul Bisby, our harbor master, was the first on the island to get his peas in - planted the seeds during a snow storm which is a tad much don't you think - even for a Mainiac?"

Why my parents would be interested in knowing that morsel was beyond me but then anything pertaining to boats was beyond me. However I agreed, laughing along with her, but not daring as much as a wiggle for fear of breaking her train of thought. When she finished her lemonade I knew the end was in sight.

"It seems, Serena, the family from Delaware who purchased the old Condon place, that's the gray one on the bay, you know, that looks like a cormorant drying its wings, has incurred the wrath of Mr. Teddie Howard."

I couldn't stop from sucking in my breath. "No!"

Mrs. Linette leaned towards me. "Yes."

Her voice lowered to a whisper. "He runs a nice dump, as you know, and woe be to any of us who puts a bottle in the wrong place or doesn't obey the 'Dump Here' sign."

I nodded, urging her on.

"Well, it seems the new family, Grindel I think, committed the absolutely, positively, unforgivable sin of depositing their trash at the dump gate on a closed day. Mr. Howard, not to be hoodwinked, went through the trash, found their name on an envelope and promptly gathered it all up again and then proceeded to drive down here to the Point, where he carefully deposited it at their front door. According to Abel, who was delivering a truck load of wood at the time, a heated verbal exchange took place with Mr. Howard definitely the winner."

Mrs. Linette sank back into her chair, chuckling. "Isn't that priceless?"

"Priceless," I agreed adopting her gleeful expression. "Mother and Daddy will love it. Simply, love it."

The slamming of a car door followed by Caesar's barking brought to an end "The Children's Hour." "That will be Abel, Serena, coming to pick me up."

"Hey! Where is everybody?"

"Everybody is right here, in the kitchen sipping lemonade!" As it turned out there was no need for me to have shouted a reply to Mr. Linette. We collided at Times Square, Adam's name for the area in the hall at the foot of the circular staircase, a hazardous spot during our childhood because of the French doors opening into it from the dining room and of course, the kitchen beyond, always the source of divine cookies and other tantalizing goodies. Adam could just as easily have dubbed the spot Haymarket Square or Quincy Market because of the telltale train of crumbs we three always left behind but the presence of a stately grandfather's clock clued him otherwise. Even way back then Adam was always disgustingly logical!

13

Our greetings to each other also collided, Mr. Linette's, "Well, well, well, look what washed in with the tide," drowning out my, "It's nice to see you again."

I liked Mr. Linette too, as did Gloria and Adam. Daddy and Mother had always said to us, "The island community couldn't exist without Abel's brand of expertise." We weren't sure, way back then, just what was Abel's special brand of expertise other than the explanation Adam, being older and therefore wiser, came up with, importantly telling us, "A jack-of-all-trades."

Actually Abel was self-employed, a lobsterman during the season and when winter roared in he put a pencil behind his ear and became a carpenter. In between times there was no job too small or too large for him to tackle. He and Mrs. L. seemed quite happy to me, always taking a trip to the Caribbean for a couple of weeks in the dead of winter and for the past couple of years to Martinique, Abel having said, "Being of French-Canadian stock it gives me a chance to practice speaking our native tongue. "Voila!"

Today Mr. Linette was a carpenter, a bright red pencil tucked behind his ear enough of a clue for even me to recognize. Also a good Samaritan for he had thoughtfully brought in all my luggage from the car.

"Never known a woman to tote more junk than the Mrs. That is, up till now. Serena, I do believe you take the cake!"

Seeing his wide smile I exclaimed as innocently as I could, "But, Mr. Linette, we girls require more luggage. After all we have to cart extra essentials to keep ourselves beautiful for you men!"

Mr. Linette arched his eyebrows. That caused his forehead to wrinkle up, sending creases across his bald head while his eyes sort of crinkled in at the corners. "And all this time I thought John Bradford was the only one in your family full of malarkey."

I laughed, mostly at myself, for everyone always said I was slow on the uptake, this time being a rare exception. "I'll pass the compliment on to Daddy."

My fling at being witty over I retreated quickly back into my true self of being ever mindful to perform the proper p's and q's. Somehow in my make-up that also included never forgetting to dot the i's and cross the t's which is why I ended up telling him, "It was so considerate of you, Mr. Linette, to bring in everything from the car. Not an easy task I know since it took me forever to stuff a week's supply of staples including a 25 lb. bag of dog chow in between the luggage."

Mrs. L. joined us at Times Square, coat-sweater on and purse in hand, obviously ready to call it a day and just as obviously enjoying our repartee. "Don't go spoiling him with all those kind words, Serena. Next thing you know he will be expecting me to give him breakfast in bed, when it should be the other way around. Besides he needs the exercise. Speaking of which we will be late for Running Start at the school if we don't leave now."

Abel laughed and pointed to his corpulent waistline. "Never let it be said that I need to exercise."

Fortunately I was spared the trauma of having to dream up an appropriate reply, Mrs. Linette laying claim to our attention. "I promised your mother, Serena, that I would come every other week, beginning today, to lend a hand. So mark it on the calendar and in case you aren't here just leave the key underneath the seat cushion on the porch swing."

I nodded. "My family seems to have thought of everything."

"One more item of note, Serena, that I forgot to mention while we were having our lemonade. Don't be startled during the night if you hear a low flying plane. It's only the Coast Guard scanning the beaches, rivers, and harbors for drug runners. During the day they search the countryside for marijuana growers."

"Yeah," added Mr. Linette. "First it was the pirates, then the Russians, and now it's drug runners. According to the gobs for some strange reason the island of Georgetown is suspect as being the 'In' place to be this coming summer for the crime set."

I thought his tone slightly ominous but I laughed anyway and walked along with them out to their van. "I wonder if the crime set knows about our offensive army? If they did I'm sure they would go elsewhere."

Mrs. Linette looked at me somewhat mystified. "What army, Serena? Why Georgetown doesn't even have a constable!"

"Oh, yes, we do! That is we have an army. Actually a rather formidable one."

I tried to dead-pan it, being witty twice in such a short span of time quite a chore for me. "It musters in the spring with the arrival of the black flies, adds to its ranks in June with newly hatched mosquitoes, fleshes them out in July, literally, and then swells to a Genghis Khan size force in August with the induction of the greenheads."

I received an indulgent smile from Mrs. L. "You forgot to mention the no-see-ums, Serena."

"Yeah, dang miserable fly-ins," Abel shouted over the hum of the van's engine. A wise-acre expression flitted across his face as he put the van in motion. "Of course we can always arm you, Serena, with a can of repellent and let you lead the charge."

I knew better than to try and top his joke. All I could do was laugh and to once again remember my manners. "Thank you both, many times over, for your help in opening up the house. The Barnacle looks just great!"

Mrs. Linette waved, her words, "See you in a couple of weeks; don't hesitate to call if you need anything," mixing in with one of Abel's twisted homilies, "Do put off till tomorrow what you don't want to do today," drifting back to me as they left the driveway.

This time my fatigue didn't vanish as I climbed the stone steps to the porch and went back into the house. Caesar was like a shadow, following me in and then following me back and forth between the hall and the kitchen as I put away the perishables that I had brought with me. It was while putting the last brown egg from the carton into its designated white cradled spot in the refrigerator that Mr. Linette's words came home to roost.

"Do put off till tomorrow what I don't want to do today sounds like very good advice to me. Don't you agree, Caesar?"

He agreed, his bark seemingly loud enough to be heard across the way in Spain.

"What I really want to do is to go to bed and sleep forever," I said giving his ears an affectionate rub. "What I don't want to do is unpack the luggage in the hall. As far as I am concerned, as of right this minute, it can stay there all summer."

Immediately I felt better. I had made a decision worthy of complimenting it with a sigh of relief. Even Caesar was happy, wagging his tail, nuzzling his cold nose into my hand. "However, there is one suitcase I have to unpack. Right, Caesar? Right," I answered for him and headed back to Times Square to unpack his belongings.

I smiled like an indulgent mother for traveling with Caesar did have its drawbacks. Not only did he take up the entire back seat of my car but he almost required as much paraphernalia as a new born babe. First item unpacked was his oriental rug which I dutifully spread out beside the grandfather's clock, his chosen spot near the foot of the stairs. Next was his nylon dog bone and an old wool blanket he liked to sink his teeth into and growl. Finally I took out two mammoth stainless steel bowls which I promptly carried to the kitchen and filled one with water and the other with dog chow.

My self-given reward for following my own advice, aided and abetted by Mr. Linette's, was to then climb the stairs and thankfully fall into bed.

It took a week of hibernation for me to satiate my desire for sleep. During that time my conscience went on a holiday but with the dawning of June 7th, eight days into doing my penance, it returned inundating me in guilt. So I tackled the rest of the luggage in the hall, put all my clothes away into a very proper chest-on-chest and closet, and after surveying the contents of the refrigerator and pantry decided I best make the ultimate sacrifice of driving into the town of Arnold for supplies. I also needed to purchase a Maine tide chart at the bookstore so I could plan precisely for my daily walk to Griffith Head. Contrary to what members of the family have said, I really don't believe I can walk on water and though my crazy system for measuring the tides by adding 45 minutes every day and then taking away fifteen every third day is good enough for me, I do admit there are times when accurate tables can be beneficial.

I also do admit to being a creature of habit. Indeed, as Gloria constantly tells me I could not survive without a note pad and pencil in one hand and a clock in the other. So being most unwilling to break the habit of a lifetime I sat down at the kitchen table and made a detailed list of everything to buy, listing the items methodically in purchase order, beginning with A the Supermarket, next B the Bookstore (naturally) and finally, quite clairvoyantly for me, C for Charlie Burdett's Market. Not wanting to flirt with survival I slipped on my wrist watch and then in a very weak moment told Caesar, "We will have to make an afternoon of it;" my reason for bringing him along somewhat fuzzy but then it's hard to ignore a 180 lb. Great Dane with soulful brown eyes.

Our run into town was uneventful and in record time I was able to cross A and B off my list. However downtown Arnold, home to Charlie Burdett's Market, was proving to be a different story. I had never seen the traffic so bad - no doubt due to we "summer complaints."

I mentioned this traffic problem to Charlie. In return he gave me one of his famous broad winks while tallying up my bill, saying, "Now we natives like to think the traffic flow has been improved. At least, that's what the town fathers have told us to think when they changed all the streets that were always one way to two ways and the old two ways to one way. Of course, they can't seem to make up their minds - rumor being if they change the streets often enough the fines gleaned from you frustrated drivers will pay for our new waterfront dock."

Charlie's stories were good, every bit as good as the meat from his butcher shop which was why I persevered in making the stop. However, if I had known then what I know now and if I had been thinking like one of the natives I would have forgotten Charlie Burdett's Market until dawn on a rainy day; they, wisely knowing better than to try and cross the Arnold Bridge at four o'clock. Me - I had completely forgotten about the existence of the Arnold Iron Works and was justifiably complimenting myself on being able to stuff three months supply of food into the trunk and front seat of my car when the four o'clock whistle blew.

Of couse, I was caught under the bridge having made Burdett's Market my last stop. Of course, traffic lights had been newly installed under the bridge which foiled the stimulating challenge of besting a shipbuilder from the Works in getting onto the ramp. Of course, on this particular day the traffic would be moving slower than usual, finally coming to a complete stop.

The honking congestion that followed reminded me of returning to Boston on a Monday morning and trying to wedge your way off of the expressway in order to get to Haymarket Square. It was also hot! In fact, for a day in early June it was unseasonably hot, which I'm sure did much to fan tempers for it wasn't long before motorists were abandoning their cars and shouting at each other the choice obscenities read in the novels that Gloria and I had always kept hidden under our beds.

Poor Caesar was drooling all over the car as well as down my back so I too gave way to curiosity and joined the frenzied pack on their trek to the waterfront. I couldn't believe it! There were about 20 sailboats circling in the Kennebec River each waiting for their turn to pass under the drawbridge. At four p.m., no less! Such unmitigated gall!

My sentiments on boating are well known. It has always boggled my mind how anyone could waste a precious summer away by vegetating in a boat. Not only that, but it has always seemed to me "yachtzie" people are a little bit crazy. How else can you possibly explain the reason behind paying a fortune for the dubious privilege of getting wet and freezing to death or broiling yourself to a scarlet lobster shade in the sun.

Anyway, not being one to belabor a point, I stood there - mesmerized - like everyone else watching the boats maneuver. And yes, grudgingly, I can attest to their bird like beauty as the family so often described them for indeed, at this precise moment, they did seem to me like graceful swans stretching their necks to catch the sun and warm breezes.

A lot of shrieking and hollering interrupted my reverie. Before I realized what was happening the crowd parted in front of me, in what had to be the same way the Red Sea must have opened for the Israelites fleeing from Egypt. Only instead of Moses leading the way it was Caesar, joyfully galloping towards me just like I was the finish line at the Kentucky Derby.

I didn't know whether to laugh or cry, my first thought upon seeing him being voiced to no one in particular, "Oh no, and I don't have a horseshoe wreath of red roses to hang around his neck," and my second thought being private, "Oh, no, he is going to injure an innocent bystander in his hellbent-for-leather playful mood."

One thing for sure, once the crowd caught on that I was the object of his attention they all focused on me, shouting, most of it good-natured though I could hear a few catcalls; "Hey, Red, drop dead," and "Hey, Carrot Top, why don't you hitch him up," being the most expressive. I ignored those, drawing upon a reservoir of dignity that absolutely amazed me. I stood firm, this not being the moment for wallflower timidity, calmly calling, "Come on, Caesar. Come on!"

He crossed the finish line at what had to be fast-forward speed, sat down promptly when I said, "Sit" and "Woofed" when I petted him on the head. An honest-to-goodness real mother could not have been prouder of her offspring for doing as told than I was of Caesar.

"Pride," however, "goeth before destruction, and a haughty spirit before a fall." So I had read, courtesy of Sophocles, and by the time we got back to the car, after I apologized to everyone on the way who had been traumatized by his wagging tail, the destruction was evident by the groceries spilled in and out of the car and my haughty spirit fell to below sea level upon discovering my favorite rum-raisin ice cream had melted like flowing lava over everything including the leather car seat.

A distraught policeman offered his commiserations while helping me to pick up the litter. He also appeared genuinely relieved when I said, "I will never set foot in Arnold again."

Someone else was helping me too; a someone sporting a very expensive wrist watch like Daddy's and Adam's, a someone with sinewy forearms that made me think fleetingly of a marble statue of Heracles that I had seen in Athens while touring Greece. My vision blurred; too many tears. I was so ashamed of myself for crying I ended up by not looking up, instead inadequately saying "Thank you."

Chapter 3

By the time I got back to The Barnacle I was a basket case. I had even given serious thought while on the way home to committing hara-kiri! However after cooling off for a few minutes sitting on the porch swing I decided the family wouldn't approve of such a drastic measure and so I got up and feverishly tackled the mess. After all I had no one to blame for leaving the car door open but myself. Besides, with me gone who would take care of Caesar?

It took a bit of doing but by seven thirty I was no longer basket material. By then I had managed to free all the goodies of their stickiness and cache them away, to scrub the leather car seat so it was once again "sitable," to whip up a fresh crab salad for dinner and, after reassuring myself that Caesar was indeed asleep on his magic carpet, to fix a very stiff gimlet. It tasted better than usual; no doubt, because I was sipping it while relaxing in the cushy green chair that Gloria and I always squabbled over. Only this time I didn't have to wait to take, "My turn to curl up and watch the sunset!"

This evening the sky was a crystal blue with a few tiny white puffy clouds hovering over Seguin Island. I watched them slowly change to pink, then to a hot pink and finally to a soft magenta; while on the far horizon beyond the Black Rocks, dark heavy thunder heads were forming and once in a while I could see lightning stab the ocean. The tide was about five hours in and the surf was splashing and sparkling like millions of diamonds dusting the beach. Not a soul was in sight - anywhere. It was all so pristine.

Enjoying this jewel-like sunset was also conducive to letting my thoughts roam at will. One minute I seemed to be mumbling, "Wouldn't it be nice if I could wipe my sins away twice a day just like the tides sweep the beach," and the next, "Wouldn't it be nice to go through life practicing Mr. Linette's philosophy of putting off till tomorrow what you don't want to do today," and then on to, "Wouldn't it be nice if I could blot out forever my marriage to Britton Peabody, who by the time he had reached the

21

ripe old age of 30 had handed down so many decisions that sitting on The Bench in Washington like Grandfather would have been a drag."

Knowing my soul as well as I do, I immediately recognized these heretic thoughts as symptoms of the rebellion I could feel building within me against the status quo. I obviously needed a change - not only from Boston - not only from the cloistered walls of the museum - but from life in general! Perhaps I had lived too long in a canvas world filled with painted vignettes of life - imaging what it might have been like to ride the prairies with Remington and Russell, or to walk the streets of Rome with Bernini, to visit the Sistine Chapel with Michelangelo, enjoy an aperitif with Toulouse-Lautrec or even during a Paris spring to stroll along the banks of the Seine with Monet. Perhaps it was time for me to sample life in the real world, to become a doer instead of a dreamer?

A deep restlessness overcame me. My hand brushed against the ever present notebook and pencil - my wrist watch was still on my arm - and before I realized what I was doing I started another list. Only this time I penciled in the heading "Things I Will and Will Not Do This Summer."

My list grew like a perennial weed, almost faster in my mind than I could write: #1, I will not set foot in Arnold (best be careful or else I could become homeless), but buy the necessary supplies from Graves: #2, I will take my favorite walk to Todd's Point and Griffith Head, everyday, regardless of the weather: #3, I will not set my alarm clock: #4, I will saturate myself with mysteries and good historical novels and ignore the stack of art books brought with me to study: #5, I will become a summer hermit: #6, I will not make anymore lists.

I must have dozed off after jotting down such a tremendous edict and then eating dinner for I woke up with a start and an orange headache. The source no doubt being a giant orange ball of a moon which had appeared on the dark horizon and was casting a mesmeric orange path across the cove, over the dunes and then lengthening onto the ocean. It continued on to the Black Rocks where the orangey waves stopped - giving the rocks an illusion of a giant step - and then the path continued on into

22

oblivion. It is hard to tear one's self away from such splendor and so I sat watching the moon climb higher and higher into the sky; watching the orange path widen into a street of silver and finally melting into an enormous glistening pool of reflected moonlight.

It was after midnight when I collapsed into bed. I did not have a very good night's rest. The stressful moments of the day had definitely taken their toll and by three-thirty I was wide awake and up; such a ghastly time to fix breakfast - but I did.

It was drizzling and in the putty gray pre-dawn I could see that during the night a thick chilling fog had blanketed the ocean. But the tide was just right for crossing the channel with about two hours to go until low, and so mindful of the #2 item on my list to take a walk regardless of the weather I dug out my old yellow slicker and sou'wester and braved the soupy elements.

The sand was cold and clammy against my feet as I trudged beside the channel to its mouth and once there, being the creature of habit that I am, paused to study the fog shrouded ocean and listen to the comforting yet haunting, melancholy warning sounds of the Seguin and Pond Island Light horns. Automatically, I turned and started to walk towards Todd's Point; letting the surf lap gently over my feet; relishing its cleansing action as each wave seemed to wash away my many faceted problems, old ones as well as new ones, such as the identity of the man who had helped me yesterday afternoon.

He now seemed more phantom than real, my recollection of him more like the composition of a surrealistic painting drawn from my subconsious mind - sinewy forearms bronzed by the sun, an expensive Breguet wrist watch like Adam and Daddy owned, a swatch of clean blue oxford cloth and a faceless head.

I shuddered, the coincidence of mind meeting matter uncanny, for by now I could see that I could not see the headland at Todd's Point. It too was faceless; the thick fog that had blanketed the ocean during the night had sneaked in, effectively camouflaging the dangerous shelf-like ledge jutting out from the promontory and the slippery rocks below. However the fog hadn't penetrated the chasm at the base. The mist had stopped short of it, creating a temporary roof over a short cut to Mile

Beach and Griffith Head. I had named the chasm Devil's Walk because of its dank rocky sides and accessibility only at low tide and most importantly only during the summer when it filled part way up with sand.

And so I ran through the passage, not daring to look back in case the Devil had appeared, ignoring the nagging thought that if I fell and hit my head on a piece of jagged rock he would claim his just due.

I was spent by the time I breached the tranquility of Mile Beach, but the drizzle had stopped and inland the sky appeared to be brightening to a blue-gray. My spirits lifted! Willingly I gave myself over to the pleasures of the early morning; to once again walk the magnificent stretch of sandy beach, to hear and see the long line of white tipped breakers thundering in and though no one was there for proof I made it legal I had walked a mile by touching with my toes the special spit of rock that juts out like a table at the base of craggy faced Griffith Head.

The sky by now was blue above and the thick fog dissipating over the ocean. I turned to head back home. Tendrils of curling sea smoke were beginning to appear far out on the water and every once in a while the dune grass shimmied like wheat being winnowed on a vast field. As I reached Todd's the same sort of deep restlessness I had experienced the evening before overcame me and I felt compelled to climb to the top of the promontory where I sat down to wait for the splendid second of the sun's resurrection.

For me there has always been a sacredness about the first hint of sunrise. Maybe it's due to the accompanying hush of the land spotlighted from above by the solitary twinkling Venus? I don't honestly know the answer, but I do know that I don't need man-made accouterments to embellish His being for I have yet to see a stained glass window to compare with His own dark blue-black ocean silhouetted against the ever changing first rosy streaks of the sun or to hear a church choir's hosannas sung more joyfully than His waves lapping against the sand.

And so, as restless as I was, I willed myself to sit patiently - to watch and to wait. All the heavy black clouds I noticed had now been swept out to sea where they had formed what appeared to be an impenetrable fortress-like wall on the horizon. The sun it seemed was struggling valiantly to try and climb the wall of clouds and at last its red rays tinged the top giving them an illusion of turrets. A gentle breeze stirred my hair; it moved on ruffling the sea lettuce clinging to the rocks, then it seemed to stiffen as it rippled the tops of the waves creating a would-be cobble stone path to the wall. The breeze seemed to stop for a moment, as if knocking at a door, and then slowly - very slowly - a brilliant tiny jagged magenta hole appeared in the wall of clouds. No longer rebuffed the breeze seemed to push through and escape - enlarging the fiery jagged red hole - giving it shape - the shape of a Norman castle door.

I watched and waited - spellbound - scarcely daring to breathe - afraid my breath would add momentum to the escaping breeze. Escaping - escaping to where and from what? My thoughts were nebulous as I pondered about an escaping breeze: Was it like an eagle escaping the bondage of earth to soar with the wind?; Was it like a wave escaping from a watery grave only to dash itself to droplets on the shore?; Was it like a boat straining to escape her mooring?

The thought startled me! Even more amazing, Grandfather's boat was christened *Escape*! Why I should think of that now, perched as I was on top of the world waiting for the sun to rise, was beyond me.

And yet, "Why not think of it now - no longer able to challenge the sea he had given *Escape* to me. Could I be that boat trying to escape my moorings? Is that why he gave her to me - knowing that someday I might need her for my very own escape?"

The answer seemed to come with a blinding yellow blaze as the sun catapulted over the wall, quickly reducing it to rubble and just as quickly swooshing it all away. How long I continued to sit on the promontory - my thoughts in a turmoil - I will never know. However I do know what had to have been a rogue wave cascading in against the rocks, leaving its afterwash foaming and licking at my feet, made me aware once more of time and tide. Slowly I stood up - profoundly moved and realizing that another decision appeared to have been made for me.

Chapter 4

The decision agreed upon at the summit between Him and me began to crumble like a cookie when I got back to The Barnacle. Of course I was the one to waver - not Him. I kept chiding myself. "Do I really want to get into a situation I might not be able to handle? Am I going from the frying pan into the fire?"

After letting Caesar out to, "Go chase a rainbow," I fixed myself a cup of coffee which I really didn't want and devoured an entire package of Pepperidge Farm chocolate mint cookies which I did want - my lust for them always insatiable when caught in a web of circumstance beyond my control. By then I had accepted my fate! "A promise is a promise."

It was still too early to make the necessary phone call so I went outside and furiously weeded the tulip bed. Then I decided to start on a new mystery novel but couldn't concentrate and after reading the same page four times deemed it fruitless and put it down. At last the clock chimed nine - the hour of reckoning had come - I could procrastinate no longer.

I gave up counting the times I nervously picked up the telephone, started to dial and then put the phone down. Finally I let the call complete itself thinking, hopefully, maybe the boat has been mistakenly sold or has been put on the auction block such as they do unclaimed baggage. That would honorably, I reasoned, let me wiggle out of my pact with Him.

"Good morning! Rigg's Marina! Miss Collins speaking. May I help you?"

Her words coming over the line were brisk but friendly in tone. I took heart. "Yes, if you please. I would like to speak to Mr. Macintosh, the yard manager."

"Of course. One moment please."

I thought I might faint, such was the effort on my part. However, the writing on the card I was clutching stiffened my spine. Having lifted it earlier from Daddy's file of often called local numbers the card had the aura of a court order.

"Macintosh, here!"

My reaction to his efficient greeting was a brief case of tongue-tie. Finally, with fingers crossed and with my eyes raised in supplication towards the ceiling thinking, "Dear Lord, please don't let the boat be there," I blurted out, "Mr. Macintosh, this is Serena Bradford from Boston, Massachusetts. Our family has done business for years with the marina and I'm wondering if the boat *Escape* belonging to my grandfather, Judge Bradford, is still there?"

"It is a pleasure to hear from you, Miss Bradford. If I sound surprised it is due to the timing of your phone call. You see we just received a letter the other day from the law firm Bradford, Bradford and Bradford advising us of the change in boat ownership from Judge Bradford to you. And, to answer your question, yes indeed, *Escape* is here."

Mr. Macintosh, unfortunately for me, could not have been nicer. If he had been crisp or snappy like his apple namesake I could have added that on to my honorable wiggling out list, a list of this nature permissible, and gotten off the hook once more. However, he was a wealth of polite information, all of it given freely in a maddening, calm way.

"She is still shrink-wrapped and still on the same blocks where she has been for the past two years though, Miss Bradford; Judge Bradford electing not to have *Escape* commissioned."

I wasn't sure what shrink-wrapped meant; however, a vision of left-overs covered with plastic wrap in the refrigerator did pop into my mind. Fortunately Mr. Macintosh assumed I did know since he continued his briefing. "Both engines have been properly maintained, the auxiliary kept in storage, of course!"

"Of course," I echoed, but to myself; the question as to why one engine should be left out in the cold just begging to be asked. Mr. Macintosh continued, sparing me a comment. "A check has also been received, Miss Bradford, to cover not only next year's storage but for any expenses she might incur this boating season. In fact, I was just discussing *Escape* with the dockmaster and we were wondering, since a check has been received if she should be prepped for the season?"

I should have realized, being the kind of person Grandfather is, that just in case the possibility of me becoming a sailor materialized every avenue for my boating enjoyment would have been covered. He had placed only one restriction on his generous gift the day *Escape* was given to me. "Serena, " he had said tenderly while taking my hands into his, "I know you hate boats and I know you have a fear of the open ocean but there comes a time in all our lives when we have to shed a bit of the past in order to move on into the future. I trust you will recognize the interlude."

Grandfather had winked then. "You must give *Escape* a fighting chance! You must promise me not to sell her; we will renegotiate the terms in a couple of years."

My pledge, "I will," to his, "Give *Escape* a fighting chance," and my vow, "I do," to his, "Promise me not to sell her," had been declared in a dewy-eyed manner reminiscent of when I took my marriage vows. Those, of course, had been irreconcilably broken.

I was determined not to break faith with Grandfather. The interlude was over! So I took the plunge, wide-eyed, and said (honesty being the best policy I thought), "I am the black sheep of the Bradford family, Mr. Macintosh. By that I mean I am the non-boating member of the family. I know absolutely nothing about boats but I have decided to put *Escape* into the water. Do you have a mooring available?"

His affirmative reply was coupled with the statement, "You will want to have the boat's bottom painted."

I was shocked! "You mean the boat isn't already painted?"

There was complete silence. I could just see him putting his hand over the phone and saying to that person, whoever, he is, "I have a live one on the line." To Mr. Macintosh's credit he finally replied to my stupid question in an extremely business-like way. "Algae grows very quickly on a boat's bottom and that in turn reduces her performance - that is she wouldn't be able to perform well - her speed would be reduced."

Speed! Here I was literally trying to muster enough courage to get into the darned boat when he had me entered into the America's Cup race. Thankfully, before I could make another stupid statement he made the decision for me. "Judge Bradford always had that done."

Naturally I acquiesced adding, "Please do whatever surgery is necessary to get *Escape* ready for the summer."

Mr. Macintosh again replied in a very business-like way. "As usual her dinghy will be placed on the float ready for use."

The dinghy! I had forgotten about the dinghy. Of course, one does need some mode of transportation out to a mooring. As innocently as I could I asked, "Couldn't I use the tender service?"

Silence! Once more I could see him putting his hand over the phone and saying to that person, whoever he is, "I have a real live flake on the line." However, again to Mr. Macintosh's credit, he answered my question politely though this time in a painstakingly business-like way. "The marina does not provide tender service, Miss Bradford."

"Oh," was my intelligent reply - not at all worthy of a Phi Beta Kappa.

Well, I was now down to the nitty-gritty. I had one more hurdle to overcome and so as Daddy would have said, "Bite the bullet." I did, timidly asking, "Mr. Macintosh, would you know of anyone who would be willing to give me boating lessons?"

Once more there was silence! This time I tried hastily to fill the void. "As I mentioned before I am the non-boating member of the family."

Mr. Macintosh could have sarcastically replied, "Obviously," but instead - very kindly - almost fatherly - said, "I'll scout around for someone. In the meantime, not to worry."

Not to worry was easier said than done, especially after we had agreed upon the date, "A week from today," for *Escape*'s launching. However, after hanging up the phone I decided to follow his advice of, "In the meantime," since between now and then a lot of good things could happen. Why, I could fall and break a leg; a solution to my dilemma worthy of Solomon.

"Ha! Then the cookie would really crumble."

#

30

I had been raised to try and be honest with myself. Down deep in my heart I know I wanted the week to stretch into July before *Escape* was launched. In my mind this wasn't possible - business being business - which is why when the phone rang exactly seven days later and at precisely nine a.m., I knew it was going to be someone calling from the marina.

"Bradford residence," I answered, my speech somewhat slurred from still being half asleep.

"This is Simon Mont, Miss Bradford, from Riggs Marina. I hope I'm not calling too early in the morning but I did want to let you know *Escape* is ready. She was launched late yesterday afternoon."

He was very polite but an authoritative tone in his voice sent a slight chill down my spine - quite reminiscent of the way the headmaster at school always affected me. I reached down and pulled the quilt closer to my chin. "Thank you for letting me know."

"I have given her mooring number 100 and her dinghy is tied to the float."

It has always baffled me and at the same time always irritated me how people talk about boats as if they are viable. You would think a boat has a soul and heart instead of a smelly engine and a bunch of nuts and bolts. The surfacing of this heretic thought caused me to pause a moment and before I had a chance to murmur another thank you Mr. Mont continued.

"Miss Bradford, I was in Mr. Macintosh's office when you phoned the other day to discuss *Escape*. He mentioned at that time you were interested in taking boating lessons. I've given it a great deal of thought and if you still wish to do so, I will be pleased to work up a twelve week course of instruction for you consisting of two lessons weekly. Since the marina is not usually rushed in the evenings, I thought we could begin at six p.m., say on Thursdays and Sundays. Also, since the boating season is short in Maine we could begin tomorrow which is Thursday, the 17th; that is if you don't have a previous engagement. How does that sound to you?"

My salubrious, euphoric bubble that I had been cocooned in for the past few days burst as I quickly remembered "that person,

31

whoever he is" was the dockmaster. I wasn't quite sure what that meant but the title of position and his first name immediately caused a flashback of the old Simon Legree movies that I used to watch with Gloria on the Late, Late Show; Simon always appearing wearing black boots and carrying a long black whip. To add insult to injury that also meant he had been privy to my scintillating conversation with Mr. Macintosh. I felt like the last cracker in the barrel - whatever - but not wanting to do any more damage to the Bradford family name I thought it best to go ahead and commit my soul - body too - to further the cause. I replied courageously, "Yes, that's agreeable and I do appreciate your generous gift of time."

"My pleasure, Miss Bradford. See you tomorrow evening then, six o'clock sharp! That way we can take advantage of the sun."

#

It was mid-afternoon and I was well into reading a Gothic novel when the "I don't have anything to wear" syndrome materialized - prompted no doubt by the heroine in the novel having been thrust out into the cruel world when her home burned to the ground.

Luck was with me for after rummaging through an old steamer trunk belonging to Gloria and me I found a couple of old white cotton fisherman knit sweaters - the kind I could lose myself in - plus a couple of pairs of white cotton knit pants - drawstring waist. Being the female, female I am (I could almost hear an exasperated "I know" from Gloria) I decided that, "If I'm going to drown at least the coroner will not be able to put in his report anything derogatory about the way I'm dressed." So much for positive thinking!

I spent so much time rummaging, modeling different outfits and reminiscing over the snapshots and momentoes of past beach parties and summer amours hidden in the bottom of the trunk, that I was almost tardy for the opening of the exhibit "John Sloan and the Ashcan School." His paintings of everyday life in New York City during the early 1900's had always aroused empathy in me, but it was my promise to Mr. Smythe that forced me to make the run into Brunswick; driving through Arnold on the highway permitted in order to get to Bowdoin College's art museum.

I had attired myself accordingly, electing to wear a pastel but predominantly pink multicolored silk Mandarin dress with scandalously long side slits, my favorite summer high-heeled sandals, and after a frustrating period of time while I fussed piling my hair on top of my head in a Geisha style hairdo, a tiny delicate ivory bird cage hair ornament that Gloria had given to me. Perhaps too avant-garde I thought, after checking out my image in the Times Square mirror, but Mr. Smythe had said, "Having just packed off Renoir, Serena, it will do you good to view an exhibit without a headache and to be treated for a change as a special patron of the arts. Besides, I have told their director you would be there representing our museum."

So I did my duty. I certainly suffered no pain; the panacea of munching on big juicy strawberries and petit fours, sipping champagne, viewing fine paintings and enjoying someone else's company quite the cure for my before boating lesson jitters. Which is why I decided on the way home to stop by the marina. I guess?

Anyway, it was just one of those crazy spur of the moment I have nothing better to do decisions just like it had been for me to bring Caesar along for the ride into Brunswick. I knew I should have known better, but he had been such a good dog ever since his parting of the multitude in Arnold.

So we two drove merrily down the highway and when I got to Georgetown turned down the road to the marina. It was such a beautiful evening - in the low 70's - that I opened the sun top for Caesar. He was in his glory with his head protruding out from the top like a periscope and every once in a while I could hear him let out a yowl when the strains of Claire de Lune blaring from the tape deck hit a high chord.

It was sevenish when we crashed the marina. There were not too many cars at the restaurant and there seemed to be no activity on the docks and floats; in fact, the office, chandlery, dock house and storage buildings appeared to be locked up for the night. It

33

was so quiet and after making sure no one official looking was around - the last person I wanted to run into this evening being "that person" - I decided to let Caesar stretch his long legs - mine too - and putting him on a leash we strolled around the grounds.

I finally stopped, sitting down on the front porch of the marina office. From here it was easy to enjoy the sparkling beauty of Riggs Cove and Knubble Bay. I couldn't help but remember how everyone in the family always commented about this being such a snug little harbor ringed as it is with tall dark pines and with the added protection of a small spit of land so aptly named The Knubble. I started to remember too the tales - tall or not - of negotiating the two channels to and from the Bay. Everyone had seemed to like a different tide time with four hours out winning the prize for most fun at Blind Rocks Passage and three hours out for sheer marvelous terror at Lower Hell's Gate.

Once again, I found myself asking, "Do I really want to get into a situation I might not be able to handle?" I knew *Escape* was a sturdy seaworthy boat, but looking out at her now - bobbing and tugging at her mooring - her sleekness and raciness evident even to a novice like myself put butterflies in my stomach.

I decided I better go find the dinghy; having already made far too many faux pas I at least could familiarize myself with her. From the porch it was hard to distinguish between all the white dinghies turned upside down on the float to say nothing of those bouncing in the water. Grandfather, I recalled, had painted in aqua letters the word *Escape* on her stern to put an end to his griping about their sameness. He also used to gripe about not being able to tell Gloria and me apart until we got into a boat - me always sitting as if glued to the floor boards and Gloria always egging to go faster.

The minute I started down the ramp - Caesar in tow - I knew I was being foolish! Although the tide was high, making the ramp not too steep, a brisk breeze had come up causing the water to become quite choppy, which in turn made walking on the float a lot like crossing on a swinging rope bridge; especially for an idiot like me in high heels.

Caesar was becoming quite excited; sniffing and in turn sneezing at all the tantalizing salty smells as well as woofing at a few ducks having their own sailing school and no doubt all the time thinking that I was going to take him for a boat ride. I finally found the miserable thing tied to the float just as "that person" had said. For a few seconds I stood there, dumbly frozen to the spot, looking at it - her - the blob - whatever! At the moment names were not important. What was, was the water; so dark, so menacing, so full of childhood nightmares with creepy crawly monsters.

I released Caesar. I don't know why. Just like I don't know why I stooped down and untied the dinghy, nonchalantly looping the rope around a light pole. It was as if I had been hypnotized and responding to an oblique signal. It was either that or temporary insanity, for I took off my shoes thinking it might be a good idea to practice getting in and out of the dinghy having always been so awkward at that, never quite mastering the body English of stepping straight up and down to and from the boat.

The float was still quite teeter-tottery but it felt firmer now that I was in my stocking feet so not wanting to waste any more time I lifted my right foot off the float and with a determined thrust hopped into the bow. My lapse of memory over where to step into a dinghy - wise folk boarding in the middle - was soon apparent: for of course when I hopped into the bow instead of into the middle I pushed the dinghy away from the float. This caused my left foot to scrape against the oarlock.

Terror overtook reason. "Sit down! Regain your balance! Act logical," I kept telling myself.

Instead I did the opposite. I panicked and lunged for the rope I had looped around the light pole. Only the rope wasn't there. Instead, it was dangling in the water. In my so called hypnotic state I obviously had forgotten to secure the dinghy properly.

Neither was I secured properly - my upper half hanging over the side like I was trying to shampoo my hair and my lower half spread out like a throw rug over the front half of the dinghy.

I looked up hoping to see Gabriel standing on the float, his wings opened wide in preparation to rescue me. What I did see was Caesar, all four legs in tuck position, ready for blast-off.

35

He shot into the air like a starwars missile and from the set look in his eyes I knew I was the target. I inched aside as quickly as I could. My, "Stay, Caesar," left unsaid as the stern of the dinghy arched above me and I was hurled into the cold, dark, pitch blackness of the cove. Slimy wisps of seaweed seemed to grasp my legs and for a split second I felt the ooze on the bottom suck at my feet. I must have screamed with the force of a hundred screech owls because when I finally bobbed up several people were on the float; all talking at once and all shouting instructions.

Hysteria being somewhat akin to laughter I started to swim towards the float. I was joined quickly by my boating buddy; snorting and barking with all four legs plus wagging tail propelling him at top speed. Instead of Gabriel it was Caesar to the rescue!

#

I had often wondered when a child what an author meant by describing a female character as, "A lady in distress." Now I knew. I had become one as soon as my hands touched the float. Two men, not bothering with a customary, "How do you do?", reached down and grasping me firmly under the arm pits pulled me out of the water just like a lobsterman would haul a trap. To their credit they deposited me safely and gently onto the float, their concern for my well-being mirrored in the actions of several other men now dashing around. All of them seemed to be asking me the same questions at once. "Are you hurt?" "Are you okay?" "What happened?"

I managed, "I'm f- f- fine," and, "Th- th- thank you." To say anything else would have been impossible. I had started to shiver, my teeth chattering along in sympathy.

To add to my distress water was streaming from every pore; forming a puddle beneath my stocking feet. I could feel my hair clinging to my neck and shoulders. I reached up and tried to squeeze out some of the water. My Geisha style hairdo was gone; so was the tiny ivory bird cage ornament Gloria had given to me. In its place was a soggy mess which felt like a clump of

36

slippery seaweed. Not only a clump of seaweed but seaweed with twigs, for I could feel some of the bone pins protruding. I blinked back a few tears, the vision of me as a giant red pin cushion too much to bear.

My hair wasn't the only thing clinging to my body - so were my clothes. They were stuck to me like I was a participant in a wet T-shirt contest. Having always been self-conscious about being overly endowed I blushed; not even a dime could have been wedged between the fabric and me.

I distinctly heard one of the men mutter, "Jesus." At that remark I could no longer hold back the tears.

A lady, definitely not one in distress judging from her svelte appearance, stepped forward and helped me into a voluminous yellow slicker which had been produced from goodness knows where. "This will help warm you up, my dear," she said kindly, her eyes conveying a sensitivity to my plight. "I've also a couple of clean tissues in my purse I think you could use. That scratch on your foot looks nasty. Are you sure you aren't hurt?"

God had not forgotten me after all. He had not sent Gabriel, but he did send an angel to help me out of my misery. I smiled back at her, making good use of the tissues to wipe away my tears. "I'm fine. I do appreciate your thoughtfulness. You are truly an angel of mercy."

She laughed. "I've been called many things before, but never an angel!"

Her gaiety accentuated by a jovial man boisterously calling, "Amen to that," restored my sense of humor and once more I became aware of my surroundings. It was still light enough for me to see that the dinghy had been righted and was being tied up at the far end of the float by a very tall man. He was also motioning to someone on the shore and though his back was towards me I heard distinctly his shout, "Grab Caesar! Grab the God damned dog! He can cause more havoc in one minute than the Romans did when sacking Troy!"

Caesar! Dear sweet Caesar who is afraid of a raindrop! I had been so full of self-pity that I had momentarily forgotten him.

I turned towards the shore. It was almost dark but sensory lights near the dock had flicked on giving the area enough

37

illumination for me to see another couple standing near the water's edge trying to coax him in. I picked up my shoes plus Caesar's leash and hurried towards them, expressing a grateful, "Thank you for your help," to everyone on the way.

By the time Caesar made it to shore I was there to greet him and to immediately put him back on his leash, whereby he promptly disgraced me by shaking himself all over everyone. Fortunately laughter seemed to be the standing order for the evening. At least it was while we made our way up to the parking lot.

It is not often that a gal can lay claim to the dubious distinction of being "a lady in distress" twice in less than two hours which is why, I guess, my "Thank you again for your help" sort of slid into a groaning, "Oh, no, I've locked the keys in the car."

It was just as well that it was dark. This way I couldn't see the expression on their faces; their silence being far more damaging to my ego than the uttering of a hollow platitude could ever be.

Then I remembered. "All is not lost," I said cheerfully to them and to another man who had appeared out of nowhere carrying a very large flashlight. "I always keep an extra set in a magnetic box underneath the left front fender."

The man with the flashlight stepped forward. He seemed perturbed, like he had had one problem too many to solve during the day, yet his voice was calm as he spoke in a kind - almost fatherly - way. "Let me get the keys for you."

He didn't wait for an answer and after a thorough search of the left front fender - after a thorough search of the remaining three fenders and the hood - came up empty handed. Then I remembered. I had forgotten to replace the magnetic box when I last locked myself out. It was the night of the Renoir opening, a nerve wracking evening if there ever was one!

Tensions were beginning to build! I could feel it in the air. I couldn't think of a thing to say - except the truth - and under the circumstances what good would it do now to air my past mistakes.

As luck would have it I was spared the agony of a confession for the man with the flashlight was adroitly climbing to the top of my Porsche. Then I remembered. I had left the sun top open for Caesar; a perfect way to gain access to the inside of the car.

By now our ranks had swollen! The atmosphere became more like that of a crowd witnessing a performance under The Big Top as Mac, so heralded by another man, lowered himself half way down head first through the sun top and a few breathless seconds later surfaced with my keys.

His return to earth was greeted by a round of applause and several lusty shouts of, "Well done," and, "Good show." My welcome, as I accepted the keys from him, was very subdued. I was so miserable in my wet sticky clothes and so mortified over all the trouble I had caused that no matter what I said I knew it would be inadequate. Finally, I said just that. "I can't think of any words adequate enough to thank you for your help this evening."

Caesar, however, did rise to the occasion. I had often wondered if he could reason, such was his uncanny sense of timing. Now I knew, for no sooner had I finished speaking than he raised his huge front paw to Mac for him to shake. An ultimate gesture if there ever was one!

I heard several, "Oh my," including mine, a couple of, "How about that," and a high pitched, "How darling," as Mac leaned down and solemnly shook Caesar's paw saying, "Always happy to help out man's best friend." He straightened up then, smiled and added, "That also applies to ladies in distress."

I smiled back, a little on the wane side, but none the less a smile that I hoped was filled with gratitude and appreciative of his courtliness.

Now that the show was over the crowd scattered quickly. None of the bystanders could have possibly been more eager to get home than I was, a feat I accomplished in record-breaking time considering the tortuous route taken over rutted shore roads. Once there I couldn't get into the shower fast enough. I didn't even bother to remove my clothes or to take the bone pins out of my hair before stepping into the tiled enclosure. Instead I chose to rid myself of their glue-like existence while standing under the full force of the spray as if somehow that would wash away the memory of an ill-begotten evening. Finally I was down to being in the altogether, my hair was shampooed and I was thoroughly enjoying letting the water beat against my skin until I could now feel it beginning to tingle. My mind, however, was still not functioning on the proper plane.

Unlike Gloria, who always sang when showering, or Adam, who whistled a fine tune, I had always used the time to mentally go over my mistakes, trying to figure out the, "I should have done this from the why did I ever do that." Tonight was different. Tonight I was too tired to think of anything beyond what I had seen and heard, which in reality was nothing more than a mishmash of confusion from start to finish that began with the two men pulling me out of the water and ended with the very tall man shouting, "Grab the God damned dog. He can cause more havoc in one minute than the Romans did when sacking Troy." It was an unusual comment to say the least. That is the part about sacking was unusual considering the time and place; not the part about "Grab the God damned dog." I had heard Daddy and Adam plus several other people say the very same thing on numerous occasions.

I was too tired to think about any one thing anymore. I turned the shower off. It was just as well; I had let it run for so long that the cold water was no longer needed. What I did need though was a good night of rest being that tomorrow was the beginning of an adventure I already knew I was going to regret.

It was almost midnight when I finally made it into bed having taken a few extra minutes to rinse out my clothes and, just to reassure myself that Caesar was indeed asleep on his rug, to climb the stairs down and back to Times Square not only once but twice. As I slipped in between the smooth sheets a divine thought occurred to me, and although it had been a long time since I had said my prayers at bedtime I couldn't resist murmuring a short one. "Please, God, could it rain for the rest of the summer?"

Chapter 5

As prayers go the one I had murmured last night was certainly on the trivial side and if heard was deemed not worthy of attention for the day was one of the most beautiful I can ever remember in Maine.

It started in a blaze of glory at precisely 4:59 a.m. From then on it was the kind of day that makes you reluctant to do anything else but sit on the beach and saturate yourself in the splendor of nature's panorama; somehow trying to stamp it forever in your mind.

Dominating the scene was the vast sky. Most of the day it had been a clear robin's egg blue but by mid-afternoon as I leisurely strolled towards Griffith Head the color had deepened into a Delft blue. The ocean, as always sensuous, reminded me of a floating iridescent turquoise sari; its intricate border designed of sand and glistening mica flakes, tiny periwinkles and shell fragments, a snail's tracings and my own following footsteps, and even bits of sparkling sea foam clinging to a moiré like water line. Larger than usual breakers were cascading onto the shore; their thunder reverberating against the cliffs and beach. Each wave was spuming an illusion veil type mist which was then captured by the breeze carrying it high into the air. Once there, touched by the late afternoon sun the mist became woven with rainbows of incredible hues - cerise, jade green, soft yellow, pale pink, and forget-me-not blue.

Such was the ethereal beauty of the scene that I felt compelled to linger for a while. Walking a few feet away from the surf I stretched out against the hot sand. I could feel its heat slowly penetrating into my body, melting a myriad of tensions away. In the recent past it would have been hard for me not to reflect on life and its many problems, but now my mind only concerned itself with the soaring terns and gulls and the enormous pleasure of toying with the sand; taking great delight in the coarseness of it - letting it trickle through my fingers in hourglass fashion.

41

It was the joyful shrieking of two small children toddling after a scurrying sandpiper that brought me back into being in tune with the real world. However it took their mother's firm order, "Let's go home now for dinner," to make me aware of the time and to remind me of the prior commitment that I had made for the evening. So as much as I hated to leave the warmth of the sand and the splendor of nature's panorama I did what I had to do: I got myself up and headed towards home, the anxiety of taking my first boating lesson hovering over my head like the threat of a persistent rain cloud.

#

I had been raised to be punctual, to never, ever, waste another person's time by being tardy, so it was exactly "Six o'clock sharp" when I left the marina office and half-heartedly trudged down to the float in search of Mr. Mont. I say half-heartedly because I had just been recognized by the very kind man known as Mac, one of the last people in the world I ever wanted to see tonight in view of last night's debacle.

I came upon him unexpectedly while trying to return the yellow slicker to its proper owner. He was seated behind a large desk, elbow deep in paper work and his instant recognition of me coupled with his warm greeting, "I'm Bruce Macintosh, Miss Bradford; there was so much confusion in the parking lot last evening that I don't believe I introduced myself properly to you," completely undermined my confidence for I had spent the last few minutes before leaving The Barnacle camouflaging myself into as much of a non-entity as possible. Having recently become paranoid over well-fitting clothes I had decreed the mode of the evening to be the baggier the better. Fortunately the bulky knit sweater and the drawstring waist pants that I had found in the steamer trunk filled such a bill. As for my hair I had non-entitied it too, at least I thought I had, piling the mass on top of my head in Buddah-like fashion and then covering it all up with a multicolored babushka that Adam had brought back from Russia. I had tied it at the nape of my neck, the over-all impression being of a lost Nellie just getting off of the turnip

42

boat. I had been pleased! "No one will be able to recognize you," I had said to myself while plastering my face with sun block cream.

Well, I was wrong; for the first time, of course!

Just like over the phone Mr. Macintosh had been a wealth of polite conversation: "A beautiful evening for boating," he had said to which I had replied, "Yes indeed;" "I trust you will find *Escape's* performance up to par," he had said to which I had replied, "I'm sure I will (there was no need to add I would not have known the difference);" "I'll see that Simon gets his slicker back," he had said to which I replied nothing (the news that the slicker belonged to Simon Mont having rendered me not only speechless but hapless for that meant he had been one of the men on the float and therefore privy to my almost skinny dipping swim). I had smiled, nodded an acknowledgment of his offer and then made a hasty retreat out the office door. Just before I closed it behind me I had looked back over my shoulder. An inquisitive look had crept into Mr. Macintosh's eyes and his brow had become furrowed, as if something worrisome was on his mind. As it is with all of us there are times when we can seem to read a person's thoughts, when we can seem to sense a person is too polite to ask the necessary questions in order to restore their peace of mind. So it was with me.

I had laughed deliberately, trying to lighten my spirits as well as his, before saying merrily and hopefully, charmingly, "I'm sure you and the entire staff will be happy to know the marina is now off limits for Caesar and that on the way here this evening I stopped at Graves General Store and had two extra sets of car keys made. One of the sets I will leave here at the marina with Miss Collins. You know, just in case of another emergency."

Fortunately Mr. Macintosh had responded to my behavior with several short belly laughs. However I noticed the same expression on his face that the thoughtful policeman in Arnold had on the day Caesar went joyfully galloping along the waterfront; one of genuine relief!

So it really wasn't any wonder that I had little enthusiasm for finding Mr. Mont or that my feet felt like they were encased in lead sneakers or that by the time I reached the center of the long float the large duffel bag I was toting seemed as heavy as Caesar's 25 pound bag of dog chow. By then the only man in sight was a handsome hunk loading supplies onto a large powerboat with the intriguing name *Savannah's Revenge* emblazoned in bold red letters across her stern. Gloria would have faked a swoon at the sight of his bulging biceps but I was made of sterner stuff and instead willed myself to ignore his physical attributes. I will admit though to a palpitating heart and to glancing at his forearms to see if he was my Heracles. Just why I did that, I don't know. Anyway he wasn't; his skin tone being more olive than bronze.

Faint heart subsiding I dropped my gear beside the boat and stepped forward. "Excuse me, but by any chance are you Mr. Mont?"

He straightened up; a stretch of ten feet it seemed. "Why no, I'm not."

"Oh!"

He chuckled. "Is that an 'Oh' as in how wonderful or an 'Oh' as in disappointed?"

The question caught me by surprise. Neither was I prepared for his Casanovian come-with-me-on-a-gondola-ride type of wink nor was I prepared to be confronted by a diminutive woman with startling black eyes the color of shiny jet beads gushing, "Or maybe, Sugah, its 'Oh' as in flustered?"

I watched as she slipped her arms possessively around the hunk's waist, fluttering her fingers so I would be sure to notice the diamond studded wedding ring on her left hand. She was right, I was flustered! But not for the reason she thought, that I was enamored by her handsome husband, but because of the ordeal ahead of me. "I'm starting boating lessons this evening," I blurted quite out of context.

She laughed and let go of her husband long enough to squeeze my arm in an affectionate way. "That explains why you're so nervous. There's nothin' to it, Honey. You just hop into the boat, turn the key and go."

Of course I knew there was more to it than that, but she had succeeded in making me smile a little which seemed to prompt

44

her drawl into becoming more pronounced. "Why that's what we've been doin' every moseyin' minute since we left home. Home as in Savannah, Georgia, that is! Isn't that right, Leroy?"

Leroy managed to extricate himself from her clutches and climbed on board. "Right, Missy Sue, nothin' to it."

She followed him, giving my arm another squeeze just before boarding. "Lovin' every cotton pickin' second of it too, especially the lobstah and seein' the Maine coast for the first time. Isn't that right, Leroy?"

Leroy, having stowed away some of the supplies below by then, stuck his head out of the hatch and sort of half chuckled and half guffawed. "Right, Missy Sue!"

He had such a jovial smile on his face that my somewhat aloof New England reserve - that I have been wrongly accused of having - melted a bit more; especially when he teased, "Why old King Neptune would nevah dump a lady like you!"

I couldn't help but laugh for by then Leroy had emerged from below and was busy getting ready to cast off. "That's not to say mam," he drawled in a bantering tone, "that Davy Jones wouldn't like to tuck you away in his locker for his pleasure on a rainy day. No sireee! It's just the scalawags like me ole Neptune likes to catch in his net and keep forever."

"Oh, Leroy," oozed Missy Sue, "you do carry on so."

Leroy winked and purred back in a scandalously wicked tone right there in front of me, God and everybody, "Why Missy Sue, I thought that was one of the main reasons you married me."

Missy Sue was obviously pleased at this suggestive remark but I was embarrassed. I felt like I was peeking into their bedroom. I stood there illogically thinking no wonder the South lost the war if they couldn't be more circumspect; that maybe it was due to the cloying red dirt that made them all seem so degenerate.

For a few seconds Missy Sue and Leroy busied themselves about the boat - he turning the engine on, intent on listening to its sound, she hauling in the bumper guards, fenders, whatever. Her parting words to me as they pulled away from the float being carried by the wind. "Bye you all. Come see us now."

Leroy's were a little more prophetic. With a grand bow and cavalier sweep of his white sailor's cap he shouted, "I do believe your Mr. Mont has arrived. Remember now, Miss Fledgling, there's nothin' to it. You just hop into the boat, turn the key and go!"

I gave a final wave to them and then turned (like I had been full-rigged Gloria would have said) and practically knocked Mr. Mont down. Definitely not an auspicious beginning! Neither did his appearance help me to smooth over my clumsiness. He was the reincarnation of Simon Legree himself, even to the black boots; all that was missing was the coiling black whip. He was tall, so tall and lean too, that all I could think of was a ship's mast with a Jolly Roger pennant flying for he had a full black beard.

His words, "Shall we begin, Miss Bradford," or at least those that I heard, wafted down from the crow's nest so to speak and stirred my stomach into a quivery mass of Jello. For of course not only was he the dockmaster and "that person, whoever he is," not only was he the owner of the yellow slicker and witness to my soggy performance of last night but he was the "Grab the God damned dog" and the "Sacking of Troy" person. I recognized his broad back the instant he turned around.

"Sure," I replied; my choice of word out of the many available not very witty but what else could I say after just being stripped of the famous Bradford dignity which has been accumulated through the years like the polish on the fine antiques at home. So having set the wheel in motion there was nothing left for me to do but grab my duffel bag and follow Mr. Mont, hopefully not into Davy Jones' locker.

"What the heck," I grumbled a second later though strictly to myself, "why not come right out and say it. Hopefully not into Hel !"

Anyone watching would have thought I was carrying the crown jewels from the way I was clutching onto my old canvas bag. However, at the moment, it represented survival stuffed as it was with two life jackets, a waterproof windbreaker, a flashlight (one never goes anywhere at the Point without a torch), my purse size cosmetic kit containing a comb, extra aspirin (a current addition), band aids plus other essentials and a couple of candybars and cokes. I had tossed those in at the last minute in case of shipwreck after having decided while having breakfast that it would be prudent not to have dinner before going out into the briny Deep. This was definitely a negative approach but a practical one; the odds being heavily stacked towards me getting sea sick. How humiliating that would be I had thought, especially with a stranger looking on who no doubt was cast out of iron and who probably had never, ever, been sea sick. Looking at Mr. Mont now, me dutifully walking several paces behind as befitting pupil to instructor, I decided I had made a wise decision.

Much to my astonishment he walked past *Escape's* dinghy and stopped beside what appeared to me as a working boat since it was filled with sundry bits of marine paraphernalia. "We will take the marina's skiff out to the mooring this evening, Miss Bradford. It will save us some time."

I couldn't hide my relief over not having to drive; my, "Whatever you think best," sounding too eager.

We got into the skiff. Actually Simon Legree stepped adroitly into the blooming thing while I thudded onto her for once again I was faced with the problem I have always had of fear that the boat would float away from the dock just as I was boarding and there I would be doing a split between the two. I should have been brave enough to discuss this fear - right here and now - after all he was the instructor - but pride, false as it was, interfered. Finally, with a grace not like that of a gazelle, I grasped his outstretched hand and gingerly sidled on board, he making sure my landing was squarely in the middle of the skiff. He also had the foresight to stow my duffel bag in the bow. Me, I was just plain grateful to sit like I had been glued to the spot.

The ride out was uneventful. We talked about such momentous things as the weather and the infamous Georgetown mosquitoes. He said, "I understand the mosquitoes are worse than usual this June than those past. So far they don't seem to me as bad as those buzzing around in the arctic tundra or along the Newfoundland coast." I said, "I understand the town has set aside a few dollars for spraying some of the salt marshes this summer in hopes to control their breeding. A new kind of insecticide which kills only the male."

"Poor bloodied devils," he said midst a spate of coughing. "To sacrifice their lives for mankind is truly the most noble of pursuits."

I didn't know whether to laugh or cry. Mr. Mont's eulogy for the mosquitoes was said with such sobriety that it should have been accompanied by a requiem mass. I thought of saying, half thinking of Britt, my pompous ex, "I call it poetic justice for all the misery they cause." On the other hand I had just met Mr. Mont. I didn't know if his tribute to the mosquitoes was delivered tongue in cheek or offered like a prayer. For all I knew he could be a follower of Vishnu or belong to some freak outer fringed religious group that does not believe in killing bugs. Studying him under the guise of making polite conversation I decided it would be best to say nothing; his face at the moment being a masque of oriental inscrutability. Besides, he looked far too Prussian for my tastes.

I came to this conclusion, finally, because seated as we were in the skiff we were now on the same eye level and although I could not see his eyes shielded as they were from the sun by dark glasses, it was the combination of the glasses and the beard which gave him such a formidable countenance. As to what he thought of me or my appearance it was just as well I didn't know. Anyway, it couldn't have been very flattering swathed as I was like a "loony bird" in white cotton.

A few minutes later I could just as easily have substituted whooping crane for "Loony bird" since I was giving a good imitation of a crane perched on one leg as I tried to leave the skiff to board *Escape*. It was almost as bad as leaving home for the first time!

Upon arriving at the mooring Mr. Mont had moved quickly to tie the skiff to *Escape* before cutting off the engine. Of course I noticed this had been done stern to stern, that is the skiff's right side snuggled up against *Escape's* left side. Lesson number one had begun immediately!

"You must always remember, Miss Bradford, when planning to tie up at a mooring to never cut off the engine until at least one line is secured, be it to the mooring itself or to a boat already in place. This is a safety precaution against being set adrift in case the engine fails to start."

I had nodded, my heart skipping a few beats at the thought of being adrift.

"You will also notice, Miss Bradford, the skiff's sides are well padded so as not to damage another boat. Your dinghy isn't, so I have left a couple of fenders hanging over *Escape's* sides. If you make a practice of hanging them out when you disembark from *Escape* it's one less frustrating thing you will have to worry about when getting ready to board. Of course, once on the way you will want to lift them into the boat."

I had nodded, appreciating his tact in not coming right out saying, "As a precaution against you damaging *Escape*."

Mr. Mont had smiled. I decided he didn't look quite so Prussian.

"One more thing, Miss Bradford, before you begin to unsnap the canvas from the stern. It's strictly a matter of preference if you choose at a later date to board *Escape* from the starboard rather than the port side as I have planned for us to do today. There is no set marine rule governing this procedure. It's not like having to mount a horse from the left."

This had been said in an open for discussion school room type of manner but all I really heard was "before you begin to unsnap the canvas." Now a person would think that would be an easy job to do – after all a snap is a snap even if they are oversized grippers - but it turned out to be harder than I anticipated. In fact, after breaking three perfectly manicured nails while pulling apart four salt corroded snaps I decided the task ranked in frustration with trying to zip the back of my dress up.

It was while struggling with the fourth snap that I suddenly realized the stern canvas was zippered to another canvas covering the midsection of the boat and that part would have to be zipped open before we could board. I was the nearest. I was the logical one to perform this simple task. But it meant having to stand up! It meant having to leave my safe amidship perch! It meant coming to grips once again with my engulfing fears of being sandwiched between two boats and the water swallowing me up forever! I knew I should discuss this fear with Mr. Mont; after all as the instructor he might provide a logical solution for my seemingly insurmountable problem. But pride, mixed with a little bull dog tenacity that everyone mistakenly says I have, intervened. I gulped back down my plea for, "Help!" As it turned out, somehow, Mr. Mont heard my silent cry.

"If I had been alone today, Miss Bradford, I would have first tied up from the bow. However, in lieu of doing that, I elected to tie an extra line amidship from the skiff to *Escape.*"

I nodded slowly, quite apprehensive as to where his explanation was going to lead.

"Please notice how the extra line closes the gap between the two boats. It creates a relatively safe step; not easy for anything to fall in between."

Now I knew where the explanation led. I also knew Rasputin must have had the same kind of resonant hypnotic voice as that of Mr. Mont for he had figuratively taken me by the hand and quite successfully mesmerized me into unzipping the canvas and climbing aboard.

So here I was, finally, straddling the side of the boat "in lieu of," to borrow Mr. Mont's expression, giving my imitation of a crane perched on one leg. This position was most uncomfortable! My left leg just skimmed the skiff but my right leg had no where to go! For of course when unzipping the canvas I had not thought about giving myself enough room to maneuver in when on board. At that moment, being as I was into legs, I had the absurd thought that to have long legs was not the asset I had been brainwashed to believe. So they look nice in sheer hose and elevated with high heels - so what - history has proven that only gets a girl into trouble. Short and stubby legs are more practical and right now definitely the way to go.

Well, long and slender or short and stubby I had to do something pretty darn quick so I leaned far to the right until my right foot was firmly on *Escape's* deck and by holding tightly to the sun top managed a few one footed hop-scotch hops until I finally got my left leg clear and also onto the boat. Rejoice! However, it was a short celebration since there was a gas tank for the auxiliary engine on the floor and I ended up stumbling over it, beam-ending onto the seat behind the one reserved for the Almighty Captain.

I looked up. Mr. Mont was peering down at me from the skiff like I was a specimen on a slide. "Are you okay, Miss Bradford?"

No, I wasn't okay! My bottom hurt or perhaps it was my dignity, what there was left of it to hurt. I was also royally miffed, his question about my well-being sounding rather perfunctory and his manner not at all chivalrous. Why Leroy would have jumped on board, swooped Missy Sue into his manly arms and kissed all her miseries away. The fact that I had just officially met Mr. Mont had nothing whatsoever to do with the price of eggs. Whatever the saying!

But on the other hand it did! I had just met Mr. Mont a few minutes ago and for him to do anything else but inquire about my well-being, especially since I wasn't bleeding to death, would be most improper. My sense of reasoning restored I forgave him for not kissing my aches and pains away and chose instead to make light of my mishap. "I'm fine, but I'm not sure about the seat."

I even managed to laugh as I got up to help him remove the rest of the canvas and to open up the cockpit. "I believe my sister Gloria would say that I had just launched myself into the enthralling world of boating. At least that is how she describes sailing. Right now her description defies believability."

I was surprised to hear Mr. Mont join me in laughing. Actually it was more of a chuckle that sounded a lot like that of an indulgent parent before proceeding with a lecture. I was right!

"Miss Bradford, I've thought a lot about these lessons and since you have stated that you are a non-boater I have decided the best way for us to proceed is for me to use the old tried and true system of show and tell."

I immediately claimed the seat across the aisle from the Almighty Captain's. It only had taken one glance at the dash board to convince me I had nothing to "show and tell" but my ignorance.

Mr. Mont was very patient as he continued with my first lesson which was about the gasoline engine, a subject that normally would have put me right to sleep. However, sensing that survival might be at stake - especially after catching his word, "Explosion," - I paid strict attention to his explanation of the blower.

"Its function is to expel highly combustible gas fumes that can accumulate in a buttoned up boat."

He flicked on a little chrome switch to show me (fortunately labeled blower) before adding, "Let it run for about three to four minutes before turning the engine on," and then got up, walking back to the stern.

I followed him in a puppy dog fashion, watching carefully as he pulled back what I thought was a seat but turned out to be a cover for the engine. I had never really looked at an engine before except for one at the science museum and only then because I had been with Grandfather Horatio and wanted to be polite. But here I was - staring at the smelly thing - not really understanding it - but appreciative of its power to propel *Escape* through the water and most of all to get me safely back.

We returned to our respective seats, me nervously perching on the edge of mine and he obviously at ease behind the wheel. Mr. Mont turned off the blower and then flipped on another little chrome switch labeled Pump. This of course was easy to figure out - even for me - as I visually saw and plainly heard water draining from the boat's bottom. "The bilge," as he said, "Always be sure to let it run until dry!"

I ventured to make an innocuous comment on this part of the lecture. Maybe because I was getting restless or perhaps it was because I found myself daydreaming about strolling my beloved beach instead of jeopardizing my life on such a foolish adventure. "You know, Mr. Mont, I have always hated the word bilge. I think it stems from sympathy for the sailors who were always ordered below to 'Man the pumps.' On the other hand maybe it's because I flunked the word on a vocabulary test." I did not add that by flunking the word, bilge, I ended my perfect score for a month and lost my gold star to egghead Britt. To this day he still gloated over my loss.

Mr. Mont responded to my declaration by reaching into his pants pocket and pulling out a key attached to a darling orange fish float. "How cute," I gushed. Fortunately I was able to throttle the phrase in mid-air, sort of sliding over the syllables, propitiously changing them into something more appropriate like, "How clever!" I even became bold enough to add, "Especially for someone like me who has a penchant for losing keys."

This time I was rewarded with a grin wide enough to erase my image of Mr. Mont as being a Prussian Simon Legree. I relaxed! I didn't stress out when he motioned for me to exchange seats with him. I remained laid back while he continued in a very clear and concise way to comment upon the dials and all the other switches in a rather cursory way; explaining as he did that at the proper time he would discuss their use in greater detail. I panicked when he handed the darling orange fish float with the key attached to me!

Mr. Mont, however, was cucumbery cool. "I believe the best way for you to get the feel of *Escape*, Miss Bradford, is to talk you through the process of turning on her engine."

I could not have agreed - less! Missy Sue had said, "You just hop into the boat, turn the key and go." Leroy had said, "Nothin' to it. You just hop into the boat, turn the key and go." Well, I had already proven them to be wrong about just hoppin' into a boat and if all you had to do was "turn the key and go" why was it necessary for Mr. Mont to talk me through the process of turning on an engine? Who was right and who was wrong?

It took the rest of the evening for me to come to the conclusion I finally reached while driving home that there was no pat answer to my question. All three of them had been right, Missy Sue and Leroy because they were such experienced boaters and probably had forgotten what it was like to be a beginner, Mr. Mont correct in talking me through the process of turning on *Escape's* engine. After all he couldn't help it if I had been cursed with the "Damning Defect," Grandfather's famous name for my being a Southpaw, so that everything I was told and shown to do became awkward for me to carry out.

First there had been a struggle with the lever located to the right of the Almighty Captain's seat. It looked like an oversized inverted handle on a food grinder and was just as hard to use. Mr. Mont had said, "Grip the lower part and pull it towards you. That disengages it from the gear shift. This is a safety feature of the boat. In other words, Miss Bradford, the engine will not turn over until this step is taken."

I had nodded. It had seemed like a straight forward enough command and one certainly within the range of my capabilities. I was wrong! Heavens to Betsy was I ever wrong for it became readily apparent as I struggled in vain to release the lever that *Escape*'s blue ribbon award winning design was a fluke, that she had been obviously designed by a right handed marine architect for only right handed mariners. Not only that but a marine architect who probably lived in a Peoria, Illinois farm house and whose experience with boats consisted solely of sailing one in a bath tub, for how else could a person possibly explain why everything important was installed on the right.

I had asked a tad testily, "I wonder why boats can't be specifically designed for left handed people?"

I hadn't really expected an answer to my question as I finally reached in front of myself in order to get a firm grip on the lever and to pull it out. Nor was one forthcoming from Mr. Mont. Instead he settled deeper into the leather seat, a hint of a slump appearing in his bearing, replacing the square off set to his shoulders. I immediately recognized the posture as the same taken by my former Algebra teacher when he knew he was slated for a long session explaining to me why X plus Y equals Z. Whatever!

My mathematical thought had been interrupted with his next order. "Now, Miss Bradford, insert the key into the ignition switch but don't turn it on."

Like a robot I did just what I was told to do and then waited, poised for action, for his next order.

"Now then, push the lever forward with your right hand and with your left hand turn the key like you are going to turn on your Porsche. The engine should turn over."

Again I did just what I was told to do but nothing miraculous happened. Instead the engine sounded like the straining one in my car on a bitter cold morning.

"Pump the lever a couple of times, Miss Bradford, just like you would pump the gas pedal in a car to help get it started and then turn the key on once more."

Again I did just what I was told to do and pumped the lever a couple of times, adding three or four more quick ones for good measure.

"Var -r -o -o -o -m!" It was the most gosh awful humongus roar belched out of an engine that I had ever heard. The sound echoed around Riggs Cove, supplanted quickly by my blood curdling scream and seconded by someone on the dock shouting through a bull horn, "Simon, everything out there okay?"

Not one hair I noticed had "boinged up" on Mr. Mont's head but every strand of mine had stood on end. I had survived - barely - my breath having a hard time catching up with my palpitating heart. He spoke, finally, his voice patient but firm, his manner cucumbery cool. "You can take your left hand off of the key now, Miss Bradford, and using your right hand pull the lever back, slowly, until you hear the engine start to idle steadily. Then let it slip back into its original warm-up position. You will hear a faint click as well as feel it slide into neutral."

My reward for doing precisely what I was told to do was hearing *Escape's* engine calm down into a low contented cat-like drone. I calmed down too, to the point where I was able to apologize. "I'm sorry about the scream, Mr. Mont. I guess you could say in the spirit of 'show and tell' I demonstrated quite vocally a classic example of the left hand not knowing what the right hand was doing."

I received another award. This time it was from Mr. Mont in the form of a laugh so rich in quality that I curled my toes into my socks. "It was a good learning experience, Miss Bradford. You won't forget it."

He got up then and went to the bow, his marvelous laugh echoing back mixing with his shout, "Nothing wrong out here, Mac. Just trying to cope with a cold engine."

At first I thought he was implying to Mr. Macintosh that I was a cold engine but by the time he returned to the cockpit I decided his comment sounded more like one Grandfather would have used to cover up one of my many mistakes when on board his boat. However I did notice a briskness in his movements that was not present before, also in his voice as he said, "We are going to lose our sun soon and I still have a couple of things I want to include in this lesson such as the correct way to cast off and tie up to a mooring. I also thought you might enjoy taking a short spin out into Knubble Bay to get a feel for *Escape* so instead of talking you through this procedure, Miss Bradford, why don't we exchange seats and I'll just give you a quick run through this evening."

Feeling absolutely washed out and blah after my struggle with the lever I had no regrets, what - so - ever, over giving up my seat to Mr. Mont for the remainder of the lesson. I admit to a flurry of jitters as I watched him go forward and perform some form of mumbo jumbo with the lines and toss them into the water before taking the Captain's seat. He lost no time in continuing with his lecture. "You must remember the engine should always be idling in neutral before casting off and by the same token when returning to the mooring at least one line should be secured before turning the engine off! These are basic precautions, Miss Bradford, for keeping your boat under control."

Having said that, Mr. Mont moved the gear shift putting *Escape* into reverse. I was surprised. "Why not just go forward?"

"Because the drive shaft and propeller could sustain damage from becoming entangled in the mooring lines. That's why upon returning to the mooring you always face into the wind. This is easy to tell because of the way the dinghy will be floating."

It was then I decided Mr. Mont must have been a teacher by profession for only someone schooled in the art of explaining routine procedure could possibly have succeeded in instructing someone like me who never dreamed that a painter could be anything else but an artist instead of a line attached in a bow of the boat.

And by the time we finished cruising Knubble Bay and were meandering slowly back through the marina, me continuing to add to my meager storehouse of nautical knowledge with such trivia as 5 knots translates into approximately six miles per hour which is the proper no wake speed to maintain, I decided that the feel of *Escape* which Mr. Mont seemed to think so important for me to have was one of vigor like that of her former owner. And by the time *Escape* got tucked in for the night and we tooled back to shore I had decided the lesson had not been a disagreeable experience. In fact I was able to say what earlier on would have been impossible. "You know, Mr. Mont, I have never been at ease in a boat. I have this terrible fear of being sandwiched between two of them and the water swallowing me up forever!"

He didn't laugh or grin or crack a joke about my fear like Britt always did. Instead he picked up my duffel bag and somberly walked me to my car. "I appreciate you taking me into your confidence, Miss Bradford. Now that I'm aware of your fear I will try my best to help you overcome it during our lessons."

I immediately felt better; being honest with him had definitely been the right way to go. It was also right I decided while following my duffel bag in to the front seat of the Porsche that he should know my first lesson was not quite as bad as I thought it would be. "Being the non-boating member of the Bradford family, Mr. Mont, I can and will admit to pre-boating jitters, having qualms about the lesson and starving myself beforehand as a precaution against getting sea sick. However, none of the afore mentioned was necessary since the lesson turned out for me to be quite painless and in some ways pleasant. Especially when we returned to the dock."

He laughed! I curled my toes into my socks.

"I'll see you Sunday evening, Miss Bradford."

I nodded. "Six o'clock sharp?"

"Six o'clock sharp it is."

"Rain or shine, Mr. Mont?"

"Rain or shine, Miss Bradford!"

"Even if it's raining cats and dogs?"

I thought I would be home free with that question since he appeared to be mulling it over. The boyish grin on his face, however, should have warned me that I was wrong. "It depends, Miss Bradford, if it's raining more dogs than cats. If that happens I will call you just to be sure there isn't a mix up."

"Oh."

So it really wasn't any wonder that by the time I actually got home and out of the car I had changed my mind over the conclusion previously reached while on the way, from "There was no pat answer to my question of who was right or wrong, Missy Sue and Leroy, or Mr. Mont," to Mr. Mont was correct in talking me through the process of turning on the engine. Neither was it any wonder that the lesson made a terrific impact on my subconscious mind for later that night I had a terrible nightmare and awakened with a very unpleasant case of mal de mer.

The nightmare was vivid. I had produced it in glorious Technicolor accompanied with full stereophonic sound. For some goofy reason there were two beds pitching and tossing side by side on a vast dark green ocean. I was in one of the beds trying to keep dry from the rain while on the other bed Caesar was snoozing in the sunlight. Determined to get dry I kept trying to climb into the other bed but every time I did the beds parted until finally I fell between them. Down and down I plummeted until I bumped into Leroy who was caught in a huge steamer trunk. The water around us was churning into a giant whirlpool and the harder I kicked to free myself the faster I was sucked towards the apex which looked like a mammoth butterfly net. I kept kicking; trying to swim away from the net which was slowly being lowered over me by a smiling black bearded King Neptune complete with gold crown and seaweed covered pitchfork. "No, No," I kept screaming. Fortunately I awakened then - my stomach heaving in protest.

I spent most of the next day in bed sipping light carbonated beverages and munching on saltines. By dinner time I had graduated to chicken broth, an English muffin and tea. It was while wolfing down a second muffin smothered with a huge consoling pat of butter that I decided to reaffirm my commitment to pay my dues and to become a full ranking member of the Bradford family.

Out came the forbidden note pad and pencil; not to make a list but instead to start a private journal in which I would jot down at the end of each lesson what I had learned. I scribed a title on the cover in calligraphy, The Perils of Serena. "And some day," I cooed to Caesar who was standing watch by my bed like a threatening head nurse, "when I'm old and gray and all bent over with ague, I will take the journal down from the shelf to read and to marvel that once upon a time I was young and agile enough to embark on such a foolish trek."

Chapter 6

Sunday, like this past Thursday, arrived in a blaze of glory at precisely 4:59 a.m. too, and by five p.m., when not one decent raincloud was visible on the horizon I camouflaged myself and drove to the marina. This time I arrived hungry and with qualms about my second lesson - but without my former pre-boating jitters.

Mr. Mont was already there. He was kneeling down at the far end of the float, well distanced from the hubbub of activity going on near the gas pumps, and engaged in an obviously serious conversation with a man in what else but a white dinghy but bearing a Canadian flag. As I trudged down the ramp and headed towards them, this time my feet not feeling like they were encased in lead sneakers and my duffel bag feeling a good 15 pounds lighter, I saw Mr. Mont fold up a chart and hand it to him; their exchange of words loud enough, though spoken softly, to be picked up and carried by the breeze back to me as the man rowed away. Not having a morbid curiosity I was nevertheless intrigued by this lengthy tete-a-tete since it was being spoken in well articulated French. Though I was proficient in the language they could just as easily have been speaking in Greek for the bulk of their talk it seemed was filled with nautical terms which I didn't understand. I didn't have long to ponder, Mr. Mont's warm smile and friendly tone of greeting, "Good evening, Miss Bradford, shall we begin," effectively stopping my curiosity.

"And a good evening to you too, Mr. Mont," I replied. A second later, being as I was into lighter feelings this evening, I expanded my vocabulary from Thursday's just plain, "Sure" to, "I promise, no screams tonight."

He acknowledged my promise by jauntily picking up my duffel bag and putting it into the skiff. "We will take the marina's boat out to the mooring again this evening, Miss Bradford. It will give us the necessary time needed to make up for what I wasn't able to cover last Thursday."

Unlike before I tried to hide my relief over not having to drive. Instead of being repetitive and saying, "Whatever you think best," I said, "What a splendid idea."

We got into the skiff, Mr. Mont adroitly and me more gracefully than before for he had secured her broadside to the float by using two lines - one from the stern and the other from the middle. "Tying a boat up this way probably isn't done by experienced sailors like yourself, Mr.Mont, but from my point of view and being from the extreme opposite end of the spectrum I think it's great!"

The same kind of boyish raining more dogs than cats grin that I had seen before flooded his face. "As long as it helps you to overcome your fear of falling between two boats, Miss Bradford, it is a worthwhile procedure."

The ride out was uneventful. This time we talked about such momentous things as the unprecedented fish kill on the nearby New Meadows River and the shortage of Marine worms. Ugh! He said, "The official word out from the state is that the kill is due to lack of oxygen in the water." I said, "It's because of the nuclear power plant and its discharge of warm water into the ocean."

He said, "I understand from local diggers the harvesting of worms is well below normal, particularly in the upper reaches of the Sheepscot River." I said, "It's because of the nuclear power plant! Why we don't have anywhere the number of star fish and crabs on our beach since it began operation."

"I gather you have a vendetta against nuclear power plants?"

Our arrival at the mooring spared Mr. Mont from having to hear my answer to his question and my two dollar lecture on what I considered to be the evils of nuclear power. By this time we had snuggled up against *Escape*'s starboard side, by design I felt sure, thereby spelling me from the anticipation of falling over her auxiliary gas tank. There was also no doubt in my mind that I was expected to open up the canvas and to be first on board. I accomplished the task successfully because my left hand knew exactly what my right hand was doing! No where was this more evident than in the neat hair ribbon type of bow I made to tie a line amidship from the skiff to *Escape* in order to create my safe step to board.

Mr. Mont must have been impressed with my tying up job. He said nothing.

After we finished opening up the boat and storing all the canvas he broke his silence. "Let's go forward. Before we cast off this evening I want to show you *Escape*'s mooring lines and at the same time a method often used for securing a dinghy to them." He paused. "Using a different kind of knot."

I followed dutifully - as befitting pupil to instructor - and stood at attention by his side. "Please notice, Miss Bradford, that *Escape*'s own heavy line coming from the mooring divides into two and that each one is then pulled under and over the large cleat on both sides of her bow."

I nodded. "Why, the line looks just like the running martingale type of harness sometimes used on a horse."

Mr. Mont didn't blurt out, "Weird" or say "R-e-a-l-l-y Serena" in an infuriating you are a nincompoop tone of voice that someone I know would have done and whose name I was desperately trying to forget. Instead he studied the lines for a second or two. "I hadn't thought about it before, Miss Bradford, but now that you mention it the lines do look like a running martingale type of harness."

I realized Mr. Mont didn't know that he had just paid me a compliment. It made me want to concentrate harder on what he was saying.

"Please remember that under normal circumstances you would have the engine idling, warming up, before proceeding with what I'm going to show you. It's just easier not to have to talk and demonstrate at the same time over the drone of the engine."

"I'll remember," I said in what I hoped was a reassuring manner.

Mr. Mont seemed satisfied with my answer. He turned around and I watched as he removed the starboard line from *Escape*'s bow and transferred the line to the port side by inserting it under and over the cleat on top of the one already there; like he was going to fuse the two lines together.

63

"You will see why," he explained, "in just a minute."

I nodded and continued to watch as he nimbly reached over *Escape*'s side and grabbed the long painter from the skiff's bow. He then poked the free end which was in his hand through both of the loops where they went underneath the cleat. It was just like threading the eye of a needle that had a bent head. Even a novice like me could see his clever method eliminated a step or two of unnecessary tying of lines and that by electing to have the starboard line tied to the other when casting off meant they were all together when being hauled out of the water. "I see the 'Why,' Mr. Mont. What a neat idea!"

And another big plus for his method, though I decided not to share it with him for fear of being labeled a typical female, had to do with my disgust as a child over touching a slimy green rope that had sprouted algae after having been in the water for a while. I had found it to be the same as when reaching into a rusty can of wriggling worms being used for fish bait and when emptying a warm mousetrap - one of stomach heaving propensity.

Mr. Mont smiled as if he had read my thoughts. Heaven forbid! He said, however, as he was making a big to-do over marrying the lines together with his special knot, "And then the final step, Miss Bradford, is to do a bolin."

His instruction sounded a lot like an order to learn a new dance step. I thought it best to ask. "What's a bolin?"

Mr. Mont flinched! He actually flinched at my question that I had asked in all innocence. To his credit he quickly recovered and with the forbearance of Job explained, "The word is spelled b o w l i n e and the bowline or bolin as it is often called is considered to be the king of knots. If done properly it positively will not come undone. Let me demonstrate it to you, slowly, once again."

Therefore, having established myself as not being worthy of even the underpinnings on the totem pole I watched closely as Mr. Mont undid his special knot and proceeded to demonstrate how to tie the infamous bowline. "Perhaps the best way to learn how to tie a bowline, Miss Bradford, is by following the jingle I learned in the Bobcats."

That word I recognized from Mother's involvement in the Scout movement because of Adam, for that was when she "Did her duty" and became a den mother to a bunch of hyper little boys running around in short pants who were aspiring to become Wolves. Not wanting to be outsmarted by any six or seven year old I tried to memorize each step Mr. Mont was doing with the confounded jingle.

Having already put the painter through the loop where it went underneath the cleat Mr. Mont said as he demonstrated, "Make an overhand loop in the line while holding the end of the rope towards you." Then passing the end up through the loop to the words, "The rabbit looks out of its hole," he continued to pull it through saying, "The rabbit comes out of its hole." Still holding on to the end of the line he passed the rope behind the painter with the words, "Runs around the tree," and then poking it down through the loop again ended up with, "And goes back into the hole." He then drew the knot up tight and, "Closed the door;" the door looking a lot like the figure eight to me.

Mr. Mont looked up. "Why don't you learn how to tie the bowline in time for your next lesson. Now then, Miss Bradford, shall you put into practice what we discussed and learned to do on your first lesson?"

Although his order was cushioned politely in the form of a question I knew it was no nonsense 'Show and tell' time. I kept telling myself as I settled into the Almighty Captain's seat, "Don't be nervous, you are not going to drown, you are just going to turn the key on and go."

I told him, "I'll do my best to try and remember everything."

Well, wonder of wonders, that's just what happened! Mr. Mont seemed pleased over my not forgetting to run the blower first then the bilge and a slump still hadn't appeared in his bearing after I went through the agony of turning on the engine. I even managed to slip the lever into idling position, the steady drone of the engine telling me I had succeeded.

Mr. Mont's calm demeanor was my reward for this remarkable accomplishment. "I'll cast off now, Miss Bradford. As soon as I return to my seat I want you to put the engine into reverse by pulling the lever back towards you, very slowly. You will hear and feel it click into gear."

I had not anticipated that order. I had expected him to treat me to another shake down cruise around Knubble Bay, to say something like, "We are going to lose our sun soon so perhaps I'll just give you another quick run through." The cat definitely caught my tongue; being desperate loosened it quickly.

"Suppose it doesn't click into gear? We would be adrift! We could smash up on the rocks, hit another boat or worse float out to sea!"

I could hear the tremor in my rising voice. A rivulet of perspiration trickled down the small of my back. My heart beat accelerated to coffee perking tempo. "On the other hand if it clicks into reverse I may never be able to push the lever forward and we could end up forever and ever going backwards. I really think we should exchange seats and you take *Escape* out to play this evening."

It was a slip of the tongue. It was typical me, always making a flip remark when the occasion demanded a serious comment. I could almost hear Daddy say, "Serena, dear, some day you are going to talk yourself into serious trouble."

Unlike an indulgent parent, Mr. Mont chose not to acquiesce to my Pitiful Pearl wail. His black eyebrows I noticed rose to an expressive height above his sun glasses. His mouth did turn up at the corners though not quite easing into a full smile. "I don't believe that would be in your best interests, Miss Bradford."

"Oh!"

An hour later, my best interests having been well served by me putting *Escape* into reverse and by Mr. Mont talking me through the process of piloting *Escape* forward out into the bay and back to home base, we once again trudged up to the parking lot and I gratefully followed my duffel bag into the front seat of the Porsche. "Next Thursday evening, six o'clock sharp, Mr. Mont?"

He nodded and closed the car door behind me. "I believe you handled today's lesson admirably, Miss Bradford."

His praise surprised me. From my point of view I didn't really deserve it. I looked up at him and decided his best interests would be served by me thanking him for his sincere compliment and by not repeating my former rain or shine, cat and dog question. So I said, "Thank you, Mr. Mont. If I did well it is because of your patience."

I added quickly sensing a slight embarrassment on his part, "I promise I won't forget about learning to tie a bowline in time for my next lesson."

Chapter 7

A promise being a promise I wasted no time in trying to fulfill the one I had made the evening before to Mr. Mont. So as soon as I finished breakfast I went out to the boat house and after fishing an old piece of rope out of a trash barrel high tailed it over the dunes to Elizabeth's cottage for a freebie lesson.

Fortunately for me Elizabeth had arrived from her home in DC, earlier than usual for the summer social season and being a staunch friend as well as an astute boat person I knew she would be "Delighted" to hear about my boat lessons and would help me all she could. "I just have four days, Elizabeth, to learn how to tie a bowline," I explained further while sitting down on her deck with my rope stretched out in front of me.

"I'm delighted to hear you are taking this step, Serena, and of course I will help in any way I can. However, not with that piece of rope! It is simply too unseamanlike to use."

Considering where it had come from I didn't argue with her as she whisked mine up from the deck and threw it into a wastebasket. Elizabeth, being a retired Navy commander and therefore well versed in all things nautical excused herself then, returning a few seconds later with a new piece of rope. Sitting down beside me on the deck she stretched her rope out in front of me. "Now, Serena, a rope has three parts: the end, the standing part, and the bight."

I also learned that a standard rope has three strands; a strand being made of a number of yarns twisted together and that the lay of a rope is the direction in which the strands are twisted. I also came home an hour later quite chagrined after spending a most frustrating time trying to make the end compatible with the bight while keeping the standing part inactive. Elizabeth's parting words, "Serena, my dear, I want us to remain the very good friends we are so I really think it's best if I don't try to teach you anymore," leaving no doubt in my mind that I had flunked her course.

It was while sitting at the kitchen table having lunch and commiserating to Caesar about my scouting deficiencies that I

69

decided my problem was at least three-fold; that being the deja vu number for the day. First of all, I had been looking at Mr. Mont's demonstration sort of upside down, and secondly that "Damning Defect" was causing me to do everything backwards. And last, but not least, I accepted the fact that it really might be easier to chase a rabbit around a tree than an end and a bight.

Now that I had analyzed my problem what I needed was a good place to practice. Caesar, as he often unknowingly did, came up with the solution when he knocked a kitchen chair against the refrigerator door handle in his haste to accept a table handout; that of tying one end of the rope to the back of a kitchen chair thereby making it my dinghy and to use the refrigerator handle as a mooring.

No sooner said than done, so to speak. However, no matter how many times I tried during the afternoon to secure my dinghy in proper style I wasn't able to get that miserable, elusive, cotton-tail out and back into its hole; for every time I tried to draw the knot up tight to, "Close the door," it just came apart.

By dinner time and still luckless I removed the line from the kitchen chair and stuck it into the hand towel drawer. "Out of sight out of mind! Besides tomorrow is another day." I brightened for tomorrow being Tuesday meant that Mrs. Linette would come and she, I knew, being a dear and always sympathetic to my cause would help me tame the hare.

#

I had forgotten how fast the spoken word spreads in Georgetown. No sooner had Mrs. Linette walked into the house than she said, "Abel and me weren't the least bit surprised to hear you were taking boating lessons, Serena. It was obvious to us you needed a change of pace and according to Abel, Mr. Mont seems a nice enough young man, for a foreigner that is, to teach you even though some folks here t'bouts think he's strange, keepin' to himself so much. Still there's no doubt locally he knows his way around a focsle."

That was indeed high praise for an outsider! I was about to say, "That's good to know," but Mrs. Linette, still on the same train of thought, interrupted me. "And the fact that Mr. Mont speaks fluent French is quite an asset to the marina especially with so many Frogs from Quebec, and to quote Abel, 'flotsaming and jetsaming, up our waterways.' Course they do buy our lobsters so the flotsam, again quoting Abel, is well worth the while. Now then, Serena, why don't you go do whatever you have to do this Tuesday afternoon. I'll busy myself with the usual and as soon as I'm finished we will sit down and I'll teach you how to tie a bowline. As I told Abel your trouble has to do with you being a Southpaw, not being slow as the rumor has it."

I did as I was told and went outside to weed the garden, too dumbfounded to say anything.

Sure enough Mrs. Linette called me from my therapeutic weeding around four o'clock. She had put two glasses of lemonade on the kitchen table, plus a clam bucket and a small piece of rope. Motioning to me she said, "Sit on my right, Serena. That way I will close to your left hand, better able to see through your mistakes and to help you correct them."

We both sat down, took a sip of lemonade and sighed. I picked up the rope. Mrs. Linette began, "now then, dear, imagine the bucket is your mooring."

After three of four tries and Mrs. Linette's step by step prompting I got it.

"I got it!" I jumped up like a released toy jack-in-the-box, almost taking the kitchen table with me. "I got it, Mrs. Linette, I got it!"

"I never doubted you wouldn't, Serena. Now then you just sit back down and practice. I must run along otherwise I will be late for exercise class."

"Is Mr. Linette still joining in the fun?"

"That's not what he calls it, Serena." She laughed, picked up her oversized tote bag and headed for the door. "Abel calls it work, every bit as sweaty a job as settin' out and haulin' in lobster traps which by the way is why he won't make it today. Had to make a run to Boothbay to pick up something. Just what, I'm not sure."

I decided against sitting back down and walked out to the van with her. "Thank you for coming and thank you ever so much for teaching me how to tie the king of knots."

"I was happy to do it, Serena." She winked at me before climbing into her van. "However, when I return in two weeks I will expect a progress report from you including such details as where Mr. Mont takes you to practice, how late he keeps you out, what color are his eyes, his approximate age, etc."

For some strange reason I blushed. Thinking about it later I decided it must have been because we shared the same thought.

#

Practice makes perfect and so I practiced and practiced tying a bowline - not Elizabeth's way, not Mr. Mont's way, not Mrs. Linette's way, but my way - by sort of coming in through the back door. What I did was to run my right hand underneath the rope palm side up and then to create a loop I simply turned my hand, knuckle side up. I kept hold of the rope's end with my left hand; the end laying against my upturned palm. I then transferred the loop to my left hand; holding it tightly against my fingers with my thumb on top where the line crossed itself. Then with my right hand I reached underneath, grabbed the end of the rope and transformed it in my mind to a fuzzy little rabbit. My reasoning, quite valid in my rule book for doing it this way being, that as long as I got the blasted rabbit to look out of its hole, to come out of its hole, to run around the tree, to go back into its hole and close the door what difference could it possibly make as to how I got it there.

#

When it was time for lesson number three I arrived at the marina early, camouflaged and hungry, but amazingly free of butterflies in my stomach and eager to show off my bowline.

The ride out to *Escape* in the skiff with Mr. Mont was eventful! We discovered a shared empathy for whales after he said, "I understand a 24 foot, male Minke whale washed ashore

72

on the beach at the state park. Fortunately, death was due to natural causes and not because of abuse."

I asked, "Do you know if the Coast Guard is going to carry it back out to sea? That certainly would be a far more fitting burial for such a magnificent creature than to let it rot on the beach!"

"I agree. However I'm not sure what will be done, the world of officialdom moving so slowly at times. They could of course elect to bury the Minke in the sand," he answered seriously.

"Well, at least that way the poor thing wouldn't suffer the indignity of being eaten by predators," I said emphatically.

Our arrival at the mooring silenced our discussion. In no time at all it seemed I was demonstrating my bowline to Mr. Mont in preparation for casting off. He was pleased. "Not quite the way the Bobcats do it, Miss Bradford, but the end result is the same. That's what counts! Don't you agree?"

Having already reached that conclusion I agreed whole heartedly, even going as far as nodding my head up and down so there could be no mistake. I also had made up my mind beforehand not to tell him about my difficulties in learning to tie the knot but now, standing beside him, his straightforwardness so obvious, my decision seemed dishonest. I said rather sheepishly, "I think you should know Mr. Mont, that it took me four full frustrating days to master the bowline."

Right away I felt better, telling the truth obviously being good for my soul.

A second later I was regretting my honesty, Mr. Mont having said admiringly, "Such perseverance deserves recognition! If you would like to do so, why don't you take *Escape* out into the bay? From there I'll take over. It's flood tide, just right for an evening spin up the Sasanoa River. I think you would enjoy it."

I had never, ever taken a spin up the Sasanoa river. I wasn't sure if I wanted to spin up it this evening. It meant having to force through the roily waters of Upper Hell's Gate and Lower Hell's Gate. It meant, according to Adam, being willing to be shaken up until your teeth rattled especially when plowing through The Boilers. It meant courting disaster for Gloria had always said, "The river is turbulent and the giant whirlpools formed by its eddying currents are capable of smashing a boat to bits."

Of course through the years Mother and Daddy had consistently tried to soften the impact of Gloria's and Adam's words by saying, "That only happens when the tide is about three hours out, Serena. Otherwise a ride up the Sasanoa is very pleasant, very tranquil."

Grandfather had tried to alleviate my fears too by trying a semi-scientific approach saying, "The river is only risky when the outgoing tidal waters meet the incoming tide from the ocean. Only then is it like a head on collision."

However childhood bugaboos die hard and so as late as last summer I was still saying, "No thank you, I'll stay home," to a spin up the river or for that matter to any boat ride.

I looked up at Mr. Mont. He was so relaxed, so at home in the boat, so seaworthy. Just why that word popped into my mind, at this distinct moment, I wasn't sure. The next second I was, for it had been no more than three months ago that I had seen an oil painting of a black bearded man standing at the helm of a schooner who bore a strong resemblance to Mr. Mont. The artist had done a superb job by using vibrant colors to make the viewer sense the man's virility, the inner strength of his character. This sense of integrity had been heightened not by stern features but by the hint of mirth lines around the eyes and mouth and by the artist's subtle title of his painting, "Seaworthy."

It was an omen! Once again it appeared a decision had been made for me in a most uncommon way. I said, "That would be nice."

An hour and a half later I said, "The ride up the river was nice, very pleasant and very tranquil. I particularly enjoyed seeing the eagle's nest and the seal that kept following us was just too cute for words."

"I'm glad you enjoyed the run."

He gave me a broad smile. "However I have a sneaking suspicion, Miss Bradford, that other than seeing the eagle and the seal the best part of the trip is now while we are tying up at the dock."

I blushed and even through I knew he was joking I said quickly, "It's not the company I assure you! It's just that unlike you I have always been so ill at ease in a boat that it's always a relief to know I have made it back to shore one more time."

"Once you gain confidence in your boating skills that feeling will pass."

By then the sun was beginning its decent. Soon all that would remain of its brilliance was the fiery afterglow. Simultaneously Mr. Mont took off his sunglasses. More than before he resembled the black bearded sailor in the portrait. Mrs. Linette's parting sentence of the day before yesterday which she had so playfully accentuated with a wicked wink came back to me. I would have to tell her that Mr. Mont took me up the Sasanoa river, that he kept me past my regular lesson time, that I put his age around 33 and that his eyes were blue. I would not tell her they were a deep lustrous blue like Mother's award winning delphinium. Neither would I mention that Mr. Mont's eyes were focused on me in a very kind, warm way.

Our conversation which had had such normal overtones all evening suddenly stopped. I took off my head scarf and lightweight windbreaker, the stillness of the marina and a balmy breeze wafting in from Knubble Bay seeming to warrant the change in my attire.

It was Mr. Mont who broke the silence. "I have something that belongs to you."

I was surprised. "Belongs to me?"

He gave me a rather shy smile, reached into his shirt pocket and pulled out the tiny ivory bird cage hair ornament that I lost the evening of my dunking. "You found it, " I exclaimed in a very unfashionable girlish way.

"I found it floating in a bed of seaweed the morning after your accident. I would have returned it sooner, Miss Bradford, but thought it best to wait for a while."

"Thought it best to wait for a while?" I asked taking the ornament from him.

"Yes, under the circumstances I thought it might cause you embarrassment if I returned it sooner."

I was touched by his sensitivity! He was right of course. I would have been embarrassed. Even thinking about my recent soggy past was making me blush. I didn't know quite what to say so I said simply what came from my heart. "Thank you, Simon. I appreciate your thoughtfulness."

His eyes and mouth sort of crinkled up at the corners. "Your welcome, Serena."

We stared at each other for a minute and then burst out laughing. I knew that he knew and he knew that I knew we had just stepped onto the threshold of what could become a fascinating Odyssey.

Chapter 8

I decided to really study for lesson number four. Not that I hadn't shed a few tears in preparing for my last lesson! It was just that this one, due in large part to Simon's insight into my psyche, held a promise of adventures to come whereas the first three had represented hard work.

We were going to go through Blind Rocks Passage at high tide and on out into the Sheepscot River. Simon had mentioned this casually last night while I was making my debut up the Sasanoa river. "Bring along a chart, Miss Bradford," he had said, "so you can begin to familiarize yourself with the different navigational aids."

I had replied instantly and definitely on the terror stricken side, "According to my brother and sister Blind Rocks Passage wins the prize for most fun while going through when the tide is four hours out!"

Simon had replied calmly, "True! But we will be going through the passage at high tide when the water is calm and then, only if the weather is good."

I had felt better.

So after taking the time this morning to bring my Perils of Serena journal up to date and taking my usual long walk on the beach, I dug out the appropriate chart from all those stacked on a table in the study and spread it out on the floor. I decided while tracing the passage with my finger tips that I might be smart to make a list of everything that I thought could be bumped into, a list being permitted to make from my list of "Things I Will and Will Not Do This Summer" if used for survival. Fortunately, all the major bumps seemed to have aids stuck on top of them. The only trouble was I did not know what all the curliewurlies, dots, squares, squiggles, triangles, triangles with tails, balloons, cryptic abbreviations, lower and upper case letters, etc., meant. "Why," I asked Caesar who had usurped three fourths of the chart to sit upon, "can't the US Coast and Geodetic Survey people elect to just spell everything out like they did Measured

Nautical Mile? Why do they have to be so danged mysterious by describing a blop of land as Qk Fl 16 ft "5"?"

Caesar, "Woofed." His bark being deep and resonant had the same effect on me as the Seguin Light foghorn did on boaters - mainly to focus on what was at hand. In no time flat I remembered seeing a rather thin publication filled with a bunch of symbols on one of the bookshelves. A few minutes later I had it in hand, the titillating title of "Nautical Chart Symbols and Abbreviations" causing my heartbeat to accelerate.

The contents at first glance reminded me of a mixture of the Greek alphabet and the chemical elements but as I dug in to try and match the brief bleeps and letters on the charts to those words in the book I found the abbreviations to be straightforward. I spent the rest of the afternoon just like a spy - magnifying glass in hand - hunting down clues and trying to fathom the Navy mind. I thrilled to the discovery that Qk Fl 16 ft "5" deciphered meant a quick flashing light, sixteen feet high with the number 5 painted on it.

Armed with my new found knowledge and hipped up enough to brave Blind Rocks Passage with Simon I arrived at the marina Sunday evening eager to begin lesson number four. As a tribute to his skill as a teacher I had eaten a bowl of cereal and an English muffin before leaving The Barnacle. As a tribute to me for having lived down my embarrassment at being dumped overboard and for having survived three lessons I didn't camouflage myself.

If Simon was surprised at my different appearance he didn't say so. What he did say was, "Serena, you have reached the stage in your lessons where it is in your best interests to use the dinghy in going out to the mooring."

"In your best interests" was a phrase I was beginning to hate. However I kept that thought to myself and said frantically, "I have never been able to row a boat properly! Perhaps it's because I have to sit backwards from where I'm trying to go or perhaps it's because I always pull harder on the left oar. Whatever!"

My wail of protest went unheeded. "You need a little practice, Serena," he said putting my duffel bag into the hated tub. "That's all."

So, that was that! The ride out to the mooring was eventful for Simon in that I reconfirmed the theory that the shortest distance between two points is a straight line by touching bases with practically every moored boat in the cove.

The ride out was eventful for me in that when I finally arrived at the mooring I discovered Simon had added a third line amidship to the dinghy. It was short and on the end of the line was a swivel toggle. He demonstrated its use by snapping it quickly onto one of the large cleats amidship on *Escape's* port side. "The toggle will facilitate you in tying up to *Escape*. You won't be at the mercy of the wind and tide. You can then, Serena, take your time in tying a line stern to stern in order to create your safe step to board."

No wonder Simon had been so adamant about me starting to use the dinghy. He had made boarding *Escape* as safe as possible. The only thing safer would be not to leave the shore. Once again I was touched by his sensitivity to my plight. I wanted to thank him! However, I didn't want to embarrass him like I inadvertently might have done the other evening when I mentioned his patience. So I said what came off the top of my head, "You are a doll! What a thoughtful thing to do!"

Simon grinned and started to chuckle. His jovial reaction prompted me to ask, "Have you ever been called a doll before?"

"No, I can't say that I have, Serena, but coming from you it's definitely to my liking."

"Oh!"

"By the way, Serena, I was happy to do it. Now then shall we begin? Did you bring the chart?"

A half hour later we were in the middle of the Sheepscot River, the engine in idling position, the chart still in Simon's hands and my list in mine discussing navigational aids when he mentioned something about how wide the river is and a fairway. The only fairway I was familiar with being an 18 hole one I looked towards the shore for the golf course. Not seeing one and with Simon still talking about a fairway I thought it best to ask.

"Where is the golf course you are speaking of, Simon? I don't see it."

A pained expression flooded Simon's face. Whatever I had said it had obviously been the wrong thing to say, though not quite bad enough to make him flinch like he had done when I asked, "What's a bolin?"

"In nautical terms, Serena, the fairway is the navigable part of a river, a bay, a harbor, a main channel. In golf, as you no doubt know, the fairway is the mowed part of any hole between the tee and the green."

Not wanting to be thought completely ignorant I said, "In other words, Simon, an unobstructed passage."

He smiled, patience personified. "I couldn't have said it more succinctly."

Our ride back to the marina through Blind Rocks Passage wasn't quite as smooth as when we came through earlier, an hour's difference in the tide readily apparent in the way *Escape* handled and in the way the three red nun buoys we passed on my right were beginning to lean towards the ocean. "Always remember, red, right, returning; right, Simon?" I half asked and half stated since we were well into charts this evening.

"Right, Serena. Don't forget though when heading out towards the ocean the red buoys will always be on your left."

I nodded. After my fairway faux pas I wasn't about to ask the question that begged to be asked, "How do you know when you are heading out to the ocean," for fear he would think me too obtuse.

The lesson ended on the upbeat side! I had survived my baptism into Blind Rocks Passage. Simon seemed genuinely pleased over my interest in navigational aids and interpreting the chart. We both seemed more relaxed now that we were on a first name basis.

I asked, "Should I bring the chart along for my next lesson?"

"From now on, Serena, you should always have the chart. Learning to use it properly will become an important part of the lesson."

I followed my duffel bag into the front seat of my car. "See you Thursday, Simon?"

He nodded. "Six o'clock sharp!"

"Rain or shine, Simon?"

"Rain or shine, Serena." An amused expression replaced his serious one as he added, "And definitely if it's raining more dogs than cats."

Chapter 9

By the time lesson five rolled around, I had mentally prepared myself for the inevitable order to row out alone and open up *Escape*. I definitely was not prepared mentally to hear Simon say at the end of the evening, "Serena, I have in my hand a copy of the United States Power Squadron manual. I believe it's in your best interests to study it."

Handing it to me he added casually, "There will be a written exam on the contents at the end of the course."

I was flabbergasted, too speechless for words. However Simon wasn't and quickly filled the silence. "Studying the manual and taking the exam, Serena, will serve to highlight the areas of boating needed for further study. You won't be graded on the exam."

The phrase, further study, really bugged me; just like his conciliatory bribe "I won't be graded" bugged me. All the way home I griped; after all, an exam was definitely not on my list of summer fun things to do. "Besides," I sputtered to the disc jockey on the car radio, "what further study do I need if all I have to do is just hop into the boat, turn the key and go?" Of course, he was of no help at all. What did help when I got home was to stash the manual under a pile of newspapers in front of the fireplace - reasoning I can always say the manual accidentally burned and with this warming thought went to bed and promptly fell asleep.

#

I did not awaken refreshed. Instead, I had a throbbing head due to a heavy hangover of guilt. So I rescued the manual and after taking a long walk on the beach where I gave myself a pep talk on the loathsomeness of doing things half way, I sat down in front of the fireplace to glance through it.

Glancing through the manual led to reading through it. By dinner time when I finally put the manual down I willingly gave the high-muck-a-mucks in the Navy and in the Coast Guard their just due, that on a rating of one to ten their paperback rated a ten. Of course some of the terminology such as "privileged versus a burdened vessel" did seem to be on the antiquated side. To me "burdened" always implied too heavy a load but leave it to the Navy to muddy up the meaning by stating it has no privilege. Why they could not come right out and say - does not have the right away - God only knows!

So having absolved - rather than unburdened - myself of guilt from last night's transgression by having read the manual I willingly gave Simon his just due, that of being right. I now realized that it would be in my best interests to study the manual, that it would be in my best interests to take the exam and that the end result would serve to highlight the areas of boating needed for further study. That is, if I ever decided to go further than, "Just hop into the boat, turn the key, and go." Only time would tell!

#

My thought "Only time would tell" I found to be true, for the passing of it was making a difference in my outlook towards boating. I was actually finding it enjoyable. Enjoyable, no doubt, because I was finding it a pleasure to practice under Simon's patient tutelage. This feeling coupled with a budding faith in myself over being able to control the boat certainly did not hinder my progress either. Before I realized it July slipped into August, my twelve week course was just about over and Simon deemed that I was ready to take my written exam based on the Power Squadron manual.

"We will meet in my office, Serena, at the usual time," he had said during my last lesson in July. "The exam will take about two hours and then we will discuss the results. Just so you know what to expect the exam will include a vocabulary test based on nautical terms, identification of navigational aids, the Rules of the Road, especially those pertaining to safety around other boats, sound signals, multiple choice on handling a boat, and _____."

"And in other words, Simon," I had interrupted, "a Blue Book exam like we suffered through in college. And in other words everything in the manual with the kitchen sink thrown in?"

"Yes, everything in the manual except the math. As I said we will take that part up at a later date."

"It doesn't sound much like a fun evening," I protested in my best wide-eyed tremulous lips technique.

Simon had just sat there in *Escape* grinning back at me in an exasperating way that signaled, "It won't do you any good to try and wiggle out of taking the exam."

"Oh, well, at least I won't be graded on it!"

"True, Serena! However, bear in mind the grading comes in the form of your own ability to survive at sea," he replied seriously.

That was a low blow, but I forgave him. As I recalled I had then handed him his windbreaker by tossing it over his head!

So here I was in Simon's office, the expected longer than usual evening not quite over, waiting for him to look up from my exam papers and say, "You have failed."

To my utmost relief he eased back in his chair and gave me one of the most admiring smiles I have ever received. "Serena, I'm really proud of you! For someone who started out detesting boating the result of the exam shows you are beginning to like it. I can tell you not only studied the manual but absorbed the information. If the test was going to be graded I would be hard pressed not to give you an A."

I could have jumped with joy. Instead I said, "Thank you, Simon. I did study! I really did want to do well." I didn't say, "I really wanted to please you!"

Purging being good for my soul I added, "However, I think you should know that I almost threw the manual into the fireplace the night you gave it to me. The next morning though I rescued it from a stack of newspapers and after glancing through it decided that you were right, that it would be in my best interests to study it."

Simon got up from the desk, walked around it to the corner nearest me and sat down. His smile I noticed now leaned towards the serious side but the hint of mirth that had appeared in his eyes as I was baring my soul a minute ago remained. "I knew you were upset, Serena, when I gave you the manual to study. The stunned expression on your face was a dead giveaway."

I began to squirm in my seat under his deep blue-eyed scrutiny. "I guess I wouldn't make a very good poker player."

"No, I don't believe you would, Serena. However, I happen to find your open expressions charming."

It was a slip of the tongue on Simon's part. I could tell because he deliberately cleared his throat, looked away from me and said in a proper instructor to pupil tone, "Now then, I know you are not going to like what I'm going to say next, but _____."

I interrupted. "But it's in my best interests?"

Simon answered me with a chuckle. "Yes, it is definitely in your best interests."

I knew instinctively what he was going to say. I panicked! "I'm not ready to solo, Simon." My voice rose. This time there was an honest to goodness real tremor in it. "I'm never going to be ready to solo. I'm not sure if I every want to be alone in a boat."

Simon stood up and walked back to his chair. It was as if he was trying to distance himself from me. It was the same kind of ploy Mother and Daddy always used when they wanted to give in to me but knew it was not wise to do so. "Serena, you are ready to solo. You have practiced coming up to the dock many times. You have practiced casting off and mooring *Escape* many times. Even if you are never in a boat - alone - you must be prepared to wing it. Just suppose the person you are with has an accident."

What Simon had just finished saying, so very calmly but firmly, of course made sense; too much sense for me. I felt like saying something illogical just to contradict his sensible approach. Nothing popped into my mind except to ask, "Is this your final word on the subject?"

"Yes, this is my final word on the subject."

"Would you consider a plea-bargain," I asked in my finest wheedling out of trouble technique that I had perfected through the years by talking myself out of countless traffic violations.

Simon saw fit to bestow on me one of those don't try your wiles on me smiles. He mouthed, "No, Serena."

Mother always said, "Accept defeat gracefully, dear." She was never wrong. Daddy always said, "Give it your best shot, then move on." He was never wrong. Adam would say, "Don't be your usual mule headed self, Serena." Gloria would no doubt say and do what I was starting to do, picking up my manual for further study and saying, "I'll do my best, though the marina may never, ever be the same."

"Don't sell yourself short, Serena," Simon said quickly. "I think you will be surprised at how well you will do."

For a moment he seemed lost in thought, a contemplative frown furrowing his brow. "I do think though, Serena, if the weather turns bad the day of your final lesson we should postpone it until the following day." He didn't wait for an answer. "No need to compound your pre-flight misery with more misery. Right?"

How lucky could I get! I spoke right up before he could change his mind. "That's a splendid idea, Simon! Who knows, maybe I will be fortunate and it will rain for the rest of the summer."

Simon laughed. "I think on that note, Serena, we better close up shop for the evening." Handing my exam papers back, "For further study," he then said, "Come, I'll walk you to your car."

After weeks of lugging my gear and all the other junk I deemed necessary for survival it felt strange to walk to the car almost empty handed. Stranger still was our parting! Instead of our usual joking about the weather Simon was very serious. His voice seemed somewhat constrained. "After your final lesson this coming Sunday is over I have to go away for a few days. I should be back around the 18th or 19th. However, Serena, it's important to me that you know I have not forgotten about your graduation present, which was my promise to take you on a special cruise of your choice for the day. The only reason I'm mentioning it tonight is because sometimes the marina can get a little hectic on Sunday and it could slip my mind."

As always Simon was tactful. I decided he just didn't want to come right out and say, "Because I could be tied up rescuing you from the briny Deep."

Still it was nice to know that he hadn't forgotten his promise made during a frustrating lesson on navigation which had put me close to tears. We were discussing the rudiments of dead reckoning when I sort of blew it by saying, "You know, Simon, as a child I thought dead reckoning meant someone was dead because they reckoned wrong."

It was then Simon had offered me the carrot of a cruise by saying, "You know, Serena, I think you should forget studying that part of the Power Squadron manual. There is a lot of math involved which entails explanation. Instead, after you complete the course and by then are more at ease in the boat I'll demonstrate how to do dead reckoning. In fact the day we take the cruise of your choice would be the perfect time. I know you will find it challenging as well as fun."

Of course I readily accepted, and though Simon hadn't put it so bluntly I recognized a juicy carrot when I saw one. I had said then, just like now, "I'll look forward to it."

"Good! In the meantime I will see you on Sunday."

"See you on Sunday, Simon," I replied.

For some strange reason a few tears began to trickle down my face as I left the marina, not at all like me since up until this moment I had always left with a smile - well, almost always. By the time I got home and greeted Caesar the reason behind my emotional collapse became quite clear. I was going to miss taking boating lessons and I was certainly going to miss being alone with Simon!

Chapter 10

I had been looking forward to this Sunday evening and my solo run with just about as much enthusiasm as a person would look forward to walking the plank or climbing the steps to the guillotine. All day Friday I had fretted about not being able to handle *Escape* properly. Repeatedly I kept questioning my capability to do so. "Would I be able to hook up to *Escape* properly? Would I be able to tie a perfect bowline? Would the engine conk out on me after I cast off?"

By Saturday I had reached the stewing stage. I had become more frazzled. "Suppose I rammed into another boat? Suppose I wasn't able to brake *Escape* at the dock by putting the engine into reverse and turning the wheel as to bring her stern in close? Suppose I then rammed into the dock?"

By this morning, after my third night of fitful sleep, I had even contemplated calling Simon to tell him, "I won't be there this evening. I've decided against taking any more lessons."

However I wasn't comfortable with that decision so I ended up doing what I have always done and took a long walk on the beach to sort out my thoughts.

I really don't know why the therapy of taking a walk or digging one's toes into the sand and letting the waves carry it away from under your feet does so much good. Maybe it's the shocking coldness of the water and the intensity of its pulling power that clears the mind so solutions become crystal clear. Or maybe it's a combination of that plus letting yourself become completely tuned in to nature's lessons; being surrounded by such beauty and wildlife that was easy to do.

Anyway, here I was standing quietly ankle deep in the surf, hoping to see or experience some phenomenon that would help me to cope with my problems of capability versus fear. However the only thing in sight was a family of ducks ambling along the shore. They kept waddling closer until finally they were near enough for me to tell that proud mama was in the lead and distraught papa was bringing up the rear. In between them was their tiny brood doing their level best to keep in line and follow mama into the surf. That is all but one who seemed to have oversized feet and kept falling onto its beak.

I immediately dubbed the chick Waddlefoot and watched in fascination as papa kept going back as if to encourage his errant offspring to follow mama and join in the fun of ducking into a wave and then popping up to ride the crest in. How I sympathized as I continued to watch poor little Waddlefoot toddle time and time again to the water's edge and then stop as if afraid to face the ocean alone for the first time.

Finally, the whole clan returned to the shore and after what appeared to be a family conference they all lined up again to take off. Only this time Waddlefoot was in line next to mama and with what seemed to me a little more bravado followed her right into the surf. Right here and now, by gum, I decided that if a dumb duck was capable of swallowing its fear of the ocean and soloing after a few lessons that I should be able to do so after practicing almost three months.

Having been naturally inspired by one of nature's domestic rituals my spirits soared kite high and remained in that heady atmosphere throughout the rest of the day and throughout the time it took for me to row to the mooring this evening and open up *Escape*. Simon's bon voyage counseling as I rowed away from the float, "I wouldn't be letting you do this, Serena, if I didn't think you were capable," adding to my ebullience and confidence.

It was while working my way down a check list of "do's and do not's" that I began to experience earthly tremors, palpitations, shortness of breath, blurred vision and ringing in the ears. By the time I was ready to cast off the one precious remaining life line anchoring me to security my spirits plummeted to below sea level.

The moment of truth had arrived. I was on the threshold of trying my wings and just as anxious to succeed in making it to the gas dock from the mooring as Pytheas must have been to make it from Greece on his ancient voyage to Thule. True, he was privy to the *Periplus of Scylax* whereas I was witness only to my hit or miss list and the United States Power Squadron manual but the principles involved were just the same.

I don't believe I ever felt more alone than at this minute. Not even when I had two flat tires on a back road in the middle of nowhere and had to hike a good five miles to find help had I felt so alone. It was a me against the world feeling, but as I finally began to pilot *Escape* forward out into the traffic lanes it changed to me against a twirp in a small outboard that had the audacity to cross in front of me and pull up to the dock for gas. "Don't panic," I told myself.

I didn't panic! Instead I reacted very calmly by putting the engine into neutral and then took a moment to assess the situation. I realized that I had just made my first mistake for the evening by not having programmed the unexpected into my mind. Not wanting to make a second mistake I decided to be prudent and to circle around a couple of large moored sailboats rather than risk the chance of plowing into the outboard - though there was enough space left at the dock to berth the *Queen Mary*. So I put *Escape* into the lowest speed possible and began to circle. I circled and circled and circled the boats until I thought I might get dizzy; all the while chiding, "You're such a whimp, Serena," and getting more anxious by the minute to get this part of my sea trial over with, done and buried.

At last the twirp left. I stopped circling. Once more the moment of truth arrived. Simon had said, "I wouldn't be letting you do this, Serena, if I didn't think you were capable." Grandfather had said, "The boat insurance is paid in full." Missy Sue had said, "You just hop into the boat, turn the key and go." I said, "Remember Waddlefoot."

It was as if *Escape* was a volatile ballistic missile instead of a pleasure craft from the way I took pains to chart her course in line with the gang plank nearest the gas pumps. My target was Simon, who by this time was standing by on the dock ready to grab a line. "Always the optimist," I mumbled.

And so, just like I was skippering a corvette I drew nearer and nearer to the dock which by now had taken on the horrible appearance of piled up bleached bones in the evening sun. Such a morbid thought to have at this precise moment but it stiffened my spine and I ended up turning the boat at just the right moment; but with too much speed!

"Don't overreact! Be calm," I kept telling myself. "Put the engine into reverse."

I did overreact! I stressed out! I put the engine into reverse but gave it too much power! I forgot which way to turn the wheel so as to bring *Escape*'s stern in close to the dock!

Simon's cucumbery cool, but firm voice reached me over the loud pulsing of the engine. "You're doing fine, Serena. Just turn the wheel to the right and turn off the engine."

In my state of confusion Simon's steady voice was akin to being tossed a life preserver. I responded immediately to his order just like I had programmed myself to do all summer. I turned the wheel to the right, turned off the engine and collapsed back into my seat.

Simon hopped on board and sat down opposite me. His smile was full of admiration as were his deep blue eyes. "Well done, Serena. I'm really very proud of you."

From Dal, a cute dock boy with wavy chestnut brown hair and soft brown eyes who I had gotten to know rather well during the summer, I received a salute and the ultimate compliment of, "Wicked good!"

I was still too numb from exertion to reply to either of them. However faint heart subsiding I managed at last a somewhat garbled, "Thank you." To my "Thank you" I added quickly in my finest wheedling out of trouble technique, even though it had failed before, "Now that this part of my shakedown cruise is over do you think we could call it a day?"

Simon grinned from ear to ear. I knew what he was going to say before he said it, so I went ahead and said it for him. "It's not in your best interests, Serena!"

Simon leaned towards me, his expression an unsettling mixture of warmth and amusement. Even his words, "You are incorrigible, you know that, don't you Serena," were being spoken in a tone reflecting the same unsettling mixture of warmth and amusement. So I waved a good-bye to Dal, put *Escape* into a No-Wake speed and sallied forth out into the fairway.

"Which way?" I asked hoping he would answer, "We will practice in Knubble Bay this evening."

"Blind Rocks Passage, Serena!"

I had checked the tide table before leaving The Barnacle. I looked at the clock on the dashboard. "But, Simon," I protested, "the tide is four hours out!"

He looked across the aisle at me and smiled. "Good experience, Serena!"

So I did as I was told, chalking up his phrase "Good experience" along side of his "It's in your best interests" and put them both under a heading of Most Exasperating.

The water was a foaming, swift mass of turbulence as I piloted *Escape* into the narrow passage. Encroaching into the channel on both sides of the passage were slimy rocks covered with snake-like tendrils of seaweed. Their presence, so effectively camouflaged at high tide, a visual testimony to Simon's constant use of a chart and to his insistence that I do too. Even the red nun buoys marking the safe way through the channel I noticed had succumbed to the outgoing tide and had been almost forced flat against the water.

I tried not to think of all the hazards and the way *Escape* was being pulled from side to side. I concentrated solely on what Simon was saying, trying to respond quickly to his instructions. "Increase your speed, Serena, while going through the channel. Not a lot but just enough so the engine doesn't sound like it's straining."

I immediately increased the speed until the engine sounded more comfy. I did this slowly, having learned the hard way that if it was done fast a person could be caught unawares and knocked off their feet.

"Mind the lobster buoy coming up, Serena. Remember the line from the buoy to the trap is long. It stretches out for some feet underneath the water. Always go to the other side towards which the buoy is leaning!"

I didn't mind! I don't know why I didn't mind! *Escape* reacted to my mistake by conking out her engine in a grinding sort of way. Simon reacted by getting up and walking back to the stern, saying patiently. "The drive shaft is caught in the line. Turn the engine off, Serena, and then press the switch to raise it out of the water."

This time I did as I was told and then went back to watch Simon unsnarl the line wrapped around the propeller blade and drive shaft. "No harm done, Serena," he said.

"Except to my ego. I don't know why I did what I did. You certainly taught me better, Simon." I glanced up at him, just in time to see a twinkle brighten his eyes. Not wanting to give him a chance to answer I added, "I know what you are going to say, Simon Mont. Just don't say it!"

He sort of half chuckled and half laughed. "Okay, Serena, won't say you-know-what! What I will say is, go forward. Quickly! Lower the drive shaft back into the water and then start up the engine. We are beginning to drift towards shore."

I moved quickly to do his bidding. Though Simon had issued his instructions in his usual cucumbery cool style I detected a vein of urgency in his "We are beginning to drift towards the shore."

Sitting down in the Almighty Captain's seat I pressed the switch lowering the drive shaft into the water. Next I disengaged the clutch, the inverted egg beater, the gear shift, the lever - whatever - and started the engine. Then I brought it back towards me and let it slip into idling position. Having succeeded in this endeavor I looked up expecting to see a pristine shoreline fringed with tall pines, soaring osprey dotting the clear sky and in the distance three green beacons showing me the way into the mighty Sheepscot River. Instead, all I could see was a huge expanse of pink.

"Oh, no! Oh -h-h, no -o-, Simon -n-n-n! It's the *Pink Lady*! It's the excursion boat out of Boothbay Harbor! She's bearing down on us! All one million tons of her!"

I didn't wait for his answer. I should have, but I didn't. I shoved the lever forward. *Escape* responded like a shooting star, almost bouncing me out of my seat. Simon, caught standing between aft and fore, spiraled across the opposite seat. I heard a sickening thud at the same time I saw his head hit the dashboard. "Sorry, Simon," I shouted so he would be sure to hear my condolences and then, remembering his lecture on navigating through waves by cutting straight into them I pointed *Escape* forward into the *Pink Lady's* wake. Too late, I remembered the

94

rest of Simon's lecture, "Always reduce your speed when cutting through a wave," as we banged into it and came crashing down on the other side, jarring me until my teeth seemed to rattle, throwing Simon down into the aisle.

As if from a sea of the dead Simon rose, clutching his head. "Jumping Jesus Christ Almighty, Serena! Holy Mary Mother of God, Serena! God damn, Serena! God damn it to hell, Serena! Reduce your speed!"

I did as I was told. Simon sat down and then, just as if God was smiting him down for being summoned in such an irreverent way his right eye mushroomed into grapefruit size and changed into glorious living, breathing Technicolor.

I wanted to jump up and mother his pain away with several kisses and a few endearing words. Under the circumstances, being pupil to instructor, woman to man, I decided that wouldn't be wise but that solicitous questions as to his well being would be in order. "Sorry about this bit of bother, Simon. Are you okay?"

"I'm okay, Serena."

His words were spaced apart, like he was counting to ten before he dared to answer. I risked another question, "No broken bones I hope, Simon?"

He shook his head slowly. I decided he must be having to count on up to twenty before answering me. "No. No broken bones, Serena."

"That's good to know." It was also good to know that Simon was human after all, that he, Mr. Unflappable, could depending upon the occasion flip out just like me.

A trace of a smile appeared on his face. It spread rapidly into a wide grin, sunny and bright like a toothpaste commercial. Even his choice of words as he said, "Serena, I shudder to think what constitutes a big bother in your book," were cheery in tone as was his apologetic, "Sorry about blowing my stack. At the moment it seemed logical to do so but then it never is. I guess you might say my blossoming eye is an example of justice being served."

I reached behind me, grabbed my duffel bag and put it down between us in the aisle. Out of it I removed a steel thermos and a clear sandwich bag holding a chocolate brownie. After giving Simon the brownie, "For bravery above and beyond the call of duty," I rigged up a plastic ice bag using the remainder of the ice cubes from the thermos. "It's going to be a beautiful black eye, Simon," I said sheepishly while handing him the rigged up ice pack. Why you will be the recipient of boundless sympathy, especially when folks hear how you narrowly escaped death at the hands of a mad woman while cruising through Blind Rocks Passage."

"I'm not going to tell, Serena, if you don't," he replied softly while gingerly pressing the bag against his blackened eye. He gave me an exaggerated wink with his other and chuckled, "Let them guess, shall we?"

I nodded, touched again by his sensitivity to my feelings. "Don't you think we should head back to the marina now, Simon? I still have to drop you off at the dock and then take *Escape* back to the mooring. It will almost be dark by the time I can get back to the shore in the dinghy." And just in case he had been weakened enough to consider a change in our itinerary I put on my best wheedling out of trouble technique smile and added, "That is unless you would just as soon go back to the mooring with me?"

Once again Simon saw fit to bestow on me one of those don't try your wiles on me smiles, even though it was a slightly lopsided one this time. "I'd like to do that, Serena. It would be easier for us both, all around. However you know ....!"

"I know! Oh, how I do know!"

"Good! Now that we agree that it is in your best interests to take me to the dock, head back to the marina."

Up until then I had been piloting *Escape* slowly around and around a mid channel buoy. Now that I had received my sailing orders I turned her homeward bound and with great pizzazz deposited Simon onto his precious dock.

This time Dal was really impressed with my parking verve paying me a double compliment, "Wicked, wicked good, Miss Bradford!"

Mr. Macintosh was also impressed telling me, "Simon said you were an apt pupil. I see what he means."

96

Both of them were so impressed by Simon's blackened, swollen eye that they said absolutely nothing!

A few minutes later after mooring *Escape* I was totally unimpressed with my evening performance. The sight of Simon standing on the dock like a wounded Cyclops had sobered me up. It had made me realize how close we had become to being a boating statistic. It had made me forgetful of proper boating procedure, the only logical explanation I could come up with for forgetting to retie the dinghy after moving it back towards the stern. It was a man in a passing motorboat who brought me back into the real world with a shout, "Hey, lady is that your dinghy floating away?"

Yes, in-dee-dy, it was my dinghy! There was no use in me denying it though I was sorely tempted to as I fully appreciated what Mother and Daddy meant when they use to say, "There are times when it would be nice to deny kinship."

I mustered up a laughing-on-the outside face while crying-on-the-inside and shouted, "I'm afraid it is!"

A few seconds later he was handing me the painter from the dinghy, his smile and jovial, "It happens to the best of families," statement helping me to say, "Thank you! You have saved me from what could have been one of my life's most embarrassing moments!"

He laughed. I laughed. However, as soon as he pulled away I turned inside out and proceeded to indulge myself in sniffling and sobbing while I finished buttoning up *Escape* and while rowing back to the shore. I almost sank from so much self pity.

It was dark by the time Simon and I got to my car. His eye was worse, even the dimness of the parking lot lights couldn't shield the width and depth of the wound. Crocodile tears began to ooze down my cheeks. "I'm so sorry, Simon," I sputtered. "What a terrible thing to happen, especially when you are leaving tomorrow on a trip. It's too bad you can't leave your eye behind for repair. Oh, my, I didn't mean that quite the way it sounded. Oh, my, goodness."

Simon answered my apology with a beaming, all forgiving, Christian smile. If he had been irritable I could have at least countered with, I-told-you-so-I-wasn't-ready-attitude, but he even made me feel worse by down grading the accident, scoring it up to, "Good experience, Serena."

I started to cry in earnest. "Hey, Serena," he said ever so gently, "come on now, please don't flatter me by crying. It's hard enough standing out here in the open beside you and not being able to do anything about wiping away those tears of yours."

It wasn't until after I got home and was getting ready for bed that the full impact of Simon's tender words hit me. At the time he had murmured them I had been trying to stop my crying by finding comfort in performing the routine tasks of opening up my car, stowing my gear, and replying my customary, "Good night, Simon," to his, "Good night, Serena." He had added, "I'll call you as soon as I get back to set up a date for our day cruise," and I had responded by saying, "I'll look forward to it." Now I realized that he too must have been as upset as I was over our parting.

I turned out the light and slipped in between the cool sheets. The silky smooth touch of them lent flight to my imagination, making me wonder as I drifted over the edge of consciousness into sleep what Simon's finger tips would feel like on my face, what his fingers would feel like if they strayed to touch my throat, what his hands would feel like if they lingered long enough to press into my shoulders and then to slowly move down to rest above my heart.

Chapter 11

I spent the next few days trying to forget about Simon's finger tips, his fingers and hands and tried to catch up with everything I had left undone these past weeks. During the daylight hours I worked on a couple cords of wood that Abel had delivered, stacking the trillion pieces in an artistic beehive shape on the side of the porch, telling myself constantly, "This is good exercise for the waistline, Serena."

I wrote a few postcards stating nothing more illuminating than, "I'm fine," or "I feel great," or "All going well." I brought my journal up to date. And finally I picked enough blueberries to make two pies, one for now - just in case I had a very special visitor - and one to put into the freezer for when the family arrived en masse towards the end of October.

My evenings were far more interesting! A couple of times I went out to dinner and to the movies with Elizabeth. Our conversations were, as always, stimulating; especially our last one as I divulged all my boating mistakes to her including the big one, losing my dinghy. She laughed before saying, "It's a mistake you will never make again," and then like a wise sage added, "Good experience, Serena." I groaned privately.

As for my other evenings I spent them happily at home in the study, a good half of the time as an arm chair dreamer reading Bowditch's *American Practical Navigator*, Chapman's *Piloting* and *Celestial Navigation for the Simple-Minded*. It was the title of the latter book that had caught my eye while shopping in Camden one day. However after wading through the pages and spending a few darkened hours on the deck I put it aside. What I needed, I decided, was to find a book one step lower down on the scale.

The other half of the time I spent as a make-believe navigator perusing the several charts I had laid out on top of a large library size table. Finally I chose the appropriate chart for my epic voyage and with a red pencil marked my course for the day run with Simon. On a piece of yellow paper from a legal size notepad I then wrote down in large letters every navigational aid that I should look for on our cruise. I did this in sequence so I would know precisely where I was. I also made a column for the time and one for my speed. I debated with myself about adding another one for distance, that spacey word having come up time and time again in the reference books. I decided against it, my reasoning being that although I was into distance nee space I had enough of it left on the paper to include the column if Simon so desired.

By the morning of the 18th, my homework for our cruise and self imposed chores completed, I started to wonder when I would hear from Simon. By the evening of the 19th I was beginning to worry that he had forgotten me. Of course after almost being killed by yours truly I really couldn't blame him if he never called. On the other hand Simon didn't impress me as a man given to making false promises. Having reached that conclusion I decided not to turn in until after the late night news show and during the interim to watch a lengthy movie on the Civil War, *Gone With The Wind*.

The movie was one of my all time favorites, under normal circumstances guaranteed to keep me awake, but tonight my circumstances must have been abnormal because I woke up dreaming that Scarlett was on the telephone talking to Rhett. Definitely being on the groggy side I picked up the portable phone, which by then must have been on its tenth ring, and managed to wake up enough to say, "Hello. Bradford residence."

"Serena, Simon here. I apologize for calling so late in the evening. From the sound of your sleepy voice I'm afraid I got you out of bed."

Immediately, I perked up!

"Oh, no, I wasn't in bed, Simon. I was watching a movie and must have fallen asleep in the chair. That's all." I glanced up at the old school clock hanging on the wall. "Besides, it's just ten thirty. That's not late."

"I'm happy to hear you say that, Serena, because I actually did debate about calling you at this hour. You see I just got back from my trip about a half hour ago and since I had said I would call you on the 18th or 19th I didn't want to wait until tomorrow. I didn't want you to think I had forgotten."

"Oh, no, that thought never crossed my mind," I lied, thankful he couldn't see the guilty expression on my face which I knew was there. Never, ever again would I doubt him!

"That is good to know, Serena. Now then I took a few minutes before calling to listen to the marine weather forecast. It is supposed to rain, heavy at times tomorrow, followed by general clearing the next day. Tuesday, the 22nd, is supposed to be fair and sunny with clear skies, perfect cruising weather. Is that a free day for you?"

"Yes, Tuesday, the 22nd, will be fine with me, Simon."

"Okay! Now then, now that the date is settled I guess the next question is have you decided where you would like to go for the day?"

I wanted to give the flip reply, "You mean where would I like to go in order to enjoy my juicy carrot of a cruise," but Simon's query had been asked in his customary scholarly way so I said seriously, "Yes, I thought I would like to go as far off shore as Shipwreck Island and then come back to the marina through Booth Bay and Townsend Gut."

"H'm. That's a very ambitious run, Serena. A very long one too, I might add."

I could visualize Simon standing in his office studying the enormous blown-up chart of the Gulf of Maine that covered one entire wall. By now his brow would be furrowed in thought, his eyes reflecting intense concentration. He spoke finally. "It's not that I mind the run, Serena. Actually it would be very enjoyable. If I seem hesitant it's out of concern for your well being since there will have to be a brief span of time spent on open waters. I'm sure you noticed that on your chart."

"I do appreciate your concern, Simon, and yes, I did notice on the chart that if I took the wrong turn we could end up in Spain," I said sincerely, "but I'd like to give it a try. I also thought, that is, if it is agreeable with you, that we could break the run by having a picnic lunch on Bald Head Island. You see my brother and twin sister have always picnicked there as well as making the run out to Shipwreck Island. I'd like to surprise them when they get here in late October by being up to joining in their fun."

There was another long pause. Then, at last, I heard, "Okay, Serena, we will follow your plotted course but on one condition!"

I was miffed, Simon's "On one condition" sounding too much like home rules during my adolescence. "Oh -h -h?" I said, my voice rising along with my eyebrows.

I could hear him chuckling. That meant he was grinning from ear to ear and that his eyes would be all crinkled up at the corners. "Now, Serena, don't get into that killing the mosquitoes, doing away with nuclear power, and taking *Escape* out to play mood of yours. All I want is to reserve the right to change my mind after lunch about heading further out to Shipwreck Island. You know the weather is fickle, a sea could begin to build, a fog bank could sneak in on us. It would be very foolish not to take such variables into consideration or we really could end up in Spain. Don't you agree?"

Of course I agreed. What Simon had said was true. It would be foolish to ignore a change in the weather. So as much as it hurt me to admit that I was a possessor of moods and even though I knew he was half way teasing me I took advantage of our momentary lapse in conversation to reflect on my behavior - childish at best - and ended up by saying, "Eating crow pie is not one of my favorite pastimes, Simon, but I do agree that you are correct. As always!"

He laughed. I curled my toes deep into my old slipper socks. "Let's plan to meet on the dock at ten o'clock, Serena. It will be close to flood tide, a good time to leave. Also, now that you have proven to yourself that you are capable of bringing *Escape* in I will have Dal do the honors, see that she is fueled and give her a last minute check-over to be sure everything is on board that we might need."

"I don't know if I deserve such special treatment, Simon, but I'm not about to ask you to change your mind." His subsequent rich laugh subsided slowly, enticing my mind towards more agreeable thoughts. "I'll prepare the picnic lunch, Simon. Is there anything special that you would like me to bring?"

"No, Serena, I can't think of anything at the moment."

I detected a sudden tiredness in his voice. It made me feel guilty for keeping him on the phone. "I best hang up now, Simon. It's late and I'm sure you must be exhausted after your trip."

"I confess to being a little tired, Serena. It's rather a long haul from here to Montreal, from Montreal to Ottawa, from Ottawa to Newfoundland, and from Newfoundland back to here even if my journey was by plane. However all in all the trip went well and I shall look forward to telling you the particulars during our picnic lunch on Tuesday."

I was stunned. I was speechless. I had been dying from curiosity for the past several days, wondering where he was going on his trip, not daring to ask for fear of being considered rude and now here he was volunteering the information. Though he couldn't see me smile, I did. "I shall look forward to hearing about your trip, Simon. You know I have never been to Montreal and Ottawa or to Newfoundland."

"I'm sure you would like all the places, Serena, even though they are as different as night and day. Ottawa and Montreal as you might suspect invoke an image of old world charm and grandeur, whereas Newfoundland, especially the rural area of Rouge Baie where I was, is a quaint hodgepodge of cultures."

I heard him give a deep sigh. "Now then I must hang up, Serena, and let you get some rest. See you Tuesday morning."

"See you Tuesday morning, Simon."

"That's the 22nd, Serena."

"The 22nd," I repeated.

"At ten o'clock sharp, Serena."

"At ten o'clock sharp," I repeated, not quite able to keep my voice as sedate as his for we seemed to be falling into our customary raining cats and dogs routine.

"Good night then, Serena."

I was wrong this time. Simon's "Good night" had been said with a soft, almost caressing nuance. I broke out in goose bumps. "Good night then, Simon," I repeated slowly, trying my best to match my voice to the same inflections as in his. "May you have sweet dreams," I whispered to myself as I hung up. "I know I will now that you are back."

103

Chapter 12

Tuesday, August 22nd, arrived in a quiet blaze of glory at precisely 5:45 a.m. Being on a more relaxed time table I managed to arrive at the marina in a blaze of squeaking tires a little before ten, wanting to be sure all my gear was stowed on board in time for the anointed hour, wanting to be sure that Dal in checking over the boat had left the blower on until there was nothing left to blow and that the bilge was dry enough to pass a white glove inspection. I was feeling lighthearted, capricious, effervescent, call it what you will and undaunted by the prospect of once more being perched on the threshold of trying my wings.

At the sight of Simon walking down the float the devil in me that I always keep carefully bottled up for fear of reprisal in one form or another blew its cork. I felt just like doing one of the crazy madcap things that I always do periodically it seems, especially after some harrowing experience - jetting off to have lunch in Paris after my divorce came through being a prime example. So with my solo lesson definitely qualifying as having been harrowing, I was due for another madcap fling.

Out of my duffel bag I grabbed the red blanket that I had thrown in at the last minute for Simon and me to use on our picnic. It was old, well used by family members throughout the years and each one of its numerous mended tears a testimony to a festive beach party including the last big tear contributed by me when I celebrated my college graduation with a summer amour. Perhaps it was the memory of that wild evening that prompted me to bring the soon to be rag along. Who knows? Anyway, just as Simon was getting ready to board *Escape* I threw the blanket onto the dock in front of him and with exaggerated obeisance quickly knelt down and humbly salaamed him aboard with the exalted greeting, "Your Eminence!"

Dal, who was close by bailing out a dinghy, immediately cracked up at my irreverent salutation. "Jesum! Wicked good, Miss Bradford," he snickered.

I looked up. Simon was taken off guard. For a split second or two I thought he had become completely unglued at my spoof, but then much to my relief threw back his head and roared his marvelous deep laugh that infected everyone within range with a good case of well-being. I heard one fellow shout, "Hey, Simon, what's your secret for rating the red carpet treatment?," while another bellowed, "Yeah, some guys have all the luck!"

Simon acknowledged their jests shouting back, "Good, clean honest living," which was immediately greeted disparagingly by the men with a lot of hoots and hollers. To me, however, he said, "Wow, Serena, this is quite a welcome for so early in the morning."

It was strictly business as usual after we boarded *Escape* though I sensed a change had taken place between us for there was an emotional charge in the air. I could almost feel its surge as I put the blanket on the seat behind me and brought forward my marked up chart and the basic dead reckoning diagram I had made. A quizzical smile flooded Simon's face as I handed them to him and then for the first time I detected a slightly bantering tone in his voice as he asked his two standard questions: "Did you run the blower?" and "Did you pump out the bilge?"

All of a sudden it seemed easy to verbally spar with him. Not that we hadn't joked before but it was always as instructor to pupil - more or less. Perhaps that was why when I started to answer his questions just like always in my most dutiful school girl manner, my "Yes" flip-flopped and came out sounding more like an acquiescence to an invitation by him for a thousand and one nights of heavenly joy. I burst out laughing. Simon did not. He just sat there shaking his head, the boyish grin on his face and the twinkle in his eyes easily conveying his thought, "May God help me, what next?" He said, "Boy, you are really wound up today, Serena."

Talk about an understatement! I wasn't just wound up! It was more of a feeling like my body was a rubberband and that with each exciting twist I would wind and elongate until the snapping point. So it was with great will power, coaxed along by me taking several deep breaths, that I capped my frivolity and asked, "Is my dead reckoning diagram accurate enough to use, Simon? As you can see I've made a column for navigational aids, listing every one in sequence along the way out to

Shipwreck Island. Next to that list I made a column for distance and another one for direction but in my mind the two seemed to overlap even though Bowditch in his book showed all four headings in the chapter on dead reckoning. So I didn't!"

Simon arched his eyebrows. "I'm impressed, Serena. Anyone who studies Bowditch's *American Practical Navigator* has got to be serious about boating."

I sighed. "I finished struggling through it while you were away. Believe me it was a struggle, most of the practicality bit being impractical for me to use. Especially since I didn't understand most of it."

Simon's answer to my lament was to hand back my diagram along with a pencil. "Add the other two columns, Serena." Then, much like a magician pulling out a string of weird objects from a hat, delved into his own duffel bag and pulled out a notepad, a red pencil, dividers, a parallel rule, compass, and a piece of pliable plastic with a lot of lines and the name Courser printed on it. He placed them ceremoniously on the carpeted aisle between us saying as he did, "The tools of the trade, Serena, necessary for me to accurately demonstrate and to explain your question on dead reckoning."

I was flabbergasted! "All this paraphernalia is necessary for you to tell me if my dead reckoning diagram is accurate enough to use?"

Simon smiled. "All we are going to use is the Courser," he replied in a maddeningly calm way.

"Oh?"

"Since I was running late this morning I didn't take the time to remove the excess paraphernalia from my duffel bag." He went on to say, "In such limited space as there is here on board *Escape*, the Courser is definitely easier to use to determine direction than to use the parallel rule in plotting a course on a spread out chart, which is, under the best of conditions, unwieldy to handle!"

Though Simon's explanation was said in his usual professorial style his emphatic pronunciation of "Paraphernalia" was not lost on me. I decided I had committed a sacrilege by not using the proper nautical terms. Having been duly chastised I replied in my best school room manner, "I understand," and then dutifully added two more columns to my diagram labeling one Distance and the other Direction.

Simon picked up the Courser and my chart, putting the other tools of the trade back into his duffel bag. "Let me show you. We will place one line of the Courser over the red pencil mark you have made on the chart. Please notice, Serena, that when you do this another line on the Courser crosses near the middle of the big circle which is called a compass rose. This determines our direction which, as you can see from the arrow within the circle, is East."

I nodded and leaned closer to observe what Simon was doing. "By the way, Serena, the positioning of a compass rose varies from chart to chart and after studying the manual I gave you I'm sure you know that the compass rose is nothing more than a circle divided into 32 points numbered clockwise from true north. Its purpose, of course, is to determine the course of a vessel."

"Of course," I quipped giving him an intelligent nod even though I didn't know what I was nodding about. I couldn't resist adding, "Leave it to the Navy, Simon, to steal the perfectly good word rose, a flower of such divine scent and fragile delicate beauty, and distort its meaning into a circle pock-marked with degrees, points, numbers, and arrows pointing to the magnetic pole."

Simon gave me an askance look. Even his smile was sort of lopsided and tucked in at the corners of his mouth. He pointed to my diagram obviously trying hard to ignore my tweaking of the Navy and said, "You should enter, East, Serena, in the column under Direction beside the first navigational aid you listed which, according to your diagram, is the green flashing beacon "5" warning the skipper of the dangerous reef off of Dead Man's Point."

I did as I was instructed to do. Simon eased back into his seat. "Now then, Serena, I have made the run to Bald Head Island many times and know from experience that we are going to head East through Blind Rocks Passage until we reach the middle of the Sheepscot River which, according to your diagram

108

is marked by can buoy C "13" indicating the location in the fairway of Humpback Rock. From there we are going to turn and head South until we reach Bald Head Island. So mark on your diagram beside can buoy C "13" in the column under Direction, South."

I did as I was instructed to do and then with my pencil poised for action waited for his next order. "Once we clear the marina, Serena, try to keep *Escape*'s speed at six knots all the way out to the island. That's about 25 RPMs on your dial so in the column labeled Speed enter six knots or 25 RPMs. On such a calm day we can easily maintain this speed."

I entered 25 RPMs into the Speed column. "That leaves two to go, Simon; Time and Distance."

"Time is the easy one for today, Serena. What you will do as you pass each aid is to simply glance at your watch and record the time of passing. Distance takes longer to compute since you have to use the dividers to measure the space between each navigational aid or in many cases between specific landmarks and then translate the information into nautical miles, a nautical mile being 6080 feet whereas a statute mile is 5280 feet. It also helps to have a flat surface to work on which is why, Serena, I've decided we can wait until we return late this afternoon and go over this particular phase of dead reckoning in my office. However, for our purposes today and since I have made this run many times I know it is quite close to two miles out to C "13" and from there out to the island a couple of feet shy of three miles. So under the Distance column enter two miles in the space between the green flashing beacons "5" and buoy C "13" and enter three miles in the space between C "13" and Bald Head Island. Once we are underway and you are entering all the appropriate information on your diagram the rudiments of dead reckoning will become quite clear."

Simon was obviously on familiar turf. As for me, my head was spinning from trying to remember everything he had said and from trying to swiftly carry out his instructions, all the while thinking navigating by dead reckoning must be a lot like trying to find your way home by rote in the dark and without the benefit of a flashlight!

A few more sobering thoughts occurred to me. "I guess you could say, Simon, navigating by dead reckoning is similar to the counted steps taken by a blind person to get from point A to point Z?"

Simon gazed off into the space of Knubble Bay. He said nothing, the gentle lapping of the water against *Escape*'s hull only accenting his self imposed silence. Finally he answered, "You have made a very poignant comparison, Serena, and taken in the broadest sense quite true."

He was so serious in demeanor that I just sat there with my hands at rest in my lap. A minute later he smiled broadly, the hint of solemnity that had tightened his facial muscles a moment ago when I asked my question erased it seemed by a pleasant thought. "Now then, Serena, it's ten thirty and since this is supposed to be a joyous occasion I suggest you cast off and take *Escape* out to play."

Simon's last few words were spoken with exaggerated levity. I laughed. "Aye, aye, Captain! Out to play, it is!"

Seven minutes later, as I passed the quick flashing beacon "5" on my right marking Dead Man's Point, I made my first entry on the diagram writing beside Qk Fl 16 ft "5", 10:37 a.m. Two minutes later I passed a red nun buoy on my left, entering on my diagram beside R N "1", 10:39 a.m. By now Simon was in the bow, his long and lanky frame stretched out across the cushions, his back propped up against the left side of the cockpit making it easy for us to converse.

"I'm beginning to understand, Simon, what my grandfather meant when he told me, 'It's the challenge of navigation which puts the thrill into boating.'"

"That would be Judge Adams, Serena; the former owner of *Escape*?"

"Yes! He used to and still does tease me a lot, always telling me navigation is what puts the yo-ho in the heave or something to that effect."

"He sounds like a rather salty individual."

"Oh, he is!" I paused long enough to enter 10:43 a.m., beside can buoy C"3" on my diagram before saying, "My grandfather is also a walking encyclopedia. Through the years he has tried to interest me in boating by catering to my passion for history. I've never forgotten some of his choicest tid bits!"

Simon got up and returned to the seat across from me in the cockpit. "Such as, Serena?"

"Well, for one thing he told me Noah used a dove to locate land. For another he said Columbus goofed up in his quest for a shorter route to the East Indies because he used Ptolemy's *Cosmographia* as a basis for his calculations that the earth was 18,000 square miles instead of 24,000 square miles as measured by Eratosthenes in the 3rd century BC."

Simon grinned. "You do seem to have been an apt pupil, Serena."

I took time out to make another entry on my diagram marking 10:48 a.m., beside green beacon G "4" before answering. "I don't know how apt a pupil I was, Simon. Don't forget I was a captive audience of one, so what I remember is probably due to osmosis. By the way, look at that huge osprey nest built on top of the beacon we just passed. You know those birds must tarnish the spit and polish right off the Navy brass to say nothing of driving them berserk for defying regulations. For some diabolical reason I find their behavior most delightful!"

Simon bestowed on me another one of his quizzical glances. "I'm beginning to think, Serena, that in addition to male mosquitoes and nuclear power that you also have a vendetta against the Navy. Now then what other choice tid bits do you remember?"

"He told me about the giant clock in Greenwich, England, whose beep can be heard anywhere in the world by simply tuning into it. He went into great detail about an international agreement in 1884 which established an imaginary north-south line on the earth's surface with 0 degrees longitude in Greenwich."

"Yes, that was an important stop for navigation, Serena. You realize that up to then no one really could go accurately from east to west or from west to east."

I nodded. "So he said. My grandfather also did a lot of soliloquizing about the great navigators of the past, especially his favorites which as I recall were Pytheas, Magellan, Cook and Nansen."

By now we were leaving the narrows of Blind Rocks Passage, a trio of green beacons consecutively numbered G "7", G "8" and G "9" marking the way out into the wide expanse of the Sheepscot River. I paused long enough in my story telling to enter 10:50 a.m., 10:52 a.m., and 10:54 a.m., respectively before continuing. "He also likes to champion his love of the sea, constantly telling me that a tryst on the ocean is as easy as meeting a boyfriend in front of the Trevi Fountain, Times Square, or even at the corner of Hollywood and Vine. He even went so far as to sit down one wintry afternoon a few months ago and figure out that it would be nice if I would meet him this summer on a specified day at 69 degrees, 41 minutes, 40 seconds West Longitude and 43 degrees, 51 minutes, 10 seconds North Latitude, and that if I did rendezvous with him he would take me on a special safari to Kenya, something I have always wanted to do."

Simon picked up my chart and opened it wide. He reached into his duffel bag and took out another chart, a large one of the New England coast. After studying them for what seemed like an eternity he asked, "Are you sure of your readings, Serena? That's a lot of numbers to commit to memory."

"Oh, yes, my grandfather wrote the rendezvous points down for me and I copied them on the back of my chart in the off chance I might have a moment to discuss them with you."

Simon folded up his chart and put it away. He doubled mine over twice, to where I had it originally folded and handed it back to me. "Well, Serena, I can't be absolutely sure without making some calculations but after looking at the charts and doing some mental gymnastics I'd say if your grandfather was with us in *Escape* today, that you had just won your trip to Kenya."

"You're kidding? You mean his rendezvous point is here, at can buoy C "13" at Humpback Rock?"

I put the engine into idling position, too dumbfounded to say anything but, "I don't believe it. I don't believe it."

Simon grinned. "I'll be happy to sign a sworn affidavit stating that you were here, Serena. However, from what you have told me about Judge Adams I have a sneaking suspicion that he wants the satisfaction of being with you and to share in your achievement."

Truer words were never spoken. My eyes misted over as I recalled Grandfather Horatio telling me, "There comes a time in all our lives when we have to shed a bit of the past in order to move on into the future."

Well, I had indeed shed a bit of the past. It was the moving on into the future that was the bother. Simon helped to get me underway again, saying thoughtfully, "I know your grandfather will be happy to hear the news of your accomplishment, Serena, even though he might want you to repeat the run with him. However, don't lose sight of your immediate goal which is Bald Head Island so best record your time up to this point and then turn *Escape* towards the ocean, heading due South."

After almost three months of being programmed I did as I was told. I entered beside C "13", 11:02 a.m., making a scribbled note on the side of the diagram that we arrived at 10:58 a.m., but lost four minutes due to idling at Humpback Rock, and then gradually increased *Escape*'s speed up to 25 RPMs, turning her as I did until her sensitive compass pointed the way South. Several playful seals popped up beside us, their antics sidetracking me for a moment before I asked, "How long will it take us, Simon, to reach the island?"

"If the seas remain calm as they are now, Serena, you should pull into the harbor in about thirty minutes, that's an estimate based on maintaining the same speed you traveled while coming through the passage out to Humpback Rock."

"In other words, Simon, it took me twenty minutes to travel two nautical miles at a speed of six knots. So, based on that fact, it should take me thirty minutes to travel three nautical miles at a speed of six knots. Therefore, if I was returning home and the conditions were the same, it would take me the same amount of time and as a backup confirming my way home I would have all the aids documented with the appropriate time of passage."

Simon smiled. "That is correct, Serena."

We retreated into our private thoughts. The seals followed suit, no longer interested it seemed in cavorting beside *Escape* once I passed Green Island. A breeze freshened as we passed Dogfish Head and feeling every bit as light I breezily determined to someday do my own deed of "daring do" and then apply for admittance into that small, inner golden ring of mariners linked together by luminaries such as my buddy Pytheas along with Cook, Magellan, and Nansen. We passed Hendrix Head Light which was on my left. On my right was Five Islands, the red and white Grave's General Store sign plainly visible to me in the bright morning sun. In the distance I could see the bell-buoy marking the entrance into the mouth of the river and on the far horizon I could see nothing but the ominous emptiness of a vast blue-black ocean.

Simon was totally at ease. I was too, that is until the river broadened into the bay and *Escape* was hit by a series of white capped rollers that sent us backwards in rocking chair motion. A chill with definite yellow side effects traveled right down my spine. It ended up concentrated, like cold fat in left over gravy, in the pit of my stomach which began to erupt like the epicenter of an earthquake, sending out shock wave, after shock wave, after shock wave. I decided to exercise my woman's prerogative. I decided not to apply for admittance into that small, inner golden ring of mariners and to once again content myself with just being an ordinary landlubber! I decided Magellan could bloody well have his foggy Strait and that if Pytheas was mad enough to paddle all that distance in an oversized canoe he well deserved the stiff neck he no doubt had from following Polaris. As for Nansen - only a nerd would risk freezing his tootsies off in order to have the dubious privilege of dallying in the arctic. And for Cook - only a besotted sun stroke victim would risk death in order to bring back a few potted palms. With that thought in mind I decided Cook earned his comeuppance from the natives by letting his eyes linger a smidge too long while navigating around another kind of mesmerizing, soft, undulating, warm South Pacific swell.

It was also the persistent undulating swells or rollers or whatevers and their on-again-off-again rising to white cap proportion that were going to earn me my comeuppance. Like some menacing supernatural force reaching out to smother me I could sense the water churning and tugging at the boat's bottom. Its eerie vibes penetrated my sneakers, coursed up through my legs and through the wheel into my hands and arms. Heaven forbid! I was going to be seasick!

Self preservation, I guess, or maybe it was primeval instinct that forced me to grip the wheel until my fingers numbed and my knuckles whitened. Trillions of white dots danced in front of my eyes. Their brilliance was mesmerizing, their rapid movement compelling! I willingly let myself start to slip away into their world of peaceful serenity.

Intense pressure on my left arm stopped my flight. "Serena, you are as white as a Cloroxed ghost. Are you all right?"

I turned and found myself staring right into Simon's intense blue eyes. It was the first time he had ever touched me in an intimate way - perhaps it was the understanding and genuine caring reflected in his eyes - perhaps it was the firmness of his grip on my arm - but the combination was quite a panacea for I felt the knot in my stomach dissolve and the after shock waves of fear slowly subside. I was able to relax my vise like grip on the wheel. "I'm fine, Simon; just a good case of stage fright. That's all!"

"I think you are doing remarkably well, Serena."

This time he gave my arm a gentle reassuring type of squeeze before removing his hand. "In fact, Serena, I couldn't do any better navigating through these ocean swells than you are doing today."

From then on I was okay and able to concentrate solely on the business at hand, mainly entering the time 11:15 a.m., on my diagram as we passed the red and black bell buoy marking the entrance to the river and a few minutes later 11:25 a.m., beside the last navigational aid I had listed before we reached the island, a mid-channel black and white short-long flashing lighted bell buoy written down as BW "CH" S-L Fl Bell. Why I even merited a booming, "Well done, Serena," after bringing *Escape* into a small barren cove which served as the island's harbor and another, "Wicked good," after docking her at an old minuscule wharf no bigger it seemed than a banquet size dining table.

Though I was thrilled over Simon's compliments I didn't let them go to my head. I took a moment - brief as it was - to enter the time 11:32 a.m., on my diagram beside Bald Head Island and afterwards being a dutiful pupil reported, "You were right, Simon! It took us thirty minutes traveling at a speed of six knots per hour to get from Humpback Rock to here. Then I let the compliments go to my head. I jumped up, threw my arms around him, shouting so the whole world could hear, "I did it, Simon! I did it!"

Perhaps if the family had been on the wharf to welcome me I wouldn't have reacted so wildly, their presence and comments always bringing me back down to earth. Adam, of course, would have said, "God damn it to hell, Serena, it's only taken you 28 years to get here;" his proper Brahmin upbringing having been tainted by gutter language absorbed from the nooks and crannies of the underworld. Mother would have frowned her displeasure over Adam's unseemly conduct, then giving me a loving maternal embrace would say, "It was just a matter of time, Dear." Gloria, my dear twin, would have said, "You've done well, my pet." Grandfather would have said nothing, his pride in my achievement evident by a prolonged wink of his right eye. Daddy would have helped me ashore being careful I didn't slip between the boat and the dock, then after giving me a loving fatherly embrace would say, "I'm proud of you, Little One."

As it was Simon did the honors helping me ashore in much the same careful manner as Daddy would have done. However their similarity in behavior stopped there, Simon wisely having the foresight to keep our relationship, at least for the minute, strictly on a platonic plane for after I was deposited firmly on the wharf he removed the picnic basket and red blanket from *Escape*'s stern and then distanced himself from me by tying a couple of extra unnecessary lines onto her. Finally he turned around, the warmth reflected in his eyes and smile a telltale give away that he had thoroughly enjoyed our brief encounter. On the other hand the ramrod straightness of his back signaled that his response to my jubilant outburst was going to be dictated by the practical and serious side of his mind rather than his heart. "Serena, we will never make it to Shipwreck Island and back to

116

the marina before dark unless we have our lunch now," he said earnestly. "It appears we have the entire island to ourselves so where do you think you would like to picnic?"

I looked around. "Gloria said there was a rise in the land not too far from the wharf that offered a good view of the harbor and a magnificent bird's-eye sweep of the mainland. That might be a nice spot for our picnic."

Simon picked up the basket and blanket. "I know exactly the place she means, Serena. It's actually a flat rock about the size of a football field and weathered smooth by the elements. In fact, the rock's barren, wind polished smoothness is what prompted the island's name of Bald Head."

"Oh!"

"Now then, a person almost has to be part mountain goat to get there but the view is well worth the climb. Do you think you are up to it?"

A touch of Gloria's women's lib glib unconsciously edged into my reply. "If you can do it, Simon, so can I! So, lead on McDuff!"

Simon shook his head and chuckled. He could just as easily have said, "You're hopeless, Serena."

Chapter 13

What is it about being on an island alone with someone that makes you believe you are in a confessional? For by the time we had climbed to the top of Bald Head and finished our chicken salad sandwiches I was divulging to Simon my life history - dwelling mostly on the good such as, "I have a neat twin sister named Gloria and a big brother named Adam," and skimming over the bad such as, "I was divorced over a year ago from Britton Peabody. Our marriage was heralded in all the newspapers as being the wedding of the decade but it lasted only two years."

"I'm sorry, Serena. From the sound of your voice and the anguish in your eyes the break up of your marriage must have been very painful."

"Oh, no, Simon! It was a relief! I don't want to bore you with all the tedious details but Britt and I were mismatched from the beginning. He never was able to understand the logic of buying a yellow hat just because it was a rainy day nor could he ever comprehend how anyone could be so moved by a painting or a piece of sculpture that it rendered them into sobs - in public no less! Unfortunately while we were in Rome I broke down completely when viewing Angelo's statue of Moses. My teary scene, even though carried out behind sun shades, embarrassed the heck out of Britt. In fact, he never quite got over it."

Simon, being a perfect conversationalist, never said a word while I paused to collect my thoughts. He just sat there, his face a masque of controlled emotions, and politely waited for me to continue the purging of my soul. "On the other hand," I said, "my side of the ledger has several black entries. Being a procrastinator is one of them. Running a close second would be my stubborn streak."

"An irreverent behavior towards the Navy brass must be the third black mark on your side of the ledger, Serena," Simon interjected quickly and jovially, obviously trying to dispel my gloominess.

I laughed at his wry sense of humor. "Right you are! If not irreverent towards them, then certainly irreverent towards their confounded rules and regulations."

This time Simon laughed. "Spoken like a true disciple of *Cosmo*."

I immediately forgot about Britt and focused on Simon's espousal of the slick women's magazine, the two of them somehow not seeming to jibe. However my mind, cluttered up as it was with nautical chart symbols and abbreviations, permitted no leeway from the task at hand so I concentrated on lifting out of the basket the remainder of our repast. "How about a fresh peach from our garden and some double fudge brownies from Mrs. Linette's kitchen? That's Abel Linette's wife who I'm sure you know since he moors his fishing boat at the marina."

"Everyone knows Abel, Serena. He's quite the wheeler-dealer! Into a little bit of everything it seems. As for Mrs. Linette I've talked to her twice this summer, once in the middle of July and then again a couple of weeks ago."

"Oh?"

Simon grinned. "The first time she gave me quite the once over, from head to toe. Then I was told in no uncertain terms that you had been very ill this past winter and spring. She went on to say that you had taken a six months leave from the Boston Museum of Fine Arts in order to 'Reee-cuper-ateee' and that she and Abel had worked for your family for years on end."

"Oh, no!"

By now Simon's grin was widespread across his face. Even his body appeared to be caught up in the act of grinning, relaxed and laid back as he was against the red blanket. "In other words, Serena, please don't touch the merchandise."

I just about choked on my peach. "What did Mrs. Linette say the last time you talked to her?"

"She said very warmly and graciously, 'The bloom had been restored to your cheeks.'"

Simon sat up. "Of course, I could have told her that, Serena. I also could have told her that you have fifteen new freckles across the bridge of your nose."

I could feel the blood surging to my face. My heart beat accelerated. "But you didn't?"

"No, I didn't, Serena."

His tone was caressing, his words bantering, his eyes tender yet mirthful or was it that they were mirroring my own sense of longing to reach out and touch? I asked quickly and weakly or was it desperately, "Would you care to know what Mrs. Linette said about you?"

A hint of speculation replaced the longing to reach out and touch look in his eyes. It was as if he knew I was trying to switch the subject, which I was! "I don't know, Serena. Is it safe for my delicate ears to hear?"

Our amorous mood was broken! Thank goodness, for in my on going capricious state of mind and seated as we were on the infamous red blanket no telling what might have happened with too many reaching out and touching kind of looks. "I guess it's safe enough for you to hear," I replied unable to keep a straight face. "She said, 'Mr. Mont seems a nice enough young man, for a foreigner that is, to teach me even though some folks here t'bouts think he's strange, keepin' to himself so much.'"

Simon just sat there shaking his head, a frown like he had been affronted creasing his brow. "Being Canadian, the foreigner part of Mrs. Linette's statement doesn't bother me. However, being labeled strange does!"

I had expected him to laugh, to not be serious, to accept Mrs. Linette's words in the harmless way they were intended. "You know, Simon, I never would have told you if I had thought your feelings might be hurt," I explained hurriedly. "There isn't a malicious bone in Amie Linette's body to quote Mother. She meant you no harm. In fact, she paid you two very nice compliments; the first being, 'There 's no doubt locally he knows his way around a focsle,' and the second being, 'The owner of the marina considers you quite an asset because you speak fluent French, a big plus during the summer with so many sailors from Quebec cruising in our waters.'"

Simon's frown gave way to a look of chagrin as he said contritely, "Thanks for telling me, Serena. It's always nice to know of course that folks think well of you. I guess at times I can be a little thin skinned. If she had just said aloof, instead of strange, I would have understood but there is a connotation at least in Canada to the latter that makes me uncomfortable.

Actually though, now that I am thinking about her description of me, I have kept to myself this past summer. However my reclusiveness was for a very good reason. Which brings me to what I wanted to tell you about my trip to Ottawa, Montreal, and Newfoundland."

At last! I was beginning to think he had forgotten his promise. I should have known better, experience being the perfect teacher.

"I have a master's degree in marine archaeology from McGill University in Montreal, Serena, and have spent every evening this summer writing a dissertation to present towards receiving my doctorate. I finally finished it, thus my trip to Montreal."

I felt a twinge of guilt when he told me this. I glanced quickly away, hoping he wouldn't notice my sudden fluster for I had often joked to my museum contemporaries and to Gloria about archaeologists and anthropologists being only at home among the anthropoids at the zoo since all of them seemed to be happy only when having a platter full of bones in front of them to pick over. Now here I was caught in my own concocted web of prejudice - munching not on bones, true, but peaches and brownies - and with someone who definitely was not picky or fossiliferous. In fact, after a discreet side long scrutinizing glance, I decided Simon was definitely and always had been on the debonair side. So once more I exercised my woman's prerogative, changed my mind about archaeologists and anthropologists and after forgiving him for having chosen such an archaic field of endeavor asked, "What subject did you choose for your dissertation, Simon?"

"Eric the Red!"

"Eric the Red," I repeated. "If my school room memory serves me correctly he was a great Viking explorer and opened up the western coast of Greenland during the late 10th century."

"Your memory serves you well, Serena. You know Eric the Red must have been similar to your Abel Linette, a very likable

122

wheeler-dealer, for Eric probably was one of the first great real estate developers of all times having coined the name Greenland to describe a territory covered mostly with ice in order to entice people into joining him in the establishment of a colony."

"Was it his son Leif Ericson then who coined the name Newfoundland during his exploration of the North American coast?"

"I'll keep you in suspense, Serena. You will have to read my dissertation in order to solve the mystery."

Simon paused long enough to help himself to another brownie. "However to make a long story short my thesis ties in with my soon to be employment in a special branch of the Canadian government called Parks Canada, thus my trip to Ottawa."

Not being too familiar with Her Majesty's inner committees I thought it best to ask, "What exactly is Parks Canada?"

"It's the branch that manages her federal parks and historic sites. It's the latter located on an island in the Strait of Belle Isle just off the coast from Rouge Baie, Newfoundland, that is of major interest to the Parks Canada people for a Basque galleon has been found believed to have sunk around 1565."

"Thus your trip to Newfoundland, Simon?"

"Right! Thus my trip to Newfoundland and to the tiny village of Rouge Baie, Serena. You see for the next several summers a determined effort is going to be made to learn not only more about the Viking impact on the area but about the Basque settlements, the whaling trade and the reasons behind their demise. Some of us like me will be diving, hoping to salvage artifacts from the galleon, while others will be applying their skills to excavating the site. Who knows, Serena, maybe we will find the Basques were here long before Columbus."

"It sounds absolutely fascinating, Simon. I gather then the winter months will be spent on the tedious details such as research, preservation, cataloguing, and so forth?"

Simon smiled. "And so forth, Serena."

Curiosity finally got the best of me and I decided to venture into unexplored territory. "Simon, how on earth did you ever find your way to Georgetown, Maine, and to Riggs Marina?

Both places seem so off the beaten path for you, especially since your interests are centered in somewhat of a straight line between Ottawa and Newfoundland?"

"Georgetown is not really off the beaten path for me, Serena. Ever since I was knee high to a grasshopper I've been cruising the New England coast and that of the Maritime Provinces during the summer, first with my parents and then during college as a crew member and finally as an instructor on several educational schooners. It is only natural that through those years I picked out a few favorite places, Georgetown being one of them. When I heard the summer position of dockmaster was open at Riggs and when, at the same time mind you, I was looking for a quite place to pen my dissertation the coincidence of them both materializing in Georgetown was hard to ignore. Then too there was the added plus of Bowdoin College and their superb arctic museum being near-by in case I needed to do some extra research. So, all things considered, I simply applied for the position at Riggs, obtained my work permit and here I am."

Simon's explanation about his past and future endeavors intensified my interest in him. I began to pack away our picnic items, to busy myself in a routine of picking up while trying to decide how best to ask the kind of personal questions to obtain the answers that I was dying to know but always too shy to ask but that Gloria would normally not hesitate to come right out and ask such as, "Are you married?" or "Are you engaged to be married?"

As it turned out I didn't have to make that difficult decision, Simon volunteering the pertinent information in a roundabout way while finishing his brownie. "Abel's a lucky man his wife is such a good cook. Being a bachelor I take the easiest way out but certainly not the tastiest by buying them at the market."

Simon's abrupt rising from the blanket and terse statement, "Someone's in trouble, Serena," effectively put an end to our peaceful interlude and to any follow up questions I might have had. I immediately stood up too, my eyes following his gaze down to the harbor where a large power boat was being towed by a tender size orange rubber one. The boats were close enough for me to make out that a man was rowing the tender and having a difficult time battling the chop of the water as it churned near the dock and at the same time trying to control the slack of the line attached to the bow of the larger boat. Brief snatches of words shouted to a person on board like, "Tighten up," and, "More slack," drifted up to us.

Simon took off with the speed of a jack rabbit, scurrying sure-footedly down the rocky path to lend what assistance he could. I followed in my own inimitable way, his former lecture, "Towing is difficult and quite dangerous when larger boats are involved," causing me to want to hurry to their aid and yet a sense of deep foreboding holding me back, slowing me down, making me overly cautious, making me pick and test the firmness of each rock before taking a step forward.

A brisk breeze had come up during these past few minutes - definitely not the balmy kind which had been forecast - and that coupled with the shifting tide was pushing the larger boat straight towards the dock much faster than idling speed. In what had to be the heroic spirit of John Paul Jones, Simon started to shout commands and from the way we all responded even a casual observer would have thought we were seasoned crew members and used to working together; even a plebe like me.

"Use the tender," Simon shouted to the man rowing, "as if it is a permanent fender on a dock."

The man waved his acknowledgment of the order.

"Make ready to secure an extra line to the stern and one for amidship," Simon shouted to the person on board the boat.

The person on board saluted.

"Serena," Simon shouted, "run and fetch two of the extra long dock lines from *Escape* and then stand by."

I did as I was told, thinking as I ran to do his bidding that he could at least have said, "Please;" Mother always saying, "There is never an excuse for poor manners." Be that as it may I lost no time in grabbing the dock lines out of one of *Escape*'s cubbyholes in the bow, then rushed back to Simon's side to stand by in an "Attention" like stance as ordered.

The boat turned suddenly away from us, the tide pushing her stern emblazoned with the scarlet lettered name *Savannah's Revenge* towards land and into prominent view. I gasped.

"Simon that boat was at the marina in June. Why that must be Leroy (I thought it best not to say muscular acquaintance) rowing the dinghy and Missy Sue must be the person on board."

I wanted to run and greet him; to say something original like "It's a small ocean," but Simon sprinted across the dock in front of me, helping Leroy to tie up quickly.

Standing where I was I couldn't hear the ensuing conversation but necessary haste was apparent in their gestures. Leroy, I noticed, nodded in acquiescence and then to my utter amazement after tying a stern line on the dinghy climbed back into her and released the tow line - not letting go though but instead looping the line onto the dock by making a timber hitch.

The next thing I knew Simon was taking one of my dock lines. With a mighty heave he threw it out to Missy Sue, holding on to one end, shouting, "Secure the line to the stern," and then handed the end to me with the redundant words, "Don't let go."

Not being "Out to lunch" I didn't really need to be reminded not to let go! I also felt sure Missy Sue, being an experienced boater, did not need to be reminded to tie the second dock line amidship that Simon was heaving out to her along with his order, "Tie it amidship!"

Gloria, having a fiery streak in her nature, which of course made her a good lawyer, would have shouted back, "I heard you the first time!"

As it was, after Simon exchanged lines with me - he making a big to-do about taking over *Savannah*'s stern line - there was just enough of Gloria in me to ignite a slow burn. My about to be indignant protest, "I am capable of holding onto a stern line," was squelched though by Simon's shouting, "All together now. Pull!"

Pull we did. It was over in a second. Leroy had pulled steadily on *Savannah*'s tow-line so that she was beginning to turn slightly towards the dinghy when Simon and I started to tug. It was then I fully realized what Simon had in mind when he had shouted to Leroy "Use her for a fender." What first had appeared to be a crazy idea actually made a lot of sense for the rubber dinghy would sustain the blow and far better to risk puncturing her bright orange skin than ramming a hole into *Savannah*'s

126

expensive turquoise hull. Finally, just like a very recalcitrant child being thwarted in a dangerous attempt she slowly came along side; just grazing the dinghy and doing no damage.

Lines were quickly tied. Then, all of a sudden, it was like homecoming. Everyone was talking at once; laughing and congratulating ourselves on a job, "Well done."

Missy Sue and Leroy remembered Simon, she telling him coquettishly, "I nevah forget a handsome man;" he telling Simon, "Jesus, you sho' nuff were a sight for sore eyes standing on the wharf."

Neither of them remembered me, so I stepped forward and reintroduced myself, taking my sailing hat off in a manner similar to Leroy's grand bow and cavalier sweep of his sailor's cap on the day I met them. "I'm Serena Bradford, the nervous ninny you met on the dock at the marina," I said to Missy Sue and then to Leroy, "The one you dubbed, Miss Fledgling."

Leroy looked at me as if he had just encountered a strange apparition. His eyebrows arched in surprise. "Why I nevah would have recognized you," he drawled in the same speculative tone as on the day I had met him at the marina.

I laughed before replying. "No wonder with my hair trussed up like a chef and my face plastered with sun block cream."

It was my turn to be completely surprised for Leroy stepped forward and tousled my hair; riffling it through his fingers and toyingly pushing it back from where it was falling over my shoulders. "Why, Simon," he said cajolingly, "you sly old dog. You have gone and captured yourself a mermaid."

I was nonplussed at Leroy's boldness and acutely embarrassed as well. Never having been able to control my blushing I could not stop the hotness of my blood from surging up and flooding my neck and face beet red. Simon was not amused! Neither was Missy Sue who snapped tersely, "Stop it, Leroy! There's no time for that!"

The atmosphere on the dock changed speedily from conviviality to downright hostility and in what was a rather adroit move Simon wedged himself between Leroy and me and brusquely asked, "What's the problem with the boat?"

I could tell this manipulative move on the part of Simon was not lost on Leroy for he continued to insolently leer at me like I was the mouse and he the Cheshire cat before matter-of-factly replying, "I'm not sure. The engine just stopped turning over near that mid-channel marker."

Talk about out of the mouths of babes! "Gee whiz," I said in all innocence. "You were lucky not to have smashed up on the rocks. Instead of towing the boat ashore why didn't you just tie up to the bell buoy and send out an SOS for assistance? Sooner or later someone would have answered your call and come by."

If looks could kill I would have been dead on the spot as Missy Sue sarcastically asked me, "Hindsight is always better than foresight, isn't it my deah?"

A sort of furtive look was then exchanged between Missy Sue and Leroy which in turn seemed to prompt her to arrogantly ask Simon, "Would you take a look at the engine?"

Simon stiffened and stared off into space. Her imperious tone made me stiffen too, but instead of staring into the blue yonder I focused on Simon. Anger was evident in every measured breath and I had been with him enough during the past weeks to recognize a change in behavior from his customary warmth and kindness to one of coldness and controlled hostility.

Missy Sue stepped forward, her hands came to rest on her hips like a top sergeant at drill. "Well, Simon, don't take all day to make up your mind!"

Simon looked down at Missy Sue as if she was a smelly piece of spoiled fish fit only for lobster bait. From his disdainful expression I half expected him to give her a proper New England style dressing down, saying "I'm Simon to my friends. To you I'm Mr. Mont." Instead he took another deep breath and looked over her head at me. His eyes softened noticeably, the pupils widened as if to let me peek inside his mind. It was strange, but I knew then that it was his concern for my well-being that was going to be the compelling force behind his decision. He ultimately said to Leroy, not to Missy Sue, "Let's see what we can do."

So in Pied Piper fashion Missy Sue, Leroy, and Simon clambered aboard and sprawled out on the floor by the engine. I meandered nonchalantly behind, quite confidant with my knowledge that I wouldn't be consulted re the vagaries of a diesel engine. That was really okay, for it gave me the freedom to scout around *Savannah*'s commodious interior without being too obvious.

After moseying around the cockpit admiring the tasteful decor and fine fittings I sat down in the captain's chair. It was quite comfy, especially the way the contour of the seat and the thick foam padding snuggled up to my body, and just right for indulging myself in a favorite childhood pastime of swiveling lackadaisically back and forth. The seat was also just the right height for me to notice all the electronics on board, the extraordinary amount of them more in keeping with the *QE II*, than with a 36 foot pleasure boat. Then there was the ship to shore radio. It too appeared to be larger and more powerful than necessary.

My eyes drifted to a chart laid out on the table. Curiosity, I guess, as to how Leroy and Missy Sue marked up a chart prompted me to get up to scrutinize it. I could feel Missy Sue's beady black eyes - by now they had become beady instead of jet - boring into my back as I traced the pencil markings with my fingers. It appeared their destination was Halfway Rock, not too far from Eagle Island in Casco Bay and as the crow flies not too far out from Portland harbor. Aiding in my assumption were several neatly printed numbers beside that particular rock - the most visible being 1300.

One of those fancy no-prick-the-paper kind of dividers Grandfather used was on top of the chart. Even though I recognized it, I couldn't resist trying it ghoulishly out on my finger. Just as I couldn't resist moving a parallel ruler and a large magnifying glass out of the way in order to read what was scribbled on a notepad. I knew better, of course, but boredom can make a person do strange things so I wasn't the least bit perturbed over peering down at the doodling to see what was written in between the curls and swirls which turned out to be the names of a few harbors with French names along with a couple close to home; Haddock Bay and Blueberry Cove being two of the familiar ones that caught my eye. There was also a small

129

batch of letters and postcards stacked on top of the chart. Fortunately, I hadn't become bored enough to read their mail. Heaven forbid! Unfortunately, I accidentally knocked it all onto the floor - deck - whatever - making it impossible when gathering it up not to see a few postmarks such as Port aux Basques, Bar Harbor, and Portland, and to enjoy the scenic postcards. One in particular caught my eye, that of an old Victorian house that at first glance reminded me of The Barnacle. In fact the similarity was so great, that even though I knew I shouldn't, I turned the card over hoping to discover its location. However that part of the card was badly stained, impossible to decipher; the remaining part though was quite clear, showing no postmark, neither was there a message, just a signature B and a telephone number.

After restoring their mail to its proper spot on top of the table I tried to walk around the cockpit a bit more. In such a confined space it was really impossible to do just as it was impossible to ignore the several stuffed green plastic garbage bags stacked at the foot of the companionway. Just like the over abundance of electronics on board it seemed to be more like the accumulation of trash from the *QE II*, than that of two people.

By now I was getting very restless as I often do when having to kill time. Snatches of sentences - uttered in exasperation and anger - finally caught my attention. "I don't have the where-with-all to fix it here, " Simon said emphatically.

A few seconds later I heard Missy Sue. Her voice was loud and strident. "I told you, Leroy, to get that damn part replaced before we left home but you obviously were too busy with your stable full of women to bother."

"Mind your own God damn bloody business," sparred Leroy. "What's done is done!"

"We will take their boat to the marina and pick up the part," Missy Sue said a few minutes later, her voice stripped of southern charm.

A chill traveled right down my spine and then reversed itself as indignation swept over me at her high handedness. I started down the ladder, ready to quip, "Over my dead body," when I heard Simon very coldly say, "That won't do. The repair work required needs the facilities of a machine shop."

The next thing I knew they were beside me. I had never seen Simon so frigid. His distaste for them was so very obvious that it upset me. On the other hand Missy Sue's and Leroy's hostility towards Simon was so very obvious that it frightened me. I ended up nervously wringing my hands together in dismay but still expecting Simon to make the courteous offer of towing *Savannah's Revenge* back to the marina. Was I ever wrong! Instead he said sternly, "Serena and I will go for help!"

Like a spoiled brat Missy Sue stomped her foot in defiance at Simon and then in the same arrogant obnoxious twang countered, "That won't do! We are on a very tight schedule."

It was a stand off. The only thing missing from the scene seemed to be the bar at the "Longbranch Saloon" and a few rummies nearby playing poker. Then Leroy muscled his way forward like a swaggering 19th century gunfighter out to make a name for himself. "Yes, Boy," he added insultingly. "That's totally unacceptable!"

As insults go I had heard worse but Leroy's was bad enough to spark a good old fashioned donnybrook between the two of them. It ignited in me the urge to patch-things-up-at-any-cost syndrome and without really thinking what I was doing I just reached over and flipped the switch on the ship to shore radio; saying blithely, "Let's see if we can't fix the radio. That way you can call the Coast Guard out of Boothbay for assistance."

There was a crunchy rice-crispy, snap, crackle and pop sound and then quite clearly we heard, "Come in *Savannah's Revenge*. This is Beauregard. Do you hear me? Over and out." The message was repeated again. Unconsciously I glanced at my watch. It was one o'clock. It was 1300 hours. It was the exact time that had been neatly penciled in on the chart.

Talk about being speechless! In fact, I was so speechless that all I could think of to say was to blurt out, "Why your radio works just fine."

"We never said it didn't my deah, did we Leroy," answered Miss Clinging Vine caustically, causing me to experience one of the most infuriating moments of my life. Leroy's response was nothing more than a diabolical chuckle but it served to underscore my naiveté when confronted by people of deceit and guile.

I turned and looked up at Simon. His face appeared to be chiseled out of weathered granite and if he had been startled by the voice out of nowhere there was certainly no indication. My eyes and mouth though opened saucer wide in disbelief, but fortunately before I had the opportunity of putting my foot into my mouth once more he interceded. "I strongly suggest you call the Coast Guard and give them your position. As soon as they confirm and permission is received from them we will leave. Under the circumstances I'm sure Serena feels as I do that we are under no obligation to stay longer."

Simon's suggestion was in reality a command. All that was missing was the "Now hear this" booming over a loudspeaker. Missy Sue and Leroy, however, did not respond like members of the crew. Disregarding Simon's order she reached inside of her nylon windbreaker, pulled out a small gun and after taking dead aim at Simon's middle snarled, "Can the holier than thou attitude."

Leroy's hulking presence backed her up. He gave a sadistic sigh and added, "You will damned well leave when we tell you to leave. Now shut up until we decide what to do!"

I shut up! Believe you me a gun outweighs the threat of no Santa Claus any day of the week. Simon though I thought might blow a gasket - being as how we were also into engines. His face turned almost the shade of an eggplant and for a split second I was afraid he was going to have an apoplectic fit. However I should have known better than to doubt Simon's self control for after clenching and unclenching his fists a few times the purple pallor of his face changed slowly to sunburnt normal. Why, I could almost see a rewarding halo wreath his head as he intoned in what I had learned to be his professorial voice, "It seems to me you don't have a choice; especially since you are so reluctant to accept help from the Coast Guard."

Missy Sue, the former Miss Clinging Vine but currently known to me as Vinegar Head seethed back at Simon with, "As I recall no one asked for your opinion."

Simon ignored her and spoke directly to Leroy. "It won't do any good to take *Escape* and go pick up a part because to reiterate it will take the facilities of a machine shop to repair *Savannah*'s engine."

"We have only your word on that, Boy," Leroy replied evenly.

Listening to their repartee was like witnessing the skirmish before Armageddon. Why I thought of that battle at this particular moment I will never know. I do know that I was beginning to get claustrophobic, club-sandwiched as I was between two warring Goliaths, a black Maria and the instrument panel. Swooning I thought might gain me a little more space but then blacking out would mean missing a minute or two of the action. Furthermore my neck was beginning to ache from staring up so I changed venues and admired Leroy's topsiders which must have been at least a size 13. Just the perfect size for stepping on, which I promptly did murmuring politely, "Oops, I'm sorry."

Leroy and Simon were startled, but Simon took advantage of the momentary break by edging back a little and out onto the deck - though still very watchful and respectful of Vinegar Head's great equalizer.

At last I was able to gasp a free breath even though my heart started pounding harder as Simon shrugged his shoulders and said curtly to Leroy, "True, but if I was on your tight schedule and carrying the amount of drugs you are I wouldn't want to waste any more time before unloading them than I had to."

An audible hiss, much like a leaking balloon, escaped from Missy Sue's mouth. Leroy stiffened and with his fists raised moved in a stalking pugilistic way closer to Simon. "As if I care what you would and would not do!"

Simon shrugged his shoulders. "Suit yourself!"

Leroy moved closer, his chin thrust out like a battering-ram, his manner belligerent. Simon didn't budge so much as an inch, his chin tucked in like an impregnable fortress, his manner combative. Even his choice of words as he railed against Leroy were the same as if he had thrown down the gauntlet. "We have a schedule too you know, and it will only be a short matter of time before the Coast Guard is alerted to a possible mishap."

Simon's revealing word, "Drugs," had struck home. How he knew for sure was beyond me but I was too much in awe of my own newly discovered knowledge to be speechless. I simply could not contain myself and spouted out, "The garbage bags - you're taking them to Halfway Rock." Not content with leaving well enough alone I triumphantly added, "The notepad with its list of harbors. Why you've made pick ups and deliveries all along the coast."

Ah, how sweet was the taste of making Vinegar Head and Leroy eat crow pie. I truly savored the moment as I watched them both blanch and then immediately regretted my outburst as I realized that if there ever was an apropos time for playing dumb this was certainly it. "Ninny," Gloria would have scolded, "for letting yourself be drawn into playing a trump card so early in the game." Well it was too late for crying over the spilled milk - whatever - for by then the astounded look which had flooded Simon's face was replaced by one of deep anxiety; whereas Missy Sue's and Leroy's had changed to a sinister grimace.

In fact, so intense was the evil emanating from them both that it seemed to permeate the air - creating a vacuum - suffocating me until I finally stepped backwards and accidentally bumped into Simon.

Simon's reaction from the sudden impact was like that of anyone else trying to prevent someone from falling. His arms automatically encircled my shoulders, gripping them for a second or two while I regained my footing. It's odd, it has always been truly odd that a fleeting moment can change a person's life forever, but our touching at this instance was electrifying and every bit as potent as the surge of delight I felt when experiencing the protective hardness of his body against mine.

Missy Sue's reaction to Simon's firm but tender grip on me was not like that of a normal person. She obviously sensed what had just transpired between Simon and me. Her black eyes narrowed - the pupils became dots of hatred and an expression of malevolent cunning possessed her face. Motioning with her gun she shouted at me, "Move aside!"

Now I have never, never, never liked shouting. Indeed, I always tried to avoid it, even to my detriment at times. This day was different! There had already been too much shouting. I felt the hair rising on the back of my neck and with the devil still in control of my soul I threw caution to the wind and shouted right back, "I'm not programmed to do that!"

Leroy burst out laughing at my defiance but Vinegar Head was definitely not amused. In one swift stride she struck me across the face with her hand, commanding Leroy at the same time to, "Shut up!"

It was such a hard blow and I was so unprepared for it that I staggered against the table, falling quite hard onto the deck. I felt a spurt of blood inside my mouth which gushed out as I gasped from the jolt.

Simon became enraged. He lunged forward like a charging bull, roaring as he attempted to knock the gun out of her hand, "You God damned whoring bitch. You'll pay for that!"

Leroy jumped forward, swiftly whipping a revolver out from underneath his windbreaker. He rammed it into Simon's ribs, his threatening words, "Don't try it, you bastard," lingering ominously in the air.

There was complete silence. Even the sea gulls stopped quarreling over a dead fish that washed ashore. The four of us were sort of at a standstill; only our deep and uneven breathing testimony to the previous struggle. No longer was there any need for secrecy on their part for we knew what was camouflaged in the garbage bags. What remnant was left of their thin veneer of civility which they had used to masque their faces was slowly peeled away. For a brief crazy moment the scene reminded me of seeing laundry blowing on a line. It was all there for all to see.

Simon and Leroy, it was easy to see, were sizing each other up. From my reversed bird's-eye view they reminded me of two boxers circling in the ring; searching for each other's soft spot and just waiting for the bell to ring. Both were strong and though Simon was taller by about an inch, Leroy it seemed did have a slight edge when it came to weight. Both had been cast in a Paul

Bunyan type of mold, though Leroy's muscular build appeared to be that of a body builder toned from working out in a gym whereas Simon's build seemed to reflect the honing that only a life spent challenging the elements of sea and land can produce. He was lean - all muscle. There was no evidence of fat or softness in his belly area (like Daddy would say in describing a boxer) as there was in Leroy's which was now becoming apparent to me after closer scrutiny. This hint of pudginess stood out like a flare; signaling endurance wise he would not be able to keep up for even his breathing was still labored after such a short scuffle. Somehow I knew Simon had also discovered this weakness in Leroy's armor and had carefully stored this knowledge away for future use.

What Leroy was thinking of Simon as he continued to threaten him with his revolver was a mystery to me, just as what Simon was thinking of Leroy was a mystery. However judging from the wary look on both of their faces, their thoughts must have been along the same wave length of treating each other as formidable adversaries. The sought after prize of course being their respective freedom.

So here I was sprawled on the deck nursing my bruised pride; trying to keep tabs on Simon and Leroy and trying to mind read Missy Sue. She was a challenge and she definitely was no clinging vine or some dumb so called "Southern Belle" just out for a Maine cruise. Vinegar Head was positively in charge and I had discovered the hard way that Leroy obeyed her orders.

Looking at her and her small pistol, literally from the ground up, I was surprised to not be the least bit surprised when she said, "We will tow *Savannah's Revenge* back to the marina."

It was logical. It made sense. In fact, it was the only thing it seemed to me they could do for everything Simon had said was true and apparently Missy Sue had thoroughly digested all the facts. We would be missed if not back by a certain time. Our destination for the day was known by many and it would just be a matter of time before the Coast Guard was notified with a description of *Escape*. Known by many included Mrs. Linette. Today, being a Tuesday, she would be at The Barnacle. I had left the key on the porch swing as per her instructions if I wasn't home. I also had taken the time to scribble a note detailing my planned run for the day and knowing about her romantic soul I had also written I would call when I got home around dinner time to give her a blow by blow description of all my boating mistakes. I even had added a postscript, "To also let you know if Simon and I become better acquainted!!!"

I felt certain that Missy Sue knew that the area between Boothbay and Portland was well patrolled during the tourist season, to say nothing of all the lobstermen who would pick up an SOS on their short wave radios. Being no fool, she would have also realized that *Escape*, being the much smaller boat, didn't carry as much fuel as *Savannah's Revenge* so if they left Simon and me on the island and commandeered *Escape*, she and Leroy would have to pull into a marina sooner than planned for fuel. They too would have been notified. There would be delays too in towing *Savannah's Revenge* to another marina for repairs because at Riggs Marina, Simon had carte blanche and could order work to be done immediately.

All this information I'm sure was being sifted rapidly through her warped mind for she began to tap her foot nervously against the deck. Poor deah! For a twinkling I felt sorry for her as I wondered what kind of sadistic person she and Leroy had to answer to. However, it was a very quick twinkle. After seeing my blood drip onto my new white fisherman's knit sweater I muttered, "That's their problem; Simon's and mine is to survive."

Though I sounded confident - at least to myself - surviving I knew was not going to be easy. Especially after Missy Sue motioned to me with her pistol and ordered in a scathing tone, "Move it!"

Now I have never, never, never liked some slang expressions and "Move it" is one of those near the top of my list. Even though I knew I had acted before in a very stupid way - definitely not worthy of a Bradford - the stubborn streak which I admit to having started to rear its ugly head. Right here and now, I decided, that if I am going to have to "Move it," moving "It" will be done on my terms.

I glanced up at Simon. His murmured counsel, "Stay cool, Serena," accompanied by a look much like the withering one I used to get for misbehaving in public effectively squelching my about to be impetuous behavior. So instead of provoking Vinegar Head with another, "I'm not programmed to do that," I procrastinated in getting up. I redid both of my sneaker laces and then slowly picked myself up and as I did wiped the oozing blood away from my mouth with the back of my hand. The sight of it fomented a rebellion in me - the seeds of which I had been told are present in all Bradford women, according to Grandfather, but only seem to sprout mysteriously every other generation in one member of the Yankee side of the family. So being the cursed one with the "Damning Defect" - after all, it was the only logical explanation the family could give for my running off to France - I stood impatiently on the deck but listening intently to the great debate that was following her "Move it" edict, as to who was going to tow *Savannah's Revenge*.

As so often happens in the real world a discussion mushrooms into an argument, such as the dispute now raging between Vinegar Head and Leroy. Finally, Leroy stepped back a couple of feet from Simon, though he kept his gun aimed at him. He looked quickly at me and licked his lips in a manner reminiscent of Caesar licking his chops in anticipation of a forthcoming treat before speaking forcefully. "I'll take Serena with me in *Savannah*. Simon can go with you, Missy Sue, in *Escape*."

"No you will not," replied Missy Sue emphatically.

Hallelujah! This was one of her orders that I could live with for the thought of being alone on a boat with Leroy had as much appeal as being in a cage with a hungry tiger. Missy Sue must have been thinking of this too though her thoughts, I was willing to bet, were more along the line of me being alone in the cabin with a lustful Leroy. Finally, she ordained with eyebrows raised, "Leroy, you and Simon will go in *Escape*. Being experienced skippers that's the logical boat for you both to be in."

"It's too risky," bellowed Leroy. "I can't watch Simon and pilot the boat at the same time. Just as it's too risky if Simon

138

does the piloting. That's giving him control of our only functioning engine."

At this point my mind began to wander, not from the problem of who was going to do the towing from *Escape*, but from having to hear their haranguing each other. Back and forth, forth and back they went: Missy Sue suggesting they encapsulate Simon and me in *Savannah* while they did the towing back to the marina in *Escape*; Leroy nixing that idea as not being smart since it would give Simon the opportunity to send out a Mayday over the radio. Neither of them mentioned gagging and tying us up which seemed to me like such a perfect solution - having been into whodunits the earlier part of the summer.

Simon was still standing stiffly in front of Leroy, alert and mindful of his gun and that of Missy Sue's. He was also watching me, his eyes still signaling, "Stay cool, Serena."

Well, I was cool and during this highly vocal interval I was definitely not just standing there doing nothing but occupying deck space. I had been listening intently and the seeds of rebellion sprouted a few seconds ago had germinated into a plot - not just worthy of a Bradford - but truly touching on the stature of Lucrezia Borgia.

Again, I went over the plot in my mind, probing for flaws. I could find none since it was based on the simple premise that of the four of us I definitely was the novice. To my way of thinking I would be permitted to do something only because Missy Sue and Leroy would consider me incapable of doing anything brilliantly devious. That was Simon's and my edge.

So, I stood a little straighter and boldly asserted myself. "I will tow the boat."

The three of them just stared vacuously at me. I, in Brahmin arrogance stared right back at them. "Simon has given me several lessons this summer on boat towing," I lied brashly and then added quickly before my courage ebbed, "I know I'm quite capable of towing *Savannah* back to the marina especially with the three of you to mind the lines."

I didn't dare look at Simon while telling such bald faced lies. When I finally did I was sort of half expecting him to be eggplant purple but instead he appeared quite calm as his eyes met and held mine in a very steady gaze. I crossed my fingers and silently murmured a prayer for their approbation as I continued to try and put my plan into action. "We could go in *Escape* together," I said earnestly to Missy Sue. "Why you could drive and I could follow the chart."

Then with what I hoped was just the right amount of guileless soft-soap I asked, "Or perhaps you would prefer to navigate since I'm such a beginner and am just now learning about the different buoys?"

It appeared I had struck gold, for after Missy Sue and Leroy held a whispered conference she took on a very superior air. "Simon, you will go with Leroy in *Savannah*," she said curtly. Then brandishing her gun at me she announced, "And as for you, My Deah, you will go in *Escape* with me. You will pilot the boat and I will do the difficult navigating."

Touché!

Chapter 14

It seemed like a decade was going to pass before we were ready to cast off from the wharf at Bald Head Island, but working under such threatening surveillance was slowing us down. Of course it would have helped if Missy Sue and Leroy could have made up their respective minds as to how they wanted to get three boats away from the wharf at once. After Missy Sue screamed, "Be sure the lines are secure, Leroy; sometimes you tie a sloppy bowline," Leroy asserted himself and certainly did speed up the business at hand with a yell, "God damn it to hell, Missy Sue, shut up and let me handle this problem. You just keep your gun aimed at where it will do the most good. At Simon's middle!"

A ludicrous picture of Leroy bending down and struggling with a bowline jus' like po' little ole me flashed through my mind. I giggled. It was a faux pas on my part of course.

Leroy turned towards me, his expression mean and frightening. "Serena, go turn the dinghy around so she is facing the river and then stand by." Shaking his finger at me he added sharply, "And I don't want to hear any more of 'I'm not programmed to do that' crap from you! Understand?"

I understood, just as I understood the warning behind Simon's contrived fit of coughing that it would be wise to do as I was told. So I turned to do Leroy's bidding but not quite fast enough to suit him. With one arm he grabbed me around my shoulders and neck, pulling me close, close enough for me to feel his hot breath on the back of my neck. With his other arm he circled my waist, making a point of stopping half way around to ram his gun into my side. "Okay, Mont, if you value your mermaid's life you will do exactly as I say!"

Leroy tightened his grip. He was so close that I could feel him speaking. "One more body stuffed in a green garbage bag means nothing to me." He laughed fiendishly. "Besides I have always wanted to witness a burial at sea."

This time, if Leroy hadn't been holding onto me, I would have fainted; no wonder one of the bags on board *Savannah* had been so bulky. As it was I winced from the pressure he was exerting on me. I tried not to, but I did.

Simon's eyes seemed to send out blue sparks of flame so great was his anger at Leroy. The muscles in his neck and across his back and shoulders tightened noticeably. Even his hands betrayed the turmoil raging within him for he kept them clenched like they were two hammers. However he stood in front of us, suggesting an image to me very much like an object in a still life painting which would have had to be labeled "Self Restraint." He had no choice!

Missy Sue on the other hand did have a choice and showing no restraint whatsoever shouted, "Enough of your stupid theatrics, Leroy! The man is right! Time is of the essence so let's get this show on the road! We still might be able to make our rendezvous with Beauregard though we dare not make radio contact to let him know that under the circumstances we will be running late."

Somewhat surly, Leroy released me from his grip. This time I raced to do his bidding while Simon moved to follow Vinegar Head's order, "Turn *Escape* around to face the river and then walk her up to the end of the wharf. Be sure she is well secured!"

Leroy shoved his revolver into the side pocket of his windbreaker and swaggered towards Simon and *Savannah's Revenge*. He issued his own orders. "As soon as you quit foolin' around, Boy, turn *Savannah* in the same direction. Be quick about it. As the lady says, 'Let's get this show on the road.'"

I detected in Leroy a bundle of resentment when he said, "As the lady says;" his emphasizing of the word lady leaving no doubt that he was royally miffed at Missy Sue for dressing him down in front of Simon and me. This thought made me bolder and after the three boats were turned around and the towing lines in place I risked the wrath of Missy Sue literally coming down on me again by reaching out and gripping Simon's arm. "Try to throw your chart away," I said as softly as possible.

Simon replied quickly in a barely audible voice. "Don't forget you have to adjust your speed in order to keep the lines taut between the boats. Try to keep three wave lengths between *Escape* and *Savannah* and above all, Serena, don't do anything foolish! What I said before about delivering drugs was just an educated guess. Now we know for sure! They are desperate and will let no one stand in their way."

I gave Simon my best pixie like smile and squeezed his arm, the feeling of his strength beneath my fingers giving me the courage I needed to go on just as his touching of my arm a couple of hours ago had done. "Trust me," I murmured.

There was nothing murmured about Missy Sue's next order. Her, "Let's go," came through loud and clear. She and I boarded *Escape*, me first, she showing me the way to the Almighty Captain's seat with a wave of her gun. Simon and Leroy boarded *Savannah*, Simon first, Leroy showing him the way to the bow with a wave of his gun.

So here I was beginning my second epic voyage of the day. Buoyed up by such inspiring thoughts as Simon and I are the guys in the white hats and Missy Sue and Leroy in the black I turned on *Escape*'s engine, quite confident that it would turn over promptly which it did. Sneaking a quick glance at Missy Sue reminded me that I had forgotten to check the bilge. I did. It was dry.

For the next couple of minutes Missy Sue and I worked as a team while we responded to Leroy's shout, "Cast off," and then, "Take her out!" She untied *Escape*'s dock lines and hauled in the fenders. As soon as her task was done I took *Escape*'s engine out of idling position, pushed the lever forward slowly to No Wake Speed and set our floating caravan into motion.

Escape responded quite well to her flagship status but I could not say the same for me, her dauntless captain, for by the time we cleared the harbor and passed the black and white mid-channel marker I was muttering, "I want my mommy!" Everything seemed to be going wrong at once. The waves, though not high, were not dividing themselves properly so I couldn't tell if *Savannah* was one, two or three wave lengths behind me. I got a crick in my neck from glancing back so much. All of a sudden, all I could see through the windshield was a swirling foggy wall of white. Ruefully I remembered Simon's warning, "You know the weather is fickle, Serena. A fog bank could sneak in on us." That made me think of Vinegar Head so I

143

sneaked another quick glance at her. She was holding my chart that I had drawn my course on, peering at me just like a giant squid peers at its prey before devouring them in inky darkness.

I panicked, breaking the first Rule of the Road. My heart started to fibrillate. I couldn't remember which switch turned on the wipers so I could clear away the soupy fog from the windshields. It was engulfing us, completely swallowing *Savannah*, darkening the sky like a huge shade being lowered in order to blot out the sun. I forgot which way I was going! North? South? Somewhere in between?

The blatant sound of *Savannah*'s horn followed by a sharp shuddering tug triggered my return to intrepidness. A minute later *Savannah* tooted again, her one long blast followed by two short ones completely defogging my mind. The series of blasts also ushered in the memory of my lessons on sound signals and I remembered that this sequence of blasts was the died-in-wool approved one by the Coast Guard for motorboats underway and towing another vessel. Goodness knows I had spent hours and hours trying to memorize the Rules of the Road as set forth in the United States Power Squadron manual only to learn from Simon that sound signals it seemed were hardly ever observed by small craft and that unfortunately the only signal everyone did remember was the three short blasts for "Come and pick me up."

So I decided to take a chance on Missy Sue not accurately remembering the different warning blasts and to capitalize on her startled behavior by trying to put Phase II of my plot into action. "Perhaps they want us to check the tow lines," I said knowing full well she couldn't really check the lines without examining them which meant either the gun or the chart would have to be momentarily set aside. I gambled on it not being the gun, my recently acquired fear of them being almost as paranoid as was my fear of the ocean. Besides I had not programmed a gun into my grandiose scheme for the Battle of Riggs Cove.

To my relief Vinegar Head nodded in compliance. I crossed my fingers and held my breath as I watched her get up and head towards the stern. Miraculously she put the chart down on the open side of the boat behind me and when she bent down to examine one of the lines I aided the wind by pushing it overboard. Having accomplished this bit of skullduggery I turned back around in my seat and busied myself by finally figuring out which switch was the one for the windshield wiper. I turned it on, mentally congratulating myself for at last realizing that if I had come Southerly down the river I had to go back by a Northerly course.

After giving myself a big pat on the back for remembering where I was I risked taking another peek at Missy Sue. She was standing in the bow staring at the water, shaking her head, an expression of disbelief on her face. "My God, I've lost the chart," I heard her say. She repeated herself but in a louder voice to me. "My God, I've lost the chart."

How utterly too, too divine it was to hear those words. How sweet it was to hear the tremor in her voice. "Never mind," I consoled in what was obviously a successful deadpan manner for she returned to her seat beside me, "I have my own detailed navigation list we can use."

Mindful of her gun I pulled the list out from underneath the extra cushion I used on the pilot's seat to boost myself higher. "This was my lesson for today," I explained handing it to her. "Every navigational marker for my course between here and the marina is written down. Also the time it took me to reach each one traveling at six knots; for you see I was trying to learn the rudiments of dead reckoning."

"I'm not blind," Missy Sue snapped while perusing the list. A few seconds later she ordered waspishly, "Mind where you are going!"

So I minded where I was going and not wanting to press my luck I blocked out the presence of the rapacious Harpy seated next to me and concentrated solely on what was obliterated ahead. I checked the compass reading to be sure it pointed North for that would mean sooner or later some spit of land or marker that I was familiar with would pop into view. However, in the interim, I had to be sure whatever it was - land or marker - didn't pop up under the boat until I was ready.

So we continued very slowly on to homebase, *Savannah* faithfully heralding our progress and every so often Missy Sue checking her phantom like umbilical lines just to be sure they were okay. And then such is the magic of the Maine coast the curtain of fog lifted leaving our caravan basking in the mid-afternoon sun on a dazzling frothy blue ocean. Being a most grateful neophyte I watched the silent, swirling grayness of it float on towards land, hugging the water and then every once in a while lifting a bit to let me peek underneath.

A person would have thought that I had been at sea as long as the "Ancient Mariner" from the way I reacted to the unveiling of Hendrix Head Light. "Hallelujah," I shouted to no one in particular. "Saints be praised! It's the lighthouse!"

Even Missy Sue seemed to unbend and thaw under the warmth of the sun. She forgot to scowl when Dogfish Head appeared through the mist and by the time we reached Humpback Rock she had managed a fissure of a smile. It was fleeting at best.

A muffled shout from Leroy caught her attention. Vinegar Head stood up, changed her mind and sat back down. "If you are thinking, Serena, of continuing up the Sheepscot River from here instead of heading West into Blind Rocks Passage, don't!" She raised her gun to my left temple and lowering her voice to a snake-like hiss whispered, "It could prove to be unhealthy for you."

I nodded and obediently began to turn *Escape* into the passage, not making a sharp right angle turn like I had done on the day of my graduation run but a gradual one that spread our wake out into a large semicircle. Satisfied with my performance, Missy Sue got up and went back to the stern shouting, "I didn't hear you, Leroy!"

"Maintain your same rate of speed while going through the passage," Leroy shouted back and at the same time shortened up the tow lines between *Escape* and *Savannah*.

That was definitely not what I wanted to do! I wanted to get the agony over with by going full speed ahead through the narrow stretch of hell. I was sorely tempted to retort, "I'm not programmed to do that," when Simon reiterated loudly the same order, "Maintain your same rate of speed while going through the passage, Serena." It was as if he knew what I was thinking.

Vinegar Head must have been reading my mind too for she acknowledged their order by moving to the seat behind me. "More power is not always the best way, my deah," she quipped. "I'm sure you don't want anything to happen to your friend," she added in a chilling tone a second later.

That was the first true statement she had made all day and it sobered me up to the extent that I became more determined than ever to put Phase III of my plot into action. But first I had to get through Blind Rocks Passage.

I glanced at my watch as our caravan started through the passage. It was approximately two hours before low tide - the peak of the ebb as Gloria would say - and naturally the outgoing rush of water was racing like a mad dervish on its way to the ocean. We passed by as if on parade the three green beacons marking the safe way to enter Blind Rocks with nary a squawk of protest from the feathered sentinels perched on top. We passed beacon G "4" successfully, the tide visibly swifter, Missy Sue pursing her lips as she checked the beacon's number against my list. "Leroy and I came to the marina in June by cruising down from Arnold so this branch of the river is not familiar. However, so far your diagram appears to be accurate, Serena. For your sake and that of Simon's, let us hope so!"

I had never seen a more perfect sneer. Her voice, bare of civility, could not possibly have been more menacing. A couple of hours earlier the combination would have sent my heart pounding but I remained calm. Grateful too, for the unexpected knowledge Missy Sue had unwittingly given to me that they were not overly familiar with their surroundings would make it easier to carry out Phase III of my brilliant plot.

We began to pass can buoy "3" marking the junction of the Little Sheepscot River and the Sasanoa, its green color reminding me of the new green road signs that had sprouted up recently all over the island. The installation of them had caused a furor, we "summer complaints" wanting the anonymity that comes from having no signs, the locals wanting just the opposite. In the end the fire department settled the dispute, had its way and won! And in the end, if I didn't stop my daydreaming the frenzied river would settle our dispute with Missy Sue and Leroy, have its way by claiming us and win!

As we pulled away from the buoy the full force of the tide battered the boats. The river spumed up like a pan full of boiling water, creating whirlpools that eddied in frightening suction. It felt like riding on a giant roller coaster and the Whirling Teacups at the same time. I couldn't grip the wheel tight enough. The tender it seemed was going to wrap itself around the red nun buoy - pulling all of us behind and down in a twirling, top like spin - while *Savannah* appeared determined to moor us on the seaweed covered rocks on our left. *Escape* began to shudder and buck as the lines holding the two of us together became quite taut. I thought for sure her stern was going to be ripped apart heaving us out along with her splintered remains to float down and die on the cold muddy floor of the underworld among all those lurking, creepy, crawly unspeakable creatures. But being true blue to her colors *Escape* rallied and her engine steadily purred us forward past beacon "5" marking Dead Man's Point and away from the turbulent water into the calm of Knubble Bay.

Giddy with success I triumphantly turned around to receive my due accolades - flowers strewn gratefully at my feet would be acceptable. Instead there was a glowering Missy Sue wiping the spray off of her face like a dampened cat and in *Savannah*, Simon and Leroy were once again busy shortening up her tethering lines. Strictly business as usual!

"Take the boats to the furthest mooring, Serena," shouted Simon. "That's the last one to the left of the marina as you head down into the cove."

I didn't argue since his order dovetailed quite nicely with my devilish plot. Having already turned *Escape* left towards Riggs Cove when I passed Dead Man's Point, I throttled her down to a slower pace and after Leroy's shout, "Not so fast, Serena," to almost No Wake Speed and plunged confidently forward humming, "Onward Christian soldiers, marching us to war."

The refrain had somehow sneaked in over the transom and though not being a blasphemous person I thought for sure I could see, "The cross of Jesus going on before." It appeared brilliantly in the distance, beckoning me forward into battle to right a wrong.

As I reached the marina my guiding bright light that was "going on before" merged into the green day beacon that I had learned separated Part A of Riggs Cove from Part B, and far more importantly for me marked the rocky ledge visible only at low tide that jutted out from the shore. It was this limish-green beacon, this reed of truth, this symbol of nautical integrity flaunted as usual by a squawking feathered friend on top which had become the sublime object of my attention; not only of my attention but the sublime object of my direction.

Once again Missy Sue sat down beside me, taking the time to carefully scrutinize my navigation list. I took advantage of her momentary lack of interest in me by slowing *Escape* down to No Wake Speed and then keeping my eyes on the red mooring, slightly altered my course so it was dead ahead and to the right of the beacon. Satisfied my course was correct I looked across the aisle at Vinegar Head. She was staring right back at me, a sardonic grimace on her face that twisted her lips as she began to speak. "Your list of navigational aids seems to be rather incomplete, my deah."

What she said was true! My list was incomplete for I had started it with the flashing beacon marking Dead Man's Point. I had seen no reason when preparing my diagram for entering the one which was home base. After all I knew the slinky rocks were there, especially after witnessing one mind boggling smash up when a zippy red cigarette type boat jutted over the ledge a little before low tide due to pilot error and ended up reduced to a stub. That mishap had happened just a few days prior to my last lesson and I could still see in my mind the hullabaloo it caused which was probably why after being clobbered by Missy Sue the idea projected itself for demolishing *Savannah's Revenge*. Of course I didn't want to go that far - Simon was on board - but a few shattered boards and a severed drive shaft would do quite nicely.

I took a final peek at my watch - a little less than an hour and a half to go before the drain out. The tide was now perfect for me to accomplish such a splintering task! *Escape*, according to my squirreled away snatches of conversation would just barely skim over the tip tops of the rocks whereas *Savannah*, being larger and drawing more water, would come to a grinding, screeching halt beaching herself right on top like a huge whale. So I ignored Missy Sue's caustic comment about my list and with the prospect of being able to salt away forever two thugs from Hel radiated as much sweetness and innocence as I could stomach and asked, "Would you mind grabbing the mooring line?"

I didn't give her a chance to say, "No!" Reaching behind me I removed the boat hook from its proper storage spot and handed it to her. In so doing my eyes met and held Simon's for a brief moment. It was as if he knew what I had in mind for he sat down on *Savannah*'s starboard side and gripped the railing.

Victory was now within my grasp! Like a nervous Nellie I watched Missy Sue march forward to the bow toting the boat hook as if it was a spear. Her absence from my side was like a breath of fresh air, relieving me of any doubts I might have harbored about not succeeding. Mustering up all my courage I pushed the throttle forward slowly, watching the little wand on the RPM dial start to climb higher. *Escape* responded to my touch like a cup winner. *Savannah*, of course, had no choice but to tag along behind.

Vinegar Head did not acquiesce so graciously. She started screaming. "You damned idiot, you're supposed to be going slower not faster." That compliment was followed rapidly by a stamp of her foot. "You dimwitted moron, mind the beacon. Rocks could be there."

Having kept quiet for such a long time I couldn't resist retorting, "I can't hear you, if you shout!"

Missy Sue's eyes started to roll back into her head. "Go to the left of the beacon you God damned slut," she screamed like a cat at rutting time and in a furious fit threw the boat hook right at the windshield.

Being by now a tarnished cherub I shouted right back to her. "That oversized twig. Don't give it a second thought. It's just a decoration for the restaurant at the marina."

With that lie I shoved the lever as far as it would go. Nothing happened! For a suspenseful second it seemed like a life or death game of tug or war was being waged between *Escape* on one end of the tethering lines straining to go forward and on the other end *Savannah* aided by the ebbing tide reluctant to give way. The contest lasted as long as the blink of an eye before the full power of *Escape*'s engine took over and thrust us forward.

Like lightening we swished safely over the rocks leaving behind my breath and a very substantial wash. Halfway during the swish *Escape*'s bow shot almost straight up into the air sending Missy Sue flying across to the other side of the boat and sending me into hysterics for fear of being pitch-poled right out of my seat onto the top of *Savannah*. A shuddering, terrific jolt shook *Escape* and our aerobatics over the water stopped abruptly to the most glorious, delightful, exhilarating tune of a boat's bottom and engine being run aground.

The impact set Missy Sue careening back and forth in the boat like a yo-yo while pitching me forward against the wheel and then back against the seat. She ended up dangling over the port side, silent for once, and I ended up with the presence of mind to turn the engine off and then dashing forward pushed her and her gun overboard.

After that I too was quiet for once, taking a moment to bow my head in silent tribute to *Escape*'s stalwart seaworthy soul. She wasn't just a tub of nuts and bolts and chrome dials. She wasn't just a smelly engine. She did indeed have heart!

My silent tribute to *Escape* over I looked up, seeing what Adam would have called in his adolescent cop and robber school boy days a mop up operation being played out in front of me. Simon, thank goodness, managed to come up smelling like a rose - being as how I was into roses this day - and just succeeded right in front of my eyes in giving Leroy a hard punch to the jaw which knocked him overboard. Missy Sue was bobbing up and down like a cork in the water, her outpouring of profanity fortunately garbled from swallowing too much water. Against my better judgment I threw her a life preserver. Simon, his thought I know more noble than mine, threw one to Leroy.

On the shore the marina came suddenly to life, positively buzzing with activity like that of an overturned beehive. On the water the different sounds of many engines being started up at once gave a promise that rescue was at hand.

The lobster boat *Amie* with Abel at her helm pulled up broadside of *Escape*'s stern. She had come steaming out of nowhere or so it seemed. That is until Abel started to shout out an explanation over the drone of *Amie*'s idling diesel engine. "You passed by me at the head of the Little Sheepscot, Serena. Saw you and Simon were in trouble so I sent out an SOS to the Coast Guard, the Marine Patrol and to the marina."

"Oh," I answered not too brightly.

No sooner said than a Coast Guard cutter emerging from Blind Rocks Passage bore down on us like a swooping eagle, horn blaring and whoop whooping, and someone on board bellowing over a loud speaker, "Heave to!"

We had already, "Heaved to," *Savannah* literally, but leave it to the Brass to be redundant.

Next to be heard from was the Marine Patrol. The dark green cruiser darted out from Knubble Bay like it had been catapulted off a carrier, their speed in bearing down on us giving credence to the scuttlebutt that the boat had the capability to go fast enough to break the sound barrier.

Both official vessels converged on the left hand side of the green beacon and their respective skippers, just like bureaucrats arguing over who gets what piece of the pie, began to verbally skirmish over who was going to pick up whom. Proper introductions then being made to Simon and me, Lieutenant Fogg of the United States Coast Guard, starchly outranking Officer Pennel of the state's Marine Patrol - in girth too - laid claim to Leroy and Missy Sue. "Stand-by to pick up survivors," he ordered crisply to a seaman obviously on the low end of the totem pole like me.

Officer Pennel being permitted to rescue Simon and I, adroitly maneuvered the patrol boat around *Amie* and alongside of *Escape*'s bow. I tied a couple of fenders and quickly put on my life jacket just so he would know that I had some smarts left. He smiled. "Always wise to take precautions. Right?"

"Right," I replied, acknowledging his smile with a smile.

"Are you okay, Miss?"

"Yes, I'm fine, Officer Pennel, though I'm not sure about *Escape*'s hull and propeller. There is a chance she could have

152

been scraped and dented up a bit when skimming across the rocks."

"Best not to take any chances! Throw us a line and then release the tow lines to *Savannah's Revenge* before *Escape* drifts onto the rocks. We will secure her to the mooring dead ahead, take you ashore and then come back to determine the damage. Any personal things on board you might want to bring along."

So precise were his orders that I almost saluted and shouted, "Aye, aye, SIR!" However under these circumstances, I decided such behavior would be unseemly. I did the appropriate and followed his orders, this time having no qualms about saying before I started to board the patrol boat, "I have a fear of falling into the water, especially when climbing between two boats."

Officer Pennel was very understanding. So was the other officer on board who stood up immediately and gallantly assisted me in making the hop from one boat to another. "Officer Baker at your service," he said. "No need to apologize. Everyone has their hang ups. Mine is a fear of heights."

Somehow I felt better, making the switch without a hitch into the stern of the cruiser, letting myself become aware once more of the drama being played out in front of me. On the shore the local fire engine had arrived, its red brilliance plainly visible beyond a grove of tall pines. Parked beside it was the island's new ambulance and next to it a white patrol car with blue lights still flashing pulled alongside. Obviously the sheriff had arrived.

On the water Missy Sue and Leroy were now on board the cutter and were swathed in blankets, both to my delight having had to suffer the indignity of being hauled out of the water looking like competitors in a wet T-shirt contest and both hopefully fretting over what life would be like in "The Big Stew Pot."

Abel, not being one to be bedazzled by the hierarchy according to Daddy, was proceeding with his own plans to rescue Simon. "None of us can get any closer," he called out to him, "and I know God damn well you don't want to spend the next five hours stranded on that damn rock! Course, you could elect to abandon ship in one of Fogg's canvas sling buckets, but speaking strictly for myself mind you, I wouldn't trust one of those contraptions as far as I could throw it which ain't far! So, I'll tie another length of line on the dinghy and then toss it to you. She's made of rubber, light in weight, has a flat bottom and should glide right over the top of the ledge. Once you are in it and if you find you can't manipulate the oars because of the low tide I'll haul you back. Comprendre?"

"Comprendre, Abel!"

That had been a long speech for Abel, Mrs.L., usually being the one to indulge herself in such lengthy dialogue. Having tied the extra line onto the dinghy while he spoke, we all watched as Abel heaved it out to Simon; Lieutenant Fogg disapprovingly from the bow of the cutter, his hands on the hips stance speaking louder than words.

I watched anxiously as the line snaked out, unable to keep from gasping just as Officer Pennel and Baker were unable to keep swearing almost simultaneously, "Christ Almighty," and, "Holy hell," respectively at the sight of Simon's bloodied face as he reached up to catch it.

"That must have been one hell of a friendly fight, Simon," Abel shouted. "You sure ain't gonnah win any beauty pageants today!"

To my surprise Simon laughed. "You should see the other fellow close up, Abel."

It appeared there wasn't a moment to spare so hastily did Simon pull the dinghy up to *Savannah*'s bow. Neither did he waste his breath on polite trivia. "Fogg, Pennel, there's a dead man on board stuffed into a garbage bag. There's also a shoot load of drugs. How do you want to handle it?"

This time Officer Pennel spoke first. "Leave the man and the drugs where they are stowed. We will keep the boat under surveillance, wait the tide out and then board!" Fogg agreed, contributing nothing to their conversation.

Simon managed to use the oars, his RPM time in getting away from *Savannah* and back on board the *Amie* greater than the speed of the cutter's or so it seemed. He stood in the stern smiling at me. His gaze was steady, penetrating; his eyes were never bluer. I felt like he was reaching out across this

154

treacherous lead of water to clasp my hand, to comfort me, to reassure me with a firm but gentle squeeze that all was well.

It had been a traumatic day! The sight of Simon's bruised, cut face and his torn stained clothes was moving me to tears. I could feel them coming. At first it was a trickle like a leak in a dyke. Suddenly it was a break in the dam and with a shuddering sob down the spillway they poured. "Jesus," I heard Baker mutter to Pennel. "Let's get the cargo back to shore before all hell breaks loose."

His thought wave must have been hooked up to the wireless since Fogg gave orders immediately to head towards the far end of the dock. The *Amie* followed and we in turn followed her in Pied Piper fashion back to the safety of land, fortunately not disappearing like the children of Hamelin.

As our flotilla pulled up to the dock a welcoming committee stepped forward to greet us like we were visiting dignitaries on an important mission. There was Mr. Macintosh, worried but business like as he greeted Lieutenant Fogg. Standing near him was Dal, eyes opened wide taking in the artillery on the cutter. Then there was the sheriff, resplendent in his brown uniform, and standing behind him the island's volunteer fire chief Rob Green not so nattily dressed having obviously come right from his potter's wheel. Mary Smith, the assistant volunteer fire chief who doubled as the ambulance driver and full timed it as a housewife, was beside him. There were also two touristy looking type men hurrying down the ramp towards our entourage. They were daringly dressed in identical navy blue suits that projected an aura of Washington and the Bureau. "Federal Fuzz," as Gloria would call them when in one of her disrespectful moods.

All of a sudden there was Simon striding across the dock, his behavior similar to that of an anxious parent pacing the floor while waiting for a child to come home. "Are you okay, Serena," he asked while helping Baker tie up. Then, not waiting for an answer as I had so often found happening when dealing with Mother and Daddy, he reached down and literally lifted me onto the dock. The proximity of him produced another body racking sob. "I'm fine," I spluttered, "but you, your face, Simon. It looks so painful."

"I'm sure my face looks worse than it really is, Serena. At least it's nothing that a little soap, water, and a couple of bandages won't cure."

The break in the dam widened, my tears came faster. "Don't cry, Serena," he whispered. "Please, not here. Not here where I can't do anything about it except to keep on repeating myself."

There was a hint of mischief in his voice when he said, "Not here, where I can't do anything about it." My tears stopped flowing. I glanced up, suspecting that by now he would be grinning and that his eyes would be reflecting the change in his mood from one of concern to one of down right merriment.

I was right! He was grinning and his eyes did have that unsettling twinkle in them. "What do you mean, Simon, by do about it?"

"You will see, Serena."

"When?"

"This evening after we have dinner. It's going to take the rest of the afternoon to answer all the questions that I know we are going to be bombarded with by the present constabulary. The Coast Guard will take even longer to satisfy and only God knows what tedious questions the drug agents are going to ask. In other words, Serena, it's going to be one hell of an afternoon!"

I was far more interested in learning about Simon's mysterious "You will see" than to worry about all the forthcoming questions. "What do you mean, Simon? How will I see?"

His chuckle was just loud enough for the welcoming committee to hear and they began to gravitate towards us. He leaned down and speaking very, very softly into my ear said, "You will see because I intend to demonstrate the Mont method for chasing away tears, something I have been aching to do every since your last lesson when I was caught facing this same kind of situation."

Sometimes I could be maddeningly slow on the uptake. It took me a full second to finally fathom Simon's remark. However I made up for lost time by asking quickly, "Where will this demonstration take place, Simon? Your house or mine?"

"Since you asked, let's make it your house, Serena. My place is a fishing camp built for a bachelor, not too many amenities though it is a very nice fishing camp overlooking Knubble Bay."

I took time out to think for a moment about my sudden problem of what to serve a ravenous man being as how Simon had said, "After we have dinner." My culinary skills were limited having been raised in a home with full time live in help and since my divorce leaned towards the lean and simple. Except of course when I went on a chocolate binge. I remembered then, Mrs. Linette having said she was going to make a big pot of fish chowder to help me celebrate my excursion out into the wild blue yonder.

Once again Simon seemed to read my thoughts. "I'll bring pizza, Serena. How does that sound to you?"

"I adore pizza, Simon, but how does a big bowl of Mrs. Linette's fish chowder sound to you? Her's is absolutely out of this world."

"Fish chowder is one of my all time favorites. I'll bring some brie and a couple bottles of wine that I brought back from Montreal." He paused long enough to smile at me in a way that made me think I was his true love before saying, "Something special, Serena, to serve on a special occasion, and only to share with a special someone like you."

You would have thought I had never before been paid a compliment. My insides began to tingle. I couldn't help but blush as I returned his compliment with one of my own. "How sweet of you to say so, Simon," and then with my next breath added, "I know I will enjoy the wine," and then with my next breath blurted out like some addlebrained school girl just what popped into my head. "Caesar, of course, will have his dog chow to eat."

I couldn't believe I had made such an outlandish statement. It was so out of context. It was so vintage me, always stammering something inane after a major crisis or even during a tense, steamy romantic moment. Simon's reaction was swift. "You mean instead of having me to eat?" he asked with just the right amount of tongue-in-cheek humor.

I cracked up! Fortunately, before I had time to put my foot into my mouth again the welcoming committed joined us, Mr. Macintosh leading the flurry of questions with, "Are you hurt, Miss Bradford?" Mary Smith was next in line. "Best come up to the ambulance, Simon, so I can attend to your face." From then on it was just as Simon said it would be, "One hell of an afternoon!"

Chapter 15

What is it about being alone with a handsome virile man in a rambling, umpteen gable turn of the century "cottage" that makes you speechless instead of confessional box loquacious like I had been on Bald Head Island? For by the time Simon and I had finished dinner - which began with the decanting of his wine and a toast, "To good experience," - and we were seated in the study sipping a snifter of brandy I was just that - speechless!

It was as if a spell had been incanted over me or perhaps my silence came because the room was home for so many of my childhood memories and dreams, and those make believe fantasies that I had spirited away from the pages of the books placed on the shelves lining its walls. Even Caesar was quiet. He had stretched out on the floor beside me in lieu of snoozing in his favorite spot smack dab in front of the fireplace. No doubt he thought I needed protection.

Poor Caesar! Poor, dear, sweet, afraid-of-a-raindrop Caesar had become completely discombobulated upon seeing and having another male in the house. He was too polite to growl or bark after being told, "It's okay." However he had let me know of his disapproval by sticking to me like a shadow, sitting beside me throughout dinner like an infatuated swain and all the while keeping a wary eye on Simon, licking his chops every time Simon so much as reached across the table for some oyster crackers to add to his chowder. Caesar had even gone so far as to eavesdrop on our conversation, flexing his ears towards Simon like antenna, intent it seemed on picking up every nuance in his voice.

I smiled, reached down to give him an affectionate rub on his back and then got up to put another birch log on the fire, taking advantage of the activity to try and recapture the stimulating conversation Simon and I had shared earlier in the evening. "I don't think I'll tell my parents or for that matter the rest of the family about our troubles today. Time enough for that when I go home at the end of October and confess that I have been spending this summer taking boating lessons. That alone

159

will put them all into a state of shock. Then, on top of that, hearing the news that I will have to testify in court against Missy Sue and Leroy and that the whole affair has to be treated so hush hush since the so called 'New England Kingpin' of the drug world is still at large will positively send them into orbit. Which reminds me, Simon, I received the marina bill yesterday and the charges for all your lessons were not on it. As I recall I discussed the marina's fee for lessons back in June with Miss Collins when I left an extra set of car keys with her at the office. She said she would make a note to discuss it with you and Mr. Macintosh. I'll have to tell her that she forgot to include them in the bill." I sighed and sat back down, delivering such a long speech for the sake of congeniality leaving me breathless.

Simon gave me an all knowing Buddha like smile. All knowing, because he too seemed to possess the extraordinary extra sixth sense necessary to understand the motives behind a person's actions. Shaking his head as if to say, "There's no need to be nervous," his expression became serious. I gripped the arms of my chair until my fingers tingled, the adventurous part of me curious to know what he was going to say and the serene part of me almost afraid to know after such a harrowing day.

"There was no mistake made on the bill, Serena, which brings up a subject that has been bothering me for some time," was his unexpected reply.

I relaxed my grip on the chair. "What ever could possibly be bothering you, Simon?"

"My conscience, but before I confess to you my sins we must do something about this seating arrangement. Either I'm going to squeeze into that small chair with you or you are going to come over here and sit beside me in this oversized wing chair where we both can be at least comfortable."

The wine and brandy having helped to put me into true form I bantered, "There is the leather sofa. It is a good eight feet long."

"That is about five feet too long for what I have in mind."

"Oh!"

Simon smiled. His smile widened into a grin and he started to laugh. I curled my toes, not into my socks, but into my

Ferragamo sandals. Caesar scrambled to his feet. "Really Serena! I'm not a wolf in sheep's clothing. I'm not going to eat you up." He winked wickedly. "Even though I might be tempted to take a bite or two, especially since I have had to sit here looking at you all evening long dressed the way you are in that green gauzy whatever you call it outfit of yours."

Talk about Caesar having become discombobulated! The poor dear's emotional state was nothing compared to mine. I had never known Simon to tease so much. Up until this minute he had always been so serious, so very proper, so teacher to student. Naturally, being me, I did the usual and blushed, taking refuge quickly behind the only defense that seemed to be at hand, that of discussing women's fashions. "The color is mint green," I corrected. "The material is nainsook, woven from 100% cotton fibers and therefore very cool to wear in the summer." Not willing to leave well enough alone I added, "It's a Hindu word, the 'nain' part of it meaning the eye and the 'sook' part, spelled s u k h in Hindi, meaning pleasure."

Well, I had said it! Yes, indeed, I had said it and in all honesty I could not blame my stupid remark on innocence, my subconscious obviously having surfaced long enough to force me to put into words what I knew to be true - that I had donned the sleeveless V-necked tunic top and pull-on pants with an eye to giving pleasure. Adam had laid the foundation by telling me, "I'd like the outfit if you were my date, especially if we were spending the evening in my pied-a-terre. However, since you are my sister I'd live in fear that you were going to be compromised every time you put it on." Gloria had built upon Adam's sentiments after borrowing the tunic and pants to wear while vacationing in Sardinia. "Paul adored it, Serena," she had confided upon returning. "He said the other guests at the resort were bound to think I was his secretary. Of course it hung a little loose around the bosom, but that's my problem not yours."

True! But then Gloria's so called problem was also my problem in reverse and depended entirely upon another person's point of view. At the moment neither of our problems were as pressing as my present one of trying to decide between exchanging the sanctity of my cozy, little chair for the worldly

161

pleasures possible to experience within the arms of Simon's spacious oversized wing chair custom designed to hold two.

I looked across the coffee table at Simon, no mean distance since the table was an enormous glass topped ship's wheel salvaged from one of great-great-grandfathers fleet of seafaring vessels. Simon said nary a word. He didn't have to, his eyes reflecting the same mixture of warmth and merriment that I had grown accustomed to seeing of late, saying it all.

Simon did look different, but then so did I according to him. Tonight, instead of his customary khaki marine garb he was dressed in all white - a sharp contrast against his tan - just as was the neat white bandage Mary Smith had used on the side of his left temple a contrast to the midnight blackness of his hair and the startling blueness of his eyes. And yet he himself, the inner person who was Simon, didn't appear different at all. There was the same patient - but not Prussian - air about him. The sense of integrity that I had noticed in his face so early in the summer was still there only more pronounced. Perhaps because his tan had deepened accentuating the mirth lines around his eyes and mouth or perhaps it was because I had learned that Simon not only personified but had lived up to the meaning I had gleaned from an artist's concept of "Seaworthy."

I made my decision! Actions speaking louder than words I got up, made a brief detour to give the fire a rejuvenating poke and then sat down beside Simon, pushing myself sideways back into the corner of the chair so I could see him as he talked. Caesar followed, laying down in front of us with an almost human like whine as if to say, "I hope you know what you are doing."

Well I too hoped I knew what I was doing, especially after Simon said, "Don't give me that innocent, eyes as wide as saucers look of yours, Serena. At least not now, not until after I confess my sins to you. Then and then only can I do something about it."

"I don't think I know what you mean," I replied, before taking a sudden interest in my nails.

Simon chuckled. "You know dog-gone well what I mean, Serena. The kind of glance that mists your eyes like they are two

162

stirred turquoise pools of iridescent tropical water. The kind of glance you kept giving me all summer long every time you tried to wheedle out of doing something while on the boat."

"Oh."

"Now then, Serena, please hear me out. What has been bothering me is that I know you are not aware that I knew who you were before I agreed to give you boating lessons."

"Say that again?"

This time Simon smiled instead of chuckling. "It is a mouthful, isn't it? To repeat, I know you are not aware that I knew who you were before I agreed to give you boating lessons."

I sat up straight. "You mean you agreed to give me lessons under false pretenses?"

Simon winced. "Under false pretenses is a very strong phrase, Serena. I can answer truthfully, no, to that. I also can understand why you are so indignant. It is just that under the circumstances, that is because of the circumstances under which we met, that I didn't see the need for telling you that we had previously met up until now and so you see that's why there was not, and never will be, a lesson billed to you."

I sank back into the chair, his pained expression making me sorry I had over reacted. "Talk about a mouthful of words, Simon. Just what is it you are trying to say?"

"I'm trying to say, Serena, that I was the one who helped you in picking up all the cans of food that Caesar had knocked out of the car in Arnold on that hot day in June. That's what I meant by telling you that I knew who you were before I agreed to give you boating lessons. That's what has been bothering me, especially of late."

It took a minute or two for Simon's confession to sink in. "So you were the one besides the policeman to help me," I managed to finally say more to the fire than to him. "As I recall I was crying and I was so ashamed of myself for giving way to tears that I never looked up."

"That's right, you never looked up. But you did say, 'Thank you.'"

"But how did you know that I was me when I spoke to Mr. Macintosh over the telephone about taking lessons?"

"You have a one of a kind Massachusetts license plate. It's hard not to notice it, especially since it is imprinted with the letters S E R E N A."

"I see." But yet, I didn't see. I turned, drawing my legs up against my chest so I could have room enough to look at him right in the face while asking, "Now let me get this straight, Simon. If I understand you correctly, what you are telling me is that you would not have agreed to give me lessons if you had not seen me before and therefore that you knew after hearing my name over the telephone that it was me calling?"

"Yes, Serena, that is correct."

"But why, with the writing schedule I now know you had, did you put yourself out, to tie up your evenings the way you did?"

"Why, Serena?" A tender smile replaced the visibly tight lines of constraint on his face. He reached over and took my hand in his, giving it a gentle squeeze. "Because I was, to quote Don Quixote or someone else like him, smitten on the spot. Because you had on a lavender and white checked gingham sun dress that revealed your many obvious charms. Because you had a huge lavender bow in your hair holding up your titian tresses. Because you had on your feet lavender flats that showed you were an under my chin size and because you were sniffling. Something I have learned this summer that you do with alluring artistry."

I didn't quite know how to react to Simon's offbeat flattery. He still had not released my hand from his grip and to make matters worse he had winked when he mentioned my sniffling. I decided to go on the offensive, to give him the pert reply, "I don't sniffle," when he interrupted my train of thought. "That's why, Serena, Miss Collins didn't make a mistake on the bill. I never intended to charge you for the lessons. I just wanted to get to know you and giving lessons seemed the perfect way after your call to Mac. I know it was devious but on the other hand the psychological impact of thinking you were paying made you work harder and to take the lessons seriously."

164

Simon paused just long enough in his addendum to his already long confession for me to notice that a humorous glint was replacing the penitent look in his eyes. He gave a short laugh before continuing. "I might add that you are a very apt pupil. In fact too apt a pupil, for what you did by pulling *Savannah* so rapidly over the rocks, no matter how noble the cause, was very dangerous and you could have been killed. Besides, Serena, I'm getting to old to handle that kind of stress."

By this time Simon was grinning at me, his tone somewhat scolding as he added, "Between thoughts of hauling you off to the woodshed for conduct so unbecoming a lady and offering numerous prayers for your safety interspersed with rantings of, 'I'll kill you for attempting something so dangerous,' at least umpteen times I must have aged a hundred years."

I couldn't resist saying, "Now that you mention it, I do see some gray hairs emerging that weren't there earlier today."

A you're hopeless glance or maybe it was a glance of exasperation like Adam always gets when he considers I am being too impertinent replaced the grin on his face. He shook his head. "I gather from your lighthearted mood, Serena, that I am forgiven?"

"You are indeed forgiven, Simon. Actually I am overcome and at the same time flattered that you went to such great lengths to be with me."

"No, Serena, I'm the one who should be flattered since you stuck with me throughout the summer. There were moments when I thought I had blown it, that I had pressed too hard in striving to help you learn the rudiments of boating, and I worried that any day you would call and cancel the rest of your scheduled lessons. But you didn't and for that reason you made my summer memorable."

That did it! Even though I was sitting down I grew weak in the knees before replying, "How sweet of you to say so, Simon." I said this from the bottom of my heart, not automatically as I had done in the past because I had been taught that a polite way of receiving a compliment was by returning one. Then I floundered. This time there was no one waiting in the wings to help me out. I was on my own. Not only was I on my own but I was seated in very close proximity to a man who once again was making it difficult for me to think clearly. However my mind was still clear enough to ask, "Do you have any regrets, Simon? That is do you have any regrets about spending your summer evenings teaching me?"

Simon released his grip on my hand just long enough to reach up and cup my chin. I could see him beginning to lean towards me, coming closer and closer to my face. I shut my eyes, the exquisite tingling torture of being in an about to be kissed state too much to bear otherwise. My heart throbbed faster as I felt his lips touch mine. It was a gentle kiss, not demanding, but reassuring as were his words, "No regrets whatsoever!"

I opened my eyes. His face was still quite close as was his hand cupping my chin. The ticking of his watch was the only sound I could hear; the others, Caesar's steady breathing and the crackling fire had faded away, forgotten. For a crazy moment I started to count the ticks of his watch per minute or perhaps it was the beats of my heart while trying to decide what to say or if just to say nothing at all. To say nothing at all certainly seemed the most exciting way to go especially since Simon was removing his hand from my chin and reaching for the back of my neck. I reached up too, not to stop him like he thought judging from the startled expression on his face but to clutch his arm proclaiming, "Why, Simon, you are my Heracles!"

To say that Simon was surprised would have been inadequate; dumbfounded, was more like it. I held onto his arm, pulling it down into my lap as I assumed a normal sitting position, all the time exclaiming, "It's your watch, Simon. Don't you see? Your watch is a Breguet! My father has one. Adam has one too and as you no doubt know since you own one the watch is rare, so rare that each is numbered on the dial. Up until how your timepiece has been a Rolex, one of those super diver's watches that's pressure proof to 4,000 feet."

As perplexed a look as I had ever seen on anyone crossed Simon's face. I couldn't seem to talk fast enough to explain my behavior. "It was just as you said on the day of the tin can episode. I was upset. All I can remember is a policeman, a blur of blue oxford cloth and being helped by a man with sinewy forearms that at the time reminded me of a statue of Heracles that I had seen in Athens and of course the watch."

I pushed up Simon's shirt sleeve. "I didn't really notice your forearms before because of the tree in the forest or is it the other way around? Whatever! Even a minute ago when you confessed that you were my knight in shining armor it didn't register. So don't you see? You are my Heracles! It's your watch that brings all the pieces together."

Simon sat there as if he had been immobilized by a tranquilizer, his perplexed look slowly giving way to one of I don't believe what I'm hearing. "Serena, I've been called a lot of things in my lifetime, many of them I'm sure not mentionable in polite society, but never a knight in shining armor and never, ever, Heracles. That's really a bit much." He paused and took a deep breath. "By the way, the watch was a gift from my parents when I graduated from college. I plan to pass it on to my son, that is if I ever have one, on the day of his graduation and the reason you haven't seen me wearing the Breguet is because I had sent it back to the shop for cleaning."

"Oh."

"Now then, Serena, knowing you as I think I do and 'Being as how,' to borrow one of your quaint expressions, I didn't have the chance to finish telling you about my trip and "Being as how' I am your knight in shining armor and your Heracles and you are my beautiful sea sprite why don't you turn around and sit facing me. This way I can have your undivided attention."

There was no denying the teasing in Simon's voice so after almost three months of being programmed to do as I was told and after having received such a charming new nickname to replace Adam's taunting, "Red head, red head, 5 cents a cabbage head," I did just that! I stood up, turned around facing Simon and then sat down close beside him listing towards his starboard side, drew my legs up so my knees touched the back of the chair and let my feet dangle over the side of the cushion we were sitting on.

Simon adjusted his position to accommodate mine, propping his feet against the edge of a leather hassock which he pulled up so it was tight against the chair. Being so very tall this resulted in me being able to lean back against his long legs which were now bent at the knees, using them just like I was resting against the back of a chair. After all this shuffling around I almost giggled, a for sure sign that I had had one glass of wine too many, and almost added, "And being as how you aren't going to eat me though you might be tempted to take a bite or two," but I didn't. A signal similar to the waving of a little red flag had materialized, warning me that this was not the time for frivolity, that he was in no mood for one of my playful quips. So I willed my hands to rest peacefully in my lap and myself to wait and listen. Simon, innervatingly for me, having willed his hands to rest upon my shoulders.

"Serena, as a way of beginning, let me say that I can understand your logic for buying a yellow hat just because it is a rainy day. It would be the same kind of armchair logic that I would use to buy a new set of sails during a down pour. I can also understand why you, being you, could be so moved by a painting or a piece of sculpture that it would render you into sobs as it did while you were in Rome viewing Michelangelo's statue of Moses. And although I have experienced the overwhelming force emanating from the magnificent sculpture, for me it was the sight of Frederic Remington's bronze *The Bronco Buster* that knocked me for a loop. Why I must have spent an entire afternoon sitting on a hard museum bench absorbing the details, admiring the sheer muscular power, the determination and grit of steed and cowboy trying to outbest each other that he captured in his bronze."

Simon unknowingly had forged another bond between us by his declaration of appreciation for Remington's prowess as a sculptor. Goodness knows, my passion for his art was as boundless as was my passion for chocolate and long walks on the beach. And so when he said, "I also find the paintings of Charles Russell very compelling, especially the one he titled *When the Plains Were His* depicting a lean and hungry appearing brave leading several women on horseback across a desolate prairie," I willingly became putty in his hands. And, when he changed positions slightly, pushing himself further back into the chair, and I suddenly found myself laying flat against his chest

168

which was shockingly rock-like hard beneath my breast, I became very receptive, literally, to everything mentioned including his invitation to, "Come with me to Rouge Baie," which would have been unthinkable a day earlier.

"Come with you to Rouge Baie?" I echoed.

"Yes, Serena. It's not something I have just dreamed up. Actually I have been thinking about it for some time, long before our conversation today of the settling of Newfoundland and the Basque whalers."

"What would I do while you are diving?"

"Any number of things, Serena, since you are well schooled in museum practices. Hopefully there will be accessioning to do if the diving team continues to be lucky in salvaging artifacts. Then there will be the tedious task of packing them for transportation to the St. John's museum."

"In other words, Simon, lend a helping hand?"

"That's right. On the other hand you don't have to do a thing. It will just be nice knowing you are waiting for me on the shore at the end of the day."

Simon had said, "Waiting for me" with such tenderness that I succumbed totally into his arms, tucking my hands behind the small of his back to achieve a closeness which suddenly seemed important to me before asking, "Where would I stay?"

"Where I am staying, Serena, at Euphy Browne's boarding house. I have already discussed this with her and she said you could have her late mother's sewing room to use as a bedroom. It's a small cozy room but far more important than its size is its location which happens to be next door to mine." Simon laughed softly. "Euphy is a sweetheart. She is also a hopeless romantic and since I have known her for a long time, ever since I was knee high to a grasshopper, she was happy to further my cause, quoting her."

In my humble opinion Simon needed no help whatsoever in any way or shape or form other than my own shape or form to further his cause, for the minute I had succumbed so wantonly against his manly chest his hands meandered slowly down my back to where they were now resting possessively around my waist. I felt an urgent need to surface for air, to grasp at any straw of reasoning, no matter how illogical that I could think of for not weakening and going with him to Rouge Baie. "I'm not sure if there is enough time for me to travel all that distance and get back by the last week in October when the entire family is due to arrive, Simon," I said hurriedly, pushing myself back into an upright position. "Then too, since I have to resume my duties at the museum November 1st, I need a couple of days to get back into harness so to speak."

"I promise, Serena, to have you back on time."

I knew he would! As for me, having been willingly locked for so many years behind the shield of proper behavior, I realized several chinks had just been made into my defenses. Soon there would be nothing left to defend. "Then too," I said hurriedly trying to stem my downward spiral into sin, "I also have the additional problem after all the trouble today of having to arrange for *Escape*'s maintenance."

Simon dismissed my feeble protests with one of his all knowing smiles. "I'm sure your friend Elizabeth as well as the Linettes will keep an eye on everything for you. As for the boat, it will be quite safe at the marina. I'll arrange to have it completely checked over for damage during the interim."

I knew he would! There was only one more obstacle I could think of to bring up for not going with Simon, definitely the pièce de résistance, my last vestige of hope for salvation. "I have C a e s a r to think of, Simon," I whispered, spelling out his name as an added precaution against waking him up. "I can't go off and leave him and I really can't board him for two months. He would pine away into nothing but skin and bones."

Simon chucked me playfully under the chin and whispered back, "I have discussed your four legged friend with Euphy and she said you could bring C a e s a r along providing you keep him under control at all times and that he does not enter her formal gardens. That sounds worse than it really is, Serena, since Euphy's house is on the outskirts of town and is surrounded by several acres of open fields where he can run."

That did it! Salvation from my about to be sin of running off with Simon to Rouge Baie no longer seemed relevant. I was practically packed and on my way. "Euphy Browne must think the world of you to make so many concessions," I answered somewhat on the amazed side.

"Well, not really of me, but of my parents. You see my father did his in surgery residence at the medical center in St. John's. I was born there and according to my mother, she and Dad spent five wonderful years on the island before moving to Ottawa. Somehow they met Euphy and Captain Bob Browne while there and the four became fast friends. The friendship has weathered the test of time and distance. In fact after Captain Browne was killed at sea during the conflict between the Falkland Islands and Argentina a few years ago they seemed to become closer, visiting back and forth quite often. I believe it was after that tragic incident that Euphy moved back to her family's home in Rouge Baie, one thing led to another and today she takes in a few boarders if the spirit moves her."

"I see." I also saw the amorous gleam in Simon's eyes as he gently but firmly pressured me forward towards his manly chest, his hands creeping upwards to the dangerous zone in the middle of my back where I always ended up melting into a puddle of passion when held there for long. I simply had to ask, "Is this the time you are going to demonstrate the Mont method for chasing away tears?"

"Yes."

"Is this demonstration going to be in my best interests?"

"Yes, Serena, I would say very definitely this demonstration is going to be in your best interests. Now then, no more questions."

I shut my eyes, the exquisite tingling torture of being in an about to be kissed state too much to bear otherwise. My heart throbbed faster as I felt his lips touch mine. It was a demanding kiss, not gentle like the one before. I melted, my toes freed from their bondage within my sandals curled deep into the upholstery, my hands slid across his broad back and found a home at the base of his neck while the rest of me responded in quivering delight as Simon's demonstration got exploringly underway.

We parted finally, reluctantly, Simon leaning back into the chair toying with my hair, twisting the tendrils nearest my cheeks around his index fingers, me plucking at an imaginary loose thread on his shirt sleeve. Neither of us said a word, we just sat there staring intently at each other, and me, being me, even outdid me with the wild thought of being at a wine tasting party, both of us savoring the aftertaste. Simon spoke first, the mixture of warmth and merriment that I had grown to adore momentarily replacing the amorous light in his eyes. "Whew! You know, Serena, for a prim and proper girl from Boston you sure pack one whale of a punch."

Of course I did the usual and blushed. I knew I should say something and from the mellow look in Simon's eyes I surmised he was expecting me to and yet my assumption wasn't quite right. I wanted to say something! I wanted to say what I really felt! So I drew the strength from deep within me and trying to forget my sudden shyness said, "It takes someone like you, Simon, to make me want to give of myself." Then, being me, I blushed again and tried to change the subject before another demonstration got underway by asking, "How long do I have to make up my mind about going with you to Rouge Baie?"

Simon's answer was to pull me close. His hands resumed their former position in the middle of my back. Another melt down began immediately even though I was trying to concentrate on what he was saying rather than concentrating on his heart beats throbbing against my breast. "I would prefer an on the spot decision while I seem to have you under my spell, Serena. However, knowing you as I think I do, you will want to sleep upon it, take a long walk on the beach tomorrow. Maybe even take another full day to make up your mind so taking all things into consideration if you could let me know by Thursday evening, Friday morning at the latest it would be a big help. You see I have to be in Rouge Baie by Sunday evening and ready to begin diving Monday morning, weather permitting of course, which means I have to catch the eight a.m., ferry out of Bar Harbor for Yarmouth Saturday morning in order to make the ferry from North Sydney to Port aux Basques Sunday morning."

"That's not quite two days for me to think about the trip, Simon!"

"I know it's short notice but I didn't want to mention it before, not until I knew for sure you could stay at Euphy's home.

I talked to her as soon as the federal agents left the marina and she assured me you are welcome just as I want to assure you that if you decide to come and after getting there, no matter how soon after arriving, you want to come home I will see that you and Caesar get back to here."

Being seaworthy, I knew he would!

Once again the memory of the painting had sneaked in over the transom. It was an omen! How else could I possibly explain the phenomenon of the descriptive word having popped into my mind at this very moment. The fact that my thought was accompanied by a violent clap of thunder and a sheeting of rain pounding against the windows only served to pave the way for my about to be decision to go with him. It also intensified my desire for another demonstration of the Mont method for chasing away tears. I clasped my arms tighter around the small of Simon's back saying the obvious, "It's raining."

"I hear it, Serena."

"Do you think it's raining more cats than dogs?"

"Definitely more cats than dogs," he whispered back while nibbling on my ear.

"A person could catch their death having to go out on such a night when it's raining more cats than dogs. Don't you agree?"

Simon became very quiet. One of his hands slid down to my waist while another found its way caressingly across my left breast until finally he let it rest at the pulse spot on my throat. "I agree," he said at last. In the interim, I gasped!

"Under the circumstances, Simon, perhaps it would be in your best interests to spend the night, just so you wouldn't catch your death by having to go out into the rain. Then too, it might be in my interests if you spend the night. Your being here just might help me to make up my mind about the trip. We would have more time to discuss the details. Do you think that can be arranged?"

I shifted my position slightly more sideways so I could see his face, covering his hand with mine as I did so he wouldn't take it away. He began to chuckle. I was so close that I felt the tremor in his chest clear through my nainsook tunic top and custom made imported French lace bra designed to fit the well-endowed femme before I heard him say, "I think that can be arranged, Serena. Now then no more questions while I get down to the business at hand."

"Which is?"

"Which is to demonstrate to you the modern Canadian version of your old-fashioned New England style of bundling. To be properly executed it will require a change in venue but that will come in due time." He winked mischievously at me. "Shall I begin?"

I shifted my position again, this time moving onto his lap and snuggling up tighter against his chest like I was a cooing homing pigeon returning to its nest. "You may begin," I whispered.

"Oh, my," I exclaimed rapturously a few minutes later, "your business is certainly well - in - hand."

A few breathy minutes later Simon replied, "I believe the due time has arrived, Serena, for us to have a change in venue."

I might as well have lapsed into a coma so great was my momentary stupor over Simon's voicing what I knew was coming down the way. It didn't last long! Being as how I was me I rose to the occasion, harkening back to something Simon had said earlier in the day after we had arrived on Bald Head Island, making a play on his words, giving them a different kind of twist. "I know the exact place to go for our change in venue, Simon. It's actually my bedroom which is about the size of a small classroom and weathered comfy cozy worn by the passing of time. A person has to be part mountain goat to climb the grand staircase to get there but the view of the fireplace from my huge canopy bed is well worth the effort. Do you think you are up to it?"

Simon broke our embrace by leaning back into the chair. His hands remained heavenly in place, one in the middle of my back and the other toying with the very top button of my deep V-necked tunic. His smile was as provocative as his eyes were merry. A touch of male macho lib glib edged into his reply. "If you can do it, Serena, so can I. So, lead on McDuff!"

This time, being as how I was playing the role of McDuff, I unwound myself from my pretzel-like position and began to lead the way out of the study and into the hall. In an instant Caesar was on his feet, dashing ahead of us out into Times Square, his wagging tail and abandonment of me a visible sign that he was beginning to accept Simon. "Tell me, Serena," Simon asked softly after witnessing this frisky display, "where does C a e s a r sleep?"

Now it was my turn to chuckle. "He sleeps on his oriental rug at the foot of the stairs. C a e s a r doesn't like to climb them unless absolutely necessary."

"That's a relief to know," Simon replied while putting an arm around my shoulders, "especially since I am a firm believer in the old adage, 'Two is company, three is a crowd.' However, because I am the possessor of an inquiring mind and because I believe it is in my best interests to know in regard to my future behavior just what does constitute a necessity for C a e s a r?"

"Being summoned to defend my honor does it every time." I added quickly, "Which I can assure you is something you won't have to worry about tonight." I saw no reason to elaborate, to explain that Caesar would definitely not be called upon because I didn't want my honor defended.

Simon paused at the foot of the grand staircase, his eyes and facial expression suddenly solemn and thoughtful instead of teasing and jovial. "Serena, up until this moment you and I have been having a jolly good time of playing cat and mouse but there does come a period when games must be put aside to make room for what is meaningful in life. This change in venue we are about to take is an important step in that direction. Are you positive you want to take it? If you don't I will understand, just like I hope you will understand and believe me when I say that regardless of what we do or don't do, here and now, I still want you to come with me to Rouge Baie."

Simon's profound philosophy on life, so poignantly spoken at this moment, sobered me up and swept away any reservations I might have had about accompanying him on his trip; especially after he said so impassionately, "I want you to come, regardless of what we do or don't do."

I paused at the foot of the stairs too, looking up at Simon like I was gazing at the stars; Britt, my not quite forgotten former

175

half, never having been so understanding or sensitive enough to comprehend what Simon was calling, "Meaningful in life." It had been a very difficult day. Simon and I had come within a hair's width of being shot. I had personally almost killed four people. I had single-handedly demolished one boat and damaged another. Perhaps that was the reason a few tears began to well up or perhaps it was because I was deeply moved by Simon's eloquent speech. Either way I couldn't hold them back and they started to trickle down my face.

Unfortunately I sniffled while saying, "I'm positive, Simon, about taking this important step." Having recently been told I did this with alluring artistry I tried to hide my teary emotional state by starting up the stairs, on the first step telling Caesar, "Stay;" on the second step telling Simon, "Don't you dare say a word about my sniffling;" and halfway up I looked back telling him saucily, "Besides I always believe in doing what my teacher tells me is in my best interests to do," and of course to see if he was following me.

He was!

Chapter 16

Simon's modern Canadian version of old fashioned New England bundling had worked like a charm on me and by late Sunday evening we three weary travelers were seated in Euphy Browne's kitchen getting rejuvenated after a very long trip to Rouge Baie, which I had discovered was designated on the road map by nothing more than a tiny dot situated on the outer fringes of the civilized world. Euphy and Simon were doing most of the talking, Caesar and I doing the listening and just plain looking around.

The kitchen was exactly as Simon had said, "Big and old fashioned," and furnished I decided in the folksy style of a Norman Rockwell painting that could have been titled A Visit to Grandma's House, circa 1930. He had also said, "It's always cheerful because of her ample presence, Serena, even on a cold rainy day. 'Euphemenia is my given,' she will tell you, 'but everyone staying in my house calls me Euphy.'"

I had been told this immediately upon meeting her, word for word, just as I discovered during the next few days of our so called shake down getting acquainted time that nothing much escaped her eyes, that she reigned supreme over her domain and that she was as generous with advice as she was with the bowls of thick oatmeal placed in front of us for breakfast each morning.

Simon had also been correct when he told me, "Euphy is a sweetheart and a hopeless romantic." Indeed she was and from my point of view still is, for it now being just a week later Euphy had more than lived up to her reputation, constantly enthralling me with spicy tidbits about the locals as Mrs. Linette always did, only this time her gossiping seemed to be taking a sudden turn towards the personal side. Seated outside as we were in her picturesque garden overlooking the harbor and sharing a very proper English tea she leaned forward, a confidential air replacing her outgoing manner. "Now that we have become friend-girls, Serena, even though I'm sure I'm well past your mother's age I did want to say that it was the way Simon described you when he was here earlier in the month, sort of stammering over his words instead of straightforward like, that said to me he was sweet on you. Of course now that I have met you I can understand why."

"Oh."

"Course even if Simon hadn't told me about your background, your work at the Boston museum and how he met you I would have guessed from the faraway dewlike glow in your eyes that you were not part of their scientific world. Then too, you were toting fashionable leather luggage instead of the canvas duffel bag type favored by other archaeologists. You know, the kind pictured in the mail order catalogs that are double stitched and have seams bound for durability."

"Oh," I again replied.

"That's why I put you into the room next to his, above the inside place."

"Oh," I replied again sounding somewhat like a broken record but in what must have been a questioning tone because Euphy explained coyly, "I believe you mainlanders call it the living room but it's a room we Newfoundlanders use only for formal occasions, like a wake. No one ever goes in there so you see it makes the room upstairs nice and private."

I blushed, sort of choking on a cup of very hot tea Euphy had poured with great pride from a pewter teapot. "The pot has been in the family for a long time, Serena. My grandmother brought it over the seas with her from England way back. I use it only when serving tea to people I like."

Coming from a family imbued with tradition I understood her sentiments. I spoke right up. "I am honored, Euphy."

#

By early October having a cup of tea with Euphy had become a ritual, a special part of my daily routine that I looked forward to after fulfilling my self-appointed duties of helping her in the garden for two or three hours beforehand and helping Simon along with the other archaeologists in the morning with my curatorial skills. Even Caesar helped to earn his keep by maintaining a constant surveillance over all activities, including mine.

Up until then evenings in Rouge Baie were spent pleasantly outside and usually began by Simon and I, Caesar too, taking a leisurely stroll on the beach and then ending up at Teweks General Store down in the village proper where we spent a while in the company of the many others associated with the project. However as the daylight hours grew shorter so did our walks on the beach and now most of our time was spent in Euphy's kitchen playing checkers or chess, or joining some of her other boarders or friends in a wild game of Trivial Pursuit.

The days also had become crisp. It was now too cold to sit in the garden. I discovered heavier gloves were needed to work outside mulching and readying the flower beds for the approaching winter and I definitely found the warmth near a large pot bellied stove in the kitchen a far more preferable place to sit for exchanging pleasantries and the daily ritual of sharing a cup of tea with Euphy.

Only by now a cup of tea had been switched around in my vocabulary to a cup of switchel, one of the many quaint Newfoundland words and expressions having been absorbed willingly by me during these past weeks. I had picked up another choice word when finishing a late breakfast this morning, Euphy answering my question, "What ever possessed you to serve pancakes instead of oatmeal and figgy bread today?" with, "My bangbellies have always been a favorite with the boarders, Serena, and after the mishap yesterday I thought everyone needed a bit of extra cheer in their stomachs before taking off for the day."

She was right, of course; a bit of extra cheer was needed for the day and for the few remaining ones safe for exploratory diving before the weather snugged everyone inside for the winter. I smiled; inwardly at her colloquialism for pancakes which actually did hit your belly with a bang and outwardly at my four legged, 180 pound mishap curled up at my feet. Dear, sweet, afraid-of-a-raindrop Caesar had done it again! Only this time he had compounded his previous felonies of overturning a boat and scattering a car load of food on the streets of downtown

Arnold by playfully absconding with a priceless piece of wooden scrimshaw Simon had miraculously salvaged from the galleon sunk in the mud on the bottom of Rouge Baie. We were both in disgrace, me for having brought him along and Caesar for not recognizing the difference between a 16th century bite size stick and a fresh contemporary one. That was just one of the reasons I had elected to stay behind for the day, to try and unearth what Caesar's dirty nose told me he had buried. The other was more prosaic having overslept and being told by Simon, albeit good naturedly, "The tide, Serena, contrary to what you Bostonians think, will not adhere to your time schedule!"

I was just about to excuse myself and head outside to hunt for the missing artifact one more time when Jacques, Euphy's very likable, loquacious, risque and sometimes disrespectful boarder from France breezed into the kitchen. "Euphy, ma cherie," he greeted like she was his long lost love, "I came back early to spread tidings of good will throughout the village and to deliver a message of great importance from Simon."

Always teasing, Jacques gave her a bear hug then untied her apron strings. "Simon has asked me to tell you, and of course you too, Serena, that Chris, our illustrious CEO and hailed by some as our dauphin in residence, has decreed that if the seas continue to rise and if the fog becomes as thick as pea soup, that he and his merry crew will shelter down at the campsite tonight rather than risk crossing the channel from Backbone Island and ending up in Davy Jones's locker."

"Humph," Euphy grumbled shrugging her shoulders, a pretense of irritability betrayed by the soft warm glow in her eyes. "Lucky for you, Jacques B. Labelle, you got here when you did else I would have wasted time preparing a mess of fresh cod tongue for dinner tonight."

Jacques grinned. "Euphy," he said solemnly, "wasting time is a tool of the devil. May heaven forbid if I was responsible for your downfall."

Well, heaven did forbid! A deluge of rain pushed by a shutter-banging nor'east wind splattered unexpectedly against the windows causing Jacques to quickly make the sign of the cross before wickedly saying, "Serena, since you already are a fallen woman, I don't need to worry about your soul. However, Simon does and adjures you not to take your usual walk along the shore this evening for fear you might be spirited away in the fog."

Simon's concern conveyed by Jacques made me feel almost as good as having received absolution from the Pope. Not only was I forgiven and that meant Caesar, too, but I had been spared another meal of cod tongue. Of course it wasn't Euphy's fault that I detested the sliver-like morsels cut out of the cod. The fault lay with a wayside restaurant outside of St. John's that had served the entree immersed in a bland white sauce that accentuated its slimy texture. The taste thrill immediately elevated cod tongue to the top of my hate list, replacing the olive, forcing it down into second place. To Euphy's credit she did serve her borders this so-called North Atlantic treat in a swallowable way by dipping each piece into an egg batter and then frying it to a golden cripsness. Being extremely hungry I had found helped to make the cod, when served this way, at least palatable; but unfortunately for me by the time I reached that state of grace I had earned a reputation for being a taffety eater. Consequently I was always trying to mend my fussy image so when Euphy said, "We will have fish chowder tonight," I scrambled to help chop up the potatoes and onions.

Cheerfully, Jacques picked out another sharp knife from Euphy's arsenal of cutlery and joined our cooking bee, the three of us noisily making light work of the vegetables until Euphy stopped and sighed, "Out with you now; too many cooks will spoil the chowder. Besides it's my time of day to collect my thoughts."

Euphy's self-allotted thought-collecting time was taken seriously by all the boarders. It meant the difference between having tea served with jam-filled tarts or having tea served bare-legged. It meant the difference between sandwiches being made with mouth-watering homemade bread or prepared with a commercial loaf of baker's fog. And, it meant the difference between having glazed carrots or boiled carrots a' la nude, the latter, because of their long shelf life, tasting to me somewhat like a nibbled eraser on the end of a #2 pencil. So Jacques and I, with Caesar padding along behind, made a hasty but respectful exit and headed upstairs to change for dinner, a civilized ritual strictly observed by the entire research team even though it only meant, after bathing, exchanging grubbies for a pair of clean jeans and an unpressed shirt, ironing being a problem due to an antiquated fuse box.

The topside part of Euphy's house I had discovered upon the day of my arrival was a visual testimony to her seafarin' father in that every bedroom offered a view of the water, be it the wharf lined harbor, the turkey neck shaped bay with Backbone Island lodged in the gullet or the Strait of Belle Isle. My view was of the Strait and, though Simon's room was adjacent, because of the angle his was of the bay. Jacques', on the other hand, was down the hall and boasted a small balcony which showed him a fascinating bird's-eye look of the busy waterfront.

I had always felt comfortable when walking down this hall to my bedroom; the portrait hung walls reflecting Euphy's past also serving as a constant reminder to me of my parent's home and my own heritage. But today I felt ill at ease. The portraits were no longer friendly. Instead the painted eyes seemed to come alive, the pupils narrowing accusatively, following me down the hall, registering stern disapproval. Even the still lips appeared to move in unison, all voicing dismay over my fall fling, at my flaunting of proper convention.

I didn't know if this daytime nightmare was due to indigestion from eating too many bangbellies, the apprehension over spending an evening on my own or Euphy's erratic grandfather's clock chiming 24 times. I do know the result. A wave of homesickness washed over me and like the surging of an incoming tide gained in momentum until I knew tears were going to well up, embarrassing me and perhaps causing Jacques to ask the reason for my unravelling at the seams. Quickly I blew him a kiss as an answer to his murmured make believe, "Parting is such sweet sorrow," routine and thankfully shut my bedroom door behind me. It was obvious I needed a few moments for my own thought collecting time.

I liked my room and today more than ever I appreciated its special ambiance. It was small and cozy, not overly fussy but still feminine, the decor harkening back to a gentler era when pin cushions, lace doilies and smelling salts were in vogue. Euphy had told me on the day of our being introduced, "This was my mother's sewing room. It was her retreat from the foul weather, especially when the men's boots and slickers dripped onto her clean kitchen floor. It was her snug harbor when *The Mary Jane* got caught in a gale and not knowin' if my father had gone to his reward. It was the place she always came to when out-of-sorts, just how out-of-sorts I could tell by the speed she ran her sewing machine. And, when the need arose to voice an opinion to the Lord, she did so while standing in front of the bay window."

Euphy had paused a second or two before adding in a rather wistful tone, "I can see her now, gazing out towards the Strait, one hand resting upon her right hip, the other hand invoking His help to get her through the day."

Then, Euphy had smiled at me. "The furniture is as she left it: the sleigh bed for taking a catnap, the cherry chest of drawers she used to hold her sewing supplies and her favorite rocking chair." Giving it a fond push she said, "It still squeaks you know."

I attested to the chair's squeakability as soon as I had finished unpacking on that memorable day. Now having been here a little over a month I not only understood why Euphy's mother had chosen this particular room out of all the others in the old Victorian house for her citadel, but to her reasons I had added two of my own. The first being the room was above the inside place, therefore quiet and as Euphy had said, "Nice and private." It was also because of the spellbinding sunrises and the daily parade of awesome icebergs, nomadic humpback whales and boats that I continually witnessed from Euphy's mother's pulpit, the bay window.

In truth it was now gospel with me to rise early, long before Simon stirred, and tiptoe back to my room in time to witness the unveiling of a new day. Bundled up against the morning chill in an old flannel bathrobe of Simon's plus a pair of his woolen socks, I would sit in the rocker, comforting myself with its soothing, lullaby-like motion while watching for the sun to peek from the edge of the earth. Some days it would rise slowly,

183

appearing to rest for a moment on an altar of bloody red waves before giving me its offering of warm golden rays. At other times I believed I was watching The Master painter in His studio at work, His canvases being as vast as the blue sky, as deep as the far horizon and as wide as the mortal eye could see. His strokes were rapid, sure and bold, the subtleties of color breathtaking and everchanging. Even on a rainy, dismal morning there was stilll the gray dawn to observe just as during the day a familiar panorama of sea and land to enjoy; even if it meant looking through rain streaked windows like I was about to do this afternoon.

I say, about to do, because for some strange reason I changed my mind. Not that changing one's mind is a sin, it's just that I am a creature of habit. For instance, I always floss my teeth before going to bed, put my right shoe on first, make my bed with hospital corners and since arriving at Euphy's head straight for the bay window upon entering my room. Now here I was stretched out on the bed, instead of looking out on the view, and patting Caesar on the head."Poor, dear, sweet, afraid-of-a-rain drop Caesar," I said consolingly, "you are going to have to go into therapy when you get home."

As always Caesar understood me, his tail wagging in response when he heard the word, "home." The trouble was no one else seemed to understand me, but on the other hand if I didn't understand myself who could? Getting up from the bed to start changing for dinner I decided being a creature of habit did have merit, but a creature addicted to making spur of the moment decisions left a lot to be desired.

Why the word desire had to pop into my thoughts just as I was pulling off my clothes I didn't know. Gloria would have immediately said, "A Freudian slip, Serena." Simon would have laughed in his inimitable way, making me feel lovable and very special. Jacques, I had learned, would have winked and whispered sweet nothings into my ears, making me crave _____ goodness knows what!

And yet Simon and Jacques were alike in so many ways: both tall, lean and dark-haired; both witty and charming; both complimentary to each other. Simon having told me, "Jacques is a welcome summer gift from Spain to the Canadian government, a sort of lend-leasee sent from their Basque region to help unearth the truth behind the demise of the 16th century whaling fleet in America." Jacques having told me, "Simon is like a seasoned oak keg holding fine Madeira that has aged well."

Now that I was down to my bare bones the main difference between the two of them suddenly became quite clear. It was in their behavior! Jacques' manner was ebullient, always making me feel lighthearted; whereas Simon's quiet demeanor always made me feel tranquil. However at the moment I was feeling nothing but the cold. Euphy had warned me, "Come October the bedrooms get chilly. I can only afford to heat the bathrooms so unless you want to get the bivvers and catch your death, don't tarry putting on your clothes."

Bivvers, shivers, whatever, Euphy was right and not wanting to, "Catch my death," the phrase quite naturally popping into my mind since it recently had been a motivating force behind my acquiescence to the trip to Rouge Baie, I quickly donned my robe and headed across the hall to a warm bathroom where I readily slipped into my regular routine of mentally going over my mistakes both past and present. Stepping into the tub, I turned on the shower full force, letting the water beat against my skin until I could feel it beginning to tingle. Normally there wasn't enough time, nor hot water, to enjoy this bit of spa-like rejuvenation but with most everyone battened down at the campsite I could not see any harm in treating myself to a little luxury. I even had with me a hotel size bar of pure castile soap to help wash away my rainy day problems which currently seemed to number three and a half; Simon, Gloria and me, Jacques being the other half! There was no doubt in my mind I was the one of the three and a "halfsome" with the tortured soul and so, with the water streaming down my face and through my hair, my solution to one of my problems became quite clear. I simply had to take care of me first, then the two and a half remaining to be solved would fall neatly into line.

As I saw me, from my position underneath the shower-head, I had become a fallen woman, a tool of the devil for wasting time, a taffety eater and by my own admission a procrastinator.

There wasn't much I could do about the fallen woman bit except head for home which I fully intended to do within the next couple of weeks. True, my taffety image was improving; it was the procrastinator in me I had to purge. Once I exorcised that being from my soul I would no longer be a tool of the devil.

I was now squeaky clean, my course of action clear. Tonight, with Simon gone, I would perform the necessary ceremony. I would need Euphy's permission to use the kitchen, the big oak table and a hurricane lamp for the ritual. I would supply a pen, notepaper and as a precaution against giving in to the devil a stamped envelope already addressed to Gloria. Having been raised to "Waste not, want not," I knew once that stamp was licked and in place I would finish the promised letter containing all my recent comings and goings, well not all, even if it took me all night!

Having rinsed away the problem of Gloria and me which left one and a half to go, I got out of the tub and started to dry myself off with one of Euphy's soft lavendar scented towels. Enhaling the fragrance ushered in another wave of homesickness, not only for the rock gardens at The Barnacle where the plant grew in profusion but also for the formal pruned beds of it at home, the latter at the moment symbolizing an orderly and proper way of life; definitely not the kind I was seeing fit to live today. A few tears of alluring artistry trickled down by face. These drops of remorse were accompanied by a spontaneous loud sniffle or two or three. Unfortunately for me Simon wasn't present to witness either since I felt certain that he would want to demonstrate again the Mont method for chasing away tears. Fortunately for me Caesar's whining and scratching at the door along with a shout from Jacques, "Are you okay, Serena? I heard you sniffling half way down the hall," effectively stopping my daydreaming.

"I'm fine, Jacques!" Hurriedly I pulled on my lacy undies, another bit of luxury stuffed into my suitcase at the last minute along with the 100% cotton long john's guaranteed by the world's great outdoor outfitters to keep you warm under adverse conditions. "Guess I just got slightly carried away in trying to sort through my problems."

"Well, sort them out downstairs!" He added cajolingly, "I'll be glad to help. You know, Serena, mon petit chou, in addition to my good looks and many hidden charms, helping damsels in distress solve their problems is a specialty of mine."

I laughed quietly to myself, thinking, "Ah, Jacques, my pet, do I dare tell you that you are one half of a part of my problems," but called out, "I'll be right down. In the meantime don't forget, 'I love thee with the breath, smiles, tears, of all my life.'"

His chortled response was lost to me. Perhaps it was just as well for our lighthearted repartee filtering through the door paved the way for me to focus on my remaining problem and a half, Simon and Jacques. This time I wiped the steam off of the mirror before beginning a poignant soliloquy.

"Yes," I said to my reflection, "I do declare I like Jacques. I find his outlandish attention to me flattering and very pleasant. And that's my problem! Is it wrong for me to enjoy Jacques' flirtatious behavior when I am in love with Simon? After all isn't that why in the end, and after all was said and done, I came with him to Rouge Baie? I wanted to be sure. I didn't want to make another mistake, especially when both of our futures are at stake?"

I blinked my eyes slowly several times. It was during the sixth blink I knew Rouge Baie and the confines of the bathroom were not the places for me to make such weighty decisions regarding my future or Simon's future, what is right and what is wrong, if I'm in love or not in love. Any monumental decisions of such magnitude had to be decided, I decided, while walking the beach in front of The Barnacle or while treading on hallowed Boston Common in front of my parents' ancestral gray stone home on Beacon Street, the familiar turf of the latter being conducive to solving problems when one considered the erudite conversations that must have taken place there between John Hancock, the Adams men, Sam and John, and Paul Revere.

Mentally putting myself in their company was comforting. After all they had made the right decisions. So, having dispensed with my remaining one and a half problems by postponing my decision I cautiously opened the door, bracing myself for

187

Caesar's charge which I knew would be like that of the final dash at the Super Bowl with goal-to-go.

I was not disappointed.

Chapter 17

I could not find anywhere in my repertoire of excuses, not even a one, for pigging out the way I did over Euphy's fish chowder and cloudberry pie for dessert. Euphy was pleased; Jacques was amused, pointedly saying, "You will become your own Personal Flotation Device, Serena, if you keep on eating that way."

On the other hand Robert "Sonofagun" Barrows, widower, retired sea captain, local story teller par excellence and a close friend of Euphy's late husband who always seemed to "Come by and pay a visit" at mealtimes - tonight being no exception - pithily said, "Hell's bells! Another new name for life jackets coming down the way."

I braced myself for the forthcoming gale. Euphy, long accustomed to riding out the storm, poured Sonofagun another cup of coffee. Jacques managed to quickly fortify himself with a second piece of pie before the blast hit. "Why is it," Sonofagun roared, "in today's society we can't call a spade a spade? What is wrong with calling a life jacket, a life jacket? If the word, life, is offensive and if the word, jacket, is bothersome what is so gall-darned great, I ask you, about Personal Flotation Device? It sounds like a plumbing fixture to be kept hidden away in the head. Even worse are the initials: PFD! Makes you think of a piece of sewer pipe!"

"Now, Bob, remember your high blood pressure," Euphy interrupted. Putting her hand on his arm she squeezed it hard. "The doctor said you were not to let yourself get upset, especially over trivial matters."

The effect of her touch was like oil on water. Turning to me he winked. "Euphy's right, you know. No need to let myself get ticked off by some asinine name. It's just that in my heyday we called PFDs 'Mae Wests' named after the actress whose bountiful charms were undeniably shapely." He started to laugh softly, a mischievous twinkle kindled in his brown eyes. "Why it was the vision of being hugged by Mae West when cast out into the brinish deep that keeps a man's spirits up. Of course she was before your time, Serena, but I believe Simon could appreciate the comparison."

Being me I blushed over his remark. However, I forgave him instantly for by now, after so many, "Come by and pay a visit" mealtimes, I found Captain Barrows to be utterly charming, to the point of doting on his every word. He had even tendered me the compliment not long after our having been introduced of, "You're okay, Sis, for a landlubber." The bond had thickened between us when he found out I was the granddaughter of, "One of Mac's boys." A far away look had come into his eyes when he told me, "I, too, have the honor."

This bit of family history had been divulged during one beautiful September afternoon when I literally ran into him at the town wharf. I had been helping Simon unload several small cartons from the *Avon*, each one containing a priceless artifact laboriously salvaged from the bottom of Rouge Baie. I was completely absorbed in my task, well aware of the excitement these bits and pieces of pottery and wood would create when unpacked at the Newfoundland Museum in St. John's. That was why I hadn't seen Captain Barrows approach us or heard his conversation with Simon until I caught the words, "Wait a minute." Thinking he meant me I stopped dead in my tracks. Both of them thought this uproariously funny. However I wasn't able to share in their laughter until after Simon informed me, "Matches, Serena; wait-a-minutes are sulphur tipped matches. Sonofagun came down to buy some at Teweks General Store."

"Oh," I had replied, which for some strange reason prompted Captain Barrows to launch one of his stories.

"Reminds me of a sailing friend I had many years ago. From Boston he was. Had a funny accent and was so tall his feet stuck out of his bunk. We both had signed up, or I guess I should say our father's had paid for us to be a crew member on the *Bowdoin*, a gaff-nosed schooner belonging to the late Admiral Donald MacMillan. MacMillan had made a practice in the mid 1930's of taking young whippersnappers, like us, along on his scientific expeditions to the Arctic. We were green when we embarked out of Wiscasset, Maine, and we got greener the further north we sailed into turbulent seas."

"But by gum," he had added proudly, emphasizing each word by pounding his arthritic right first into the palm of his left hand, "by the time Horatio and I returned, our mettle had been tested; we were men, physically and mentally fit to challenge the world. We also had earned the right to our respective nicknames; mine being Sonofagun since that was my favorite epithet every time I fumbled a line, which was often, and Horatio's being Waitaminute since he had a habit of saying during a weighty discussion,'Now wait a minute, there is another side to consider.' Horatio went on to become a lawyer. A damn good one too since he is now whittling his time away sitting on The Bench in your capitol. Has the highfaluting title of The Honorable Horatio Adams Bradford, Chief Justice of the United States Supreme Court. As for me, as you know I chose a life at sea. Always had to see what lay beyond the next sea. Anyway, old Waitaminute and me kept in touch and after I became master of my own ship *The Invincible*, his son John crewed for me on several of my expeditions."

I had stood in front of him, speechless. Captain Barrows had finally asked, "Serena, is there something wrong? You're as white as a new sail!"

"No, nothing is wrong," I managed to answer, my voice barely above a whisper. "It's just that your long time friend Horatio is my grandfather and his son John is my father."

Captain Barrows comment was predictable. "Well, I'll be a son of a gun," he exclaimed loudly. "You're Horatio's granddaughter and John's little girl. Well, I'll be a son of a gun!"

Simon and I had spent the rest of the afternoon listening to flash backs about, "The good old days;" Captain Barrows confirming what I had long suspected that my father and grandfather were not always the saints they proclaimed to be when growing up. For some strange reason finding this out on that now memorable afternoon not too long ago made me feel closer to both of them than ever before, if indeed that was possible.

This evening though, with the blush from Captain Barrows backhanded Mae West compliment lingering on my cheeks mixing with the jovial atmosphere created by his customary hearty mealtime greeting of "Come by and pay a visit," my thoughts were not focused on my family's past exploits. Instead they were focused on what he had just announced in his 'Now hear this tone' and was out of necessity due to my dumbfoundness having to repeat. "Serena," he said again, "I've decided to load up Old Bess and drive you and that monster of yours back to Boston!"

Euphy gasped. "Such a long drive Bob!"

"Nonsense! The ferry will take us part way. Then with the two of us standing watch at the wheel we should have a pleasant trip. Meeting Serena has given me a hankering to see old Waitaminute and John one more time before I get deep sixed. Besides an unexpected legal matter surfaced in Boston that requires my attention, so to my way of thinking this is the perfect time to go."

Captain Barrow's brown eyes crinkled up at the corners and his voice became teasing as he asked, "What say, Sis? Shall we give it a whirl? Do you think old Simon would mind me spending so much time with his girl?"

I was deeply touched by his offer. It was, as Euphy had said, a long drive not only for him but for his Land Rover as well since Old Bess would soon be able to qualify for antique status. As for Captain Barrows joshing about spending time "With Simon's girl" I knew Simon would be genuinely pleased over this surprising turn of events.

In truth the logistics of getting myself and Caesar back to Boston by November 1st had become a thorny issue between Simon and me. What had seemed like such a good idea in the beginning, to leave my car at The Barnacle and pick it up on the way back, had fizzled due to the unusually good fall weather; so many sunny days prompting the entire research team to extend their hours of endeavor. It now appeared Simon could not easily leave before the middle of November, he staying behind to help Chris, "Close up shop," - hopefully before the first glitter storm paralyzed the area - and to make the necessary arrangements for their work to continue the following summer. This included coordinating their efforts with those undertaking the land excavations on Backbone Island.

In the privacy of the bedroom Simon had become quite vocal, in his quiet way, about me renting a car and traveling alone back to Georgetown. If he had said it once, he had said it a hundred times, "Serena, it's not safe! Not until after the preliminary hearing! Even then you still could be in jeopardy."

"But," I always countered during our arguing sessions, "I can't spend the rest of my life being afraid of my own shadow. And, it goes without saying if I am in jeopardy so are you. Besides I am of age, or haven't you noticed? I am quite capable of making my own decisions. Also I will have Caesar with me."

Those remarks got me absolutely nowhere. His answers were always the same. "You're too trustworthy. You take people at face value and we both know you take too many chances. Besides you should have learned by now neither you nor Caesar can stand up against a gun."

"But!" I always managed to edge that word in one more time before Simon would forcefully interrupt saying, "There are no buts about it, Serena. I brought you to Rouge Baie. It is my responsibility to see you get home. Safely! I will figure something out."

Round and round and back and forth we went, hashing over the same stupid subject, both of us trying hard not to let our squabble become switchel time gossip. That was up until a couple of weeks ago when Simon told me flatly, "I have decided you and Caesar will fly back to Portland with a friend of mine who runs a charter service out of St. John's. Your friend Elizabeth, I'm sure, won't mind meeting you if by then your parents aren't at The Barnacle."

I had protested. "It is too expensive. Besides I have gone ahead and made arrangements to rent a car."

"You what?"

I didn't like the indignant tone of his voice or the way he suddenly risen to his feet. I spoke slowly, softly and I admit defiantly. "I said I have gone ahead and made arrangements to rent a car. This way I won't be a bother to anyone."

Simon had stood in front of me for a few seconds before replying, an enigmatic expression on his face but I recognized the intrepid look in his eyes. I had seen it before under dire

193

circumstances. "Serena Margaret Bradford, I expect you to cancel your rental tomorrow. As I have said you and Caesar will fly back to Portland. Furthermore I don't give a damn about the expense. And furthermore I will decide if and when you are ever a bother to me."

That did it! All semblance of reasoning disintegrated; so did my calm, Boston, Brahmin composure. As icily as I could I said, "I find your attitude to be Neanderthal, Simon Stewart Mont; so why don't you pack up your club and crawl home to your cave."

Not willing to let well enough alone I then summed up my haughtiest expression adding, "Furthermore I do care about the expense. And further, furthermore I will not cancel the car rental."

After both of our edicts had been chillingly delivered I had found the sleigh bed in my room to be quite comfortable. I no longer needed Simon's old bathrobe and wool socks to keep me warm in the morning chill; I just didn't plan on getting out of bed in time to watch the sunrise. Instead I just laid there, seething, muttering to myself over being treated like a child. Caesar was most understanding, wagging his tail in agreement when I said, "I'm a grown-up, intelligent woman! I have a responsible position at the museum! I can find my way around Europe blindfolded; different languages, no problem! I have no ties! I am free to come and go whenever and wherever I please!"

"But," I reasoned, that word having become 'on a holding pattern' with me, "Mother had taught Gloria and me on one tearful afternoon a long, long time ago that to be totally free could mean a lonely existence. It meant being labeled egocentric. Heaven forbid! It meant, ultimately, being a person who didn't care enough about anyone or anything to warrant being cared about in return."

Mother had smiled when she rather provocatively added, more to herself than to Gloria and me, "It could mean you might never know the esctasy of compromise."

At the time I didn't know what Mother meant, the word esctasy not being in my vocabulary. She had not been her usual proper self upon arising that day, sort of dreamy, sort of in another world. Gloria and I had attributed her unorthodox

194

behavior to a rare disagreement with my father the day before. However, a tiny box delivered by messenger from Tiffany's later that same day did seem to make everything right. Compromise, I had understood, having reluctantly agreed on that tearful afternoon to go sailing with my parents overnight in return for a weekend in New York City.

I had often recalled that mini-lecture, thinking as I grew older and wiser the word, bribe, could be a good substitute for compromise.

The days of my self-imposed exile soon slipped into a week. I had not come up with a compromise or a bribe. Neither had I canceled my car. Simon and I simply avoided the problem by avoiding each other like the plague, becoming extremely polite when a situation forced us to be together. No one suspected we were having a fight. This is, no one but Euphy!

She had called me aside after breakfast, feigning to need an extra pair of hands for a minute or two. "Serena, it's been a week now since you and Simon started your lover's quarrel. I don't mean to butt in, but if I can be of help?"

I unraveled. I let it all hang out. I finally started to sob. "Oh, Euphy, I'm so ashamed. I was so mad at being ordered around that I called Simon a Neanderthal and told him that he should pack up his club and go home to his cave."

Euphy laughed. "Is that all? Here I have been worrying this past week that you and Simon had a really serious tiff. Why, that's nothing compared to the rounds my Bob and I had."

"Is that all," I echoed. "Euphy, I don't think you understand. Simon ordered me to change my plans."

"I understand perfectly, my dear. I don't think you do."

Her words startled me. "Whatever do you mean, Euphy?"

She shook her head, the friend-girl smile on her face, I noticed, changing into one of concern, even motherly. "Serena, Simon obviously cares about you, deeply. Perhaps he wasn't as tactful as he should have been but his solution to a potentially dangerous situation, if what you have just said is true, has merit. His heart was in the right place. Is yours? Do you care enough about Simon to overlook his highhandness? If your answer is yes, then accept some advice from someone who is older, from someone who wishes she still had a man to fight with. Don't be ashamed to be the first to extend an olive branch."

It took me a couple of minutes to digest thoroughly the meaning behind her words, even though there was a familiar ring to them. Of course she was right, just like my mother was right. I wiped my tears away, blew my runny nose. "Yes, I do care about Simon. Perhaps more than I realize."

"Well, then, I suggest tonight you tell him, I'm sorry. That's all, just those two little words." Euphy winked. "Nature will do the rest."

I had gone around the rest of the day humming, "On the seventh day of Christmas my true love said to me." At midnight I was just about to get out of my bed and tiptoe to Simon's room, a make-up kiss on my lips to be offered with the words, "I'm sorry," when I heard the door open. Caesar didn't bark or growl so I knew immediately it was Simon.

"Serena, are you asleep?"

"No, I'm not asleep, Simon."

I could sense his nearness. It wasn't until he sat down beside me on the edge of the bed though, that I could see the outline of his muscular body. His facial features remained masqued by the darkness but I knew by the long, deep breaths he was taking that his brow was furrowed, his expression one of anxiety, his eyes tender.

I laid there, waiting, my heart beginning to beat rapidly. Simon did not say a word. Instead he pulled the quilt away from my shoulders, reached down and pulled me towards him, his arms tightening like a vise around the small of my back. My meltdown began immediately! There was no escape. Not that I wanted to, especially after he murmured in a voice husky with emotion, "I'm sorry. I should have asked you, Sprite, to cancel your plans, not ordered you. I should have discussed with you the real possibilities that we are being searched for by members of the Colombian cocaine cartel. For all we know a member could be a passer-by on the street, maybe an acquaintance, perhaps a friend. New England and the Maritime Provinces encompass only a small area; there are only a few major roads tying the cities together. You would be easy to spot; you with your long, wavy red hair and traveling alone with a gray Great Dane."

I interrupted him with my make-up kiss, actually several make-up kisses all fervently and lingeringly bestowed in the true spirit of compromise. Just to be on the safe side I even whispered into Simon's ear several times, "I'm sorry," though it didn't really seem necessary, actions speaking louder than words.

The dawn was more spectacular than ever. Perhaps because Simon squeezed into the rocking chair with me to watch the sunrise; his excuse, "I forgot to bring my robe and I don't want you to get the bivvers." Perhaps because we both were caught in the afterglow of an ecstatic compromise. We had spoken barely above a whisper to each other that morning out of respect to The Master in His studio, both of us unwilling to disturb His concentration while brushing the sky with vibrant reds and purples and both of us unable to keep the old rocking chair from crooning its special lullaby. By the time the sun's golden rays warmed the pulpit, our plans had been made. I agreed to fly back to Portland. Simon would drive Caesar and me to St. John's a couple of days ahead of time so he could show off some of the historic sites, and eat at a few favorite restaurants. Simon's back had stiffened when I said, I would prefer to pay for the flight back; his voice taking on a steely edge as he asked, "Why?"

"It's a matter of principal, of my honor," I answered carefully, not wanting to break the romantic spell, not wanting to hurt his feelings. "It has to do with the way I was brought up."

"A matter of principal and your honor, Serena, are rather heady subjects to discuss before breakfast," Simon finally replied before relaxing back into the chair.

We sat quietly for a few minutes watching a distant iceberg cut through the channel, its crushing force camouflaged by sheer pristine beauty. Simon started to toy with my hair, coiling it around his fingers. "Tell me, Serena," a gently, teasing tone having eased into his voice,"would this matter of principal and your honor be tied into Victorian mores? Could I have here, seated on my lap, an old fashioned girl worrying about what others might say, or harboring silly thoughts of being considered a kept woman? Worrying, that if I pay for the charter, my friend might think you were being compensated for favors received?"

I had nodded my head, yes, to his questions. Simon started to laugh, tightening his grip around my waist. "Tell me, Sprite, is there a bit of that old saying, 'Beware of men bearing expensive gifts,' mixed up in all of this?"

Simon's deep laugh was infectious. "Beware of handsome men bearing expensive gifts," I corrected.

Simon threw back his head, his laughter bouncing off the walls of my small bedroom. "You win, Serena. I can't argue against principal and honor!"

I swear I heard Euphy's mother laugh along with us. In fact, I know I did after Simon winked and nodded a yes to my, "Did Euphy by any chance talk to you, too?"

So that was why this evening, after Captain Barrows jolted me back from daydreaming by a good poke in the ribs with his elbow, I answered sincerely, "Simon will be pleased for me to have such a gallant escort. As for me, I can't imagine a more dashing and charming traveling companion. Caesar and I accept your very gracious and generous offer."

"Good," he bellowed. "One thing though, Sis, now that that's settled I want you to know I have already discussed our trip with Simon. He was lamenting to me privately the day before yesterday about some of your difficulties. One thing led to another and before I knew it, I up and suggested I drive you back. Old Simon was all for it, but said I should ask you."

I smiled at Euphy, a knowing look passing between us.

"Another thing, Sis, I want to leave earlier than you had planned, no later than October 20th. That gives you one week more to spend here in Rouge Baie."

"That will be fine with me, Captain Barrows."

"Good, we will press out the details later." Getting up from the table he excused himself with his usual aplomb and accolade, "Thanks for the light lunch, Euphy."

The kitchen seemed empty when he left, but not for long, Jacques filling the void by provocatively canting one of his impromptu poems:

"Ah, Serena, wouldst that I could take thou home
Alas, I am but mortal man, temptation would be great
To clutch thou to my manly bones
Ah, Serena, tis best I fly with the phoenix, west."

I smiled at Jacques, not knowing quite what to say, but Euphy never seemed to be at a loss for words. "You are the limit," she chided indulgently, "and speaking of bones I don't think you have a serious one in your body."

Jacques pretended dismay. "Thy barb cuts into me deeper than an arrow."

"Humph!"

Euphy started to rise from the table, then suddenly sat down. There was a hint of irritation on her face and she began to tap the table with her fingers. I had seen her in this state of annoyance several times before, always when she had forgotten something very important.

"Jacques, I'm sorry. I forgot to mention I took a phone call for you this morning."

Jacques arched his eyebrows in surprise. "For me, Euphy?"

"Yes. It came through just after you left for Backbone. At first I thought it was for Serena, since it was a Boston operator, but it turned out to be a call from your cousin Sue and her husband. She seemed upset."

The name Sue startled me; a name that as far as I was concerned, "Would live forever in infamy." Jacques appeared to be startled too, for seated as I was directly across the table from him, I noticed his fingers gripping the cup of coffee he was holding turning pale from the pressure. His question to Euphy, "Did my cousin leave a message?" appeared to be asked with exaggerated nonchalance, almost as if he didn't care. On the other hand, I decided, if I turned the coin over, perhaps that was his way of not showing emotion. After all I didn't know Jacques' inner soul that well. In fact, I didn't know his soul at all. I only knew his flattery and charisma which, admittedly, was considerable.

"Yes," answered Euphy, "she did leave a message, Jacques. Rather involved so I jotted it down."

This time Euphy did make it up from the table. "I stuck it over here on the bulletin board where it would be in plain sight so I wouldn't forget to give it to you. I best read it outloud though, since it's in my own form of shorthand."

I had seen Euphy's shorthand. It was a mixture of doodling, recipe symbols, nautical terms and Newfoundlandese that defied normal deciphering, so I immediately understood the horror behind Jacques' muttered, "Oh, no."

"She said, Sue that is, said, due to unforseen events they would be unable to rendezvous with you as planned before you return to Spain. Sue said to be sure and tell you, she accented the word sure, Boston lived up to their expectations and they particularly enjoyed the historic waterfront district."

Euphy paused, frowning at her notes. "Her message became garbled, there was a lot of static on the line. Suddenly it cleared and she said they were extremely disappointed with the southern Maine coast. They had an accident of sorts there, which dampened their trip. This problem, or maybe it was these problems, she said, were described in a letter that is on the way to you."

An enormous sigh of relief escaped from Euphy's lips. "Thank goodness that's over with. You know sometimes I have trouble reading my own writing. Be that as it may," she exclaimed sympathetically, "I do hope your cousin and her husband haven't been hurt."

Jacques smiled disarmingly. "I appreciate your concern, Euphy, but knowing my cousin and her husband, as I do, I suspect they had engine trouble. That's all!"

I had succeeded in remaining silent during Euphy's recitation, studying Jacques as intently as he was watching her deliver the message. Though visually relaxed his smile seemed forced, his eyes betraying the tension within him. At first I thought this was a normal reaction to having heard some bad news but I changed my mind as Euphy matter-of-factly stated, "I didn't know you had relatives in the states, Jacques."

By this time Euphy was busy at the stove so she didn't see Jacques' smile give way to an expression of shrewdness or witness the cunningness that had sneaked into his eyes. I did! It shocked me into holding my breath for a minute or two, and though his sly look was fleeting it was long enough to reveal an unsavory side of his character which I never dreamed existed.

Luckily Jacques didn't notice my discomfort, neither did Euphy. For that I was glad, since their on-going lighthearted banter tended to belie my thoughts, making me wonder if perhaps what I had seen was nothing more than Basque mystique couched in a different guise.

I felt better for having come to this conclusion, the benefit of doubt restoring my peace of mind. I even let myself laugh along with Jacques as he countered Euphy's question of kith and kin.

"Ah, Euphy, light of my life, I must keep you guessing. I must keep you in suspense so you will always beg for more."

"Humph! That will be a day you will never see, Jacques B. Labelle."

Chapter 18

Now that dinner was over and the culinary side of the kitchen put to rest for the night Euphy closed the cottage style curtains covering the old mullioned windows, a nightly before bedtime ritual that she always did with the same kind of gusto as a stage hand pulling the ropes for a final curtain call. "It's a foul night, Serena. Not fit for man nor beast to go roamin' and although the evening is young I've locked the front door. So, anyone, with an attack of wanderlust and itchy feet better not forget their key."

I nodded in agreement.

"Now, Serena, mind the pot bellied stove. It's as temperamental as I am."

"I will, Euphy."

"You might have to add some wood in a couple of hours to keep the kitchen toasty while you write your sister."

Euphy, by then, was standing in the doorway to the back hall while talking to me, her hazel eyes suddenly appearing tired, her shoulders beginning to slump a bit from the day's chores. "Either way, Serena, be sure and add some wood before you turn in and turn the damper down like I showed you. That way the kitchen will be warm when I get up to start breakfast."

A lump started to form in my throat as I heard the weariness in Euphy's voice. I was going to miss her. She had touched my life in the profound way a fond memory is born, her courage in facing adversity having become an inspiration to me. Unable to stop myself I walked over and gave her a hug, as is so often the manner of friend-girls, saying, "I appreciate you letting me use the kitchen tonight. Wood is precious, I know, so I won't forget to turn the damper down."

"Humph! Not to worry. Besides, having you help me to put the garden to bed for the winter will more than make up for the few logs you use."

Euphy turned and left, her parting words, "Best start on your letter for according to Jacques wasting time is a tool of the devil," being quite-germane to my problem in that I had

203

struggled after dinner to keep the old scalawag at bay and not give in to his tempting offers. The first one had come in the form of a Civil War novel guaranteed by the publisher to, "Titillate one's senses." It had been returned to Euphy earlier in the day by Jane Teweks, proprietress of Teweks General Store, with a note stuck inside on which was written one word in all caps, "STEAMY!" I had persevered by placing the novel next to the bible on the book shelf, making sure the book's Gothic type jacket of a half naked woman rested against the gold cross embossed on the bible's cover.

The second tempting offer had come disguised in the form of Jacques wanting to play checkers. Again I had perservered by telling Jacques the barefaced lie that, "Euphy lent the checkerboard to the next door neighbor." Seeing as how I was fighting the devil I had said this without batting an eyelash or crossing my fingers.

Congratulating myself on having prevailed over not only one but two pleasured enticements I finally sat down at the big oak table, adjusted the wick on the hurricane lamp for brightness and with my daily journal, pen, notepaper, and pre-addressed as well as stamped envelope laid out in front of me began to exorcise the devil from my soul.

Chapter 19

It soon became apparent to me that the devil is a formidable adversary and that he wasn't about to relinquish his hold on my procrastinating soul without a fight for as soon as I picked up the pen the electric lights went out. Although I had planned from the beginning to use the hurricane lamp as a prop, to sort of keep me in the mood for writing, it now became an obvious necessity if I was going to get a letter off to Gloria.

Determinedly I turned the wick higher, the glow of its white flame momentarily hurting my eyes, forcing me to glance away from its sphere into the encroaching darkness. The kitchen walls it seemed were now papered with monstrous shadows instead of the cheerful multicolored vegetable print Euphy had chosen while the bygone era clothes tree, a catchall for an assortment of foul weather garb, appeared like an obese witch riding on a broomstick, complete with pointed hat no less.

I shuddered, a symptom I had learned to immediately recognize as one preceding a good case of the bivvers unless properly doctored. The prescription was easy and well within my grasp. I simply and finally picked up my pen and started to write.

> *October 13*
> *9:00 p.m.*
> *Euphy Browne's kitchen*
> *Rouge Baie, Newfoundland*

Dear Gloria,

At long last the promised letter!
I know you must be exasperated with me for mailing virtually blank postcards to you this past summer, stating nothing more illuminating than, "I'm fine," or " Feel great," or, "All going well." Even my occasional phone calls, I know, have been sort of worthless and vacuous, leaving a lot unsaid. Especially the last two when I casually mentioned I was staying

at Euphy Browne's boarding house in Rouge Baie, while touring Newfoundland with one of my museum friends.

As always you were circumspect, not asking, "Which museum friend?" or "From which museum?" You didn't even ask, "Touring with a she or he?" Such virtue must be rewarded!

Well, it's going to be a long letter and I shall probably develop a severe case of writer's cramp before finally being able to put down my pen. I will save my present comings and goings until the last and begin my tale with the immediate past, the immediate past being wild, exciting, and at times frightening compared to the romantic and ecstatic present. As for the future, who knows?

So go put yourself in a receptive mood for catching up with my life by following a suggestion to splurge with a bottle of Mumm's champagne and then to curl up in the cavernous wing chair of Paul's that you always retreat to for solace with my voluminous letter in hand, SHOES OFF - of course!

Now are you ready?

Then, as we used to say when we were kids - on your mark, get set, GO!

To begin with, let me assure you that I am in the best of health and not "Out to lunch" as you so often call my contemporaries at the museum. In fact, after a shaky start during the first week of June, when as you know I arrived in Georgetown, I have now built up to a daily walk of about six miles. How about that? On the negative side, I have produced the best crop of freckles - ever. Not to worry lest you think I have become completely flaked out for I have not forgotten to be kind to Mother Nature and have faithfully lavished myself with a broad spectrum sunscreen lotion. As for my jumpy heart I rarely have pains now and when I do, can readily attribute it to a stressful moment of the day. So as much as I hate to admit the family was right, returning to the beach and home I love for the summer did indeed restore the bloom to my cheeks that my bout with pneumonia and sundry illnesses had taken away.

I really don't know what has possessed me to do what I have done or perhaps I should be honest and write, to do all the strange inconsistent things that I have done since leaving home.

You know I have never been the one for spur of the moment decisions; that is almost never. Ha, Ha, Ha! Well, my peculiar behavior began about a week after I arrived when I was taking a pre-dawn walk to Griffith Head, and YES, anticipating your devilish thought, Sis, I did remember to change clothes. Getting caught on the beach in my nightgown is not something I care to repeat. To this day I will never know how everyone in Georgetown knows that I have a penchant for airy blue nighties. The only explanation I have ever been able to come up with is that gossipy Mrs. P., must have been up earlier than usual; binoculars around her neck - you know what a commanding view of the beach she has. To make a long story short by the time I got back from my walk having done a lot of soul searching while on the way I had decided to take boating lessons. Having made a commitment to the Higher Being while I was on the beach I had no recourse but to call Riggs Marina and to chart my course for the summer.

How's that for an eye opener or are you still in a state of shock? Will give you a moment to recuperate while I take time out to check the wood stove.

Having written in my letter to Gloria, "Time out," I was honor bound by one of our childhood covenants to do just that. So with a grand flourish I crossed the "t" in the word, stove, and got up from the table. My timing was uncanny, maybe even clairvoyant for as I opened the cast iron door to check if another log was needed a rush of cold air chilled my back and momentarily fanned the crackling fire into an inferno-like roar. At this second the addition of another piece of wood would be definitely incinerating.

Caesar growled a protest and scrambled to his feet. "It's the front door, Caesar. That's all! The last person to go out simply did not give the necessary tug needed to keep it from blowing open."

"Or, the last person to come in," I whispered a few seconds later, Euphy's emergency flashlight taken from the kitchen hutch clearly illuminating a path of wet footprints heading across the carpeted foyer and up the stairs.

I curled my fingers underneath Caesar's collar. "Strange, that whoever it was didn't come into the kitchen and say hello. The hurricane lamp is plainly visible from here as we also must have been seated at the table." Letting go of his collar I shut the door against the pelting rain, giving it an extra nudge with my shoulder until I heard the lock click over, then I twisted the knob for the dead bolt into place. "That is unless the person was an intruder or unless the person was coming to visit someone and didn't want to be seen."

Caesar, as if in agreement rumbled like a disgruntled elephant, and started to sniff at the footprints, doggedly following them to the foot of the stairs. I followed him, playing the beam of the flashlight from side to side and up and down, wondering if I should shout out a warning that an intruder was in the house and that we were all going to be murdered or if I should pause, take a breath, bring my over active imagination to heel and resort to logic.

Logic won, for after I paused and took a deep breath I recalled something Euphy had said just before she left the kitchen to go to bed. "It's a foul night, Serena," she had complained. "Not fit for man nor beast to go roamin' and although the evening is young I've locked the front door. So, anyone with an attack of itchy feet and wanderlust better not forget their key."

At the time I really hadn't thought about her threat muttered in such a bone-weary manner since I had committed myself to an evening of exorcising the devil. Now that I was thinking about it the open, now closed, door looming in front of me took on the aspect of an exciting mystery to be solved. I turned off the flashlight. Immediately everything became quite clear.

Euphy had said, "I've locked the door." I had learned not long after arriving in Rouge Baie that if Euphy said she had done something she had done it with a capital D! So, that meant that one of the two people upstairs, Jacques or Euphy, supposedly nestled in their beds, had tiptoed down the stairs and unlocked the door for someone I wasn't supposed to see. The one set of wet footprints heading topside confirmed that as a fact.

I breathed a sigh of relief. I had just saved myself from what could have been one of my life's most embarrassing moments, running through the rooms screaming a murderer was on the loose. However, there was someone in the house who didn't qualify for sleeping over.

Of course, it was none of my business as to who was entertaining whom in their boudoir. However, Caesar thought differently. He bounded up the stairs, his manner far too playful for me to ignore. I followed quickly, Simon's words, "Grab the God damned dog," shouted in frustration a few weeks back under soggy circumstances haunting me.

With Caesar finally and firmly in tow I sat down beside him on the landing. The hurricane lamp in the kitchen was giving off just enough of a glow for me to make out the familiar objects placed along the walls below. Slowly my eyes adjusted to the darkened upstairs hall. There was a miniscule streak of soft flickering light visible underneath Euphy's door as there was coming from Jacques. There was also a third shaft of light coming from a tiny bedroom beyond Jacques, next to the stairs leading to the attic and seldom used. Euphy called it The Chart Room, "Being as how," she had said, "my father and my Bob stored their charts and ship logs in there."

"Ayah," I murmured into Caesar's pointed ears, "obviously from yon wee glimmer of light filtering through The Chart Room door the new boarder has arrived."

Euphy had said in a rather off hand way or maybe it was in a vague way that an acquaintance of Captain Barrows or maybe it was Jacques would be spending a few days. Her explanation, "He will seem more phantom than real, Serena, his hours different from that of the rest of my boarders and he won't be taking meals," somewhat garbled due to the blender whirling at top speed.

Perhaps the phantom was the guilty culprit. Perhaps it wasn't Euphy or Jacques tiptoeing down the stairs to let someone in for a clandestine meeting or a romantic rendezvous but rather it was the new boarder coming in and not being aware of the temperamental front door, that you really had to push it shut.

After all, being qualified to sleep over he would have been given a key.

I had "perhapsed" myself to death and, though the temptation was great to investigate the home of the faint murmer of voices I could hear, there was a louder voice nagging at my conscience telling me, "Procrastination is a tool of the devil." Even the grandfather's clock chimed its ten strikes worth, proclaiming the young evening had ticked into night.

"Come on, Caesar," I ordered, "let's go back to the kitchen. We have solved the mystery, for whoever is here is friend not foe. Besides, I'm never going to finish my letter to Gloria sitting here on the landing."

As silently as possible we made our way down the stairs, the high winds and steady rain buffeting the house fortunately helping to deaden Caesar's rambunctious retreat to underneath the kitchen table. A few seconds later, my retreat from the landing having been accomplished in a more sedate manner, I sat down at the big oak table, picked up my pen and started again to exorcise the devil from my soul.

Now, my dear sister, to continue on with my letter; the wood stove doing okay!

Of course taking boating lessons meant I had to get Grandfather's boat into the water and then find someone willing to risk their life by taking mine into their's. The first part of my dilemma was easy to solve, I simply dialed the marina number and spoke to the manager, a Mr. Macintosh, whose name I had discovered in the card file. I admit to being somewhat flabbergasted when he told me that correspondence had been received regarding the boat's new owner and a check to cover all expenses incurred for her maintenance and storage. Being me, and _Escape_ being considered a she, I almost quipped, "You mean just like a kept woman?" Rest at ease, I didn't.

It was Mr. Macintosh who also solved the second part of my dilemma by finding an instructor for me, a he, but best spelled in all caps, a HE. Now then, I want you to think of this HE as someone who in June when I began my lessons looked like Simon Legree since at the time I met him he was wearing black fishing

210

boots and had a full black beard; his name being Simon having fueled my overactive imagination which you say I possess. However, from now on I want you to think of this HE nee Simon as a HUNK, his transformation in my eyes having occurred slowly throughout the summer as I struggled to cope with my lessons.

It is also important that at this time you forget what I told you, oh so many, many months ago after my divorce from Britt came through, that "I'm off men, forever!" and that "What a grand world this would be if the men were all transported far beyond the northern sea!"

You see, I'm in love! At least I think I'm in love and don't you dare to even think or to say "Serena is off on another summer fling." This time it is for real! At least I think, as of now, it is for real since that's why I came to Rouge Baie with Simon Stewart Mont, my so called museum friend to you.

How's that for another eye opener? Are you having trouble keeping up with me? If you are I'm not the least bit surprised since I'm having trouble keeping up with myself, not only with myself but also with the amount of stationery I need to finish this letter so time out to fetch more.

I visualized a smile coming to Gloria's face as I wrote, fetch. The word was seldom spoken back home in Boston or at The Barnacle, our family having learned the hard way that Caesar considered it an invitation to bring whatever was nearest to him on the floor regardless of its status in the world of objects. Even writing the word was dangerous for at times he seemed to possess a sixth sense like Simon and Buddha.

I looked up, guilt I know written all over me, and stared straight into Caesar's big brown eyes. "Don't give me your hound dog expression look," I admonished, but softly and with a smile.

I was presented immediately with the chewed-up remains of what appeared to be upon examination a well marked road map of Nova Scotia. It was pointless to ask, "Where did you find it?"

Instead, I got up from the table and threw the map into the stove making a mental note to tell Euphy of its loss in the morning, then taking advantage of the open door added another log to the fire. I was tempted to linger for a moment enjoying its warmth and the spectacle of spiralling flames but again I had the fortitude for proceeding with the business at hand, namely fetching more notepaper to finish my letter.

Telling Caesar, "Stay," I grabbed Euphy's flashlight and headed for the back stairs. I regretted my decision as each step taken on the bare wooden treads seemed to creak louder than the last. However, once I reached the landing I was able to sashay down the hall to my bedroom without causing so much as a rustle.

Euphy's light was out as was Jacques' and the new boarder's. All was quiet except for the grandfather's clock tolling eleven o'clock. All seemed to be in order. Well, not quite all was in order. My bedroom door was ajar!

So many conflicting thoughts raced through my mind at once that I turned the flashlight off; for some reason the protective custody of darkness preferable to the revealing arc of light in front of me. I had shut the door, even given the knob an extra twist before going down to dinner, but I had been in a hurry - so - maybe I just thought I did. I had brought little of great value with me that a burglar might be interested in except for a single strand of pearls, a gift from Mother's late parents given to me on the day I graduated from college, but I hadn't worn them since arriving in Rouge Baie - so - no one knew they existed. I had pooh-poohed Simon's warning about being searched for by members of the Colombian cocaine cartel, but perhaps he was right in his assumption - so - a member could be a friend, an acquaintance, a passer-by on the street or, heaven forbid, someone who left wet footprints in the hall.

My heart skipped a few beats, fibrillating into over time. My breathing followed suit, deep and rapid. I had come round-robin in my thinking - back to square one - once again asking myself, "Do the wet footprints in the hall belong to friend or foe?"

I stepped forward, cautiously, very cautiously and pushed my bedroom door slowly back against the wall. It opened all the way. There was not even enough room for a self-respecting shadow to wedge in between.

Satisfied, I allowed myself to step over the threshold. In a repeat performance of what I had done just an hour before I anxiously plied the flashlight from side to side and up and down, manipulating the beam, probing into all four corners. Nothing!

Feeling a little more confident I knelt down and peered under the bed. Nothing! Not even a dust whisker!

That left the closet, a miniscule space to be sure, barely adequate to hold the few articles of clothing I had brought with me. Emboldened by this thought I got up, walked into my bedroom and jerked open the door. My reward for such bravery was in discovering the closet was just a closet and that it was not being used as a hideaway.

Still something seemed different. I thought I had hung my damp bathrobe to the left of my yellow nylon windbreaker. Now it was on the right, the hem laying against the top of one of my suitcases. Being a clothes neat-nick, that bothered me. I moved it back, chalking-up my untidiness to the same excuse of being in a hurry.

The cherry chest of drawers claimed my attention. Somehow, it too appeared different. It wasn't that the chest had been moved away from the wall but rather it was the top drawer being slightly open. Having limited storage space the top drawer was where I crammed my "unmentionables" as Euphy called my lingerie, my socks and nighties, and the object which I had come upstairs for, an exquisite Florentine leather portfolio, hand tooled in gold and holding notepaper, postcards, stamps, etc. It was part of a desk set I had picked up at a Christie's auction, the rest of the set too bulky to pack. Taking it out of the drawer I decided to a run-of-the-mill burglar it would appear worn and not worth stealing. However to a snooping foe the newspaper articles I had stuck inside the overleaf re the Colombian cocaine cartel would make fascinating reading.

Hurrying, why I wasn't sure but somehow haste seemed important, I put the portfolio on top of the chest and opened it. Nothing was missing. All was in order and yet I thought I had put the newspaper clippings face down. Now they were right side up! "Serena," I told myself, "you are not infallible. You

213

only think you put the clips face down. Just like you only think you shut the bedroom door."

For once, I agreed with myself; a major mistake on my part for there was definitely another living breathing soul in the room, though at the moment I wasn't sure if I qualified as one of the living breathing twosome. It was the sense of a presence I noticed first, then the awareness of their damp scent swept over me right before I felt the brush of death against my feet and ankles. I needed to scream, to release the pressure of fear that had reached the explosive state within me but nothing would come out except a weak gasp and finally a drawn out, shaky, barely audible, "Oh - h - h, no - o - o, Simon where are you?"

A mewing cry in answer to my plea came out of the stillness and dark of the night, as loud in my ears as the mighty roar of a tiger must sound to an intruder in the jungle. I jumped, taking one huge leap from in front of the chest clear across the room to the side of the bed. My legs gave out, quivering like jello on a spoon. I collapsed, sinking down onto the soft mattress, somewhat amazed that I had not dropped the flashlight, its glow revealing that I had survived a monstrous attack, that I was still intact.

My assailant stood in front of me, back arched in proud splendor, eyes glowing like fiery embers; nothing more alarming than Euphy's plump, big black cat, an affectionate fur ball of fuzzy fluff just waiting to pounce onto my lap. Talk about feeling foolish!

"Cobweb, you naughty pussy-cat. So you are the villain." I couldn't resist picking Caesar's nemesis up, scolding gently as I did, "You might have nine lives but I don't."

I started to laugh, giving him an affectionate rub under his outstretched chin. "The joke is on me, Cobweb. Why you must have pushed the door open when I failed to shut it properly."

Holding him tightly under one arm I put the portfolio under my other and with the flashlight showing the way once again trudged downstairs to finish my letter, this time silently via the front hall. I didn't bother to shut my bedroom door, my arms being full giving me the necessary excuse.

Caesar wasn't the least bit thrilled to see Cobweb; neither was Cobweb overjoyed at having to share the space underneath the table with him. As for the space on top of the table I wasn't about to relinquish it to the devil so once again I sat down, picked up my pen and before the old scalawag could tempt me into a switchel break continued immediately on with my letter to Gloria.

My stationery having now been fetched and stacked neatly in front of me I shall continue with my saga. I'm not going to bore you, Sis, with the details of all my lessons, only the last one that led me to travel willingly down the garden path with Simon all the way to Rouge Baie. Actually, what I am calling my last lesson was really a day cruise Simon was taking me on in honor of my having completed sixteen weeks of frustrating work trying to learn the rudiments of boating. It also represented sixteen long weeks for him in learning how to survive under extreme duress and what had to have been at times enduring death defying moments while my hands were on the tiller; though he has never complained or said so in so many words to me.

Our cruise started propitiously from Riggs Marina on the morning of August 22nd, at 10:30 a.m., with countless good wishes for a pleasant voyage from many bystanders. The sky was a delphinium blue, the same color as Simon's eyes; the sun was dazzling, appearing like a giant lemon drop as it inched its way up and over the fringed tops of evergreens circling Knubble Bay. It ended somewhat soggily around 3:30 p.m., back at the marina amid lots of welcoming greetings heralding our safe return, still under a delphinium blue sky but with the sun beginning to edge its way over the yardarm. You see it was those in between hours, the time Simon and I spent between our going from and coming back to the marina which included the time I described back on page one of my letter as being wild, exciting and frightening that launched me into Simon's scholarly world of marine archaeology; for it was during that interim that Simon and I encountered drug runners, discovered a dead body, were almost shot and I personally scuttled one boat and damaged another.

How is that for an addendum to my previous two eye openers?

Now not to worry for all is well that ends well; the drug runners otherwise known as Missy Sue and Leroy are now in the custody of the police and awaiting trial, their weapons and illicit cargo confiscated, their boat <u>Savannah's Revenge</u> which I smashed now salvaged and impounded, <u>Escape's</u> minor bumps and bruises smoothed away and the dead body, a drug agent out of Boston, now at rest in a proper burial plot.

It goes without saying, Gloria, this "mop up operation" to use one of Adam's favorite expressions, was not accomplished over night. In fact the ramifications of our ordeal are still going on, but in retrospect I do believe the first few hours after Simon and I returned from our cruise with Missy Sue and Leroy in tow were the most tense interrogation wise for us, making the next couple of days before we left for Rouge Baie a breeze to get through. Sworn statements had to be given, signed in blood - you know how you lawyers are - since most of the evidence was water damaged and some, like the charts, nonexistant because of the tides. Then the police and federal drug agents cautioned us against discussing the case with an outsider, their investigation of those involved in the northeast still being in the hush up stage. Then they had to know our exact "whereabouts" - for the rest of our lives it seemed - so we could be summoned to appear in court for a preliminary hearing, either Portland or Boston depending on which state wins the tug of war. Simon was a problem in so far as he is a Canadian citizen - this got to be rather hairsplitting - but like I wrote above, all is well that ends well. Ayah!

Now before I continue on with my letter it is important to me that you try to understand the reasoning behind my decision to come with Simon to Rouge Baie. Our day cruise might have been the catalyst for my actions since it was packed with adventure but it was the grand total of events and details experienced during my sixteen weeks of lessons that swayed me in the long run to come.

There is also another reason, a bit on the profound side, slightly mystical, perhaps unfathomable. It has to do with trust,

*the kind of trust that develops over a period of time, the kind of
trust you once described to me as being willing to put your life in
someone else's hands, the kind of deep trust, you said, that is
acutely felt when alone with someone else in a small boat
bobbing in the middle of a vast ocean.*

My fingers were beginning to cramp giving me an excuse to
put down the pen. Anyway, I was getting too philosophical in
my writing or maudlin as Gloria might say, thinking that I had
had one glass of wine too many.

The incessant ringing of the telephone gave me another
excuse to pause, to get up and stretch my legs by walking across
the kitchen floor to answer the bloomin' thing. It had been
ringing or dinging or pinging - call it what you will - all day long
and Euphy, usually very even tempered, had just about jerked it
off the wall in exasperation. She had said after answering its call
for what must have been the hundredth time and hearing no one
reply, "The trouble with the telephone, Serena, is that a tupilak
has put a hex on the line."

"A what?" I had asked.

"A tupilak! It's an Inuit word my Bob used a lot. It means,
loosely, an evil spirit. You see many years ago it was common
practice among the Inuit to go to a shaman and have him whip
up an evil charm made out of all sorts of disgusting,
disagreeable, ugh, items. The word somehow was adopted by we
Newfoundlanders."

"Oh! You mean like a voodoo doll that a person would stick
pins in to give someone they didn't like an aching back?"

Euphy had laughed. "Exactly, Serena."

However my explanation seemed more plausible, though I
didn't tell her so, that the erratic dinging was due to a
combination of high winds and Rouge Baie being in the process
of having its phone network upgraded from a predominantly four
part system to a two party line. So here I was once again
responding to a jingling of the phone, the steady ringing having
stopped, and in all probability there wouldn't be a person on the
other end to answer my, "Captain Browne's Mooring."

217

I was dead wrong. I didn't have to say a word since a conversation was in progress. I should have hung up, having been taught eavesdropping is a despicable act, but the oddity of the hour and the raspy voice, reminding me of chalk grating against a blackboard, compelled me to listen to his words.

"Now let me repeat the instructions as briefly as possible. A bill of lading is to be written acknowledging receipt of three crates for transportation. Preparations are to be made for receiving said cargo on the 20th, approximate time and location for deliver of said cargo to be confirmed that morning. Since goods will be highly perishable proper packaging will be required to prevent premature spoilage. Crate size to be roughly seven feet by four feet by four."

There was a click, like a receiver being put down and then the line went dead. I too hung up, the weirdness of the lop-sided conversation and my guilt over listening making me uncomfortable. However that feeling was fleeting, quickly replaced by my morbid curiosity, as to who upstairs was on the line or had a tupilak crossed the wires carrying a stranger's voice, as to why business should be discussed during the witching hour instead of during the day and as to why October 20th seemed to be such a popular day for exiting Rouge Baie.

There was only one logical explanation I could think of for the latter, coincidence! As for the raspy voiced comment, "goods will be highly perishable so proper packaging will be required to prevent spoilage," the only logical explanation was fish! After all what else was there to ship from Rouge Baie other than fish?

Having settled that in my mind I sat back down at the table and picked up my pen. The time had now come for me to begin writing about my ecstatic and romantic present life since I had mentioned that way back on page one of my letter. This was the juicy part, the part I knew Gloria was panting to hear.

As for writing about the romantic and ecstatic present, Gloria, I won't go into detail except to point out the ecstatic part of my life is being well nurtured. You will have to wait until I get home for me to fill in the gaps that I know you are anxious to know. Mean, aren't I?

The romantic part I am going to tell you about is a setting which heightens the senses; picture if you will a spellbinding all pink sea-smokey sunrise, a bay window overlooking what else but a bay, a squeaking antique rocking chair, a cozy sleigh bed for one but that two can squeeze into, an old flannel bathrobe and a pair of wool socks. Is your curiosity aroused? Again, you will have to wait until I get home to find out the answers.

I'm sure by now, after receiving such a plethora of postcards from me - ha, ha, ha, - that you have perused the atlas and found that Rouge Baie is located on the Strait of Belle Isle, Newfoundland side. What the atlas won't tell you: the tiny fishing village is picturesque, quaint and not yet launched into the 20th century; its buildings are predominately box-like, spartan, utilitarian and weather beaten with the exception of a few Victorian style domiciles like Euphy Browne's; its inhabitants should be considered as a major source of material for a yarn spinner, their speech and habits being salty and thrifty like the drying of cod in the sun; its lifeline is the waterfront, always busy, dominated by Teweks General Store where all the news that's fit to be heard, and not, is discussed, a true gossip lover's mecca.

Rouge Baie is also connected to the outside world via, "the scenic route," a meandering road crisscrossing the province that eventually brings you into "Sin" John's, an honest-to-goodness sophisticated and modern metropolis that I like almost as much as Boston. Once there a person can either fly regally away like the Queen, or, if time is not pressing and you are traveling with a four legged friend like me, elect to take the east coast ferry service back to Bar Harbor and to the, so called, amenities of mainland life.

The atlas won't tell you, either, about Euphy Browne's house or about Euphy Browne. Actually, Gloria, her house is a lot like The Barnacle having been constructed of wood and native stone around the early 1900's. Both houses have their share of turrets, wide porches and gingerbread trim. It's their settings where they differ; The Barnacle overlooking the ocean and isolated from the rest of the world whereas Euphy's house is perched on a high hill within the city limits. That is, if you can call the fishing

219

*village of Rouge Baie, population three thousand, a city. There is
a nice, wide sidewalk in front of her place which if traversed,
like I have been doing daily, leads you satisfactorily to all the
other important domiciles in town and finally down to a few
small stores hugging the waterfront in a smothering sort of
grasp. In the back of her place, often called the front by tourists
because of the commanding harbor view, there is a beautiful
perennial garden meticulously tended by her. "It was started by
my mother," she told me one day, "with the thought a garden is
forever, so each plant and shrub received their full measure of
peat moss, bone meal and love." Her sentiment I understood as
I'm sure you do too, both of us having been issued from a family
that treats a garden as a legacy and is willingly bound by
nobless oblige to keep historic Boston beautiful.*

*Now a brief word about Euphy. Again, you will have to wait
until I get home for pertinent details but let me just say for the
present that you would adore her, as I do, just like you adore
chocolate, rare steaks and strawberry shortcake.*

Caesar's scratching on the kitchen door to let me know he
had to go out gave me the perfect excuse I needed to get some
fresh air and to let me stop thinking for a few minutes about
what to write next. Also, to rest my eyes from the strain of
writing, the hurricane lamp which I thought would be so great
having produced nothing but eerie shadows on the notepaper.

Not wanting to waste time going upstairs for one of my
jackets, I helped myself to what was hanging on top of the
clothes tree which turned out to be Simon's slicker and
sou'wester. Just putting it on made me feel close to him.

By now Caesar was becoming vocal, his whine insistent and
probably would reach the pitch of ti and do on the musical scale
if I didn't move fast enough. Moving fast wasn't a real problem,
what was that in the dimly lit room I could not find his leash and
I discovered my george martins, Euphy's quaint name for ankle
high rubber boots with lacings, were missing from her ordained
place of storage, a huge rubber mat beside the door.

So I did what any other red-blooded American girl would do
in facing a crisis of this nature. I simply took off my socks and,

as an afterthought before heading outside in my bare feet, took one of Euphy's small copper bottom saucepans hanging on a rack by the stove to use as a paper weight for my letter. I had learned the hard way that every time the kitchen door was opened it let in a strong gust of wind coming right off the bay. Everything lightweight on the table "Not ground tackled" to quote Captain Barrows would fly away.

Fly away was almost what Caesar did as I opened the door and stepped out onto the porch. He shot past me like an arrow, his destination no doubt the meadow abutting Euphy's place known by local romantics as Sunrise Point.

To my surprise the rain had stopped. I had become so completely engrossed in writing to Gloria that I hadn't missed hearing the ratt-a-tatting of drops against the window. The wind was still strong though, bedeviling the low-lying clouds now visible thanks to a rising moon.

The wet grass was barely bearable underneath my feet, its penetrating coldness going through me like the undulating swells the ocean had on the morning of my graduation run. Fortunately Caesar came right back sparing me the trauma of having to search for him with a flashlight in the dark which could be compared to hunting for a needle in the haystack.

I felt almost special as being piped aboard ship when Caesar and I walked back into the kitchen: the lights were on, the obese witch riding on a broomstick disappeared from the clothes tree as did the monstrous shadows from the walls, and the warmth from the pot-bellied stove was almost - but not quite - as comforting as being wrapped in Simon's arms.

"Just a couple more pages to go, Caesar, I promise, then it's upstairs to bed." A promise being a promise I hurriedly sat down at the table to finish my letter. Something was different!

I thought for sure I had put the saucepan bottom side down on top of the written sheets of notepaper. Now it was shiny side up! I thought for sure I had put the used sheets of notepaper, written on side, facing down. Now they were facing up!

My portfolio appeared to be as I had left it on the table, spread open, but my journal, The Perils of Serena, was closed. I thought for sure I had left it open, to remind me after returning from taking Caesar for a walk, to tell Gloria about Captain Barrows bringing me home.

I tried to keep cucumbery-cool like Simon, telling myself, "Don't panic! There has to be a logical explanation. After all no one could possibly be interested in a letter I'm writing to my sister unless _____?"

As if on cue the grandfather's clock chimed one a.m., the lights flickered and the telephone jingled. Simultaneously the back stairs creaked and a door upstairs banged shut. Caesar "Woofed" at Cobweb; he "Sissed" back and the chunks of apple wood burning in the stove shifted position, snapping and popping. I jumped up. "Oh, my, God, a member of the cocaine cartel would be interested in my letter. That's who!"

Any moment I expected to hear a fiendish laugh, to feel a cold blade of steel cutting into my spine, to see my life's blood spilling on Euphy's table, forming a thick red pool, leaving a stain forever. I could hear her crying, almost, saying as if giving a tour of the house to a new boarder, "This is where Serena Bradford was killed. All because of what she had written in a letter."

After a minute I sat backdown. I had not heard a fiendish laugh. I did not feel a cold blade of steel cutting into my spine nor was there a gush of blood spilling out over Euphy's table forming a thick red pool. What was spilling out was a good case of "ridiculitis" for once again letting my over active imagination run away with me. Common sense dictated the answer. I had only been absent from the kitchen for about ten minutes, scant time for someone to sneak in and read my letter. I had been in a rush to take Caesar out. The room was dimly lit and what I thought I had done, I simply had not. Common sense also told me that if I was ever going to climb the stairs to bed I better get on the ball and come up with a grandiloquent finale for my letter; perhaps something about the future.

Well, my dear sister, now that you know about my immediate past and my romantic and ecstatic present status I guess it's time to tell you about my future which at the moment can best be described by a giant question mark. Now, not to worry! I'm not about to give forth issue! I will be home soon, sooner than you think! Which brings me to a grand finale for my letter!

If all goes well, I plan to leave here bright and early on the morning of the 20th which means I will be back at The Barnacle the evening of the 21st. The really super news is that I am getting a ride back, Caesar too, with Captain Robert "Sonofagun" Barrows who happens to be a very close friend of Grandfather Horatio's and a friend of Daddy's. It seems that Grandfather and Captain Barrows sailed together on the <u>Bowdoin</u> when in their early 20's and that after Captain Barrows became master of his own ship Daddy crewed for him several times. All three of them have remained in touch throughout all these years. It is indeed a small world!

When we arrive at The Barnacle, regardless of the hour, I will give you a call. After spending a couple of days closing the place up for the winter, that is unless the whole family is there as planned, we will both head for Boston, Captain Barrows it seems having some unexpected business to attend to in our fair city. So will you please be sure and tell Mother and Daddy the minute they get off the plane from London, as I know they will want Captain Barrows to stay with them; Grandfather and Grandmother still being in Washington this time of the year.

Well, Sis, I now have a good case of writer's cramp, that being mentioned on page one as a possibility, so will bring this letter to a close. Please tell Paul, that zany husband of yours whom you call "Paul, Baby" I finally took some boating lessons. Maybe it's best not to mention at this time that I injured <u>Escape</u> to him or for that matter to anyone else in the family. I'll confess my sins to all when we get together.

It goes without saying I am really looking forward to seeing you. Much, much love from your delinquent sister.

Serena

P.S. I will call you the morning of the 20th, just before we leave Rouge Baie for Maine.

*P.P.S. I felt I had to wait until the very end to let you know
Simon isn't married and never has been - else you might not
have found the strength to finish reading my letter.*

I sighed, loudly, as I put down my pen. However there was
one more chore I had to do before I was free to leave the table
and go to bed. I picked up the sheets of notepaper, tapped them
against the table to form a neat pile, folded them in half and then
stuffed them into my previously stamped and addressed
envelope. I smiled. "Waste not, want not."

The letter, now being a fait accompli, meant I was finally
free of sin. I was no longer a tool of the devil. I had succeeded in
exorcising that being from my soul. So, a promise being a
promise, breakable only by death or being hospitalized, I added
the extra wood to the stove as Euphy had asked me to do and
turned the damper down low. The hurricane lamp was next and
after stacking my writing paraphernalia together on the table I
lowered the wick and blew it out. All seemed to be in order, just
as Euphy would have left the kitchen; even the flashlight was
back in its place on the hutch as was the saucepan back in its
place hanging on the rack by the stove.

There was only one thing to do. Check to be sure the back
door was locked. It was such an easy task! So, naturally I
complicated it with the spur of the moment decision to take a
short walk to Sunrise Point. Caesar read my mind for by the time
I had put on Simon's slicker he was impatiently waiting to go
out.

The transformation from a windy, turbulent, foggy night to
one of calm, bright moonlight beauty was overwhelming.
Compelling too, as we hurried down the porch steps and headed
towards the far end of Euphy's garden where a heavy growth of
wild, thorny rugosa roses effectively created nature's barrier to a
dangerous precipice.

Having always been skittish about heights it had taken many
walks with Simon through the meadow for me to be at ease
getting to Sunrise Point. It had also taken many walks with him
for me to get there by going through the white picket gate Euphy
had erected at the far end of her garden to mark the entrance to

an almost hidden path. It was shorter this way. Prettier too, I decided, the mud path underneath my barefeet appearing like a sparkling silver ribbon. Through the years the path had been worn as smooth as glass, not even a pebble had worked its way up through the soil to provoke an, "Ouch!"

The summit proper offered no special amenities other than the old initial scarred log I was now sitting upon. It certainly didn't offer any shelter against the elements. What few straggly pines there were near the log bench were stunted in growth, their outstretched limbs bent into contorted shapes by the prevailing winds, beautiful in their grotesqueness.

According to Simon the spot historically could have boasted a stone lighthouse, perhaps built by the Vikings, similar to the one built by the Egyptians in 280 BC which had an open top so a fire could be kept going at all times. That particular one, Simon had said with a grand sweep of his arms, "Was 400 feet high and cast light about 25 miles out to sea."

According to Captain Barrows the spot offered an osprey's view of the town nestled down below at the foot of the headland and a sailor's view of the bay, Backbone Island and the Strait of Belle Isle. "Hell's bell's," he had said, "it's a sight for sore eyes to see the ships navigate through these treacherous waters."

According to Euphy it was the perfect spot to blow a farewell kiss to your lover heading out to sea. "Every time my Bob left port," she had said, "I walked here, would blow a lingering kiss out to him and wait a minute for one to come back to me."

I liked Euphy's idea!

Standing up I dared to walk closer to the edge of the precipice, not close enough to see the lights of Rouge Baie below but to try and see if there was a flickering of light visible on Backbone Island. I couldn't tell so just in case Simon was gazing across the channel towards me I went ahead and blew a lingering kiss to, "My love."

After waiting a minute I reached out to catch the one coming back from him to me. My true love's returning kiss was potent! So potent that, as I plucked the kiss from the air and brought it longingly to my lips, it sent me reeling to the ground.

As romantic as I thought it would be to believe Simon's airborne kiss packed enough punch to knock me for a loop, my prostrate face-in-the-mud-eating-dirt position was telling me otherwise. It was telling me I had been pushed!

Both of my shoulders felt numb. My head was throbbing. My chest was aching from the hard impact of the fall. To make matters worse my feet were sticking out into nothing but icebox air. That meant that one fourth of me was dangling over the precipice while the remaining three fourths of me seemed to be sliding that way. I didn't need a degree in math to figure out that if the two parts of me were added together the total would tally up to disaster.

Deliverance from a life in the hereafter came in the shape of a rugosa rose bush tenaciously clinging to its decreed spot upon the precipice. It was within my reach but so studded with thorns that Caesar must have heard my cries of pain as I grasped its branches. Perhaps he thought I had discovered a bone graveyard underneath the bush or flushed a rabbit - whatever, but suddenly he was beside me, teeth bared, snarling, growling, sniffing, snorting; fortunately close enough for me to grab his collar. I managed to gasp, "It's okay, Caesar. It's okay."

Admittedly my words were slightly garbled, a mixture of pain infused with tears, guilt over ignoring Simon's warning of not to take a walk tonight due to the storm and last but not least, guilt over not taking seriously his counsel that we were being searched for by the cartel. The last few seconds of my life proving him correct. However this was not the time to give in to pain or to feel sorry for myself and this was definitely not the time for tears! Somehow I had to get out of this mess and since Simon wasn't here to pull me from the brink of disaster Caesar would have to fill his shoes. Tightening my grip on his collar I ordered, "Home, Caesar, let's go home!"

He tried! I knew I was like an albatross hanging onto his neck, my dead weight perhaps hurting him, but at this precarious point in my life I had to take the risk. Caesar was my anchor to having a future. I decided to try a different tack. "Fetch! Go fetch your ball," I ordered in a sterner tone.

This time he hunkered down, his gray bulk looming above me in the moonlight comparable to the Goodyear blimp. His tail beat back and forth against the brush, his soft low growl telling me he was ready to play our tug of war. "Fetch! Go fetch your ball, Caesar!" I repeated.

Caesar tugged. I moved a few inches. "Fetch your ball, Caesar!"

He tugged harder. I moved forward at least a foot. Hallelujuhs were now in order as my feet came out of the icebox and all of me came to a welcome rest in the dirt.

I grasped Caesar's collar tighter. "Good boy," I encouraged. "Good boy! Now one more time for auld lang syne. Go fetch your ball!"

It was indeed a miracle when a few seconds later I actually stood up beside the old log bench. I also considered it a miracle when ten or fifteen minutes later I actually realized that I was now, at this very minute, sitting on the edge of my bed nursing the thorns out of my hands. Somehow, even though I couldn't remember how, being the misguided soul that I am, I had found my way back through the meadow. I had even had the presence of mind to batten down the kitchen before climbing the front stairs to bed, arriving "With Portfolio" in hand.

Caesar, thank goodness, appeared unharmed. He was already curled up in a ball on his rug beside the bed. A good place for me to be, I decided; in bed with the covers pulled over my head. That way I could hide my shame, for once again I had let my imagination run rampant. I had talked myself into believing that I had been pushed by a member of the cartel when obviously, after picking pine needles off my pants, I had backed into one of the pine trees close to the bench, the jolt knocking me to the ground.

As an afterthought, just before turning off the light to follow my own advice I leaned down giving Caesar a pat on the head. "What say, old boy? Shall we keep this escapade between ourselves? Simon doesn't have to know we were galavanting around tonight. What he doesn't know won't hurt him, don't you agree?"

I turned the light off then, thankfully crawling between the sheets, quite confident Caesar wouldn't say a word. In the meantime, between now and the time Simon returned from Backbone, I would think of some logical explanation for having a fist full of thorns, something like having fallen into a rose bush while searching for his precious piece of scrimshaw.

Caesar, always in tune with my vibes, rose noisily to his feet and thrust something wet and slimy into my outstretched hand. "Oh, no," I said quickly to him, "not another dead skate."

I turned the lamp back on. There, shining under the lamplight in all its glory was the piece of scrimshaw that he had so playfully buried. I might just as well have been looking at the Holy Grail so great was my awe.

Caesar! Dear, sweet, afraid-of-a raindrop Caesar had rescued me again. He had provided me with the necessary evidence to substantiate my false alibi. I accepted his gift gratefully and gave him another tender pat on his big gray head. "Good boy! recovering this bit of scrimshaw will certainly pacify Simon."

Immediately I felt guilty, lying not being one of my strong suits so I added quickly, "At the right time I will tell Simon the truth. In the meantime mum's the word. Okay?"

Caesar plopped back down onto his rug. I turned the lamp off, this time saying to myself what I had written to Gloria, "All's well that ends well. Ayah!"

Chapter 20

There was a sharp, cold bite in the early morning air on October 20th. Local fishermen, knowingly, reached for a heavier shirt to put on under their sweaters before heading out to sea. Landlubbers, discovering a heavy frost on the ground when they awakened, lingered over breakfast, their conversation invariably leaning towards the weather and the arrival of last year's first glitter storm. Euphy made an extra pot of cocoa so Simon and Jacques could fill their thermos bottles before leaving for Backbone Island. She also packed a picnic lunch for Sonofagun and me.

#

From the pulpit Simon and I could see sea smoke wafting in the Strait. Rising from the rocking chair we stood close together, encircling each other in our arms, silently watching the rays of the rising sun turn the gray ghostly vapors into a palette of soft pinks. "The pink smoke reminds me of cotton candy. It looks like swirls of it floating out to sea. Don't you think so, Simon?"

Simon responded by giving me a kiss on the head, then leaned down, kissing me gently on the lips before saying, "In truth, Serena, I was thinking the pink sea smoke is the same shade of the dress you were wearing the first evening I saw you at the marina. The evening I literally fished you out of the sea."

I started to blush from my toes up. "Please, Simon, I would appreciate you erasing that evening, forever, from your mind. I was such a mess!"

He chuckled softly, his love reflected in the tenderness of his smile and the warmth flooding his eyes. "I agree, you certainly were a mess, Serena, but a beautiful one. As for erasing that evening from my mind I know I will carry with me to my grave the vision of you standing on the float." Lowering his voice he whispered into my ear, "Especially the way that pink dress was clinging to every curve to your body."

Simon's words, though spoken endearingly, had the same effect on me as that of opening the gates on a spillway. Tears started to stream down my face. Sobs racked my body. The tighter Simon held me and the more he murmured consolingly, "Please don't cry, I didn't mean for my teasing to upset you," the deeper my sobs. Finally, between gulps and wiping my nose on a handkerchief Simon produced from his flannel bathrobe I managed to sputter, "It's not that. I know you would never say or do anything intentionally to hurt me. It's just the past few months have been so traumatic, so much has happened." I burrowed my head into his shoulder, trying to muffle my crying. "And now that the time has come to say good-by, I just can't bear to do it."

Simon's voice was constrained. "It's not good-by, Serena. There never will be a final good-by between us."

With those reassuring words lingering in the air he lifted me into his arms and walked slowly away from the pulpit towards the bed. In reality it was just a few steps away but measured against the overwhelming desire I could feel rising within him and my mounting passion it seemed more like a mile.

Laying me gently down Simon didn't say a word, nor did he while pulling a cotton coverlet up from the foot of the bed, stretching it out over me, tucking it in around my shoulders. When he finally did speak it was with obvious restraint, even his hands I noticed were thrust down deep into his blue jean pockets. "Serena, it is taking the disciplining of a lifetime for me to stand here beside the bed instead of reaching out to love you one more time before we have to part."

I looked up into his expressive eyes, reading his thoughts, understanding his self imposed exile and then turned my face away; his total commitment to me so visible upon his countenance that I was afraid to speak, afraid that if I did I might not be able to convey a total commitment to him. I needed time, time to think, time to walk my beloved beach once more where somehow I knew I would be shown the way. Desperate to ease the tension that had built up between us I grasped at the only straw that seemed to come into my mind, hoping against hope that he would understand. "Simon, don't you know, contrary to

230

what you archaeologists from Ottawa think, the tide will not adhere to your time schedule?"

It took an agonizing minute, perhaps two agonizing minutes before I heard his stretched out answer. First, there was an amused chuckle and I felt a tweak on my big toe. Second, it was the lingering touch of his fingers riffling through my hair. Third, was a whispered, "I'll take your luggage and Caesar down." Fourth, was a brief kiss on my forehead followed by, "Call me tonight. I'll be anxious to know how your trip is going." Fifth, was a kiss blown on the wind followed by, "I'll tell Euphy you will be down immediately for breakfast."

"Immediately" hung in the air even after Simon shut the door behind him. It spurred me into action for I had promised Captain Barrows I would be on time, he having informed me with proper quarter-deck authority, "The ferry waits for no one, not even The Queen."

I was glad that yesterday I had made a white glove inspection of my room, determined that Euphy and Abbie, the local cleaning lady who came to help her, would find nothing amiss. Now, all that really remained to be done was straighten the lovely wedding ring coverlet on the sleigh bed - having slept next door last night - and return the rocking chair to its original sideways position in front of the bay window.

With those two small chores accomplished, I stood in the doorway, make-up kit in hand, taking one long, last look at the pulpit and the now silent rocking chair. My vision blurred a little as the memories of the past few weeks crowded together in my mind. I couldn't help but wonder, as I sadly turned away and started down the hall, if I would ever again see Euphy's mother's citadel, the "room next to his, above the inside place."

#

Breakfast was over. Old Bess was loaded to the gills, Caesar and his paraphernalia taking up the entire back seat. I was already a basket case and it was just seven o'clock.

Caesar had been unusually difficult. "As mule-headed as you," Simon would have said. He did not want Captain Barrows

231

to touch him. He did not want to climb into the Land Rover. Apologizing, over and over again for the delay, I ended up unpacking Caesar's suitcase, spreading his oriental rug over the car cushions, putting his two stainless steel dog dishes on the floor and placing his favorite nylon dog bone on the seat, plus an old flannel blanket he liked to sink his teeth into and growl. That did the trick! He seemed happy, at least for the moment.

Captain Barrows started to warm up the engine. "Now, Serena, make your phone call PDQ to your sister and don't tarry saying, 'Fair Winds,' to Euphy. I don't want to speed all the way to Port-aux-Basques. Old Bess isn't as young as she used to be and like all you females is likely to blow her bonnet if pushed too far, too fast."

As always Captain Barrows' witty speech delighted me and since Simon was not around to view my obedience, I rushed into the house and placed my call.

While waiting for it to come through I sat down at the small French writing table Euphy had placed in the front hall. The piece was exquisite, of museum quality and as usual I found myself worrying that a negligent boarder might mar the smoothness of its surface. Euphy had told me though, after I had conveyed my concern, "Not to worry, Serena. I don't have any negligent boarders! Besides, that was where my mother placed it, under the stairwell so she could share its history with everyone, my great-grandfather having brought the writing table back from Marseilles on *The Merry Euphemenia*."

"Why, you were named after your great-grandmother, Euphy," I had replied somewhat in amazement. "So was I. For that matter so was Gloria. Our parents weren't expecting twins, you see, so our arrival sent them to the back pages of the family bible where important dates had been recorded. It was there they found my great-grandmother's name, Serenagloria. They decided to split the name, the coincidence of having two names combined not to be ignored."

Euphy had understood, nodding her head in approval. She had momentarily busied herself at the table, straightening up the stationery and the postcards depicting Captain Browne's Mooring she kept in a papier-mache box on top for her boarder's use, before continuing with her explanation to me. "My father had the floor to ceiling window put in, creating sort of an office for her. You know, a pleasant place to sit while paying the bills and catching up on correspondence. Also, so she could see the garden."

It was the way Euphy said, "See the garden," a wicked twinkle in her eyes, that had made me ask mischievously, "A compromise?"

Why that particular conversation had lodged in my mind was a mystery. Just like now it was a mystery, after passing by the table countless of times during the past weeks, why I suddenly decided to take one of the postcards home to show everyone where I had been staying. I scrutinized the card again before tucking it into my jacket pocket. Again, as before, I experienced an eerie sensation of having seen the card in some out of the way, far away place. "You are being ridiculous," I told myself.

Gloria's groggy voice came over the line. I had forgotten about the time change; no wonder she sounded so fuzzy, it would be just around 5:30 there. "Serena, I've been laying here, dozing off and on, waiting for your call. Since it's the morning of the 20th, I gather you and Captain Barrows are on your way?"

"Yes, we are leaving as soon as I hang up. If all goes well Captain Barrows and I should arrive at The Barnacle late tomorrow night. I will call you as soon as we arrive, regardless of the time."

"That won't be necessary, Serena. We will all be there to greet you."

My throat muscles constricted. "By all, you mean the entire family? Even Super-Sleuth Adam from Washington?"

Gloria laughed along with me over our very private nickname for our very dear older brother. "Yes, even Adam. For some unearthly reason he is worried about you."

I didn't mean to be abrupt. My, "Why," just came out that way.

"Now, Serena, don't be difficult! We had a family conference call via the overseas operator after I received your letter and everyone agreed this is for the best."

A family conference call meant trouble; trouble for me. My turtleneck sweater suddenly felt tight around my neck, like a noose. My voice squeaked. "The best for whom?"

"For you, of course. The papers have been full of news regarding the Colombian cocaine cartel and its vast network of dealers. In fact, it has turned into quite a local scandal, their clientele it seems reaching into some very high places and, after all, you are a prime witness. I also happen to know you are going to be served with a subpoena as soon as you return, a preliminary hearing I believe scheduled close to Thanksgiving. I also know, Serena, you are out of touch with the outside world up there in no man's land, not that you aren't always slightly out of touch with reality, but even you must realize certain precautions must be taken."

I recognized Gloria's placating tone and decided to ignore her barb about me being slightly out of touch with reality. It was true. She had always been practical, not impractical. She always listened to the weather report and dressed accordingly. I always dressed by mood or like last spring in keeping with the current exhibit at the museum.

"Serena, are you there?"

I nodded my head, yes, knowing she meant well, that she loved me; knowing they all meant well, that they all loved me; knowing deep down in my heart, in fact all the way down to my sneakers that I was lucky to have such a caring family.

"Serena, are you still there?"

Again I nodded my head, yes, thinking she sounds just like Daddy cross-examining a witness for the prosecution.

"Serena, answer me!"

Her command startled me. "I'm sorry, Gloria. I thought I had answered you. Yes, I'm still here but I have to go now. Captain Barrows is waiting and we have to catch the ferry."

"Then quickly let me fill you in on the plans we have made. Mother and Daddy are flying into Boston from London today. Adam is flying in from D.C., tonight along with Grandfather and Grandmother. We will all leave early tomorrow morning for The Barnacle. That is everyone but Paul. He has surgery in the morning but will drive up later in the day. It goes without saying,

234

Daddy and Grandfather are looking forward to seeing their friend of so many years."

"I've got to go, Gloria."

"One more minute, Serena. Adam wants to know your itinerary."

"Why?"

Gloria's voice rose. "Shades of Sherlock Holmes, Serena, don't ask me why! Just give it to me. You know how Adam is. He probably wants to put a red headed pin on his wall map along with all the other pins marking the misguided souls he has under surveillance."

I resigned myself to the inevitable, doomed forever it seemed not to be trusted out of sight. "Quickly then, Gloria. Remember Captain Barrows is waiting. He is not the most patient man in the world. We are taking the ferry out of Port-aux-Basques to North Sydney, Cape Breton Island. It's about a five hour trip. Once there he plans to take the eastern shore route to the Halifax-Dartmouth area where we will spend the night at Country Harbour Mines. It seems he has a friend anchored there who runs a Bed and Breakfast. Tomorrow morning we will get up early, continue down the coast to Yarmouth, taking the ferry out of there for Bar Harbour. From there, as you know, it's just about a three to four hour drive home."

I heard Gloria give an enormous sigh of satisfaction as if she had just accomplished the impossible. Her flat statement, "You know, Serena, there are times when you assume the qualities of a clam," proving me correct. However, she didn't wait for me to answer explaining in a very business like way, "All right, Serena, I've jotted your plans down and will tell Adam when he arrives."

"No doubt armed with his briefcase stuffed with road maps, a magnifying glass, a compass, and a box of pins."

I was expecting to hear one of Gloria's quick and snappy replies delivered in her usual light and happy way. Instead, she surprised me by her silence before saying finally, "You will drive carefully, won't you? There is a chance of snow blanketing the coast tomorrow night."

I heard the caring behind her mild admonition to drive carefully, just as I sensed her many unasked questions. After all we were of the same flesh, a part of each other having been nurtured together for nine months in our mother's womb, alike in so many ways that it was difficult, save for those few who knew us both well, to tell us apart. Instinctively, I knew what she wanted to hear and though Euphy was motioning for me to hurry, I tarried long enough to say,"It will be so good to see you, Gloria. We have a lot of catching up to do. Also, I want to tell you more about my museum friend, Simon."

Gloria interrupted, laughing, "I gather from your letter he no longer looks like Simon Legree to you?"

"No," I drawled out, her question making me feel a tad sheepish. "Actually, Gloria, it's strange that you should mention that because Simon got rid of his beard a couple of days ago, unveiling what you would describe as a firm, determined square jaw line. So now I would have to say he looks like a contemporary Paul Bunyan with the dazzle of the Marlboro man thrown in."

"Oh - my - word! You are really hooked, Serena."

There was no reason I could quickly come up with to fault her statement. Niether did I want to elaborate and say why Simon had decided to cut his beard, that revelation having been made to me during a rapturous moment when he murmured, "I shaved my beard off, Serena, for many reasons but this instance demands honesty. The main one is, though you never complained, I sensed you don't like the scratchiness of it against your face."

I paused just long enough to tease her like she always did to me. "By the way, Gloria, Simon will be spending the Thanksgiving holidays with us so you will have a chance to judge for yourself."

I heard her gasp, the holidays in our home so cherished that anyone who was invited to come and stay was to be considered as practically a member of the family. "Bye, bye now, I've got to dash. Give my love to all."

"I will, Serena. In the meantime, play it safe! Just be sure you don't give all yours away!"

236

I put down the phone, telling Euphy, who by this time was frantically propelling me out the front door, "My dear sister, always the practical one."

"Someone has to be, Serena."

We walked towards the car. I tucked my arm under hers, dreading the thought of saying good-by to her too. A gentle, reassuring hug passed between us. "Euphy, _____."

"Say no more, Serena, and don't you dare cry!" Having issued her order for me not to dissolve into tears she opened the car door, shooing me in, biding time by giving Caesar a farewell pat on his head before telling me, "I'll write to you," and telling Sonofagun, "It's time to cast off."

I looked back at Euphy from the side view mirror as Captain Barrows put the car into motion, saw her take a hanky out of her crisp, white apron pocket and dab at her eyes before turning to walk around the house into the garden. I didn't look back again, making sure I kept my eyes on the road.

It was quite a while before I felt up to speaking. Captain Barrows seemed to understand, continuing to point out scenic spots and historic landmarks along the way without expecting a comment in return. At last I was able to say, "How much longer before we reach Port-aux-Basques?"

Captain Barrows guffawed. "Lucky for me Old Simon issued a small craft advisory this morning, warned me before he left for the island that some turbulence en route could be expected, else I would have no choice but to think my company was boring you."

I couldn't help but laugh, Simon's play on words so typical of his fine sense of humor. "You are the limit! You know that? And, you know what else? All of a sudden I'm hungry. Hungry for one of Euphy's chocolate chip cookies."

"Now you're talking, Sis, and while you are lolly-goggin' around how about pouring me a cup of hot coffee from my flask wedged in beside the picnic hamper. I don't want to fall asleep while on watch."

Immediately I offered to drive. "Remember, you said, we would both take our turn at the wheel."

"Later, Sis, after we get off the ferry and out of North Sydney a piece. My eyes aren't as good as they used to be and I detest having to drive a long distance in the dark."

"Whenever you are ready then."

I quickly poured his cup of coffee and then opened the wicker hamper Euphy had placed on the floor board in front of my seat. "My word, she has packed us a feast! Look at this will you? In addition to the chocolate chip cookies which she has labeled, "Snack," there are sandwiches filled with sliced cold duck, apples, a bottle of wine, cloudberry tarts and a couple of Cadbury bars. Why there is even a doggie bag just for Caesar."

Helping himself to several cookies he said after a bite or two, "I guess Euphy was afraid we were going to starve to death going over on the ferry. Actually the chow on board isn't that bad. Nothing fancy mind you, but it will stick to your ribs."

What was left of the morning passed swiftly, Captain Barrows treating me to many of his salty yarns while I continued to keep my eyes on the road, enjoying every hairpin curve, "oohing" and "aahing" over a sweep of beach, gasping at the sheer beauty of the headlands. So engrossed had I become with the countryside that when he pulled off the road into a rest area I was surprised to learn we were just a couple of miles out of Port-aux-Basques.

"Best walk Caesar here, Sis. It will be his last chance before we embark and then disembark at the terminal in North Sydney. You know, of course, he has to stay in the car while we cross?"

"Yes, that's why I will give him a tranquilizer. It worked out quite well when Simon and I came over on the ferry. I hated to do it but the pill did calm him down and the vet said it wouldn't hurt him a bit. In fact, he slept all the way."

After attaching Caesar's leash to his collar we got out of the car, the three of us enjoying our freedom of movement. "I'll plan on giving Caesar a good drink of water and Euphy's doggie bag treat after the ferry trip, Captain Barrows. Then tonight when we arrive at your friend's home I'll give him his regular meal."

"Sounds okay to me, Sis, but I think we better scoot along now."

I couldn't resist mimicking his proper quarter-deck authority. "I know the ferry waits for no one, not even The Queen."

His answer was a wide grin and a couple of toots on the car horn. I quickly reached into my pocket, took out the pill and burying it in a piece of cookie gave it to Caesar saying the magic word, "Treat."

#

The afternoon passed as swiftly as the morning. Unlike Caesar snoozing away below in the back seat of Old Bess I had trouble sitting still. First, I had to be sure the ferry's master knew how to properly pull away from the terminal. Then, I had to be sure he knew how to navigate, that he had not forgotten his rules of the road as we threaded our way past the buoys guiding us out into Cabot Strait. Having accomplished those two important tasks, I decided it was, "Time for chow?"

Captain Barrows was in rarer form than usual in response to my query. After we had found a sunny, sheltered spot on the promenade deck and spread out Euphy's sumptuous feast he assumed the role of a sommelier, hamming it up with a broad pantomime of a wine-waiter struggling to open a bottle of bubbly. I was in stitches by the time he was through as were so many of the other passengers who had gathered around to watch his performance. As it is on all voyages of any duration barriers of reserve are quickly broken down and strangers find themselves chatting to each other with total ease. We were no different in exchanging our pleasantries, especially with a tour group from Ames, Iowa, who had recently spent a full day observing the world famous tidal bore at Truro. One gentleman describing it to me as, "A rusty wall of water coming towards you that would scare the hell out of the devil."

Captain Barrows, of course, was in his element, giving a mini-lecture on the famous tides that gorge the Bay of Fundy twice a day. "Everyone has their favorite view but dollar for dollar I like Flowerpot Rocks at Hopewell Cove; the rocks at low tide you see looking like earthern pots stuck in the sand since they have small evergreens growing on top. At high tide, of course, the so called pots look like they are going to float out to sea."

I added to the deluge of opinions proffered over the most scenic spot by saying simply, "I'm like one of the shoemakers children who has no shoes. Although I'm from New England and have spent the past several weeks in Newfoundland I've never witnessed Fundy's tremendous tides."

It took the call, "Land Ho," to disperse the crowd, Captain Barrows and I following suit of the others by gathering up our belongings and heading towards the car in preparation for disembarking. Caesar wasn't the only quadruped awake and barking when we arrived below, his was just the deepest and loudest to be heard over the din of cars being revved up to go.

Once more I marveled over the efficiency and speed with which the ferry service personnel emptied the ship of its motley cargo. We were one of the first to drive off, having been one of the last to drive on and Captain Barrows lost no time in taking advantage of the open space to get underway.

"There's a small, isolated beach about three miles down the road, Serena. It's a good place to let Caesar run, give him his drink of water and snack since you mentioned this morning that's what you thought it would be best to do."

No sooner said than done, it seemed, we pulled off of the road and clambered out of the car. At first I didn't see the beach, sheltered as it was from a cursory passers-by view with thick intimidating brush, tall pines and a natural outcropping of ledge, but nevertheless after close scrutiny, there it was in all its secretive glory. My imagination clicked into overtime, seeded no doubt by Simon's tales of pirates having roamed the Strait eons ago and Gloria's reference to Sherlock Holmes, to say nothing about Super-Sleuth Adam winging in with his box of pins. "What a perfect beach for the likes of Captain Kidd and his merry band of cutthroats to come ashore and hide their loot," I said as we picked our way over the rocks down to the shore. "How did you ever find this little hide-away? Perchance you stumbled upon an old map of his showing the X that marks the spot?"

I was expecting Captain Barrows to laugh at my preposterous question or to perhaps bellow, "Hell's Bells, Sis." Instead, he stood in front of me, wooden, like a store front Indian, the lines of his face constricted into mud pack rigidity and the pupils of his eyes shrunk into dagger-like specs. This cloak-of-another-color demeanor of his sent my pulse into double time. The man seemed more like an adversary rather than the utterly charming one whose every word I had doted upon. This man's stance was now aggressive, his tone raspy and menacing instead of booming and jocular as he said, "Actually, I didn't, Serena. An acquaintance showed me this beach not too long ago. Don't you agree that it is a good place to stretch your legs after a long drive or to come ashore by boat for a private rendezvous?"

A vision of Leroy rowing towards shore in his orange Zodiac immediately surfaced. "Or to kill someone," I blurted inadvertently.

Captain Barrows frowned at me, my words underscored by the way his bushy white eyebrows momentarily fused together and by the couple of ominous steps he took forward. "Now that you mention it, yes! It would be a good place to kill someone."

His admission caught me by surprise; I had not expected him to agree. By all rights he should have pooh-poohed my question, he should have laughed; but then he had not laughed at my X marks the spot joke. It had been a long time since I felt uncomfortable in my surroundings and the spotting of a stuffed green garbage bag ensnarled in the seaweed near-by didn't help to assuage my mounting uneasiness. Quite the contrary, the sight of it escalated my apprehension into fear, pushing my voice up an octave or two as I asked him haltingly, "I suppose a body could be left here for days before the police would find it?"

"That is possible, Serena; perhaps even never when you take into consideration the caverns in the rocks made by the washing of the tides. Why, a body could be salted away forever if lodged in one of those."

His answer was so candid that it blighted my reasoning, it ushered in the thought that Captain Barrows could be a member of the Colombian cocaine cartel, that under the guise of

241

pretending to be a friend he actually was set upon killing me. I tried to scream for help. Unfortunately, nothing came out but a mouse-like squeak, not the best sound to summon aid or to proclaim to the world that I was about to be killed, pickled in brine and then stored away forever in a cave, much like a cucumber sealed in one of Euphy's canning jars that she kept on a shelf in a darkened pantry.

However, my pitiful Mayday, "EEEk," was heard. Caesar bounded up in response, wagging his tail so furiously that we both bent over at the same time to massage our whacked legs. Our synchronization of movement appeared to strike Captain Barrows' funny-bone, seemingly giving him a change-of-heart for the tight lines in his face slackened into a lop-sided grin, the pupils of his eyes dilated, a mischievous twinkle replacing the dagger-like specs, and his voice boomed with familiar jocularity. "My, my, Sis," he said drolly, "you do have a vivid imagination! Are you planning for a murder to be carried out here? Because if you are, best plan to accomplish the skullduggery during the daylight hours since it would be mighty difficult to climb the rocks back up to the road in the dark."

For the second time, in not so many days, I felt foolish for having doubted the sincerity of a friend. First, it was Jacques, and now here I was pondering the character of Captain Barrows, a man who was, "One of Mac's boys," a former confidant of Grandfather's, a mentor of Daddy's and a present friend of Simon's. Of course, he was right, my imagination was a tad too vivid, reading something into something that was absolutely nothing but a behavioral quirk of his advancing age.

He answered his own question with a robust laugh. It was infectious, restoring my sense of humor so that I was able to laugh back before saying, "No, I'm not planning for a murder to be carried out here."

"Whew! I'm glad to hear ye say that, Sis. You had a wild gleam in your eyes there for a while, sort of a crazed Captain Ahab, 'Thar she blows,' look." Glancing up at the sky he added emphatically, "We are going to lose our sun in a minute. Best heave a line around Caesar. In the meantime I'm going to head back to Old Bess and dig out the proper road map for us to

242

follow. To save time I'll also fill Caesar's water dish and empty the rest of Euphy's treat for him into a bowl."

I saluted him what I hoped was proper tar fashion, saying briskly, "Aye, aye Sir," and then hurried dutifully away to carry out his command. Not though without first taking a surreptitious peek over my shoulder, just to assure myself that Simon had not materialized out of nowhere to witness by obedience.

#

The darkness came swiftly as soon as the sun had set. We had been driving on the Trans Canada Highway for almost two hours, chatting along the way about this and that; this being a steady commentary by Captain Barrows about the finesse needed to lure a tasty Cape Breton salmon into swimming up to take the bait; that, being my travelogue about the many scenic places along the eastern shore of the island Simon had shown me while enroute to Rouge Baie, including a day spent touring the historic restoration at Louisbourg.

Our passing-the-time-of-day conversation stopped, however, when the headlights illuminated a large road sign indicating the last exit for the Port Hastings business district before crossing over to the mainland on the Canso Causeway. A hunger pang accompanied this directive, prompting me to speak up. "I don't suppose I could talk you into getting off the highway here and having dinner in town? Simon and I had a fairly decent breakfast at a small restaurant located on the waterfront called, The Strait Cafe."

"My sentiments exactly, Sis! I've eaten there many times, usually though having arrived by boat rather than by land. You see it's part of The Canso Strait Marina." He glanced at the clock on the dashboard. "Nineteen hours. Actually we are making better time than I thought we would thanks to you spelling me at the wheel for a while. Now then if we don't tarry too long over a steak, but just long enough for us to have a piece of apple pie with a slab of cheddar cheese on top and a mug of coffee, we should reach Country Harbour Mines around 23 hours."

"Translated, that's eleven p.m.," I said, after quickly counting on my fingers, still not being at ease with nautical jargon.

Captain Barrows chuckled. He was still chuckling an hour and a half later when we left the restaurant over a few of my boating mistakes I had divulged, a pint of ale with dinner having made him receptive to listening. "What's a bowline? That's a good story, Sis! I bet Old Simon just about croaked?"

My affirmative anwer was partially drowned out by a welcome yelp from Caesar. Before we had gone into the cafe I had tied him to Old Bess with a long lead line so he could stretch his legs. I had done this many times through the years, Caesar never getting tangled up. Tonight though he had wrapped himself up on the chain so neatly that all I needed was a mailing label to send him Special Delivery. Even stranger was his refusal to gobble up the steak bits I had brought out to him.

"Poor baby," I crooned, stooping down to unleash him, "if you could only understand that soon we will both be able to rest our weary bones."

Caesar's answer to my petting of him was a lethargic wag of his tail. This too was unusual for he loved to be scratched behind the ears and underneath his muzzle. Opening the car door for him to climb in I did my best not to sound anxious. "I do believe Caesar isn't feeling well, Captain Barrows."

"Probably getting saddle sore, like me, Serena. That's all! Now then, the sooner we get a move on, the sooner we will get to my mate's place."

"I'm sure you are right," I said, settling into the seat beside him. "It has been a long day, especially for dogs."

Captain Barrows grinned. "Especially for old sea dogs, Serena."

I grinned back at him. "No comment."

Conversation became virtually nil after we crossed over the toll bridge into Nova Scotia, both of us proprietary about our thoughts. Mine were conflicting, sort of a mixed bag: on the one hand an overwhelming desire to see and be with my entire family, yet on the other a profound reluctance to leave Simon. I felt an eagerness to get back to the museum for I did enjoy my job as a curator, but then I couldn't help but wonder about my future, wondering if my world and Simon's world were too far apart. As for Captain Barrows' thoughts, I couldn't tell. His face was inscrutable. That's why I gasped when he said calmly out of the blue, "I've changed my mind, Serena, about driving down to my mate's place at Country Harbour Mines. Instead of getting off the highway at the Lower South River exit we will continue on to Antigonish. It's just a few miles further down the pike and this time of year we won't have any trouble in finding a place to stay. In fact, I know of a couple of motels that stay open all year in the immediate area."

"But, but, why?," I asked, so startled over the change in plans that my voice quivered, the tremor bringing Caesar to his feet and his head to rest protectively on my left shoulder.

"Well, now, I've been thinking about what you said to the folks back on the ferry, that you've never witnessed the tides of Fundy. No telling when you will get the chance again, so I've decided we will spend the night at Antigonish, then leave bright and early tomorrow morning for New Glasgow. From there we will go to Truro so you can see a stretch of the Minas Basin and then on to Windsor and to Digby. At Digby we will take the ferry across the bay to Saint John. It's just a three hour run from there compared to spending six hours on the boat from Yarmouth to Bar Harbour. Barring an unforseen event we still should reach your parent's home late tomorrow night."

I remembered my manners, even though my heart skipped a beat or two over the switch in itinerary, saying, "How very thoughtful of you. I'm sure it will be a trip I shall never forget."

Caesar, however, did not remember his manners for a second later when Captain Barrows reached in front of me to adjust the lever on the dashboard for heat he lunged forward, attacking his arm with a rabid fury.

#

The lobby of the Antigonish Animal Hospital was not typical. Perhaps because the clientele, if the pictures of horses

245

and cows on the wall were indicative, tended to all be of the avoirdupois size. For this I was grateful.

Neither was veterinarian, Dr. Ian McTeague, typical looking. He had a bald head, cauliflower ears and his short-sleeved uniform revealed burly arms somewhat battle scarred from bites and scratches. However his hands I noticed were like Simon's, large and strong; gentle too, like Simon's, judging by the way he was examining Caesar. For this I was also grateful.

"Now tell me again, Miss Bradford, what exactly happened? The information Joel gave me over the phone after you brought Caesar in was sketchy, that you were enroute to Maine when your dog became ill and that the toll booth operator gave you directions to get here."

Hearing the urgency in Dr. McTeague's voice I tried to be concise. "It was around eight thirty when Captain Barrows and I left the restaurant in Port Hastings. Caesar didn't seem quite his usual frisky self and he refused the steak bits I had carried out for him. This was most unusual. We had been driving for about an hour when Caesar stood up and plopped his head down onto my left shoulder. This was not unusual for it was a habit of his to do so whenever he would get restless. I could tell Caesar was upset because of the faint rumbling sound he was making. Another habit of his whenever something seemed wrong to him. You see I had been surprised when Captain Barrows suggested a change in our itinerary for tomorrow. Caesar must have sensed this and when Captain Barrows reached in front of me to adjust the heat, he must have thought I was going to be hurt. That's when he snarled, bared his teeth and latched onto Captain Barrows' arm. The very next moment Caesar collapsed. He started to whimper and his body started to heave. Even his legs jerked."

Dr. McTeague glanced up at the large white clock on the wall. My eyes followed his. I couldn't believe it was ten thirty.

"Can you tell me, as accurately as possible please, the last time Caesar had something to eat? That is, that you know of?"

"Why yes! It was about ten minutes to five."

"Are you sure?"

"Yes, Dr. McTeague, I'm sure! The ferry from Port-aux-Basques docked around four o'clock. Captain Barrows knew of a small beach a short distance from the terminal where Caesar could run, so we drove there immediately. We gave him a small amount of chow and some water that I had brought with me just before we got back into the car."

"What about on the ferry?"

His questions were so probing, so decisive, so to the point that I knew instinctively Caesar was very sick. "He slept on the ferry. I gave him a tranquilizer along with some chow and water right before we boarded. Caesar was fine, Dr. McTeague, when we disembarked!"

Dr. McTeague pursed his lips. "I suppose he could have unearthed some form of toxic matter on the beach."

"What do you mean? What is wrong with Caesar?"

He wished he didn't have to tell this worried young woman there was real possibility her dog would die. She was exquisite, like the fawn he had nursed back to health, her big eyes reflecting the same kind of fear of the unknown. Keeping his voice low and calm he said, as kindly as he could, "Your dog has been poisoned."

I grabbed the stainless steel dolly and held onto it for all I was worth, the impact of his diagnosis hitting me as hard as Missy Sue's smack across my face. "But, who would do a wicked thing like that?"

McTeague sighed. "I don't know. I have never been able to understand the mentality of a person who is cruel to animals. Now then, Miss Bradford, time is of the essence. There is a slim chance Caesar could pull through. He is a large dog. If he didn't ingest too much of the poison and if his system can be cleared with a cathartic he just might make it."

Tears spilled down my face onto Caesar's fur as I leaned forward to stroke his head, give him an affectionate scratch behind his ears. "Poor, dear, sweet, afraid-of-a-raindrop Caesar," I murmured, hoping to see some response. He remained listless, his soulful brown eyes glazed over with misery.

McTeague's eyes filled with compassion. He knew personally what it meant to lose a devoted pet. He had experienced the anger and the frustration that always accompanies such finality. Not having been blessed with eloquence he knew there wasn't much he could say to console her, just as he knew his gift to give comfort came from the agility of his hands to heal. He said what he always said under such sad circumstances, "I will do my best."

I stood there, wringing my hands together in despair, watching his assistant, Joel, switch on lights in the adjoining room. It was a blur of tile, chrome and more stainless steel dominated by a mammoth operating table large enough, it seemed to me, to accommodate an elephant. As if I was a butterfly attracted by the bright lights I started to walk toward the room. Dr. McTeague stopped me, saying, "Joel, please show Miss Bradford into my private office." He turned to me, adding sympathetically, "You can wait there. It's much warmer."

Numbly, I followed Joel into Dr. McTeague's private office. This room too, proved to be not typical. There were of course the usual medical diplomas to be viewed but the rest of the wall space was taken up by pictures of boxers, including an oversized one of a much younger Ian McTeague garbed in boxing attire and labelled, Golden Glove Champion. The sport, I decided after studying the picture, no doubt being the source of his cauliflower ears.

Suddenly, I felt weak in the knees and rather faint. The office was, as Dr. McTeague had said, warmer than the examining room and I took off my jacket, and my shoes too so I could take refuge in a man-sized wing chair remarkably like Daddy's. In my hour of travail being able to curl up in its roomy yet confined cushy comfort seemed auspicious. For this too, I was grateful, my own self-alloted thought collecting time being in desperate need of attention. I closed my eyes, contemplating how Simon would react to the same duress, summoning a vision of him to appear, preferably, as he had looked standing in the pulpit this morning, his eyes warmed with a mixture of love, tenderness and merriment, his magnificent, muscular body bathed in a soft grayish pink ghostly glow. Instead, Joel appeared, the whiteness of his hospital uniform effectively blotting out my divine stream of thought.

"Miss Bradford, I forgot to tell you, your friend, Captain Barrows, has gone to register you both at a motel, The Pirate's Cove Inn. It's just down the road about a mile. He called ahead to be sure there were two units available. He will be right back."

"Thank you for telling me." I shuddered, as if a big bag of ice cubes had been dumped down my back, not at the name of the motel but at the mention of Captain Barrows, his name in my present freaking out state having become synonymous with Missy Sue and Leroy, a stuffed green garbage bag, a black Maria and a bottle of poison. Wanting to at least appear calm I returned Joel's smile, albeit a tear dampened one on my part and asked, "How long will it be until we know about Caesar?"

Joel did not give me a direct answer as he left the office. "Try not to worry. Caesar is in good hands."

I took his advice for the moment of not to worry; Caesar, I knew, was in good hands! But, was I?

I had made the snap decision after Dr. McTeague had finished questioning me that Captain Barrows was the wicked, vile, dispiteous person who had poisoned Caesar. He certainly had had the opportunity, but did he have a motive? Now that I was alone again I felt compelled to take the snap out of my decision by logically thinking through it, step by step, as Daddy would do. "After all, Serena, you poor displaced girl," I muttered to myself, "your life may depend upon the juxtaposition," to quote him, "of a few thoughts!"

To achieve this momentous goal I reverted to a long time ploy of mine. Drawing my knees up tightly against my chest so I could rest my chin on top of them, I pressed my finger tips into the sides of my temples, pushing hard until I could feel the steady beat of my pulse beneath them. What had worked throughout the years did now! Like a colorful banner being towed by a private little Cessna, his motive for murder floated by in my mind. "Member / Colombian Cocaine Cartel."

"Now, now, now, Serena, don't let your imagination run away with you," I could hear Daddy admonish, all the way up here in Antigonish, by gosh! Next he would say, "You've got to line up the facts, put them in proper order," and Mother would counsel, gently, "Yes, dear, it would be terrible to unjustly accuse your friend of wrong-doing."

Well, from my site of view I wasn't being unjust and as far as I was concerned fact number one was obvious! Captain Barrows had no choice but to kill Caesar. Then, it would be easier to dispose of me - tonight - tomorrow - whenever - in some out of the way tidal pool, tides being a hot topic between us. That way I wouldn't be able to testify against Missy Sue and Leroy, thereby Captain Barrows' chance of being incriminated was lessened considerably.

Fact number two was also obvious. He was the last person to give Caesar food, unless someone in The Strait Cafe's parking lot slipped him a so called mickey finn. On the other hand, Caesar didn't accept food from strangers, having been taught as Gloria and I had, only in dog obedience school, that it was wise not to do so.

Now that my brain was working at rush hour speed soundings of Captain Barrows' recent conversations surfaced. He had given as his reason for driving Caesar and me back to Boston, "An unexpected legal matter requiring his attention." In his, 'Now hear this' tone he had added, "A hankering to see my old friend Waitaminute for one more time." Those two statements were facts! "But," being an important conjunction at this point, I asked myself, "Did he offer to drive us back before Simon had told him of our difficulties or was it after? If it was before, then he was being big-hearted. If it was after, then he knew of our troubles with Missy Sue and Leroy which meant I was in jeopardy." As hard as I tried I couldn't remember, so I had to relegate these two questions to the keep-in-mind side of the ledger.

Fact number five sneaked into my head. It was an insidious one! A fact so odious that I hated myself for even thinking about it! But, the truth was overwhelming! It was so staggering that it was making me nauseous! Euphy had prepared the treat for Caesar that Captain Barrows and I had given him.

That this was an indisputable fact saddened me beyond belief. I admired Euphy. She was warm, kind, tolerant and generous to a fault. We had become friend-girls despite the difference in our ages and in our backgrounds. It was incomprehensible that she would want to hurt me by poisoning Caesar. "What possible reason could she have for doing such a despicable act?"

My head started to spin, not only from the nausea, but from the obvious answer to my own murmured question, that Euphy, too, was a member of the Colombian Cocaine Cartel, that she had plotted along with Captain Barrows to get rid of Caesar and me.

My palms were becoming moist with sweat; a sudden sprinkle of tears splotched my face. This show of nerves sent me fishing into my parka for a kleenex, always an exciting adventure! I found it quickly, along with a package of gum, a couple of candy wrappers, a rubber band, two paper clips and the postcard displaying Euphy's house I had tucked into a side pocket this morning. Just like then, I was struck by the thought that I had seen the same card in some far away, out of the way place, recently, too! Now that indeed was a step forward in trying to solve the mystery of the elusive postcard. The fact that I had seen it recently had sort of sneaked in over the transom like my humming of "Onward Christian soldiers, marching as to war" on that now infamous, unholy day of days when I smashed *Savannah's Revenge*."

Turning the card over I stared hard at its blank side, running my finger tips across its smooth surface much like a fortune teller reading the past by rubbing a crystal ball, asking myself over and over again, "What do you see?"

Being an unskilled clairvoyant it took a lot of card rubbing before I began to answer myself, slowly, in proper theatrical gypsy-like style. "I see the inside of a boat. I see a chart with the number 1300 printed on it." Having picked up a little expertise in crystal gazing I rubbed the card a tad harder. "I see a notepad doodled up with the names of places and a few inns. I see a small batch of letters and scenic postcards scattered on the floor. I see a rather worn out card, coffee stained, with Euphy's house pictured on the front and a neatly printed message on the back consisting of her telephone number and the signature, 'B'."

Leaping out of the chair, I squealed with delight over my successful peeping into the past. Even Adam would be proud of my achievement, giving me a brotherly bear hug before grinning and saying his usual, "Well done, Sis! Especially for someone who can't remember port from starboard or stern from bow."

My euphoric high dissolved as I brought myself back down to earth and to the chair with the words, "No time for sentiment." It was time, instead, to try and understand this revelation, to ascertain the meaning behind the initial, B. I decided one did not need the mentality of a spy to do so. It was a straight forward conclusion, that even the likes of a museum freak like me would know, that the B stood for Euphy Browne or for Captain Barrows.

Rubbing the card again I remembered there wasn't a stamp in the designated "Place Stamp Here" spot, nor was there a penned mailing address. Trying to think like Adam, which wasn't easy because of his CIA trained brain, I came to another logical conclusion. The postcard had been hand delivered. Not only had it been hand delivered by Euphy or Captain Barrows, but it had been hand delivered to Missy Sue and Leroy while they were anchored in Esperance.

This time I rubbed my eyes, this last piece of the puzzle having fallen into place. Esperance was just a stone's throw away, so to speak, from Rouge Baie. Esperance was one of the places listed on the notepad that I had seen when looking at Leroy's charts while aboard *Savannah's Revenge*.

I reacted calmly to this diabolical twist of fate, instinctively knowing this was not the time to panic. My first thought was of Simon, my subconscious rising to consciousness, confirming what only this morning I had wondered, that I was in love with Simon and committed to him forever.

My second thought was for Simon's safety, that I had to warn him of impending danger. Not having a short-wave radio to send out an S O S in the true spirit of the sea I did the next best thing. Getting up from the chair I availed myself of Dr. McTeague's telephone placed on the starboard side of his desk, taking a measure of comfort because of its position on the

252

polished top that he too was probably cursed with "The Damning Defect."

I disliked using his phone without permission but the specter of Simon being served oatmeal laced with arsenic tomorrow morning for breakfast pushed aside etiquette. Making a mental note to tell Dr. McTeague of my trespass I gave the overseas operator Euphy's number and the one for my parent's telephone credit card, a number well ingrained into my memory after years of abuse on my part. Any remaining qualms I had over using the phone I shivered away with the horrendous thought I might never see any of them ever again!

I crossed my fingers when the phone started to ring, hoping that Simon would answer and not Euphy. There were only two phones in the house, one in the foyer and the other in Euphy's bedroom which could make it difficult to carry on a private conversation, she perhaps listening in under such cloak and dagger circumstances. I had never contemplated Euphy committing such a breech of manners, but then I had never thought her capable of murder. Such a thought was still abhorrent to me and even now, knowing that Caesar was in the operating room struggling for his life, I wished for another explanation, a kinder, gentler one so I could think of Euphy once again as a friend-girl.

The phone stopped ringing. "Captain Browne's residence." My finger crossing had paid off!

I would have recognized Simon's deep, rich baritone voice coming over the line from anywhere in the world. He had said the same about mine, being recognizable that is, only in some what of an accusing tone, "Your voice, Serena, oozes a promise of sex in every soft, melodious vowel pronounced." Never having listened to myself speak I wasn't quite sure what he had meant, but I had decided if I oozed sex he oozed a powerful image of "Come into my snug harbor and rest awhile." Be that as it may, it was propitious for me to speak up; 'Time was of the essence,' as Dr. McTeague had said. "Simon, it's me. I'm sorry to be so late in calling."

"Hello, Me! Yes, it is late, so late that we have all been worried sick you might have had car trouble. Old Bess not being what she used to be. Are you all right, Sprite?"

His voice, pitched low and caressing, like he was whispering, "I love you," into my ear resounded over the wire. I started to ache for the feeling of his arms around me. "To be honest, Simon, I'm not. Neither is Caesar."

It took one sixtieth of a minute for him to ask, gently, "What is wrong, Serena? I can tell by the quiver in your voice that you are in trouble."

"Is Euphy there, Simon?"

"Sprite, please don't answer a question with a question. Now what is wrong?"

I recognized the shift in his tone as he repeated himself. It was a mixture of caring, concern and firmness. "Please, Simon, it's important. Just tell me if Euphy is near-by or in bed?"

This time I detected indulgence and a hint of exasperation in his answer. "Euphy is in the kitchen filling several hurricane lamps for us to use. We have lost our power due to a severe glitter storm. Now once again, Sprite, what kind of trouble have you gotten yourself into this time?"

His last sentence - question - whatever - was asked with so much endearment that it brought tears to my eyes. "Oh, Simon, Euphy and Captain Barrows are members of the Colombian Cocaine Cartel. They have poisoned Caesar. You and I are next on their list."

I thought we had been cut off he took so long to answer. His voice was calm, reassuring when he did reply. "Where are you calling from, Serena?"

"Outside of Antigonish. Actually from Dr. Ian McTeague's office at the Antigonish Animal Hospital."

Another pause over the wire. "Then Sonofagun is planning to take the ferry from Digby to Saint John?"

He was beginning to sound like Adam. "Yes, that's exactly what he said, Simon. We would go through the town of Truro on the way to Digby, his excuse being so I could see the depth of the tides at different locations along the Bay of Fundy."

There was another pause, only longer. "Serena, I know how much Caesar means to you. Is he going to pull through?"

The tears came faster but I managed a weak, "I don't know, Simon."

"I'm so very sorry, Sprite. I wish I was there to spare you from the worry and grief I know you are experiencing."

His expression of sympathy was so soft spoken, so tender that it was almost like being held in his arms. "I wish too, Simon. More than you will ever know."

I could hear him clearing his throat over the line before he spoke. "Serena, I have a gut feeling there is a very logical explanation for what has happened. I find it hard to believe that Euphy and Sonofagun could be involved in anything so contemptible."

He spoke with conviction, perhaps a shade too much as if trying to allay my fears and bolster his courage. "But, Simon, Euphy prepared the food for Caesar and Captain Barrows gave it to him. And there is one more damaging piece of evidence that you might not know about. There was a picture postcard of Euphy's house on board *Savannah's Revenge*. Written on the back of it was her telephone number and the initial, B; the B obviously standing for her last name. Why, maybe it could even stand for Captain Barrows."

This time an audible sigh and several deep breaths replaced his previous silent pauses. "I must admit the circumstances seem damning, Serena, and until we know for sure you must take precautions, as I will here. In the meantime, since you might not be able to, I will call your family, advise them of the change in your itinerary, that you and Sonofagun will be disembarking in Saint John instead of Bar Harbour."

I immediately felt better. I had succeeded in warning Simon. He in turn would talk to my family, not the best way to introduce himself but by now, because of my letter and phone call to Gloria, they would at least know a little about him, that he was coming for the important Thanksgiving holidays, the revered time of the year in our home. I was about to ask, "What precautions would I take," when the line went dead and Dr. McTeague returned to his office.

I coudn't read Dr. McTeague. I couldn't tell if he was bringing me good tidings or carrying bad news. I gathered it was neither, sort of in between, as he asked, "Would you like to see the patient? Joel and I have put Caesar in one of the lambing pens where he should rest comfortably."

Not needing a second invocation I hurried to put on my shoes. "Is Caesar going to be all right, Dr. McTeague?"

"Your pet has responded well to the treatment," he replied slowly, thinking it best to side step her questions after noticing her swollen eyes, tear-streaked face and the torn bits of kleenex on his desk top. "Right now I think Caesar could use a little moral support, would like to see a familiar face and hear your voice." He smiled explaining further, "I'm sure his accommodations and his roommates are not what he is accustomed to having. Come, you will see what I mean, Miss Bradford."

His answer seemed unusual but then so was everything else at the Antigonish Animal Hospital. I slipped on my jacket and followed him past the surgery, through a set of double doors and into what insultingly would be called a barn, for this modern building had been designed and built solely for creature comforts. It was so clean and so sweet smelling from the fresh hay that even Mrs. Linette would not be able to find fault.

I followed Dr. McTeague down the concrete center strip, about two car widths wide I guessed, to the far end where Caesar was resting on a bed of straw in one of the smaller stalls. By then I understood what he had meant about Caesar's roommates, having passed a gigantic sow nursing piglets, two mammoth horses that looked just like the ones I had seen on television pulling a wagon and a couple of cows.

"Poor babe," I said, kneeling down to stroke his head. "No wonder you are frightened, surrounded by all these weird country folk." This time I was rewarded by a weak thumping of his tail.

Not being one to make snap decisions, well, almost never, I looked up at Dr. McTeague. "May I stay with him? I know that must seem strange to you, but perhaps my being here will give him the extra edge he needs."

256

McTeague smiled broadly. Many the night he had spent with a sick animal, playing the odds that his presence could make a difference. Then too the fact that he had not been wrong in judging her, that she really did care about her pet, made his effort worthwhile. "I understand perfectly. In fact, I was hoping you would ask. Now then, Joel will be on duty tonight. He will bring you a blanket since it's not warm in here. For your own protection I must insist you do not enter any of the other stalls. If there is a problem, or you need to use the facilities, just go back through the same set of doors."

His mention of the facilities jogged my memory. "Dr. McTeague, I apologize for not asking your permission to use the phone. I felt I had to touch bases with my family, to let them know where I was and what had happened to Caesar. It was a long distance call but I charged it on my father's credit card."

McTeague laughed. "Thank goodness for fathers, eh, Miss Bradford! What would the world do without them?"

Although Dr. McTeague had laughed I detected an undercurrent of sadness in his joking. Perhaps sadness is not the right word, my inner voice countered, try substituting tragedy. Well, I thought as I watched him turn to leave, his own personal tragedy could be the non-fulfillment of a boxing career. And yet as I watched him stop at each stall, give a friendly rub to an outstretched nose I knew that was not the correct answer, that his tragedy was far more poignant, like the death of a loved one. And what was really tragic to me was that I would never get to know, or to even pass the time of day, with a very special someone who had really touched my life.

Joel returned, almost immediately. He spread a bright red horsecloth on the straw beside Caesar and handed me a plaid mohair car-throw. "This should keep you warm."

"Thank you, Joel." The tears started to come. I couldn't stop them. "And thank you for being so kind to Caesar."

"Don't worry, Caesar is going to be fine," he replied consolingly.

I watched him shut the lower half of the paddock type door. "I'll be making rounds during the night. Don't let me startle you."

I nodded, appreciating his thoughtfulness.

"Miss Bradford, your friend Captain Barrows called from his room at the inn. I told him you had decided to spend the night. He will be here when we open at seven a.m. In the meantime, regardless of the hour, he will come if you want him."

"Thank you again, Joel. I believe I will be fine right here," being careful to say, fine and not, safer.

Suddenly I was very tired, the strain of the long trip and the worry over Caesar exacting its toll. Stretching out beside him, like I used to do when he was a pup, I pulled the car-throw over me, relishing its warmth and silky softness. Joel had turned off the bright lights and I could see the stars and a sliver of moon twinkling through the sky lights. A prayer coming from the heart formed in my mind, not for me, but for Caesar. Reaching out to stroke his massive gray head I asked, "Please, God, don't let Caesar die. Although he can't speak for himself, on his behalf, I would like to say he exemplifies your disciplines of devotion and loyalty. In his own way all he has every done is to show love. All he has ever asked in return is to be loved. Isn't that what you expect and pray for from all of us?"

#

Sleeping in a barn on a bed of straw covered with a bright red horsecloth and being wrapped up in a plain car-throw against the chill, even though made of soft mohair, is not by any stretch of the imagination comparable to snuggling underneath a lavender scented down comforter in a huge four poster bed complete with canopy and embracing bunk mate. However, it is a unique experience, especially at roll call before breakfast when all the barnyard dwellers vie for full attention in their own inimitable way. It can also be a joyous occasion, like rushing downstairs in the early morning to see the Christmas tree in all its sparkling splendor or like this morning, to feel a cold, wet nose nuzzling your neck and your face being washed with a sandpapery tongue.

Feeling unbelievably happy I was telling all of this to Captain Barrows, except the part about the embracing bunk

258

mate, as we rolled down the highway after taking the time for our own breakfast and for me to shower and shampoo the straw out of my hair. "Dr. McTeague said, when I was telling him good bye and thanking him for all he had done, that Caesar will be fine; just off his feed for a couple of days. But then I told you that."

"Several times, Serena."

"Oh."

Captain Barrows chuckled. "I must say the saw-bones' bill was reasonable. Coming in at night like he did and with all that fancy equipment I was expecting you were going to be charged an arm and a leg. Instead, it was just a leg."

Defensively, I replied, "Yes, his bill was reasonable and I do appreciate you lending me the extra money to settle the account." My principles and honor being involved in this transaction, since we had agreed beforehand that I would pay my own expenses plus half the fuel bill, I added decisively, "I'll pay you back as soon as we get home tonight."

"Don't worry your pretty little head about it. Just lean back and enjoy the countryside."

Gloria would have considered his remark demeaning. Mother would have considered it patronizing. To me his remark was in keeping with the Captain Barrows I had grown to like. He had also said, "Don't worry," but I really couldn't help but do just that! I was out of money, having used up the last of my travelers checks to pay Caesar's bill. Of course, I had some change left and a few one dollar bills but not enough to sustain myself in case of an emergency. Translated that meant I was in the clutches of a could-be assasin determined to stop me from getting back to Maine and ultimately to Boston.

And yet, Captain Barrows had seemed genuinely pleased over Caesar's recovery. He had been charming at breakfast, insisting after my night's vigil that I take the time to eat some bangbellies and to have an extra cup of coffee. He had been understanding when I broached the subject of my needing to freshen up. "Take your time, Serena," he had said. "I did some checking on the ferry out of Digby and as long as we get there by three o'clock we will be okay."

In fact Captain Barrows was now acting so much like his regular ornery, joshing self as we continued to speed along the highway towards Truro that I decided to give him the benefit of doubt and to do as Simon suggested, heaven forbid, by just taking precautions until we knew for sure. Of course the phone had gone dead before Simon could tell me what kind of precautions I should take. Left on my own initiative early this morning I had already managed to give Old Bess a quick search while coaxing Caesar into the back seat; coming up with nothing more incriminating than a flashlight in the glove compartment. I had even been able to go through his bulky jacket while he was checking us both out of the inn looking for a gun or some other form of nefarious weapon. Coming up empty handed, I had then decided that with Caesar once again by my side and me being fleet of foot I stood a 50% chance of holding my own. Actually 75%, for out there waiting in the wings, I knew, was Adam with his box of pins, Daddy with his network of old school boy ties and Simon, my Sir Lancelot, imbued with the courage and heart to tackle any opponent.

So, feeling quite smug, in addition to feeling unbelievably happy, I leaned back to do as I was told and started to enjoy the countryside; a colorful patchwork of blueberry fields, green pastures, and tiny hamlets glistening under a brilliant October sun. That is, until we got to Truro!

It was noonish. It was low tide. "In Georgetown, Captain Barrows, when the tide is this low we call it a drain-out."

"Every locale seems to have their own descriptive phrases. That's a good one though. I'll have to remember it, Sis. Now then, this looks like a perfect spot along the shore to park Old Bess so we can walk out onto the Minas Basin. This is the place that would scare the hell out of the devil, according to that fellow back on the ferry."

"I remember. He said when the bore finally came it was like seeing a rusty wall of water coming towards you."

Grabbing the sandwiches and cokes we had purchased in Truro and after putting Caesar on a leash we trudged out a ways onto the Basin. "Its bowl-like shape and with the cliffs and pines looming up on either side reminds me somewhat of our place in Maine, Captain Barrows. You will see what I mean tomorrow."

Nothing more was said for a few minutes, the pleasure of exercising our cramped limbs and munching on our sandwiches taking precedence over the time of day and the weather.

Captain Barrows stopped walking and sighed. "Sis, I've been thinking!"

"Oh," I said, thinking, the last time he had said, "I've been thinking," we ended up in Antigonish instead of Country Harbour Mines. Not only in Antigonish but at the Antigonish Animal Hospital where Caesar had been treated for poisoning!

"I've changed my mind, Sis, about taking the ferry out of Digby for Saint John. Hell's Bells! Why put Caesar through the trauma of another long boat trip when we can just as well take the scenic route back to Maine. I have a hunch you might enjoy seeing the Cape d'Or lighthouse and the Apple River valley. Amherst is a pretty town surrounded by lots of marshlands and blueberry fields. When we get to Moncton, that's in New Brunswick, you know, we should be in time for you to see their tidal bore which according to the tide tables should be around six p.m. We can have a leisurely dinner, then dig out the road map and chart our course from there. It will mean more driving but with both of us standing watch the trip won't be so bad. Remember, too, we are still on day light saving time and we will gain another hour when we leave Canada and enter Maine at the St. Stephen - Calais border crossing. This means we still should arrive at your home around midnight."

I wanted to scream, "Help!" The only trouble there was no one around to hear my plea, standing as we three were, on the sandy floor of the Basin. Neither was there a "reach out and touch someone" person to hear my cry for help while we climbed the steep hill to Cape d'Or lighthouse or navigated the lonely road to Amherst. Nor was help available there, since Captain Barrows elected not to go into the town, instead picking up the Trans Can Highway and driving on into New Brunswick. However, by the time we got to Moncton, had stopped long enough to witness the great wall of water rushing towards the shore and finally to, "Drop anchor," in front of the

Northumberland Inn and Restaurant, I no longer felt the need to scream for help. My fear over being killed and left in the Minas Basin had vanished into thin air. After all we were no longer there! My fear over not being aboard the 3:00 p.m., Digby - Saint John ferry, had also dissipated because of Simon's phone call to my family. I knew, without a doubt, they would have planned to meet me at the terminal in Saint John and when I didn't show up Adam would throw a net over the northeast that even a minnow couldn't wiggle through. So I played it like Simon would, cucumbery cool. Besides, I told myself, there was still the possibility that Captain Barrows could be innocent and as Mother would say, "Yes, dear, it would be terrible to unjustly accuse your friend of wrong-doing."

Looking at him now in such a relaxed state of après dinner contentment it was hard to believe he could be anything else but innocent. He was slumped against the back of the leather upholstered booth we were seated in, one hand absent-mindedly riffling his thick white hair while the other kept tapping a spoon against the road map spread out in front of us on the table. I was holding my breath and gripping the seat cushions every bit as tightly as I had held onto *Escape* the day of my first lesson, hoping he would adhere to the axiom that the shortest distance between two points is a straight line. I wasn't the least bit surprised when he said, "Sis, I've been thinking."

"Oh?"

"I've been thinking we should head right on down the pike. It's too dark now to see Flower Pot Rocks or the view from Alma. Perhaps you will have another chance."

I uncrossed my fingers. They were almost numb from being squeezed together so tightly. "What ever you think is best, Captain Barrows."

"Okay, Sis! Now then, I'm feeling a little drowsy so I hope you don't mind driving for awhile. Just in case I doze off we will take Route 2 into Essex. From there we will take Route 1 right on into the St. Stephen - Calais border crossing."

I nodded in agreement as we got up from the table. "Captain Barrows, I would like to give Caesar a walk and some of the dog chow from Dr. McTeague's clinic before we leave."

He seemed preoccupied, his answer, "We will walk Caesar together, a little strange. So strange that I started to worry if his remark about having another chance to see Flower Pot Rocks meant I might not ever have another chance, since he planned to do Caesar and I in somewhere along the pike.

For a few minutes I pushed that thought aside after we unlocked Old Bess to let Caesar out. I had decided before going into the restaurant not to chain him to the car while we were inside eating, the idea of him being poisoned again too much to bear.

Compared to the night before he was frisky, pulling me around the parking lot, even pausing to greet two men coming hurriedly from inside the restaurant by offering them his paw. They seemed pleasant, passing the time with Captain Barrows while I fed Caesar, their topic of interest a salmon fishing trip they had just taken along the shores of the Margaree River in Cape Breton.

Captain Barrows order, "Cast off," followed as soon as Caesar was back in the car. After taking a brief moment to adjust the seat, the rear view mirror as well as the side ones to my size I did just that, along with a stern warning to myself, "Keep alert."

The miles clicked swiftly by. I turned the windshield wipers on as we approached Essex, the snow storm Gloria had mentioned appearing right on schedule. Captain Barrows had been stretched out in his seat, "Not asleep, just resting my eyes," he had said not once, but twice since we passed the exit sign for Petitcodiac. My eyes were getting to that bleary stage too, but each mile traveled meant I was closer to home, family, and safety so I ignored the urge to rub away at their itchiness. My thoughts kept changing every time I switched gears: yes, he is a member of the cocaine cartel - the poisoning of Caesar and the postcard are sufficient proof; no, it's as Simon had said, "There is a very logical explanation for what has happened."

Glancing across at Captain Barrows I was inclined to again agree with Simon for he appeared more like my old ragged stuffed teddy bear than a wolf in sheep's clothing.

"Serena, we are almost at the junction where we will pick up Route 1. There is a small gas station there. Please pull in. I'd like to get into my suitcase, dig out a sweater for I feel a slight chill coming on."

I jumped, his brusque manner startling me. "Of course, Captain Barrows."

Thinking he would also want to fill up Old Bess with gas and check her oil I brought the car to a stop in front of the dimly illuminated pump. His description of the Essex Junction Gas & Lube Station was exaggerated. It wasn't small, it was Lilliputian! However what was lacking in size was more than made up for in hospitality.

"There is hot cocoa inside, Miss," the attendant answered to my query. "None of that slot machine junk but real, honest-to-goodness cocoa. You can have it spritzed with real whipped cream if you like."

"I like," I said eagerly getting out of Old Bess.

"Does he bite?"

"Who, him?" I asked.

Unconsciously I must have looked at Captain Barrows rummaging through his suitcase in search of a sweater because the attendant started to snicker. "No, the monster in the back seat?"

"Oh, him!" I replied, unable to control a giggle. "No, Caesar only bites plumbers. But I'll take him with me just to be on the safe side. He hasn't been feeling well lately." I didn't want to speak the truth by saying, "Because I'm afraid to leave him alone with Captain Barrows or for that matter with you."

As rest stops go, ours was briefer than a brief one. We were just leaving the station when several other cars pulled in, all coming from different directions. "The gas station seems to be doing a brisk business tonight, Captain Barrows. The drawing card must be the free cocoa and cookies which, by the way, were very good."

Captain Barrows ignored my comment. Instead he leaned forward in his seat and started to drum his fingers against the dash-board. "Serena, the gas attendant said a new road has just opened to St. Stephen. It's dirt and gravel but in excellent condition. By taking it we can by-pass the busy Saint John area and save ourselves about fifty miles of driving."

"Saving fifty miles is worth taking any road, Captain Barrows. Where do I turn off?"

"Just ahead. The road is supposedly marked St. Stephen Road, otherwise known locally as the St. Stephen - New York City Expressway."

"How droll!"

His voice boomed out at me. "There it is, Serena."

#

We had been on the Expressway for about an hour when I finally admitted to myself that I hadn't been thinking straight back there at the pass, that the busy Saint John area was exactly where I wanted to be, not out here in moose and Indian country. Trying to rationalize my stupidity, I confessed there really was nothing I could have done once Captain Barrows had made up his mind. But, a tiny voice nagged, "You could have tried to talk him out of coming this way."

The snow was petering out. Just enough had fallen to dust the tall pines and to show off bunny and deer tracks on the road. It was a tranquil scene, making me think of peace on earth and having good will towards men, especially towards Captain Barrows. I realized then he was no longer slouched back in his seat and that his eyes seemed glued to the side view mirror. Why, I thought, I have been paying so much attention to my driving that I haven't even noticed the pale blue cardigan he had put on. It was a shade most becoming to him and I wanted to tell him so.

"Captain Barrows, I like —"

He turned towards me, his cardigan falling slightly away from his chest, revealing a shoulder holster with a gun protruding from the top. My entire life shutter-bugged in front of me.

"Yes, Serena, you like what?"

His voice was strained. I gripped the steering wheel as hard as I could, as if trying to squeeze a quick solution out of it, the hard surface only telling me there wasn't one, just to play it cool. I almost choked on the words. "I like the color of your sweater."

265

He smiled. On the other hand, maybe it was a leer. I couldn't really tell in the dark. "Thank you, Serena."

I picked up headlights in the rear view mirror. Automatically I started to slow down. My spirits lifted, every bit as high as the eagle soared on that memorable morning not too long ago. Escape was within my grasp, just like it was before. This time it would not be in a boat but it would be with Adam in the car coming up fast behind us. "Someone else has discovered this so called Expressway, Captain Barrows," I shouted excitedly.

He whipped out his gun. "Don't slow down! That God damn car has been following us all the way from Moncton. I suspect it's those two ninnies we met in the restaurant parking lot; impostors for sure!"

"Ninnies? Imposters?," I shouted back, not quite sure which of the two job descriptions, one being a fool and the other having to have some smarts, would benefit me.

"Hell's Bells!"

I thought my ear drums would burst.

"This time of year a real salmon fisherman would never use a number ten Blue Charm fly and a nine foot for a number six weight fly rod. He would use a number two General Practitioner with a nine foot for a nine weight fly rod."

"Of course, doesn't everyone?," I murmured.

"Serena, I repeat, don't slow down!"

I reacted to his command without thinking. Old Bess sputtered at the indignity of having the gas pedal pushed so abruptly to the floor but rallied like the good girl she was with a roar. For a Hermes-like second I thought of *Escape* and how she had responded to my bid for survival. Only this time, I snappily decided, survival was behind me with the ninnies and impostors. I should have put Old Bess into reverse.

"I can see the lights of the border crossing ahead, Serena. Give her the gun!"

This time I willingly responded; the border meant people, police, whoever and whatever.

A screeching, honking, tire burning stop was the result of my following his orders to a T. I opened the car door and started to run for the State of Maine and the good old USA. Someone was pounding the asphalt behind me. I could hear labored breathing, sense two hulking presences drawing closer and closer. Caesar was yowling and barking, heralding my forthcoming incarceration as grasping fingers dug into my shoulders, pulling me to a stop.

I turned, not quite fully prepared to meet my Maker, but under the circumstances what else could I do?

"My God, Serena, I had forgotten how fast you can run!"

If I had been attending a Boston Pops concert the cymbals would have clanged together just then. "Adam, oh, Adam" I cried, throwing my arms around him, squeezing his chest as tightly as I could, receiving in return a big, brotherly bear hug.

"And, Daddy, Daddy," I sobbed, running to meet him, longing to feel the security and love of his arms around me, wanting to hear him murmur, "Don't cry, Little One;" those sweet words of endearment which had always taken the hurt away. "I knew you both would be here. I just knew it," I sniffled, holding on to both of them for dear life.

They put their arms around me, Daddy saying, "We are here, Serena, thanks to your so called museum friend."

I looked up, Daddy's expression was enigmatic but his eyes were kindled with what I always called a warm-hearth glow.

"You know, Serena, I like the way your Simon thinks."

"Yes," Adam added, "he called the shots right on target. He said you would be where you were and when you would be there. I couldn't have done better."

Such high praise for Simon made me feel happy; coming from Daddy and Adam it was unusual. Neither of them had been particularly fond of Britt; too self-centered Adam had said, while Daddy commented on his lack of compassion for the less fortunate.

Reluctant to let go of either of them I asked, "Simon obviously got through to you? I knew he would, somehow, even though the phone went dead while we were talking due to a glitter storm."

Adam spoke up. "Simon got through to us around four o'clock this morning. He had to drive to St. John's in order to phone. He would have been here except the airport is still socked in."

"Come now, dear, you are shivering and your feet are getting wet. You must get out of the snow or you will end up spending the Thanksgiving holidays in the hospital with another bout of pneumonia. Mother will never forgive me. Besides, Little One, we have days in which to catch up."

Like a found lost lamb Daddy and Adam shepherded me back toward Old Bess, Captain Barrows, and Caesar. "You must call Mother right away, Serena. Gloria and Paul are there with her as well as your grandparents. All are anxious to hear from you, to know that you are safe. Everyone agreed we had to have a back up team in place at The Barnacle just in case, mind you, Adam and I missed connections or they would have been here too, to greet you."

"You seem to have thought of everything."

"We tried to, dear. Now then, Adam, since you are responsible for our successful mission, why don't you take Serena into the customs office where she can make her calls in private. I will go greet old Sonofagun and try to calm Caesar down."

I grabbed Daddy's arm, fear washing over me once more, making me weak in the knees. "Daddy, be careful! Captain Barrows has a gun. He was going to kill Caesar and me."

"Sonofagun kill you, Serena? Captain Robert Barrows, master of *The Invincible*, member of The Explorer's club, recipient of countless medals, kill you? Never! Never in a million years! He was protecting you!" Leaning down he kissed me gently on the cheek, held me close again before saying, "You always were a worry-wart, but I love you for it."

Somehow, this time, I didn't mind being told what to do as Adam walked me over to the customs office. I could plainly hear Daddy's and Captain Barrows' voices, their greeting to each other traveling in the cold night air.

"Well, I'll be a son of a gun! My God, John, you are a sight for sore eyes. Put on a little weight haven't you? Well, I'll be a son of a gun!"

Daddy's reply was predictable. "As my Dad would say, 'Now wait a minute, Bob!'"

Glancing back before we entered the building I saw they had been joined by several other men, including the two "ninnies, impostors" who had been at the Northumberland Inn. "Adam, who are those two men talking to Daddy and Captain Barrows? They appear to be sharing some sort of hilarious joke."

Adam laughed, winked at me. "They are fellow Super-Sleuths. Though I believe we met our match in Captain Barrows."

I stared up at him, blankly. "What ever do you mean?"

"It's a long story, Serena, and I will fill you in on the way home. Let's just say for now Dad's unshakable faith in his long time friend and your Simon's gut feeling kept me from acting rashly."

"You, Adam, act rashly? You, the pragmatist! Now it's my turn to say, never!"

Adam grinned, "Come on, Serena, let's go make those calls including one to Simon. He gave me a phone number where he can be reached in St. John's."

"Still the same old bossy, big brother," I teased, deliberately messing up his hair since I knew it made him mad.

Chapter 21

The museum staff welcomed me back with open arms on November 1st. Director Smythe went so far as to host an elegant catered luncheon for me on the premises in the Renaissance Room, an impressive space furnished with exquisite antiques and then promptly sent me off to my converted storage closet of an office with a stack of correspondence and the glad tidings, "Good to have you back, Serena. Since you did such an outstanding job on the Renoir catalog I decided while you were gone that you are the logical person to prepare one covering our American landscapes going on loan to several museums. I would like the catalog to include a brief history of landscape painting including a photo of Pieter Brueghel, the Elder, and his masterpiece 'Alpine Landscape.' This exhibit will be going to Washington, Dallas, San Francisco and to Ottawa. I shall expect you to attend each opening."

"Yes, Mr. Smythe."

"In your spare time, Serena, I would like you to edit the Marsden Hartley catalog. Please have it on my desk before Thanksgiving. I have scheduled a small exhibit of his paintings for the beginning of this coming year, before we begin to gear up in the spring for our major show on South American art."

"Yes, Mr. Smythe."

"It's good to have you back, Serena."

"Thank you, Mr. Smythe. It's good to be back. I think!"

#

From then on it was as if I had never been away on a six month leave of absence. In fact my past adventures were already dimming under the work load except for the memory of Simon whose image remained larger than life in my mind. Not only in my mind but in my eyes too since as soon as I had returned home I went back to the gallery on Charles Street and purchased the painting "Seaworthy," planning to give it to him for a Thanksgiving gift to see if he knew who was his look alike, to let

271

him know during a soul searching moment of its impact on my life, to let him know why I had considered the painting to have been a good omen and how it had helped me in the shaping of my destiny. In the meantime I had hung the canvas in my office on the wall across from my desk, facing me naturally so I could gize up at it every now and then. However, my now and then moments were beginning to be scarcer by the day and today not at all.

"Serena, you have a visitor!"

I shrieked. I should have known better for in my tiny office the sound of my cry bounced right back off the wall in haunting refrain. "Oh, no, Jeannie, not today. Not today of all days."

Reluctantly I put down my pencil, knowing full well that a visitor in mid-afternoon meant another delay in my proofing the Marsden Hartley catalog, which was supposed to have been done yesterday. "Mr. Smythe, our esteemed director, will kill me, Jeannie."

Jeannie's exasperated sigh brought me quickly to my feet sputtering and explaining, "I know I have procrastinated in getting the catalog done just like I know Hartley has made his mark in the art world. It's just that his paintings don't send me. They don't move me. I find his landscapes of Maine far too harsh."

"Serena, let's face it, you have been back at the museum for over three weeks now during which time you have been moved to tears, daily, by the new show in the Adams Gallery featuring paintings of contemporary Canadian artists, especially the one titled 'Seasmoke at Sunrise.' Me thinks you need a drying out period."

As close a friend-girl as Jeannie is, I couldn't bring myself to confess there was more to that painting for me than met the eye. I thought it best to laugh. "You always did have a knack for saying just the right things at the right time."

Jeannie laughed along with me, adding sympathetically, "Perhaps after the preliminary hearing on that cocaine mess is over tomorrow you won't be in such an emotional state. On the other hand, with Simon flying in tonight you could experience a drain-out."

I picked up an eraser and threw it towards her. "Wicked girl!"

"Best not keep your visitor waiting, Serena," Jeannie charged, gracefully dodging the missile by stepping slightly back out into the hall. "I know I wouldn't! He is too dreamy of a hunk to be left wandering around on his own. In fact, I wonder if Simon would get upset to know you have a secret admirer waiting in the Adams Gallery?"

"Did you say a secret admirer, Jeannie?"

"Yes, he wouldn't give me his name." Removing her horn rimmed glasses she arched her eyebrows for emphasis. "He said in an utterly debonair and ebullient way, 'I want to surprise her.'"

"From your wanton expression and the breathless nuance in your voice, Jeannie, I can tell my surprise is well packaged!"

"Oh, my, yes. All six plus feet of him."

"Well, then, as you suggest I best not keep my visitor waiting." Pausing just long enough to carry out Mr. Smythe's directive *re* energy conservation and security measures by turning off the lights and locking the office door behind me, I joined Jeannie in the hall saying jokingly, "You do realize my reputation for dressing to reflect a current exhibit will be permanently tarnished. For such a romantic rendezvous to be properly consummated, especially in front of a backdrop of canvases depicting the pristine arctic, I should be draped in pure cashmere, preferably white like the snow and ice, with just a touch of green, perhaps in the form of emerald earrings to match the glistening sea, instead of this heavy cotton peasant type skirt from Greece I'm wearing, which by the way is so old it could have come straight out of an Attica attic."

Jeannie smiled. "Being in the bush for six months has sharpened your wit, Serena!"

I smiled back, thinking my sense of humor had been sharpened too, but asking as we walked towards the elevator, "How did my secret admirer find you?"

"He joined today's group of visitors taking my regularly scheduled two o'clock general tour of the museum. When I finished, he lingered behind and after exchanging a few pleasantries inquired if you were here."

"I must say I am intrigued. Now be a good sport and give me a clue as to what he is wearing. So far I have only his height to guide me."

Jeannie's answer was lost in the shuffle between several handicapped persons getting on and off the elevator and a class of giggling elementary school children passing by us enroute to their school bus. That is, all but the one she managed to convey from the back of the elevator by raising her voice. "Don't forget, Serena, you are giving me a lift home. I'll be ready at five and will wait for you downstairs in my office."

I nodded, quickly waved my acknowledgement and then turned to start my walk down the short stretch of carpeted hall to the Adams Gallery where my surprise package was supposed to be waiting for me.

#

Jeannie's words, dreamy of a hunk, didn't seem to describe any of the men present in the gallery. True, there were several distinguished looking gentlemen studying the landscapes but, knowing Jeannie as I did, the man I was to discover would be dark haired and handsome in addition to being tall; our tastes in men were quite similar.

"Guess who?"

I practically jumped out of my panty hose. The playful question whispered so seductively into my ear literally caught me by surprise. Having programmed myself only for a dreary day of proof reading, this bit of mischief along with having my eyes covered by someone standing kissing-close behind me sent a tingle of excitement up and down my spine. It had been a long time since I had played the childhood game of Guess Who and I was just bleary-eyed enough from proofing copy that I welcomed the change of pace. Eagerly I arose to the occasion asking right off the bat, without even thinking, "Tis the ghost of John Adams?" He muffled his answer. "No, tis not a ghost that brings thee tidings of good cheer."I wanted to reach up and put

274

my hands over his but that would be cheating, a touch, considered to be a dead give-away. There was, however, a faint aroma of pipe tobacco emanating from his hands which smelled similar to that enjoyed by Captain Barrows. Perhaps he had decided to make today the one for his surprise visit? After all he had said last evening while we were strolling leisurely down Beacon Street, "Sis, now that your father has finished with the necessary legal hoopla needed to complete my bequest to the Museum of Science, and now that those dang-blasted sawbones have fixed up my ticker to where it's almost as good as new, I'll soon be heading home."Giving me an affectionate pat on the shoulder, he had added, "Though not before I pay a surprise visit to that museum of yours."

I had felt guilty when he mentioned his "ticker," my thoughts immediately zooming back to the day on the beach when I believed he was going to kill me but in reality, I learned later, he was having an angina attack. Just like I learned later from Adam that Daddy was right, that in no way, shape or form was Captain Barrows a member of the Colombian Cocaine Cartel. On the other hand they all agreed, including Captain Barrows and Simon, that under the given circumstances I had made a logical conclusion. In fact, Adam had been so proud of my logic that he treated me to a weekend in New York City. "A time to rejuvenate familia ties," he had said. Why he had even gone so far as to acknowledge me as his sister to some of his will-o-the-wisp friends. My cup had indeed "runnith " over. But it wasn't running over now and standing here like a dodo bird reminiscing about a past weekend would in no way help me to solve the mystery at hand. Action speaking louder than words, whatever, I asked tenuously, "Captain Barrows?"

"No tis not a near-by sailor that wishes thee good speed."

As clues go even I could not have missed that one. It was obvious the person standing behind me knew Captain Barrows was a sailor and not a captain in the Army; also that he was in Boston. I thought of saying, Daddy, but ever since I had become a grown-up he played the game only in private. Adam had always liked to play Guess Who as a child, no doubt because he considered it was a prerequisite to his becoming a Super-Sleuth.

Adam, however, was in Outer Mongolia -wherever! Still, I decided, he could have slipped back into the country during the night. "Adam, it's you? You're back!"

"No, tis not that Adams fellow you keep mooning about!"

Now there was another clue! Obviously this person holding me captive was not familiar with United States history. Neither did he know about the existence of my big brother; one simply does not moon over a brother, no matter how suave and good-looking.

I could also discount Britt. Not that I hadn't already discounted him, my ex being overbearingly familiar with our country's history as well as being acquainted with Adam. Besides I knew Jeannie would never, ever, send me to meet him. Simon, I knew, was in the air somewhere between Ottawa and Boston having talked to him early in the morning. So my mind being a blank I copped a plea. "I give up. Who?"

"Moi!"

I could not believe my eyes! "Moi," being the welcome summer gift from Spain to the Canadian government. "Moi," being the lend-leasee sent to help unearth the truth behind the demise of the 16th century whaling fleet in America. For the second time in about three weeks if I had been attending a performance of the Boston Pops, cymbals would have clanged, this time accompanied by the thunder of kettle-drums being savagely pounded.

"Jacques," I squealed, unfortunately sounding a bit too much like one of the piglets at Dr. McTeague's clinic. "I thought you were back in Spain. What ever are you doing in Boston?"

"Ah, Serena, you are a sight for sore eyes."

Picking me up he whirled me around and around. "You look very chic today in your colorful blue outfit, so very, very proper Bostonianish." He squeezed me tighter. "However, your fragrance is so very, very tantalizingly French and you feel so very, very sinfully huggable."

"Jacques, please put me down. I work here, remember," I managed to gasp.

He complied, putting me down as slowly as possible while laughing in such a diabolical, delightful, roguish way that I thought my heart might burst out of its rib cage. "Serena, mon pétit chou, I can now fully appreciate the meaning behind Captain Barrows' preference for calling Personal Flotation Devices, Mae West jackets."

I blushed like the flustered bride I had been on my wedding night. Experience having been a good teacher, I talked away my embarrassment over Jacques' exuberant behavior. "Come, let's go celebrate your visit by having a glass of wine or cup of switchel downstairs in The Atrium. It's next to the gift shop and tends to be quieter this time of day than the main cafeteria. We will take the escalator since it's just around the corner from this gallery."

Quickly I assumed the role of docent, the familiar routine calming my adrenaline-charged heart, restoring my dignity at least to the point that I was able to introduce Jacques calmly to several fellow museum employees as we made our way to the café. "As you can well see from the sleek architecture, Jacques, the escalator connects the old museum to the new wing. It was completed about five years ago and houses the space necessary for large exhibits like the forthcoming one on South American art. The original museum was literally bursting at the seams. Storage facilities were cramped, putting on large shows was a nightmare and, with attendance increasing steadily, the cafeteria had become nothing but a hopeless line of frustrated visitors. Now in addition to the cafeteria there is a formal dining room on the second level overlooking The Atrium which as you can see is just above us. Then, too, the museum needed more space for the gift shop, its sales a major source of income. That's why it was moved from the old section, the powers-to-be insisting on a high visibility area near the main entrance and adjacent to The Atrium and the new dining room."

Jacques had not said a word, even edgewise. Of course I hadn't given him much of a chance due to my steady spiel of trivia while trying to put my silly school girl qualms at bay. Having succeeded, I dared a look up at him and was quite pleased with myself for being able to ignore the knowing twinkle in his eyes and the tongue in cheek smile on his lips, matter-of-factly saying, "By the way, Jacques, the gift shop has a lot of neat items in case you are looking for something different to take home to someone special."

Jacques winked, giving my shoulders another quick squeeze. "Ah, Serena, these days everyone special seems to be on this side of the great pond."

This time I laughed, recklessly sending my very, very proper Bostonian dignity on a mini holiday. Picking up a spoon from a table, I waved it at him. "To quote someone we both know, 'Humph! You are the limit, you know that Jacques B. Labelle!'"

The thought of Euphy dampened my euphoria in seeing Jacques, she still being suspect until Adam declared otherwise. However, it was just for a second, Jacques' frivolous mood denying me the time for reflection and the sadness that always seemed to accompany thoughts of the recent past. Choosing a table near the rear of The Atrium, Jacques passionately declaring with hand over heart a need for an intimate tête-a-tête, we sat down and placed our order for a bare legged tea instead of wine and cheese. Both of us started to talk at once but I won by default, Jacques bowing his head in concession and joshing, "Damsels, Serena, especially those with a titian shade of hair, bedroom-blue eyes and sassy freckles always get to speak first."

I was unable to suppress a giggle. "Well, then, once again, what ever are you doing in Boston? As I said earlier I thought you would be back in Spain, especially by now, since according to Simon all diving operations have ceased and the campsite is battened down for the winter."

"Speaking of Simon, Serena, have you talked to him recently?"

Under such given circumstances, Jacques evasiveness seemed odd. It was the second time he had side-stepped answering my question by querying me with another one. I didn't know whether to tease him about having become a prevaricator or, like I had done in the past, chalk his behavior up to the Basque mystique and let well enough alone. Our tea being served solved my dilemma, the civilized ritual prompting me to choose the latter course of action. "I talked to Simon this morning. In fact, Jacques, Simon is due in tonight on an Air

Canada flight out of Ottawa. If all goes well, he should arrive at Boston's Logan Airport at eight."

"Tonight!" Jacques' eyebrows arched in surprise. "I thought the preliminary hearing on that cocaine bust wasn't going to be held until the first of next week, just before the beginning of your country's Thanksgiving holidays."

Now it was my turn to be surprised. "You know about the forthcoming trial?"

"Everyone having stayed with Euphy through this past fall knows about the trial coming up, Serena, and that you, Captain Barrows and Caesar had a harrowing trip back to Maine."

My astonishment showed after his terse statement. "But why should the trial be of interest to you? And why were you so surprised to learn that Simon is flying in tonight? And how on earth did you find out that Simon and I are involved in the cocaine bust? I don't recall either of us discussing it with you!"

Jacques put down his cup of tea. "Wow! One question at a time please, Serena." He then leaned forward, clasping my hand, bestowing on me a smile dazzling enough to dry out any self-respecting rain cloud. "By now you should know that anything concerning you is of concern to me."

"Oh?"

"And as far as being surprised over Simon's flying in tonight, I believe my surprise is more like a sudden attack of jealousy. You see," he whispered while rubbing his finger tips across the back of my hand, "I had visualized the two of us dining by candlelight in some romantic little bistro overlooking the city. Sharing you with Simon, as hale and hearty a fellow as he is, was definitely not part of my picture."

"Somehow, Jacques, I have a feeling that it is best for me not to know or to even think about your total picture." He grinned, his eyes roving boldly across my chest. "Tis just as well, Serena."

A minute ago I would have been able to respond to Jacques' outrageous behavior in an equally outlandish flirtatious mode. Even up to a second ago, flattered by his attention and amused by his toujour l'amour attitude, I had been able to play the coquette, to play the harmless game of hearts and flowers we always had, to bat my eyelashes a few times at his winning ways. But now his gestures seemed contrived. I had detected a flat note in his rascally response, "Tis just as well," seen a false facade materialize underneath his broad smile. A subtle change had just occurred in our relationship. I could not put my finger on the why or where for it, but I was becoming increasingly uncomfortable with his hand covering mine. Seizing upon the pretense of needing some more sugar in my tea, I withdrew mine from his, quickly helping myself to an unwanted second teaspoon before saying, "This will taste better."

If Jacques noticed my tepid excuse, he didn't say so. Instead he just continued to stare at me in a provocative manner. Or was it speculative? I decided not to worry about semantics, either way I had the distinctly unpleasant feeling that Jacques was mentally undressing me, that he had just tossed my beige lace slip onto the bed and that my bra and panties were next on his itinerary. Thank goodness I didn't have a hole in my lingerie or he might have visualized that too, such was the intensity of his stare. Be that as it may, the scene was not to my liking! It might have played well, "In Padua," but definitely not in Boston. "Jacques," I charged trying not to appear impolite by mimicking an irate Euphy whose thought collecting time had just been invaded, "I do believe you are a devil incarnate. Does your middle initial B by any chance stand for Beelzebub?"

"Beelzebub!" Jacques laughed boisterously. "Mon Dieu , Serena, you do have a vivid imagination."

His laugh was infectious, momentarily chasing away my uneasy mood and irritability. However it did not dissuade me. This time I was determined to get a straight answer. "Botticelli? Your parents named you after the great Florentine Renaissance painter?"

Jacques shook his head, still laughing.

"Brueghel? That's it! They named you after Pieter Brueghel, the Elder, the 16th century Flemish painter that is being-called the father of landscape painting?"

"No." Jacques leaned back into his chair, complacency written all over him. "Best give up, Serena. You will never guess and I will never tell."

"I don't give up easily, Jacques."

"Neither do I, Serena."

There was too much smugness in his proclaimed, "Neither do I." My stubborn streak surfaced. "Both? You were named after the Dutch landscape painter Jan Both?"

He smiled back at me, mouthing a pear shaped, "No."

Again I tried. "Bernini? Your parents named you after the illustrious 17th century sculptor Lorenzo Bernini?"

"Come, come, Serena. I can think of more important things to discuss than my middle initial." He chuckled, dismissing my guess of Bernini with a wave of his hand. "Such as the weather, the time of day and your testimony and that of Simon's at the hearing tomorrow. Besides never in a million years will you be able to guess correctly!"

Of course Jacques was right, there were more important things to discuss than his middle initial. Whether he realized it or not his three mentioned topics were of considerable concern for me, the weather in that it could become fickle and delay Simon's plane, the time of day in that it was a half hour until the museum closed and I had not finished proofing the catalog which Mr. Smythe had wanted on his desk by five o'clock and that I be accurate in my testimony tomorrow recalling the myriad of events leading to the downfall of Missy Sue and Leroy. And yet, I hated to give up. I hated to have to say, "Uncle."

I looked across the table at Jacques and giggled. Simon had told me that I got silly when I started to weary of a situation, a giggle being the first symptom. He had also told me, while we were enjoying one of our many walks on the beach, that I became kittenish, spontaneously saying the most outlandish things such as the time I called the bow of a boat, "The pointy end."

I finished my tea, an attack of the "sillies" causing me to spill a bit into my saucer. Again I looked at Jacques, trying to peer behind the curtain of secrecy veiling his eyes, telling myself, "Forget Beethoven, Brahms and Bach. His middle initial stands for a name far removed from the world of the Muses. Think! Think far out. Think far, far out!"

"Beauregard." The name played on my lips as it flashed like lightning through my head. "Beauregard?" I tingled with excitement, exulation, whatever, exclaiming wildly, "It's Beauregard, Jacques? Your parents named you after an American general that fought for the South during the Civil War?"

Jacques' jaw dropped, practically to the floor.

Gleefully, I responded. "You said never in a million years will I be able to guess correctly. Well, now, you are going to have to eat your words, Jacques Beauregard Labelle."

I sat there expecting him to laugh, waiting for him to 'fess up to being outsmarted, to say something witty and complimentary like, "Foxy lady."

I could not hear his answer. Even being seated just an arms' length away, I could not hear his answer. Drowning it out was a very loud ringing in my ears that sounded ominously like a blaring fire alarm. The ringing crescendoed into a crunchy rice-crispy, snap, crackle and pop sound, capped by a voice booming, "Come in *Savannah's Revenge*. This is Beauregard. Do you hear me? Over and out!"

Having started the day by getting out on the wrong side of the bed I reacted inanely to this revelation by jumping up and blurting, "You are the person who was waiting at Halfway Rock for Missy Sue and Leroy! You are the signatory, the B, I saw neatly printed on the postcard picturing Euphy's house when I was on board *Savannah*. Furthermore you, not Euphy thank goodness, hand delivered that postcard to them while they were anchored in Espérance, that little fishing village so close to Rouge Baie. No wonder you were so upset and evasive that day when Euphy said your cousin Sue had called to let you know that she and her husband had met with an accident while in Southern Maine, an accident which dampened their trip, the accident being my destruction of *Savannah*. An accident you confirmed by snooping through my belongings and reading my letter to Gloria."

The full impact of indignant me handing down accusations came home to roost. I had succeeded in scaring myself silly and yet I was unable to stop from recklessly goading Jacques. "No wonder you are so interested in my testimony and that of Simon's! Why we could put you away forever! If not forever, at least till the cows come home!"

Unfortunately I had not jumped fast enough or far enough away to escape Jacques' wrath. With what had to be the same speed as that of a striking cobra, he grabbed my arm, twisting and squeezing it like a coiled python I had seen on a Geographic special getting ready to eat its prey. I sat down, trembling, wincing with pain and mentally flagellating myself for acting so smart that I had now out-foxed myself into the liar's lair.

Jacques grinned, his show of teeth making me think of a salivating, rabid dog. "All, of what you say is quite true, Serena, though I am disappointed in not being credited with the attempt on your life at Sunrise Point. However, it is now a moot point and to borrow your quaint expression, mon pétit chou, you will never live long enough to see the cows leave home, let alone come home. Nor will Simon."

I did not care for the finality of Jacques' prophecy, especially after hearing his chilling confession to an attempted premeditated murder on my life. What I could do about it, ensnared as I was in his vise-like grip, was another matter.

"I can read you like an open book, Serena." His voice lowered to a menacing rasp, grating on my nerves like the sound of a dentist's drill. "Don't try anything stupid."

The malicious glint in Jacques' eyes and his baleful expression fascinated and repelled me at the same time. Spellbound, I watched him reach into the breast pocket of his sport jacket, pull out a revolver and brazenly place it underneath his napkin on the table adding sardonically, "That is unless you don't mind seeing a few innocent bystanders being killed."

I gasped. "You wouldn't dare!"

"Ah, but I do dare! You witnessed Caesar's plight from my slipping poison into his food the morning you and Sonofagun left for Maine. Unfortunately, Sonofagun threw a monkey wrench into my plans for doing away with you both by changing his mind about going to Country Harbour Mines. I, along with my colleagues, had planned to welcome you with a cold dip, permanently!"

I gasped again upon hearing his horrifying admission. Up until now everyone was still guessing, hoping for a logical explanation. Now I knew. I also knew the meaning behind the "shipment of three crates." Rage replaced reason, my disdain for him spilling out in a flurry of words. "You are beyond contempt. Vileness must run in your family. What other reason could you possibly give for planning to kill innocent Captain Barrows and my Caesar?"

Jacques sneered. "I am not like your Simon, full of compassion for all mankind. When it comes to saving my life, I am merciless."

I knew he meant it, such was the venomous tone of his voice. My vision blurred into prisms of blue-white light. My fingers were tingling from the constant pressure Jacques was exerting on my arm. It was affecting my stomach, the bitter taste of bile, fear and panic starting to rise in my throat. I bit down hard on the inside of my lower lip, thinking, hoping, the therapy of self inflicted pain would restore my equilibrium. It worked! I became cucumbery-cool, able to look Jacques straight in the eye saying as sarcastically as I could, never having been a devotee of that discipline, "I must compliment you on the new high you have brought to the game of deception."

Jacques stared back, a hard uncompromising glare in his eyes. "Leroy was right. You do have a feisty streak in your otherwise patient nature. However, Serena, you best keep it in check."

Picking up the gun he slipped it into the side pocket of his jacket. "Shall we go?"

I hated to budge from my safety position. "Go where?"

"To hell, you might say, Serena." Rising from his chair, he pulled me up with him, relinquishing his grip on my arm just long enough to make a fond pretense of protectively gripping my shoulder. "Now pay attention. As we leave The Atrium I want you to look up and give me an adoring, rapturous smile. That way if anyone is watching they won't be alarmed."

I gagged at the thought. "You are asking a lot of me."

"It will do you good to suffer, Serena. Otherwise, others will."

Digging his fingers into my shoulder Jacques propelled me through the maze of exotic potted plants interspersed between the wrought iron tables and chairs. As we neared the entrance, he leaned down kissing me lightly on the top of my head, whispering, "Serena, smile sweetly at the garçon and the maître d'. Say what you have to, nothing more, nothing less."

I nodded, the intense pain in my shoulder and the fear Jacques would live up to his threat of killing a bystander making it difficult for me to do anything else but comply.

Philosophically speaking, what is it that ignites the spark of rebellion existing in all our souls? At what point do the oppressed step out from under the thumb of the oppressors? For me it was this precise moment! My defeatist thought of having no choice but to comply merged with the realization that I had inadvertently given Simon's travel schedule to Jacques. Both notions fused with his order to, "Smile sweetly at the garçon and the maître d'". Voila! Little did Jacques realize he had just illuminated a way for me to strike my first blow towards freedom and to put him in "The Big Stew Pot" along with Missy Sue and Leroy. "May the three of you bubble together forever," I muttered angrily, though strictly to myself.

Anxiously I waited for what I was hoping would be just the right moment. As soon as Jacques pushed open the heavy glass swinging doors with his free hand I turned my head towards Jerry, our garçon, pointedly saying, "David, be a doll and please put the tea on my tab will you?" Having known Jerry for several years I felt certain my calling him by a different name would be noticed. I dared not look back to see.

Jacques didn't mince any words once we were outside of The Atrium. "Listen carefully to my instructions, Serena. I will not repeat them to you. We are going to walk hand in hand, leisurely, cheerfully, through the rotunda to the escalator. Once there we will ride up to the second floor, go through the Adams Gallery to your office, pick up your car keys and then take the elevator to the ground floor parking area reserved for employees."

I could feel his inferno-like breath on the back of my neck. It fueled the rebellious flame flickering within me. "Ha, ha! You are out of luck. I walked to work this morning, Jacques."

"Don't ha, ha, me, Serena!" His fingers dug deeper into my shoulder. "I happen to know your red Porsche is parked there, plainly advertised by your license plate, S E R E N A."

Touché, I thought, mentally scratching one up for the visiting team. Not to be outdone, I quickly countered with one for the home team by recklessly asking, "Do you have a valid driver's license?"

His answer differed from those dictated permissible under the terms of the Geneva Convention. In fact, Jacques didn't answer at all. He let his fingers do the talking by walking them into his jacket pocket, pulling out the revolver and poking it against the small of my back. I immediately regretted my flippant outburst, Jacques' ominous silence almost as terrifying as the pressure of his gun digging into my spine.

Nudging me forward, we started on Jacques' prescribed leisurely walk towards the escalator. His arm fell away from my shoulder, only to end up slithering down mine giving me the bivvers. Once again I could taste that bitterness rising in my throat as his hand grasped mine, his strong fingers cruelly bending my fingers into his palm.

Tears sprang to my eyes. Jacques laughed at my discomfort. "Come, come, Serena, you are supposed to be cheerful, not unhappy. Let me see an adoring smile on your face, not an expression of gloom as we take the escalator." Bending his head, he added lasciviously, "Perhaps it will be easier if you think about it as ascending a stairway to consummate a rapturous night in Simon's arms. Unfortunately, neither you nor Simon will ever again experience such sublime bliss!"

Over my dead body, I thought defensively; the analogy, admittedly, not being the best but at the moment it was the only one I could think of as suitable. I said, as haughtily as I could, "You seem very sure of yourself."

"Serena, I can tell by the tilt of your chin and the spark of defiance in your eyes that you are not taking me seriously." He forced me closer to him with an agonizing twist of my wrist.

"Look around you. Perhaps you are not seeing the same scenes as vividly as I am, like the delightful group of school children happily queuing up for their bus trip home. Then there is the elder-hostel group collecting their belongings from the cloakroom. Do I need to mention the fellow on crutches standing directly in front of us?"

There was nothing subtle about his threats. Replying this time I meant it when I answered, "I understand the drift of your thoughts, Jacques."

"Good! Now then shall we proceed to your office, get your car keys and, of course, your coat." He smirked. "Though where you are going a coat really won't be necessary."

I decided to ignore his supercilious remark about my coat and did as I was told. Dutifully I proceeded Jacques onto the escalator and as we glided upwards to the second floor I took a measure of comfort from the lights still being on in Jeannie's office, the word Tours clearly visible on the door, knowing that when I didn't appear a few minutes after five she would investigate the reason behind my tardiness. Why, maybe she would even run into Jerry and hopefully he would tell her that I was literally bent out of shape when I called him David. Now that would be a bit of luck! In the meantime, I was on my own.

On my own! The phrase sounded like the title of a juicy soap opera. I could almost hear Simon counsel in his professorial, tender way, "But, Sprite, this is not a soap opera with a 'To be continued' tomorrow ending. This is for real! This is your life."

It was a sobering thought. However, far more sobering and important to me was that Simon's life was hanging in the balance. I had to survive to save Simon and in order to do that I had to dispose of Jacques, a dispensable person if there ever was one. But how?

My question, but how?, was as mind-boggling as playing the game Guess Who in that there were no quick, correct answers. Under the circumstances the best I could do was to be prudent, to mind my p's and q's and, as nauseous as it made me feel, to continue smiling ardently at Jacques while we walked to my office.

There wasn't a need to communicate as I unlocked the door, Jacques' watchful eyes dictating my every move. After switching on the lights I walked briskly over to the desk, removed my leather purse and gloves from the lower left hand drawer, grabbed my suede coat off of the coat tree and rapidly walked back out into the hall, pulling the door closed behind me. I risked Jacques' ire, fiddling away an extra second by twisting the knob and then dropping the ring of museum keys into my purse.

Jacques grunted his impatience. Taking me firmly in tow, he headed towards the elevator. If he noticed my excessive nervousness characterized by trembling and shortness of breath or heard my heart pounding, he didn't say so. Having just struck my second and third blows for freedom by leaving the lights on and the door to my office unlocked, I couldn't help being as skittish as a rabbit stuck in a fox hole.

Jacques appeared to accept my uneasiness as being normal, probably thinking my behavior was justifiable proof of his, so-called, great prowess as an intimidator. Indeed, he beamed with malicious pleasure, zapping the elevator button with supreme assurance, forcefully saying, "Mind yourself, Serena. If anyone is on the elevator, don't make them suspicious by being evasive. On the other hand, don't be overly friendly."

My mind went blank. It was as empty as the elevator when the doors parted to reveal nothing but cube-like space. By the time we reached the ground floor parking area, I had not conjured up an encore to my previous three bold strikes for freedom and Jacques didn't waste a minute before heading right for my car. Unfortunately, it was still there!

Jacques let go of my hand when we reached the driver's side of the car but he did not remove the gun from the small of my back. "Now give me the car keys, Serena, and don't dally. I want to be out of here by five o'clock when the museum closes and the parking lot will become even more congested with people than it is now."

For once I agreed with him. There were far too many people milling about the area, especially when one of them was a gun toting, trigger-happy barbarian. I decided on the spot that whatever I did to try and survive I had to do in private or in a safe secluded out of the way place. In Boston, the hub of the universe, this was easier said than done.

"Serena, the car keys!"

Jacques' order was curt and I immediately delved into my purse for them. Without a wicked good thought to buoy up my spirits, I pulled open the zippered compartment reserved solely for the Porsche keys and automatically reached for them. Nothing greeted my exploring fingers. Absolutely nothing!

"Oh, no, Jacques," panic being the motivating force behind my shout, "I've misplaced the keys."

Fortunately for me mortality wise, Jacques realized my astonishment was genuine, that I wasn't fudging. "Dump the contents of your purse onto the suntop, Serena. Perhaps the keys are in another compartment."

I nodded, quickly turning my purse upside down, shaking it, not wanting to provoke Jacques into doing anything rash. Normally I would have been embarrassed to do this, Mother having always called the contents of my purse a disgrace while Grandmother would tut her disapproval but at the same time avow the mess of ticket stubs, market receipts, lipstick tissues, etc., seemed to go hand in hand with someone cursed by The Damning Defect. Gloria, however, said the clutter was due to my museum training, that the collection of ephemera was far too ingrained for me to ever stop. Whatever their opinions, it mattered not a whit today, my purse being squeaky clean having changed over to a different one more in keeping with Greek antiquities. What did matter was finding the elusive keys. Pronto!

The heavy stuff spilled out first: wallet, museum keys, change purse and check book. Next came the lightweights, all cylindrical, the pen and pencil set, the lipsticks, a flashlight, all rolling off the suntop in clanging harmony. I tried to stop them, to pick them up, but Jacques had other plans. "Leave them be, Serena. I have found your car keys."

"Where?"

Jacques' free hand was resting on the car door handle. "Where else but in the ignition!"

289

Upon hearing his news I didn't know whether to laugh, cry or shout, "Hurrah," all three emotions being good bets to express my point of view. However, a little bird told me I better cry or at least appear contrite, that Jacques in his thunderous mood might not appreciate the humor behind my locking the keys in the car, that he would not interpret my forgetfulness as a stroke of unbelievably good luck. I did!

This time all kinds of wicked good ideas on how to squash Jacques, just like any other insect, immediately surfaced. I could kick him in the shins, in the movies that seemed to always produce an exaggerated flinch, or I could whack him on the head with my purse. That too might induce enough trauma to make him lower his gun for a moment. Of course, Adam always said a solid, driving punch to the lower solar plexus is unequaled for inflicting sufficient momentary pain in order to gain a slight edge against a would be attacker, but not having been trained in tai chi, fung fu -whatever -I discarded those tactics as not being practical. Having made that decision I came up with an idea that I hoped would be a winner. I would lie!

"Jacques, I always keep an extra set of car keys in my office," I said contritely, knowing full well they were right there beside me in a magnetic box stuck under the left front fender of my car. "If we hurry, we can go back into the building the way we came out using my museum key. Otherwise we will have to go through the main entrance since the nighttime security system automatically clicks in at five o'clock."

Not wanting to give Jacques time to bellow, "No," I hurriedly scooped up the contents of my purse that were on the suntop and walked decisively towards the heavy steel door painted a bright red. It was a bold move on my part and I held my breath, any second expecting to hear his gun go off and to feel what Adam called, "A hot, excruciating, pincer-like bite of pain."

To my relief Jacques followed close behind, telling me though in a sotto voice tone laced with vitriol, "Heroism in my book is not an admirable virtue, Serena; cowardice and obedience will become you more and in the long run perhaps save a life or two. Be careful!"

Jacques was bent on trying to frighten me and he bloody well succeeded! I clamped my mouth shut to stop my teeth from chattering. I started to tremble and finally, in desperation to get the key into the lock, had to use both of my hands. Once safely inside the building, I calmed down. Realizing that no longer did I have to worry about someone else being hurt, my breathing slowly returned to normal, my teeth stopped chattering and I was able to press the elevator button without even a bit of tremor. I was no longer afraid. I knew exactly what I was going to do; indeed, what I had to do, step by step, to save Simon. This was going to be my finest hour. Stepping into the elevator I took off my heavy coat, put it over my arm and then pressed the button 2G instead of 2, moving slightly in front of the control panel as I did. If Jacques noticed I had pressed 2G instead of 2, I was prepared to lie, again; telling him 2G stood for the Adams Gallery on the second floor whereas 2, similar in level to a hotel's mezzanine, stood for the new exhibit wing. Actually, it was just the reverse!

As the elevator hummed its way up to 2G I psyched myself for action, knowing the element of surprise was crucial, fully aware that I would only have one chance to make an escape, one chance to incapacitate Jacques, one chance to ever see my family again, and one chance to try and save Simon.

I could hear faintly the five o'clock buzzer ringing. Jacques was staring straight ahead, wary, poised as if to take flight as soon as the doors parted in front of him. We were almost there.

I took a very deep breath when the elevator stopped, the thought occurring to me it could be my last breath ever, so I better enjoy the thrill of breathing while I could. Having billed myself as an avenging angel, I too poised for a flight, but instead of flying to heaven to head due east straight out of the back of the elevator into the huge exhibit room which for the past couple of weeks resembled a builders supply outlet in limbo. This dual-door elevator was a godsend, in more ways than one I decided. Not only was it used for the moving of objects, priceless and otherwise, from the basement to the exhibit area, but it was also used to carry the handicapped, giving them accessibility to the galleries they would not normally have and now, for the first time, I felt sure the elevator was going to be used to commit a little mayhem.

The doors swooshed open. I flew into orbit, throwing my coat over Jacques' head, wishing I had a camera to capture the incredulous expression riveted on his face. For good measure I kicked him in the shins and zapped him one with my purse, shouting, "Now it's your turn to go to hell, Jacques Beauregard Labelle."

I sprinted out of the elevator and ran into the vast room. It was a mess. "In a state of shocking dishabille," Mr Smythe had joked, but the clutter was absolutely perfect for my escape. Ladders, scaffolding, paint, movable partitions, pedestals, Plexiglas domes, coils of rope, etc., were scattered everywhere and yet to the trained eye there was a floor plan emerging in the shape of a W.

Setting my sights on the mammoth double doors dominating the far end of the room, I ran towards them, my elation over them being closed seemingly adding wings to my feet. Normally the doors were open during the day permitting a free flow of traffic between galleries, but once closed by the guards at five o'clock an ear splitting alarm would go off the minute anyone pushed them open, summoning Boston's Finest! They would descend upon the building like swarming locusts, guns drawn, ready for a donnybrook. How wickedly wonderful!

Jacques was gaining on me. I chose not to listen to his repertoire of epithets, concentrating solely on the sound of his heavy footsteps drawing nearer and nearer. His hand grazing my shoulder sent me veering to the left, the turn forcing me to run between two enormous movable partitions that had been lined up to draw the eye to a large black wooden pedestal being prepared to hold a magnificent vessel of gold excised with Inti, the sun god in the Inca realm of deities.

My feet and legs were beginning to ache from the abuse of running in high heels. My heart was pounding, beating out an S O S, signaling me to pause and catch my breath regardless of the consequences. I stumbled, falling hard against one of the partitions. Not being permanently in place for the forthcoming exhibit, it gave way under the impact. The partition careened backwards, taking with it a scaffold holding tackle, paint and drop cloths. I followed in an ungainly swan dive spiral.

Jacques latched onto me in what had to be the ravenous manner of a vulture swooshing down to capture its victim. His talon-like fingers dug cruelly into my shoulders making me wince as he yanked me up off of the floor. However the pain was not intense enough to stop me from curling my fingers around the handle of a paint can which had miraculously fallen beside my left hand. Even though it was full, I came up swinging the can like it was a toy whirligig, not being the least bit particular where it landed as long as it struck Jacques somewhere, preferably on his head. My aim was not bull's eye perfect, his fancy foot work keeping him at bay, but finally the inertia generated by the weight of the can pulled me forward and I connected with a glancing blow to the top of his skull.

Jacques sank to the floor like he was attached to a lead line, his moaned, "Dieu," somewhat gurgled as he bent over in apparent agony. Having been whacked on the top of my head once by a swinging boom while helping to furl a sail, I could sympathize with the mush-like heaving bound to be going on in his stomach as well as the white dots zinging around in his head that the blow had caused. But I didn't; Jacques, in my frenzied state, not being worthy of anyone's compassion.

Peering down at him, I didn't know whether to run and scream or scream and run, neither choice satisfying my lust for vengeance. Not that I thirsted to see blood spilled, it was just that a lot of unadulterated pleading for mercy on his part would be nice to hear. On the other hand, if I didn't skedaddle, PDQ, quoting Captain Barrows, I would be the one on bended knee.

Still holding on to the gallon can of paint, its weight cutting into my hand as sharply as my gasps for breath were causing stitches in my sides, I noticed a long rope tied to the handle dangling down onto the floor, the end curled like a giant question mark -or -was the end of the rope more like a loose painter tossed into the bow of a dinghy?

It took me just one second to realize another miracle had been divined!

Quickly I slipped off my high heels, the feeling of flat solidness beneath my feet making it easier to kneel down beside Jacques. After a glance at his face and seeing his eyelids flutter, I knew Jacques' blackout was going to be brief, that I didn't have a moment to spare.

Grabbing the can of paint, I moved it approximately a shoe's length away from his head. As swiftly as I could I looped the rope tied to the handle of the paint can several times around his neck, in my mind the proximity of the can to his neck making a perfect mooring. I soon discovered this bit of mischief awkward to do but I rose to the situation by lifting Jacques' head away from the floor by his curly black hair, thereby gaining the necessary couple of inches needed to manipulate the rope. From then on it was as if Simon was kneeling beside Jacques and me, telling me to, "Tie a bowline, Serena;" instructing me to, "Remember the bobcat jingle, Serena;" guiding my hands to create a make-believe dinghy by pulling Jacques' wrists together behind his back, looping the excess rope over, under and around, but not to let go of the end, instead to visualize it as a rabbit desperate to find a hole in the ground.

Hurriedly I ran my right hand, palm side up, underneath the rope linking Jacques' hands and neck and then turning my hand knuckle sideup, created a loop. Having laid out the welcome mat for my fuzzy little friend, I rapidly transferred the loop to my left hand remembering to hold it tightly against my fingers by putting my thumb on top where the line crossed itself. Reaching underneath with my right hand I then grabbed the end of the rope, transforming it in my mind to a cotton-tail. "A cotton-tail which looks out of its hole," I whispered to Jacques while passing the end through the loop. He did not seem particularly interested as I continued to pull it through saying, "The rabbit comes out of its hole." Still holding on to the end of the rope, I passed it behind my so-called painter telling him, "Runs around the tree." Poking it down through the loop I started to shout. "And you will be delighted to know, Jacques, the rabbit goes back into its hole." I drew the knot up tight, closing the door, the door fortunately looking a lot like the figure eight.

It was none too soon! Jacques' interest had obviously peaked, a blood curdling cry, "I'll kill you for this, Serena," announcing his return to full consciousness.

I wasn't about to listen to his filthy words which I knew would be forthcoming; that kind of verbal abuse, which I had never expected in my wildest dreams to hear from Britt, always haunting me afterwards for days on end. A disgustingly dirty paint cloth on the floor beside me offered a quick solution and so I scooped it up, stuffing it roughly into his mouth. Neither was I about to hang around and give him the chance to kill me, though my back door bowline knot did look secure. However, even kings have been known to unravel! That thought not only brought me scrambling to my feet but sent me scooting down the ways, the ways this time being a carpeted runway leading to the double doors at the far end of the room and salvation.

My deliverance was heralded throughout the hub as soon as I pushed open the doors. I joined in the din, infused with the true spirit of Paul Revere coursing through my veins, shouting, "The Spanish are here, the Spanish are here!"

On I charged, heading nowhere in particular, just running on and on into the empty vastness of the galleries, my cries for help echoing, "Jeannie, Jerry, Mr. Smythe, anyone; is anyone there?"

The lights went out. Not that that was anything new, they always did in the larger galleries at 5:15 p.m. What was new was that sometime between nine o'clock this morning and now, the fire department's order to enlarge an exit door leading to a flight of backstairs had been started. The familiar door was no longer there. In its place was a common, ordinary, dark hole in the wall, the kind you would see at any construction site if you just happened to be prowling around in a designated hard hat area on a pitch, black night. The thought occurred to me as I found myself soaring through the air, that this was the second air-borne launching I had participated in; my first having been just this past June when I beam-ended into the enthralling world of boating via stumbling over a gas can on *Escape* and now, my second, having been just this past minute when I catapulted into the enthralling world of sky diving via stumbling over a couple of sawhorses.

Chapter 22

As masquerade balls go I thought this one a little weird. "You know, it isn't the lighting that bothers me," I complained to someone short and plump costumed as a white rabbit. "Although, I do think the lights could be dimmer, could be softer, which would make the ballroom more romantic. Don't you think so?"

I continued, the rabbit being coy and not answering. "It isn't the decor either! Although, I do think the decorations are gauche. After all, who ever heard of using green plastic garbage bags for balloons? And, in the Ritz no less!"

This time the rabbit nodded in agreement, urging me on. "No, it isn't the lights or the decor that's making this ball so weird. It's the guests labeling their costumes by hanging signs around their necks that's creating such a bizarre atmosphere. Why, who ever heard of carrying a sign to let everyone know who you are supposed to be? It takes all the fun out of guessing when midnight rolls around! Don't you agree?"

The rabbit turned its head slightly to follow my gaze, the ears somewhat askew giving me an impression of drunkenness. "For instance," I said, trying very hard to explain my point of view, "take the three men standing in the center of the dance floor. It appears to me as if they are participating in a tableau depicting an important historical event for their costumes are all from the same period, 16th century I would say and judging from the rich fabrics used in making the doublets and cloaks they are supposed to be noblemen or at least men of rank. Without even having to confirm my guess is correct by reading their insufferable signs, I would say the man holding onto the terrestrial globe and a tiny banner from Patagonia should be deemed Ferdinand Magellan. Then I would guess the one clutching a map of the world to be Leonardo da Vinci, and the other, Pieter Brueghel, the Elder, since he is holding a landscape done in pen and brown ink on white paper." I added, feeling quite smug, "It is possible you know they were acquaintances and perhaps even corresponded."

297

A couple waltzed by, distracting us from the tableau. "You see, Rabbit," by then I decided it would be best to call he or she Rabbit," the two men conversing near the bandstand? Each one is robed in a toga, they too seeming to depict an important historical event. Without even having to confirm my guess is correct by reading their insufferable signs I would say the man holding the reference book with the stick on letters 'Periplus of Scylax' and the 'Thule or Bust' banner is supposed to be Pytheas, while the other holding a small marble statue of a sensuous, curved female nude is supposed to be Praxiteles of Athens. Though one was a sailor and the other a sculptor they too could have enjoyed each other's company. Perhaps even shared a kantharos of wine? What do you think?"

Rabbit didn't answer me, instead turning to greet another guest garbed as a white rabbit, this one tall and thin. Being privy to my own thoughts for a couple of minutes while these two engaged in chit chat, I glanced around the ballroom searching for a familiar face underneath a disguise. No one in particular caught my eye; what did catch my eye was the sameness of the costumes. Sameness, in the sense that half of the revelers were dressed up as famous navigators and the other half as renowned artists. Even more astonishing to me was they had grouped themselves, unconsciously or consciously, according to their time slots in history: Columbus holding onto Ptolemy's "Cosmograpia" chatting with Sandro Botticelli; James Cook in a deep conversation with Charles Peale; Fridtjof Nansen sharing a profound thought with Winslow Homer and Claude Monet; Donald MacMillan joking with Marsden Hartley.

Someone must have heard me complaining about the lights to Rabbit. They were becoming noticeably dimmer and the band, having finished tuning up, blared out with the odd air "Onward Christian Soldiers." More couples paraded by trying to keep in step with the march, their costumes, being hilariously recognizable, needing no labels like the giant green clock dancing with the chart emblazoned by a magenta compass rose or the red nun buoy holding hands with the beacon.

298

Rabbit finally reclaimed my attention, answering my question, but, with a question. "Serena, what is it I'm supposed to think about?"

The tall, thin white rabbit chimed in with, "Serena, what is it you are trying to say? We can't hear you."

Pytheas, Columbus, Cook, Nansen, Magellan and MacMillan gathered round, forming a circle, they, too, saying, "Serena, we can't hear you."

The giant green clock and the red nun buoy joined the circle, their voices soft, tinkling like a ship's bell, whispering, "Serena, we can't hear you."

"Cast off," I shouted to all of them. "Cast off."

Rabbit leaned very close, smiling, the big floppy ears changing in front of my eyes into a tiny, crisp white wisp of a hat. "I do believe, Dr. Collins, your wife's sister is coming to now but her voice is so weak I still can't understand or hear what she is trying to tell us."

The tall, thin rabbit bent towards me, frowning, the big floppy ears changing in front of my eyes to short brown hair. "Water," I shouted. "How can I cast off without water."

They both leaned over, peering down at me like I was a specimen on a slide to be scrutinized under a microscope, fussing with what felt like sheets, pillows and a blanket. "Serena," the tall one said, "it's Paul, Gloria's husband."

I could feel the pressure of his hand on mine, gentle yet reassuring. "You are in the hospital, Serena. You were brought here from the museum in an ambulance. There is no need to worry. You have had a slight accident, but you will be fine."

Both rabbits disappeared. I tried to smile at the nurse, tried to tell Paul I understood but my lips were stiff, my throat parched. "Paul, please, water."

This time I was rewarded, the nurse wiping my lips with a moistened piece of gauze. "This will have to do for a while, Serena. In due time you can have something carbonated to sip."

I managed a, "Thank you," supremely grateful for the residue of moisture clinging to my lips. "I thought I was shouting to you."

She laughed. "Being under the influence of an anesthetic can make you think and say strange things at times! Right, Dr. Collins?"

"Right, Mary!"

Paul had nodded, agreeing affably with her I noticed, but knowing him as well as I did I could tell by his bearing that he was now standing beside my bed in a professional way. "How slight is slight, Paul," I asked, hoping to help ease him into the truth by confessing, "my entire body is aching, particularly my right shoulder and arm which I'm now beginning to realize is in a cast."

He grinned. "Well, Serena, visibly you have two black eyes, both worthy of a blue ribbon. They will fade away in due time."

"And a broken arm, Paul," I interrupted.

"Yes, Serena, a break just below the elbow. It will heal without any complications."

I sniffed, surprised by a few tears oozing to the surface. I thought I had become bone dry. "What isn't visible?"

"A concussion, slight, and a couple of cracked ribs. That was quite a tumble you took down the stairs. You are lucky, Serena. It could have been worse."

I closed my eyes, not wanting to hear anymore bad news. I wanted to sleep, to rid my brain of its fuzziness. Yet, I had to know. Yet, I wasn't quite sure what I had to know other than I had to be at the airport to meet Simon.

I opened my eyes, struggling to move. "Simon! I have to meet Simon, Paul."

"Relax, Serena, you are not going anywhere but down the hall to your room. Besides, Gloria is going to pick him up."

My head started to spin like a top, immediately sending a protest to my stomach which in turn retaliated by making a lot of nauseous waves. The pain in my arm was excruciating. I felt faint, almost too weak to speak and yet I had to know before I succumbed. "Do you think Simon will know the difference, Paul? That is, do you think he will know it's Gloria and not me? We look so very much alike."

Paul chuckled. "Serena, you and Gloria can fool a lot of people but you two never fooled me, nor will Gloria fool Simon.

It will take him exactly one glance in the right direction to know that she isn't you. Now lean back, take it easy while I wheel you into the arms of the rest of the family and a few close friends."

"Oh!"

"And, one more thing, you had better enjoy this chariot ride! I don't do this for all my patients."

#

The chariot ride had been sublime as was the comfort of being surrounded by family and friends. They were all heading home now, sent on their way by Paul's order, "So Serena can rest."

Jeannie and Jerry were the first to leave, Jeannie saying while buttoning up her coat, "Jerry had been talking to me about your irrational behavior in The Atrium when the alarm went off and we heard your shouts for help." Jerry adding to her explanation, "Yeah, Serena, I really thought you had flipped your wig when you called me David. On the other hand I should have suspected something was wrong when I saw that jerk kiss you on top of your head. I could tell from the grimace on your face that you didn't like it. Now if that had been me doing the kissing you would have swooned on the spot."

I managed to smile at Jerry's joking and a weak but heartfelt, "Thank you both for coming," as they left my room.

Mr. Smythe left next. I could tell he was concerned about my well being, pressing me for details of my encounter with Jacques but it was simply too much of an effort to give him a coherent report even though I was beginning to think more clearly. I couldn't recall ever seeing Mr. Smythe so subdued, so serious in demeanor even after Daddy paid him the compliment, "Henry, the view of *Old Ironsides* from your library window is one in a million. Of course the entire room reflects your excellent taste."

Mr. Smythe's reply normally would have been gracious and warm in content. Instead it was strained, seeming to be out of context for I overheard him say, "After the recent events of today, John, I count my lucky stars that I'm still alive to enjoy the view."

"Now, Henry," Daddy replied firmly, "no one could blame you for doing what you did under the same set of circumstances."

I must have dozed off then, just for a split second, because the next thing I heard was Mr. Smythe saying, "You know, John, I found Jacques Labelle running madly through the gallery, squawking in a patois of French and Spanish, waving a gun in the air, threatening to kill anyone who was in his way. We struggled of course and in the scuffle the gun went off. He died instantly."

Jacques dead! Unbelievable! And yet Mr. Smythe had said, "He died instantly." Something was wrong! I couldn't put my finger on it but something was definitely wrong! My mind rebelled at the news, forcing me into the safety of oblivion for the next thing I knew Daddy was shaking my arm gently, telling me, "We are leaving now, Serena, and of course will be in and out tomorrow. By the way the police want to question you about Jacques Labelle. However, Little One, I took it upon myself to tell them you were being represented by the archaic firm of Bradford, Bradford and Bradford; that it would be best to check with us first." He winked. "No complaints, I hope!"

Captain Barrows left with Daddy, his parting shot typical but a little more boisterous than usual. "Hell's bell's," he bellowed, "if you didn't want to give me a tour of your danged museum, Serena, why didn't you just say so? That would have been much easier than jumpin' off of the poop deck!"

Adam, having unexpectedly arrived home early for the Thanksgiving holidays, laughed heartily. Mother smiled indulgently and got ready to follow Daddy and Captain Barrows out into the hall. "We will be going home now, Serena, and will wait up for Simon. Gloria and Paul will bring him as soon as he has a chance to see you. Rest assured that he will be warmly received."

I nodded in agreement. It hurt too much to talk.

"Now then, dear, I hate to talk shop at a time like this but in light of what transpired at the museum I think you should know what has happened on the home front today."

302

I succeeded in asking a feeble, "Oh?," and watched somewhat mystified as Mother reached into her well organized Gucci purse and pulled out a postcard. "You received a postcard from Euphy Browne. Not that I meant to read it," she apologized while handing the card to me, "but the message on it was so odd and under these circumstances I thought I should bring it to you. So, when we left the house to come here I just slipped it into my purse."

Adam interjected a long drawn out, "And-d-d, you also got a phone call from Euphy Browne just as we were leaving to come to the hospital. Her message at first didn't make a lot of sense to me but, as Mother says, in light of what transpired at the museum it certainly does now."

I was intrigued enough to momentarily ignore my pain. "Being as how that is a toll call, Euphy must have considered her message important. What did she say, Adam?"

"She said to tell you that while having Jacques' room cleaned a small vial of arsenic was found. It had been hidden or else it had fallen accidentally behind a bureau drawer. Because of what happened to Caesar she thought you should know. That's why, Mrs. Browne said, she mailed you the postcard."

Adam pulled his chair closer to my bed, his proximity making it easier for me to talk and to listen. Mother smiled approvingly at his thoughtfulness, urging him to continue with a slight nod of her head. "Mrs. Browne also said that she discovered today a telephone number with a Boston area code written on a scrap of paper snugged into a wool sailing cap that she had loaned to Jacques. The number is an unlisted one! She checked, but in case something was drastically wrong she didn't want to call and ask to whom she was speaking. I've asked the police to investigate."

"Do you recall the number, Adam?"

"Yes, I do! However, I wrote it down for you to study just in case you might recognize it."

I took the piece of paper from Adam that he had jotted Euphy's message on. I felt like cross-examining him after his wiseacre remark about my perception, to ask him to recite the digits so I could check his memory against the numbers scribbled on the paper. However I knew better, Adam having a photographic mind and something seen once was always remembered. Besides I wasn't up to a sister and brother combat at this time. So I played it cool and replied, "It looks familiar, like a number I have dialed many times."

"The number looks familiar to me too, Serena," Mother said, "but then I'm on so many committees that after awhile they all sound familiar. Now then, on this note I think Adam and I should leave and let you rest a bit before Gloria arrives with your houseguest. We will be here tomorrow, of course."

Mother leaned down kissing me lightly on the forehead and then stroked my hair, gave a reassuring tuck to the sheet and pressed out an imaginary wrinkle on the pillow. Her touch as always was soothing. Her ministrations comforting. Immediately I felt better.

Adam leaned down giving me a kiss on the forehead too. I was overwhelmed by his solicitude. He even spared me his customary barb, instead of cabbage head using Daddy's pet name for me while saying good night. "Okay, Little One, see you on the morrow. In the meantime for Pete's sake and for mine too, please stay put, Serena!"

My mind cleared, at least for the moment, as Adam's brotherly kiss on my forehead acted on me just like the panacea of Simon's touching of my arm had on the day of my graduation run. "Adam," I whispered. "I don't want Mother to hear, but something is wrong, definitely wrong! Jacques Labelle had to have had an accomplice waiting for him inside of the museum."

Adam immediately put on his CIA face. "Explain yourself, Serena."

"I overheard Mr. Smythe telling Daddy that he found Jacques running thorough the gallery squawking in a patois of French and Spanish."

"Yes."

"Adam, I tied Jacques up and stuffed his mouth with a dirty paint rag before I ran for help. That's what I mean by Jacques having an accomplice, someone inside of the museum, someone who untied him and removed the gag from his mouth. Only then could Mr. Smythe have encountered him in the gallery."

Adam took a minute before answering. "He could have untied himself, Serena. As much as I hate to say it, especially when you are laid up and in a lot of pain, but you never could tie a knot worth a damn!"

It hurt to grin but I did. "Not anymore, Adam. I learned to tie a bowline this past summer and that's what I used. It positively would not have come undone."

I could tell from Adam's serious expression that for a change he was taking me seriously. "Okay, Sis, I believe you. I promise I will look into it right away. In the meantime try to rest and try not to worry."

#

Now that I was alone and following Adam's advice to rest and not to worry I picked up Euphy's postcard. There was just enough light coming from the floor lamp across the room for me to read her message. It began with, "Dear Serena, written in haste, I" and ended with, "Will phone to explain, Love, Euphy." In between was a mixture, very brief, of her own style of hieroglyphics consisting of a bumble bee, a pan and what appeared to be a corn stalk with a stick figure climbing it.

I wanted so much to laugh but willed my body to stop just short of the transgression since my head was continuing to send out warning vibes of protest. Instead I consoled myself with the knowledge that Euphy was indeed a friend-girl and accepted a consolation prize from myself for deciphering her message so very quickly, made easier I realized by the recent "thrill" of being pursued by Jacques, for the bumble bee obviously stood for the syllable, be; the pan, of course standing for cookware, thus creating the second part of the word, ware; together spelling beware. The rest was a snap to figure out, the corn stalk representing a bean stalk and the stick figure, Jack, or in this case, Jacques; the total message being, Beware of Jacques! How ironic the postcard should have come today and not yesterday, forewarned being forearmed and all that neat stuff!

The postcard slipped from my hand. I watched it waft to the floor, caught momentarily in a current of air, making me think back to the day so many, many weeks ago when I had been caught in a gentle breeze while sitting on top of Todd's Point and wondering profoundly about an eagle trying to escape its bondage from earth to soar with the wind. Now here I was confined to a bed, my thoughts not profound but body and soul aching to make a different kind of escape than that of the eagle, an escape right into Simon's arms and then to soar with him on an odyssey of bliss.

However an odyssey of bliss can only last so long, no matter how sublime the trip. Some thing or things or some circumstance or someone always brings it to an end. This evening it was a person standing in the shadows behind the floor lamp that ended my imaginary flight into Simon's arms to revel in a night of heavenly rapture. I spoke to the shadow." Please come in. Even though I was dozing I'm not really asleep so don't worry about waking me up."

I watched as the shadow moved towards me and into the circle of glow coming from the lamp. His voice was unctuous, void of accent and pitched low. "Good evening, Serena."

I was stunned but not quite speechless. "Why, Mr. Smythe, I thought you had gone home. I really must have been out of it a while ago to have thought so. Please, won't you sit down. This is so very thoughtful of you to come back so soon for a visit."

"I'm not really paying you a visit, Serena."

"Oh?"

"You might say me being here this evening is more like a farewell."

"A farewell? You mean you are leaving on another trip to South America? I thought you just came back from one this past August?"

Mr. Smythe walked closer to my bed until he was leaning against the guard rail. "No, Serena, I'm not leaving. You are!"

"Me? I just came back from a six month trip. Why would you send me on another trip when there is so much work to do at the museum?"

"This trip, you might say, will be a permanent one."

"A permanent one? I'm afraid I don't understand?"

Mr. Smythe laughed softly. At least it sounded like a laugh. On the other hand there seemed to be a glassy-eyed gleam of madness in his stare or maybe the gleam was actually a rosy glow from one cocktail too many. Either way, the gleam or the glow belied his laugh making it nonexistent. "You will soon, Serena," he answered provocatively to my perplexity.

I persisted. "How soon?"

This time his answer to me, was no answer at all. Instead he assumed the duties of a nurse, pulling the IV stand closer to my bed, studying the steady drops of fluid from two bags of solution suspended from the top bar as they emptied into one pliable plastic tube attached to my arm, running his fingers down the tube as if to be sure it was hanging free. "You know, Serena," he finally said, "I didn't start out in college to be a museum director. Actually I dreamed of becoming a doctor but found after a few years of study that I didn't really have the necessary compassion, that my leanings were more toward the aesthetic side. Still, I was in pre med school long enough to learn how to do a few things."

"Such as,?" I asked rather tenuously, not quite sure why he was confessing part of his past life.

"Such as, Serena, learning how to administer an IV. Such as, Serena, learning how to introduce the kind of foreign substance into an IV that leaves no trace. The kind of poisonous substance, Serena, that causes immediate but I assure you a painless death. The kind of poisonous foreign substance, Serena, that if an autopsy is performed will show nothing more than the cause of death to be heart failure."

Sometimes I could be quite obtuse, other times very naive when dealing with people. It wasn't that I was slow or stupid. It was just that my mind didn't work on a diet of deceit and tricks with murder as an objective. My mind was programmed to function on honesty and without ruse with an objective to love thy neighbor.

However this time I was neither obtuse nor naive. Mr. Smythe was going to kill me and what was I going to do about it? What could I do about it moored to my bed; true, not with the king of knots but with an IV tube attached to one arm which was just as potent as a bowline and the other arm, being broken, in a cast. To add insult to injury I was barely able to move let alone see out of my puffy eyes and it really hurt to talk, my cracked ribs protesting with every breath. However being me I did the usual and began to talk while my brain went into overtime searching frantically for a solution. Automatically I began to talk faster as Mr. Smythe reached into the breast pocket of his suit coat and pulled out a syringe, no doubt filled with the coup de grace.

"So you are the New England kingpin the federal agents were talking about, the Lord High Mucky Muck they were desperately seeking. I should have realized it the moment I heard Adam mention the telephone number. The telephone number that Euphy Browne found written on a scrap of paper. She found it you know tucked inside of Jacques' wool cap and called my home today with the information."

Mr. Smythe seemed unimpressed and he certainly did not become flustered over my news, remaining maddeningly calm while removing the emergency buzzer from within my reach so I could not summon aid. "Ah, but you didn't, Serena, thus giving me the extra time that I needed to tie up a loose end."

"The loose end being me, no doubt?"

"That's correct. I've already taken care of one loose end, Jacques. He was the only one who knew my identity, the only one who could testify against me in court, the only one capable of destroying my life, a life style which I have become addicted to and have no intention of giving up. That is of course up until you came into the picture. Now you are the remaining one person who can bring my world to an end."

"You're too late," I countered. "My parents also know about the number, so does Adam. He has the police checking it out right now. It's just a matter of time before they catch up with you."

"I'm not worried, Serena. I can easily explain away a piece of paper tucked inside of Jacques' cap, especially since you knew him and you both were living under the same roof. After all with the two of you gone who is left to disagree with me?"

I was getting desperate, seizing upon any excuse I could think of to gain a little time. "The telephone records! They will show that calls were placed to your home from Rouge Baie."

"You could have placed the calls to me, Serena. Once again, with you not around to testify, who would know? And in anticipation of your next three questions let me go ahead and answer them. First of all, Jacques made no more calls to me after you left Rouge Baie so the telephone records from then on would be useless. Next, no one saw me enter your room. I made sure of that by coming up the back stairs. And last, I untied Jacques and removed the rag from his mouth. That's when I decided I had to get rid of you too since I wasn't sure what he had divulged to you about our very profitable business adventure."

He emphasized his final remarks by reaching into the other breast pocket of his suit coat and pulling out a spotless white handkerchief. I didn't have to ask if he was going to gag me, his diabolical smile underscoring his explanation. "A gag can be removed after death, Serena. It won't leave a trace like adhesive tape. But in the meantime this handkerchief stuffed into your mouth will be just fine. It will keep you from screaming for help."

Mr. Smythe lost no time in putting his words into action. His face was menacing as he leaned over me. His voice was thick with determination. His movements were swift and sure. "Try not to fight me, Serena. Spare yourself the agony."

It was now or never time to make my bid for freedom. The never part reverberating in my mind reminding me that never meant: never again would I see my family; never again would I see Simon; never again would I walk my beloved beach and never again would I be able to run through the piles of leaves that fall in gaudy splendor onto Boston Common in the autumn.

The now part was just that, NOW! Mr. Smythe had shown me the way. I would scream, not just an ordinary scream but a scream every bit as loud as "The shot heard 'round the world." Hopefully the other patients on the floor would understand. Why, I could even get their names from Paul and send each of them a letter of apology for disturbing their slumber. With this comforting thought overriding the repelling touch of Mr.

Smythe's spiny, grasping fingers on my face I took as deep a breath as possible and screamed.

It was a beautiful scream! I could hear it echoing down the corridor, loud and long and clear.

Chapter 23

My room was full of shadows made mellow by the brightness of a full harvest moon, silent except for the distant ringing of the Angeles bell at St. Paul's Cathedral. The hoards of people who had answered my scream for help had gone, including Adam whose timely arrival by my bedside with several of Boston's Finest in tow had literally saved my day. Recalling the scene brought a faint smile to my face, a broad one would have hurt, for my relief over seeing him was obvious but being as how I was me and he was my brother I had asked between sobs, "What took you so long to get here?"

Adam, never at a loss for words, had been then! It had taken him all of one full minute before retorting, "Serena, I've never been wrong before but, here in front of all these witnesses, I'm going on record as saying I was wrong when I once said that life without you around would cause great joy! What I should have said is having you around is a fate worse than death."

I had dried my tears as best I could on the bed sheet and succeeded in widening my smile. Adam had smiled back. Not only had the evening ended on an all's well that ends well theme but everything between Adam and me was back to normal. Immediately I had felt better.

Such happy ending thoughts including the "biggie" that Mr. Smythe was resting in jail after being strong-armed to the floor by Adam should have been soothing but instead it was making me feel lightheaded and even though I was flat on my back my body was tingling all over like it used to do on a Christmas morning when as a child I laid in bed anticipating all the good things to come. Now that I was older and wiser, I hoped, good things didn't have to come wrapped in tissue paper and ribbon. Good things could be a campfire silhouetted against the blackness of a star-light night, a quiet stroll on the beach, a rocking chair bathed in the glow of a magenta sunrise or like seeing Simon walking towards me and feeling my hand in his, the soft pressure of his lips on mine and hearing him whisper into my ear, "Serena, my beautiful Sea Sprite, are you awake?"

"Yes, I'm awake!"

I pulled the cord for the bedside light, flicking it onto high beam, needing to assure myself that Simon was really here. The tears came. I couldn't stop them. "Oh, Simon, I'm so glad you are here, safe and sound. There for a while this afternoon and this evening I thought I might never see you again, that you, too, could end up in a green plastic garbage bag floating in Boston's harbor."

I accepted his hanky, making a one-handed stab at drying my tears. "Of course, we would have at least been together."

Simon was shaking his head at me, his eyes reflecting that strange mixture of mirth and love which I had come to adore in him prompting me to ask, "I suppose you think a trip to the woodshed is in order for what I have done?"

He didn't answer. Leaning down he kissed me gently again on the lips, then cupped my chin in his hand, taking a long time to study my face. There was a catch in his voice that reflected the heartache I saw in his eyes. "Gloria told me you had taken a spill, Serena; that you had fallen down a long flight of stairs. Dr. Collins, Paul that is, was more specific, describing your injuries in detail, spelling out for me what you could and should not do and the length of your convalescence. And it was your brother Adam, who I just met out in the hall, who told me about Jacques' death and of the attempt on your life by Henry Smythe. However, none of their descriptions conveyed a true picture of you."

Simon let go of my chin and began to run his fingers through my hair, his other hand occupied with turning the light down to low. He added savagely, "It is indeed fortunate that Jacques is no longer bodily with us or else I would have been the one locked up in jail for killing him. The same goes for your Henry Smythe! If I had been the one charging into your room and discovered he was in the process of injecting a poison into your system I know full well that I would not have reacted in as calm a manner as Adam. I would have killed him first and worried about the consequences later."

I almost said, "But it's not their fault the light went out and I fell down the stairs."

312

It was just as well I kept still because Simon was in no mood to hear any logic from me. He kept ranting on about Jacques being the catalyst, that if he had not been trying to kill me I would not have started to run, etc., etc., and so forth. It was when his last "and so forth" petered out with a sigh and a chuckle that I knew the storm was over. He started to laugh and then stopped, a boyish grin on his face. "To answer your question, Serena, about a trip to the woodshed being in order my answer is an unequivocal, no. I'm very proud of you, as is everyone else. What you did took a lot of spunk. I guess I have just got to get used to being constantly saved by you. In the novels, you know, it is usually the other way around."

Ignoring my cracked ribs I managed to move my legs slightly so Simon could sit down beside me on the bed. I reached for his free hand, longing to feel the warmth from it next to my heart. In the manner that had become a private gesture of love between us I clasped his hand tightly in mine and then slowly pulled it towards me until his arm came to rest across my waist and chest. "I want to tell you about a dream I had, Simon, while coming out from under the anesthetic. It was rather weird and yet made a lot of sense."

A decidedly mischievous twinkle sneaked into his eyes. "Tell me, Serena, does this dream of yours have anything to do with archaeologists and anthropologists being only at home among the anthropoids at the zoo since all of them seem to be happy only when having a platter full of bones in front of them to pick over?"

The blood rushed to my face. "Oh, no! Betrayed by own sister."

Simon bestowed upon me an angelic smile. "Don't worry, Serena. I will collect retribution in due time."

His remark was not lost to me but now Gloria was on my mind. I started to squirm. "Simon, a question before I tell you my dream. Did you know Gloria was not me when you first met her?"

"When I first met her, yes, but from a distance, no. Why? "

"Oh, I just wondered, that's all."

The mischievous twinkle in Simon's eyes faded into one of candor. "Serena, this is not the time or the place for games. I know you too well, something is bothering you and I think I know what it is. You are wondering if I greeted Gloria with a lingering bear-hug type of embrace and with, what you call, a campfire style of a kiss."

I nodded, guilt written all over me.

Simon started to laugh, shaking his head at me again, that strange mixture of mirth and love back in his eyes. "Let's just say while on the plane and knowing how close you two are, I considered the possibility of a trick being played on me. So you see I was on my guard."

He winked, his index finger sort of Morse coding across my cheeks, adding, "Do you know you have a few more freckles across the bridge of your nose than Gloria, 15 at least I would say, and then there is that hint of blue just underneath your skin near the right temple. Of course there is the obvious difference which I won't elaborate upon tonight and especially here."

Not being able to wink back I smiled, especially when he squeezed my hand.

"Now then, Serena, why don't you tell me about your dream before Gloria, Paul and that starchy head nurse arrive on the scene. For some reason she isn't about to take anymore nonsense from a junior member of the Bradford family tonight. Besides I also have something of great importance to discuss with you."

"As dreams go it's really not earth shaking, Simon, or worthy I'm sure of being recorded in a Freudian type of journal. Its value to me is in the interpretation of the dream sequences which upon review ushered in the full realization that different ideas, different endeavors, different planes of life can co-exist and benefit from each other."

An incredulous expression swept across Simon's face, his eyes opened wide. "That's what you were thinking about when coming to in the recovery room? After all you have been through today that's what you were thinking about? Now I really am worried about your state of health!"

This time I laughed. It hurt! "Please don't make me laugh, Simon. It does seem that I have put the cart in front of the horse. Whatever!"

Talking was also beginning to hurt, forcing me to be concise even if not too coherent. "I was attending a masquerade ball, hundreds of people dancing around me. I was standing with two white rabbits, a green clock and a red nun buoy waltzed by. It was weird, all the costumes reflecting the same theme, half the guests dressed up as famous navigators and the other half as renowned artists. All had signs hanging from their necks. The navigators were chatting with the artists, the artists were chatting with the navigators, all grouped together in tiny time-like-warp clusters. Columbus was with Botticelli, Cook with Peale, Nansen talking to Homer and Monet. Off to a side was Magellan conversing with Leonardo da Vinci and Brueghel. Near the bandstand were Pytheas and Praxiteles, MacMillan and Hartley."

I could see, even through my two puffy black eyes, Simon was listening intently. "End of dream, but you see that was what made me realize my field of endeavor, art history, and your discipline of archaeology coupled with a love of the sea are not a world apart, as I once thought."

Simon's reaction to my dream and conclusion was serious and professorial in tone. "I had no idea, Serena, that our different interests were a source of worry for you. They never have been for me. In fact, I have always considered navigators and artists compatible; navigators having been given the stars, the moon and the sun to pursue while artists have been given the colorful rainbows of the earth to follow. Both leave behind a visual, intellectual legacy; the navigator his wealth of charts and the artist vignettes of life on canvas."

Drowsiness was overcoming me, such a weighty subject would have to be debated another time, except for one more thought. "Simon, it probably won't make any sense to you but I decided tonight a breadth of attitude can also come from being in a hospital bed as well as strolling through Boston Common or taking a walk on the beach at The Barnacle."

A few seconds ticked by, Simon just sitting there smiling at me. "No, Serena, it doesn't make any sense but fortunately I have years and years ahead of me to try and figure out the inner workings of your fascinating mind. Which brings me to my discussion which is also important."

I thought I was going to be abandoned when Simon left my bed and walked across the room to the window. He stood there for a few moments, hands thrust deep into his trouser pockets, gazing out upon what I knew was the golden dome of the State House. A hint of humor surfaced in his voice. "You seem to have a knack for getting into trouble, Serena. That's why I've decided I can't let you run around town on the loose anymore. I came to this conclusion, by the way, after seeing the fiery red pricks all over your hands resulting from what you said was falling into a rose bush while walking Caesar the night I spent on Backbone Island." Simon chuckled, the set of his slightly tensed shoulders reminding me of the way Adam stood when he knew I was telling the truth, nothing but the truth "So help me God" -but not the whole truth.

I wasn't quite sure what to expect or to hear when he finally turned around. However, I could not help but notice Simon's solemn countenance, the tender light in his eyes, his noble bearing. It was as if I, too, had been transported back into time, once again standing in a small Soho gallery admiring a superb oil of a tall, robust man gazing out to sea titled "The Vigil." My mind balked at coming up with the artist's name. It wasn't important at the moment. What was important was listening to his words as he walked towards me.

"That's why we will get married next Thanksgiving. It's going to take that long to work out the details. In the meantime the year will fly by, literally; you playing Mother Hen to the collection of American landscapes going on tour throughout your country, me visiting you whenever possible on weekends. I've checked, you will be in Ottawa at the same time my doctorate is conferred. Boston, The Barnacle and St. John's are not that far apart by plane. We will be able to get together several times during the summer."

I reached out for Simon's hand when he got close enough, pulling him down beside me. "For our honeymoon, Serena, I thought we would take a combination land and sea trip. I've

316

always wanted to sail in the Greek islands, spend some time languishing on their beaches; you have told me many times how much you would enjoy island hopping through the Aegean Sea. We even have our first wedding gift. Captain Barrows, as part of his bequest to the Museum of Science has arranged for me to come the first five months of the following year to catalogue and supervise the transfer of his collection of marine artifacts gathered from the Seven Seas. I'll give a lecture or two on Eric the Red, the demise of the Basque whaling fleet as we know of it in North America and goodness knows what else."

Simon finally paused to catch his breath, but not for long. "However, Serena, I learned the hard way a few weeks ago that it is very wise to ask." He chucked me playfully under the chin. "What do you say, Sprite. Are you willing to exchange one kind of a canvas world for another or to at least give it a try? Shall we tie a bowline between us now that you have learned to make such a good one?"

I was speechless, my head spinning from trying to follow his projected itinerary. "You seem to have thought of every thing, including the asking."

"I tried to, Serena, and just in case you think I am taking advantage of your weakened condition, I want you to know, I am."

I loved him for saying it. I wanted to throw my arms around his neck and murmur, "I will, Simon, I will." Since that was impossible, I giggled, the urge to tease him too strong to resist. "You have thought of everything, Simon, save one. A mighty, mighty big one at that! I don't think I can say, 'Yes, till death us do part,' until we solve this problem."

Simon drew himself up, his back and shoulders became ramrod straight, a frown spread over his face. It lasted only a second, the contraction of his brows and the resulting stern appearance giving way to a wide grin. "No, Serena, I did not forget Caesar, the 'mighty, mighty big one,' although I do admit to the temptation."

Simon cleared his throat, a mannerism I had learned that always seemed to precede an important edict. "I just assumed Caesar would be going with us. It will take time, of course, to get his so called passport in order and I understand he might have to be quarantined before entering a few countries. However, Serena, we have a year to work out those major details. As for the sailing part of our honeymoon, I'm sure Caesar will do well. We both know how much he likes boats. Food and water could be a problem but not insurmountable. On the positive side Caesar will be a good watch dog, having him on board will be like having a body guard present at all times."

There was absolutely no way I could mistake the hidden meaning behind his words or fail to see the merriment kindling in his eyes. Before things got out of hand I pulled him closer, whispering, "Yes, I will marry you, Simon, and I want you to know I will try and learn to sail. Only please don't make me laugh. So far as Caesar is concerned, you win. Your snow job was superb. Caesar will stay home. The last thing I want on my honeymoon is a bodyguard."

Simon started to laugh. There was no way I could stop him, the marvelous sound filling the room bringing Gloria, Paul and the starchy nurse rushing in. I was blissfully forgotten in their verbal melee: Gloria asking Simon, "Did she accept;" Paul slapping Simon on the back saying, "Congratulations, but it's time to leave so the nurse can get Serena ready for the night;" Gloria chiming in with," I just found out, Simon, my father has arranged for your testimony to be postponed until the day after tomorrow and Serena will give hers next week;" Paul adding, "The rest of the family is anxious to meet you, Simon, so we will drive you back to the old manse. Captain Barrows will be there too, as will Serena's four legged mishap. Best brace yourself, starting now, for his charge."

All turned around facing me, flanking the foot of the bed. Gloria stooped down, picking up Euphy's postcard, putting it on the table. "A memento, Sis; another piece of ephemera for your purse." She stepped closer, lowering her voice, "I like your Simon, Serena. He is as you said, a contemporary Paul Bunyan type with the dazzle of the Marlboro man thrown in. Mother will positively swoon when she meets him, as will Grandmother when she and Grandfather Horatio arrive in town tomorrow for the holidays."

318

"Please, Gloria, don't make me laugh!"

Simon leaned down, whispering into my ear a tender, "Sleep tight, Sprite, don't let the bed bugs bite. I'll see you in the morning."

He gave me half of a campfire style kiss. I yearned for more, oh, so much, much more but all I could think of and manage to say was, "Please, Simon, don't make me laugh."

Epilogue

Serena recovered rapidly from, "My baptism into the enthralling world of sky diving," and was released from the hospital in time to be home for the Thanksgiving holidays. On the hallowed day Simon presented to the Bradford family a huge gift wrapped box containing a king size red wool blanket and a well-appointed wicker picnic basket filled to capacity with smoked salmon, a tin of Beluga caviar from the Caspian Sea, French wine and other delicacies.

The short message penned on the enclosed formal white card was scanned quickly by Grandmother Martha and then after giving Simon a decidedly affectionate wink read it outloud to all.

"To the Bradford Family,

Though this blanket and basket are missing the reminiscent rips and scratches of happy times gone by such as those visible on the ones left behind on Bald Head Island, they do come to you with the memories of a day spent with Serena that not only changed my life but gave to it meaning and a purpose.

Simon"

You could have heard a pin drop on top of the oriental rug. Grandmother was the first to speak; her warm, "We do indeed have a lot to be thankful for this Thanksgiving," being followed by a resounding, "Hear! Hear!" from the male side of the family and the compliment delivered somewhat shyly from Alicia Bradford, "Serena told me, Simon, that you were very sensitive to her ups and downs. I now fully appreciate what she meant. As Martha said, 'We do indeed have a lot to be thankful for this Thanksgiving.'"

On the same hallowed day but in the privacy of the cozy upstairs sitting room Serena and Simon exchanged gifts, she giving him the painting "Seaworthy" dampened slightly with a few tears of alluring artistry, he giving her a diamond engagement ring nestled inside a hand painted porcelain box in the shape of a dinghy and shut with a bowline knot shaped clasp from Limoges, France. After uncorking a bottle of vintage champagne they toasted each other: Serena telling Simon dreamily, "To my Heracles, may the Fates grant us a long life together and the Muses bless us as we travel along the way with their divine inspirations;" Simon telling Serena in a decidedly more prosaic manner, "To my beautiful Sea Sprite, and may Poseidon grant us the fair winds needed to ride out many a stormy sea which we are bound to encounter along the way."

From that moment on and with the old year ticking rapidly into the new the pace of activities for the Bradford and Mont families quickened noticeably, though not always running smoothly! In early January, Alicia and John Bradford flew to Ottawa to spend a long weekend getting acquainted with Simone and Stewart Mont. They in turn came to Boston near the end of the month. After the exchange of visits both families agreed that, "As in-laws go they are at least socially and culturally acceptable." On the other hand both wives after seeing their progeny together over the long weekends expressed their concerns privately to their respective husbands that Serena and Simon might not be suitable for each other: Alicia telling John, "Serena thinks with her heart, not logically like a scientist or a lawyer;" John telling Alicia gently, "Neither do you and yet we have muddled through all these years;" Simone telling Stewart, "Simon is so calm and so into details, not at all impractical or into day dreaming;" Stewart telling Simone, "A little day dreaming can cure a lot of ills."

The absolutely, positively, totally unexpected news that Euphy was going to marry Captain Barrows in April came in the mail mid February and with both families being asked to participate in their nuptials there was little time left for Alicia and Simone to fret over the suitability of Serena and Simon for each other. Horatio was tapped to be Sonofagun's best man while Stewart Mont was chosen to give the bride away. John was asked to be an usher as was Simon and Serena along with Simone and Jane Teweks attendants to Euphy. Out of consideration for those coming from the mainland Euphy and Bob decided to have the wedding in St. John's, "The airport not usually collapsing under the weight of a glitter storm, " and, "Adequate lodging to be found." Another reason, though neither would admit to being overly sentimental, "At our age," was The Chapel by the Sea, an ancient stone edifice that had been the site for both of their previous marriages, "Which survived many a stormy sea." The entire affair was a joyous occasion as friends gathered to celebrate and to witness the ceremony between two firm anchors of their community. Yet at times the solemnity of the service and the steadfast manner in which Euphy and Captain Barrows exchanged their vows moved many to tears, especially Serena whose thoughts kept drifting back to a morning when she sat upon a ledge overlooking the ocean pondering about an escaping breeze, a breeze which somehow had lifted and carried her to The Chapel by the Sea.

The Bradfords et all had not quite recovered from the stresses of the wedding when Adam shocked them by finally retiring from the shadowy world of super-sleuthing in order to, "Willingly fulfill my obligations to the family law firm by shouldering the responsibility for the international and maritime division." His private reason, "Death is not discriminating and this past year has taught me how fleeting life can be and the importance of family," was divulged only to Serena. His verbal excuse to others being, "Life seems more interesting at home. Besides, now that I am the doddering age of 35, I can no longer take the wear and tear of sleeping in a haystack one night and the Ritz the next." He shocked them even further by buying Henry Smythe's condominium, answering Gloria's, "You've gone bonkers," with, "I call it poetic justice! In addition to Henry serving a life sentence for his crimes just think how galling it's going to be for him knowing that a Bradford is living in his penthouse." After a family conference no fault could be found with his logic and Alicia, always the patient mother, agreed to redecorate his pied-a-terre, "In keeping with your unorthodox, eclectic tastes, Adam, dear."

June turned out to be the month that should have been by-passed on the calendar. It began with the conferring of Simon's doctorate degree and naturally the family flew en masse to Montreal to see the bestowing of the academic laurel. Serena, already in Ottawa and just having completed her stretch as Mother Hen to the collection of American landscapes on tour, went with the Monts to rendezvous with them. From there she planned to drive with Simon to Rouge Baie, "To spend a few days with Euphy and Captain Barrows and of course to see if any compromises had been added to the house." No one knew what she meant by compromises but it didn't really make any difference since Horatio's decision to step down from The Bench the first of July was formally announced by The President and threw any plans made or about to be made for the rest of June out of the window.

It was Alicia Bradford who called a halt to the very frantic pace by stating emphatically after the first of July, after all was said and done with by the media in regards to Horatio's lifetime of achievements, after all the farewell luncheons and dinners given in his honor including a lavish one at The White House were over and after she had unpacked her suitcase from what must have been her millionth trip to Washington, "I positively refuse to budge from Boston until Serena's wedding is over!" The fact that she meant it, the fact that for the first time in her 37 years of marriage she had put not only one but two feet down firmly onto the floor and the fact that no tempting little pin delivered by a messenger in livery from Tiffany's could dissuade her sent the family into walking on egg shells for the next several months.

The justification for her stubbornness was apparent on the day after Thanksgiving as Serena Margaret Bradford walked down an aisle carpeted with a rich Persian runner at precisely six p.m., to marry Simon Stewart Mont in the tableau-like setting of the Museum of Fine Arts' sumptuous Renaissance Room. There were no shortages of comments to be overheard about the uniqueness of the setting, Gloria explaining somewhat airily to those guests who asked, "Mother took Serena's day dreams, mixed them with Simon's wishes and logic and then came up with this practical solution."

"Oh," was the understated reply most often heard to Gloria's oblique answer. However conversations carried on between other guests across the lavishly set tables in the adjacent dining room invariably included the comment, though not spoken in an unkindly way, "Only an Adams married to a Bradford could take over the new wing of the museum for an evening."

The wedding was dutifully recorded in the Bradford family bible, as indeed it was in the Mont's. It was also duly noted in all the proper periodicals and newspapers and having been witnessed by the nine members of the Supreme Court was hailed by the press as, "The most documented wedding in the history of Boston."

As you might expect Serena took time out before she and Simon departed on their wedding trip to give Caesar a pat on the head and tell him, "Be a good boy for Adam while I'm gone." And as you might expect a couple of weeks later when the postcards mailed to family and friends began to arrive from the honeymooners, the first ones coming from Kenya due to Horatio's gift and wish that Simon fulfill for him his promise to take Serena on a photographic safari and the second ones from the Greek Island of Ios, the comment most often used by the Bradford family to express their happiness over the wedding was, "All's well that ends well."

And if you just happened to be walking alone along the shore at The Barnacle listening only to nature's music and if by chance you paused long enough to let your thoughts drift far beyond the visible sea to the Aegean you were bound to hear Serena's confirming whisper, "Ayah!," being carried back to you on an escaping breeze.

The End

ABOUT THE AUTHOR

For the past thirty years the Hardy family has called a picturesque island off of the Maine coast, "Home." Though now linked to the mainland by a network of intertwining small bridges and islands the aura of a bygone era still lingers making it a very special place to live. Alice Louise Hardy, a wife and mother, has captured this charm and ambience in her first novel to be published "Escape From a Canvas World;" a seafaring narrative drawn from her experiences while boating through the scenic and sometimes treacherous channels of coastal Maine. She is currently working on her second novel set in the fabulous Sonoran Desert of Arizona.